Bo[illegible]d, **Charlotte Hawkes** is mum [illegible] who love her to play [illegible] and who object lou[illegible]ds on the compute[illegible]ling with blocks—sh[illegible] Anglo/French co[illegible]es to hear from read[illegible]ntact her at her website: charlotte[illegible]awkes.com.

Ann McIntosh was born in the tropics, lived in the frozen north for a number of years, and now resides in sunny central Florida with her husband. She's a proud mama to three grown children, loves tea, crafting, animals (except reptiles!), bacon and the ocean. She believes in the power of romance to heal, inspire and provide hope in our complex world.

Also by Charlotte Hawkes

The Army Doc's Secret Wife
The Surgeon's Baby Surprise
A Bride to Redeem Him

Hot Army Docs miniseries

Encounter with a Commanding Officer
Tempted by Dr Off-Limits

The Nurse's Pregnancy Miracle
is **Ann McIntosh's** debut title

Look out for more books from Ann McIntosh
Coming soon

Discover more at millsandboon.co.uk.

THE SURGEON'S ONE-NIGHT BABY

CHARLOTTE HAWKES

THE NURSE'S PREGNANCY MIRACLE

ANN McINTOSH

MILLS & BOON

First Published in Great Britain 2018
by Mills & Boon, an imprint of HarperCollins*Publishers*
1 London Bridge Street, London, SE1 9GF

ISBN: 978-0-263-93373-4

MIX
Paper from responsible sources
FSC™ C007454

This book is produced from independently certified FSC™ paper to ensure responsible forest management.
For more information visit www.harpercollins.co.uk/green.

Printed and bound in Spain
by CPI, Barcelona

THE SURGEON'S ONE-NIGHT BABY

CHARLOTTE HAWKES

MILLS & BOON

To Monty & Bart.

You make me laugh louder and love deeper.

xxx

CHAPTER ONE

WITH MOUNTING HORROR, Archie stared out of the open aeroplane doors and three thousand five hundred feet down to the ground below her. As the penultimate static line jumper prepared to take his step out of the back of the plane, terror pinned her to the hard deck of the aircraft.

'You're up next, Archie.' Her instructor's words were more seen than heard as he yelled over the roar of the engines and the rushing wind.

'I can't. I can't do it,' she muttered desperately, but the sound was whipped away, unheard. Thankfully.

Throughout her entire life, those had been the only words her beloved air force father had ever flatly refused to hear... *I can't.* She glanced down at her colourful 'Make Cancer Jump' skydiving suit and felt a hot prickle in her eyes.

Guilt and regret; they had made terrible companions these last five years.

Whatever had happened to the bold, fun-loving, spirited Archana Coates of old? Even of six years ago? Back then she and her father would have jumped out of that door without a second thought. Now here she was, glued to the deck, unable to even inch her way forward.

She didn't dare look over her shoulder. She was the last of her group of static line jumpers but there was still half a planeload of tandem skydivers all ready to ascend to their required altitude of ten thousand feet. They were just waiting for her to go.

He was waiting for her to go.

Kaspar Athari.

She'd tried to ignore him from the moment she'd spotted him that morning across the vast chasm of the training hangar. Just as she'd ignored the way something had kicked in her chest, and if she hadn't already known it had died the same day her father had—almost five years ago to the day—she might have been fooled into believing it was her heart.

Kaspar. The boy who had burst into her family's life when she'd been six and he'd been almost eight, and had turned things upside down in the best way possible. For the seven years he hadn't just been her brother Robbie's best friend. He'd also been like a second brother to her, spending every school holiday from their boarding schools—thanks to Kaspar's money and her own father's career in the air force—with her family.

Or at least...mostly like a second brother. Even now, even here, she could feel the hot flush creep into her cheeks at the memory of childish crush she'd had on him that last year. She'd been thirteen and it had been the first year she'd been acutely aware that Kaspar wasn't a brother *at all.*

The same year his narcissist Hollywood royalty mother had finally tired of her latest husband and dragged herself and her son back to the States in the hope of kick-starting both their careers. But, though having once been one of the most heartbreaker child actors in Hollywood, thanks to a combination of his stunning blonde British mother and his striking, dark-haired Persian father, somewhere along the line Kaspar had turned his back on the industry.

Now he was a top surgeon who risked his life in former war zones and on the battlefield. Saving civilians and soldiers alike. Winning awards and medals at every turn, none of which he appeared to care a jot about. With the press hanging on his every choice.

'The Surgeon Prince of Persia', the press had dubbed him, as much for his bone-melting good looks as for his surgical skill.

And even though she'd devoured every last article, had known he split his time between the US and the UK, had seen the Christmas card and US Army antique he'd sent her avid collector father every year without fail, she'd never seen Kaspar again in person. Until now.

Not that he'd even recognised her after all these years.

'Archie. Are you ready?'

Snapping her gaze back up to her instructor, who was still smiling encouragingly, she shook her head, half-incredulous that, even now, even here, Kaspar Athari had managed to consume her thoughts so easily. Especially when she hadn't thought of him very much at all over the intervening years.

Yeah, a voice inside her scoffed. *Right.*

But right now wasn't the time to go there. This skydive wasn't about him. It wasn't about anyone. Just herself. Just the fact that she'd spent the last five years, ever since her beloved father's death, ricocheting from one disaster to another, and today that all stopped. It was time. She just needed to make that leap. Literally.

Edging forward she somehow, miraculously, managed to summon the strength to push herself off her seat onto the metal floor, closer to the open hatch, and peer nervously down again.

The wind ripped at her, as though it could pull in even more different directions.

'I ca…' She began to mutter the refusal again but this time something stopped her from completing it.

It was time to regain her dignity. The life she'd somehow put on hold for the past five years since her father's death. In fact, almost five years to the day since her fearlessness had seeped out of her like a punctured rubber dinghy in the middle of a wide, empty ocean.

'I can do this,' she told herself fiercely. Out loud. Safe in the knowledge that no one could hear her over the roar.

She wanted to make the jump. She *needed* to make it. Five years of mistakes and disappointments had to end today. From her marriage, which had been doomed from the start, to the baby daughter she had lost at eighteen weeks. Even the baby that her ex-husband and his new wife would bring into the world barely a month or so. It was time to stop being a victim. To erase this weak, pathetic shadow of a person that she'd somehow become and rediscover the fierce, happy woman she'd once been.

Sitting on the cold, metal floor, paralysed with fear, wasn't part of the plan. And she hated herself for it. She reached out her arms and tried to shuffle across the floor on her bottom, but despite her best efforts her body refused to comply.

'I *have* to do this,' she choked out, desperately willing herself to move.

She was letting people down. She was letting herself down. She felt exposed, vulnerable, worthless.

Her head snapped around at the movement in her peripheral vision to see Kaspar edging his way through the plane. As if he knew exactly what was going on. As if the last fifteen years were falling away and they were once again the teenagers they'd been when she'd last seen him. As if he was still every inch the superhero he'd always been to her, even when she'd been nothing more than the annoying kid sister.

She should be more shocked. Shouldn't she?

He couldn't be coming to her aid. He wasn't that boy any more.

So what was hammering in her chest harder than the vibration of the aircraft engines? Had he recognised her after all?

'Everything okay?' he yelled. Concerned but with no trace of recognition.

Archie stared helplessly, attempting to shake off the irrational hurt that needled her. Why *would* he recognise her? It had been fifteen years and she'd liked to think she no longer looked *quite* like the gangly kid she'd been when he'd last seen her. It wasn't even as though her name would mean much to him, even if he could hear it over the roar of the engines. Archie was a name she'd only settled on in her later teens, and she doubted he'd ever even realised her name was Archana. Like her family, he'd only ever called her 'Little Ant', in reference to the ant farm she'd had as a kid, and the way she'd been so proud of her undaunted, determined little pet colony.

He moved closer, his mouth nearer to her ear so that she imagined she could even feel his breath.

'You want to jump?'

'I *have* to jump, but…' she choked out quietly, not sure whether he could read her lips.

He nodded curtly in response, before turning to her instructor.

'She can come with me. I was doing a tandem jump but my guy didn't even make it onto the plane.'

So Kaspar was an instructor here? Of course he was. What did the press call him? *Playboy...surgeon...adrenalin junkie.*

Articles waxed lyrical about his trekking in the Amazon, skiing down avalanche-prone mountains, or diving off hundred-foot-high cliffs into sparkling tropical waters. Being a skydiving instructor on his weekends off would be a cake walk to someone like Kaspar.

'You need to change harness.'

'Sorry?'

She didn't mean to flinch as his hand brushed her shoulder. It was instinctive. Consuming.

Now that her instructor had closed the door for the plane to ascend another six thousand feet or so, it was possible to hear each other without having to shout so loudly over the engines or the wind.

'The tandem's easier than the static line, and I'll run you through the basics, but you'll need to change harness.'

And then Kaspar was addressing her, for the first time in fifteen years. She stared at him intently, as though willing up some spark of recognition, even if it was only to realise she was the kid sister who'd bugged him and Robbie. The one who had tried to get her brother to let her in when Robbie had far rather push her out. The one who had taught her little words in Persian, and chastised Robbie when he'd taught her swear words.

She gazed and, for a moment, she thought he stared back. Holding eye contact that fraction longer than necessary. It was as though the very blood was stilling in her veins, her body hanging for a split second. Everything seemed to tilt, to change colour.

But then he looked away, searching for the right harness, and she realised that moment had only existed in her own head. She could only watch in silence as Kaspar busied himself with the kit, slipping them both into the adult equivalent of a forward-facing baby carrier then sitting, with her perched on his lap, like the other tandem jumpers left in the plane.

It felt surreal. Nothing about this moment remotely resembled the hundreds of naïve fantasies she'd nurtured—for longer than she cared to admit—about how a conversation with him would go if she ever saw him again.

She'd envisaged beautiful clothes, perfect hair and make-up, and her sexiest smile. She'd imagined making Kaspar gasp at what he'd failed to see, right under his nose, all those years ago. She'd dreamed about making him chase her, just a little, before inevitably giving in to some all-consuming desire. Her innocent, wholly unrequited teenage crush finally blossoming into some movie-perfect moment.

She had *not* imagined being in an aircraft in the most unflattering, unshapely skydiving suit, which bunched around the crotch thanks to her heavy harness, and, to cap it all off, too frightened to even make her jump.

Well, she'd be damned if she was going to bottle this one, too. She had to make this jump. From ten thousand feet. With Kaspar.

She absolutely was *not* thinking about how close they were going to be, strapped together in a harness, her back pressed against his front.

Her blood was absolutely not racing away in her body, leaving her feeling decidedly light-headed and clammy.

She was going to concentrate on the jump and be grateful for the second chance. She had to do this well.

For charity.

For her father.

For herself.

And not because Kaspar was going to be with her for every single spine-tingling nanosecond of it. *Truly.*

Abruptly, everything faded to a blur, from Kaspar sorting out her gear to going through rigorous checks that would ordinarily have been completed on the ground. And then they were ready. Waiting. Her back glued to his chest.

Somehow that inability to face him lent her confidence.

'Why are you doing this?' she asked suddenly, surprising even herself.

Kaspar frowned.

'Sorry?'

Despite the relative quiet of the plane now the hatch door was closed, one still had to speak loudly and clearly to be heard and her murmur hadn't been nearly loud enough.

'Why are you doing this?' she repeated, grateful that no one else would stand a chance of hearing.

'Why am I doing this?' Kaspar repeated slowly, as if checking he'd heard right.

But she knew that cadence. Realised it meant he was choosing his words carefully. It felt like a tiny victory. She still knew him. Or a part of him anyway.

'Like a lot of people up here today, I'm doing it in memory of someone.'

'Who?' The question was out before she could swallow it back.

She could picture his face tightened, his jaw locked. So familiar even after all these years. The unexpectedness of it knotted in Archie's stomach and stopped her heart for a beat.

'We'll be at altitude soon.' He jerked his head to the door, clearly sidestepping her question, but she couldn't help it. She couldn't explain why but suddenly she needed to know.

'Who?' she insisted.

His jaw spasmed but, presumably because it was meant to be a charity jump and people had been sharing stories all day, he schooled his features into a neutral expression.

'His name was Peter. I knew him…a long time ago.'

He stopped curtly, as though it was more than he had intended to say. But it was more than enough for Archie.

Peter? Her father?

Archie shook her head, her lungs burning with the effort of continuing to breathe. He was doing this in memory of her own father? An odd sense of pride surged through her that even now, five years after his death, her big-hearted father still touched lives. And yet a sickening welling of emotion quickly snuffed out the pride. Kaspar clearly had absolutely no idea who she was. Despite all her earlier reasoning, that feeling of hurt, of rejection, coursed through her with all the power of a tsunami. She couldn't possibly hope to stop it, as illogical as she knew her reaction might be.

She opened her mouth, trying to find a way to tell him who she was. But at that moment the hatch door had reopened and her words were sucked out and into the ether before Kaspar had heard them. And as she sat there, her body feeling like lead, she was semi-aware of the other skydivers making their jumps even as her eyes blurred to everything around her.

The next thing she knew, Kaspar was hauling her to her feet, carrying out the final procedures, and then they were moving to the door, exiting the plane, dropping for what seemed like for ever but was probably no more than thirty seconds or so.

And without warning every thought, every emotion seemed to fall from Archie's mind, leaving her strangely numb.

At some point, it had to have been quite quickly, Kaspar tapped her shoulder to remind her to spread out her arms and legs in the freefall position as they rushed towards the ground, although it was as though the ground was rushing to them, her back pressed to his solid, reassuring chest.

There was no chance for conversation up here, they could shout and yell and the other one would never hear them, and to Archie there was something freeing in that. For all intents and purposes she was alone, even if she could feel Kaspar's rock-like mass securing her. As the adrenalin coursed through her veins, pumping along like nothing could hold it back, it was as though the wind not only blew away the stiffness from her body but the fog that had clouded her mind for so long.

Too long.

Kaspar opened the chute at what Archie knew would have been around five thousand feet, the loud *crack* ripping through her entire being as they were yanked up into a more upright position, as if breaking her open and allowing the first hints of fear and anger and regret to seep out.

And then absolute silence.

Peace.

Her heart, her whole chest swelled with emotion.

They were still descending but, with the parachute above them now slowing their rate of descent, if she didn't look at the ground, it almost felt as though they were floating. Suddenly time seemed to stand still.

Another thrill rippled through her.

She remembered what it had felt like on that first jump with her father. The life she'd intended to have. The strength of character that used to be hers. And for a moment she felt that again. Free of any responsibility for opening the parachute, steering them to the landing zone, or even having to land safely, she felt her body relax for the first time in years. And the more her body let go of some of the tension it had bottled inside for too long, the more her mind also opened up.

Lost in her thoughts, she was almost startled when a thumb appeared in front of her.

'Okay?' he yelled, his mouth by her ear.

Instinctively, she thrust both her hands out in a double thumbs-up, nodding her head as vigorously as she could, and then he was offering her the paddles to try controlling the chute for herself for a moment.

She was about to shake her head when something stopped her. For a split second she could almost hear her father's voice in her head encouraging her to do it. Tentatively, she reached up and took hold, changing direction slowly at first, surprised at just how comfortable and natural it felt. Even six years on, it was as though her muscles had retained the training her father had given her.

'Were you really going to do tandem jumps today?' She twisted her head so he could hear her easier.

Kaspar nodded. 'I was subbing for another instructor friend of mine who's unwell today. Originally, though, I was going to sky surf. Peter would have loved that.'

He stopped again, clearly catching himself.

Archie thought back to the surfboards she'd seen in the hangar on the ground and smiled into the expanse of blue. Of course a simple skydive wouldn't be enough for adrenalin junkie Kaspar, but he was right, her dad would have loved it.

Bolstered, she tried a slightly trickier turn, surprised and delighted at how comfortable and natural it felt, things that her father had taught her coming back quicker than she might have anticipated. Again and again she steered the chute, going further, trying things out, wishing she had the skill to really push her boundaries. All too soon it was time to release the paddles back to Kaspar.

Almost as though he could read her mind, Kaspar steered them into a high-speed turn, a gurgle of laughter that she hadn't heard from herself in years rumbling through her and spilling into the silent sky. She revelled in the sound as Kaspar led them both into a series of high-speed manoeuvres that thrilled her beyond anything she'd hoped for.

They held such echoes of what she'd loved until recently. For a moment it was as though she could almost reach in and touch the spirited, strong girl she'd once been.

It was transitory. Archie knew that. Soon Kaspar would have to stop and once they landed this moment, this connection to her old self, would be lost.

But this jump had done the one thing she'd desperately wanted it to do. It had finally reminded her of the girl she'd once been and—however deeply buried that part of her may be—today had helped her to begin her journey back to the old Archie.

The biggest shock of all was that it wouldn't have happened but for Kaspar Athari.

He might have no idea who she was, and once this jump was done he'd be out of her life again. Maybe for another fifteen years. Probably for good. But she was grateful to him nonetheless. Part of her longed to reveal her identity to him, but part of her was afraid of ruining the moment.

She was still gazing at the scenery spread out beneath them like the most vivid green screen image, trying to decide, when a small explosion by a truck in a layby below them snagged her attention. They were still a little too high up to see much detail but a dark shape lay on the ground. Archie opened her mouth to speak but Kaspar was already steering the parachute around for a better look.

'Is that a person?' she asked tentatively after a few moments. 'Or bins? Or bags?'

'I can't be sure. Possibly a person.'

His grim tone only confirmed her fears. If it was a body, they would likely have been caught in the blast.

'They have ambulance crews on the ground at the fete,' she shouted.

'That's true but the fete's some way away, they won't have seen the blast we saw. And I know that stretch of road, it's on the route from the hospital and Rick's Food Truck is parked in that layby six days a week, popular with both weekday truckers and with weekend walkers, all looking for a hot bacon and egg bap. For me, Rick's sausage and tomato toasties are more than welcome after a long night shift.'

'So what's the plan?' she asked, knowing neither she nor Kaspar would have mobile phones on the jump.

The decisive note in her tone was something she hadn't heard in all too long.

'There's about a mile over the fields, as the crow flies, between the truck and the fete. If we land as close as we can to the layby we can check it out. If it *is* a person, I'll stay on scene while you run back and alert the medical crews at the fete. Understood?'

'Understood,' she confirmed, caught off guard by an unexpected flashback to a time when Robbie had come off his bike, trying to do some somersault trick, and had been lying deathly still on the ground.

She'd been beside herself, but Kaspar had taken control then much as he was now. Assessing, verifying, trying to assimilate as much pertinent information as he could. Kaspar had taught her a lot, even as a kid.

Just like her father had.

Right now, she suddenly realised, she felt more like her old self than she had for years. Who would have thought she would owe Kaspar Athari part of the credit for that?

CHAPTER TWO

KASPAR VAULTED OVER the hedge and through the field. A part of him was glad to be getting away from the girl—*Archie*, her instructor had called her—with her expression-laden eyes that seemed to see altogether too much. It made no sense and yet even through her obvious fear up there in the plane, every time she had fixed that clear gaze on him he'd been unable to shake the impression that she could see past the façade he'd carefully crafted for a drooling press over the years, and read his very soul.

If he'd actually had a soul. But that had been long shattered. As much by his own terrible mistakes as anything else. Not least the one night that had altered the course of his life for ever.

And yet he couldn't seem to shake the notion that this one girl—woman—almost *knew* him. As though she was almost familiar.

He told himself it was just the emotion of the day. Five years since he'd heard Peter had passed away, the closest thing he'd ever had to a real, decent father figure. Who, even as a widower trying to hold down his air force career, had been more of a father *and* a mother to his son and daughter than either of Kaspar's own very much alive parents could or would ever have been.

Peter Coates had taught him that the volatile, physically

terrifying marriage of his own parents wasn't normal or right. He'd taught Kaspar to handle his emotions so that he didn't lose control the way his own father had. The way his own mother had, for that matter.

Hearing about Peter's death had winded him. Along with the rumour that Robbie had subsequently sold the old farmhouse and emigrated to Australia. Kaspar could understand why. With both parents dead, Robbie, only twenty-five, and with that kid sister of his to look after, it made sense to have a completely fresh start. And yet somehow, knowing the Coates family no longer lived in that cosy, old, sandstone place with its roaring open fires, it had felt like the end of an era.

'Rick? Mate, can you hear me?' Kaspar shook the memories off and called out with deliberate cheerfulness as he approached the figure lying on the ground, one eye half-closed and bloodied.

The extent of the blast damage made it almost impossible to recognise the man as Rick, but the man's build and clothing fitted. There was one way to tell for certain, though. Carefully, Kaspar ripped the man's shirt sleeve.

A clipper ship stared boldly back.

Rick. But he wasn't conscious. Pinching the man's side, Kaspar began a quick examination, surprised when Archie came running up not far behind him. Her intake of breath was the only acknowledgement that the dark shadow was indeed a person.

'Is it your friend Rick?'

'Yes. Get a medical crew,' he instructed.

'He might have a mobile,' she suggested hopefully, but Kaspar shook his head.

'He doesn't. Claims to hate them. So you'll just have to hoof it. Can you do that?'

'Yes.'

'Good. Tell them to alert the air ambulance and say we've got an unresponsive adult male, around fifty, with severe maxillofacial blast injury, including tissue loss of the right eye and nose and unstable maxilla. GCS three and his airway is going to need to be secured immediately.'

She recited it back clearly and competently despite the slight quake in her voice then left. Kaspar turned back to Rick. By the looks of it, the man was mercifully beginning to regain some degree of consciousness.

'Rick? It's Kaspar. Can you hear me?'

At least the older guy was making vague groaning noises now, even if he didn't appear to recognise Kaspar at all. He certainly couldn't seem to speak, although that was hardly a surprise. Keeping up light, breezy conversation, Kaspar concentrated on the injuries and the potential damage to the man's airway. If that collapsed, things would spiral downwards pretty damned fast.

Occupied, it felt like it was only minutes later when the helicopter landed and the on-board trauma doctor came racing over.

'Kaspar Athari.' The doctor nodded in deference. 'Your partner said it was you. I'm Tom. What have we got?'

'Adult male, around fifty years old. Name is Rick.'

'Rick the food truck guy? You're sure?'

'Sure enough.' Briefly, Kaspar tapped a bold, unusual tattoo on the man's upper arm. 'Approximately fifteen minutes ago he was changing a gas bottle on his food truck when it exploded, no witnesses except myself and my skydiving partner but we were too far away to see clearly. He appears to have been projected by the force and hit his face and neck on something, I would guess the vehicle bracket. There's tissue loss of the right eye and of the nose, unstable maxilla and suspected crushed larynx. Initially unresponsive, he's now producing sounds in response to verbal stimuli. GCS was three, now four.'

'And he's breathing?'

'For now,' Kaspar said quietly. 'But with the soft tissue swelling and oedema there's still a risk of delayed airway compromise, while haemorrhage from vessels in the open wounds or severe nasal bleeding from complex blood supply could contribute to airway obstruction.'

'Okay, so the mask is out, given the damage to his face, supraglottic devices are out because of his jaw, and intubation is out because if the blast caused trauma to the larynx and trachea, any further swelling could potentially displace the epiglottis, the vocal cords and the arytenoid cartilage.'

The trauma doctor ran through the list quickly, efficiently. He was pretty good—something Kaspar always liked to see.

'One more thing,' Kaspar noted. 'There's a possible cervical injury.'

'One p.m. So we've got a high risk of a full stomach after lunch, which means increased risk of regurgitation and aspiration of gastric contents. I could insert a nasogastric tube or I could apply cricoid pressure, but either of those procedures could worsen his larynx and airway injuries.'

At least the guy was thinking.

'Yes,' Kaspar agreed slowly, not wanting to step on anyone's toes. Ultimately, this was the trauma doctor's scene. He himself might be a surgeon, but today he was a skydiver on his day off. 'Still, I'm not confident that his airway will hold without intervention.'

'Can't intubate, can't ventilate,' Tom mused. 'Which leaves a surgical airway option. Tracheotomy or cricothyroidotomy.'

'I'd say so,' Kaspar concurred, thrusting his hands in his pockets to keep from taking over. The doctor was actually good, but Kaspar knew he'd be faster, sharper. It was, after all, his field of expertise.

It was the one thing that gave him value in this world. Every patient. Every procedure. They mattered. As though a part of him imagined that each successful outcome could somehow make up for his unthinking actions that one night with a couple of drunken idiots. As though it could somehow redress the balance. A hundred good deeds, a *thousand* of them, to make up for that one stupid, costly error of judgement.

But it never would.

Because it hadn't been merely a mistake. It had been a loss of control. The kind that was all too reminiscent of his volatile father.

The kind that Peter Coates had tried to teach him never to lose.

The memories burned brightly—too brightly—in his head. It must be why he was feeling so disorientated. He'd thought the jump would help, but jumping with that woman had somehow heightened it all.

A familiar anger wound its way inside him. Even now, all these years later. All his awards, his battlefield medals, the way the media lauded him meant nothing.

In many respects he was glad that Archie woman was gone. She was, for some inexplicable reason, far too unsettling. The way she'd looked at him on that plane. As though seeing past the playboy front and believing he would do the right thing and help her.

He couldn't explain it, but she didn't look at him the way almost everyone else in his life looked at him. She didn't look at him as though calculating what being with him would do for her career, or reputation, or fame. In fact, she'd looked at him with eyes so heavy with meaning he hadn't been able to stop himself from wondering what it was she'd seen. Why she made him feel more exposed than anyone had in long, long time.

It made no sense. And Kaspar hated things not making sense.

Just as he hated the part of him that had wondered whether, when this was over and the patient was safely on board the air ambulance, he might head back to the fete or the hangar and perhaps buy her a coffee. Or a celebratory drink that night.

For the first time in a long time the idea of a *date* actually made him feel…alive.

'Want to do the honours?'

Tom's voice broke into his thoughts.

'You're the on-duty trauma doctor.' Kaspar hesitated, fighting the compulsion to jump straight in, needing to be sure. Not to protect himself but to protect the hospital. He owed them that much. 'And you're good.'

'I am.' There was nothing boastful about the way the doctor said it. Simply factual. Exactly as Kaspar might have said it. 'But you're the oral and maxillofacial specialist, it's right up your street and this is a particularly complex patient. I can't afford to make a wrong move. If anyone is going to be able to stabilise him enough to survive the flight, it's going to be you.'

'Fine,' Kaspar acknowledged. It was all he needed to hear.

He bent his head to concentrate on the job he loved best, and pushed all other thoughts from his mind. He wouldn't think any more about Archie. He wouldn't be taking her for a drink that night. And he certainly wouldn't be attending the charity wrap party.

The party was in full swing and, predictably, people were crowding around him, from awed wannabe colleagues to seductive wannabe girlfriends.

But there was only one person from whom Kasper couldn't seem to drag his gaze.

It was ludicrous. So uncharacteristic. Yet it felt inexorable.

He hadn't been able to eject her from his thoughts since the skydive, however hard he'd tried. And he wasn't a man accustomed to failure—as a surgeon he had one of the highest success rates—which made it all the more incredible that banishing one woman from his thoughts was defeating him. If anything, with each day that passed she'd become more of a delicious enigma until he'd found himself powerless to resist coming here tonight.

Just on the off chance that he might see her again.

When was the last time a woman had done that to him?

Had *any* woman? Ever?

He tipped his head in consideration, finally allowing himself to give in to impulse.

Archie was stunning. Not necessarily in looks, although she was certainly very pretty, from her sexy pair of *look-at-me* heels to legs that seemed to go on for ever before they finally slipped beneath a short, Latin-inspired, tasselled dance dress number, showing off perhaps the shapeliest pair of legs he ever recalled seeing. He couldn't seem to help himself, but he practically imagined her wrapping them around his body as he sank into her, so deep that she wouldn't know where he ended and she began.

His body tightened just thinking about it.

Him. Kaspar Athari.

He had never wanted *any* woman quite like this.

He'd never *wanted* quite like this.

He'd had enough women throwing themselves at him on practically a weekly basis that he'd never had to lust after any woman quite so…*helplessly.* Not the most stunning supermodels, or the most worshipped Hollywood starlets. But he was lusting after this perfectly pretty, perfectly cheeky, perfectly ordinary woman. Who, it turned out, was to him most extraordinary.

A little like the woman who had been too frightened to do the static line jump but who, when steering the tandem jump chute with him, had displayed a skill and eagerness that had belied his initial conclusion that she was a novice.

Against all logic, Kaspar found himself fascinated.

There was a story there. *But what?* And why did he even care?

Sexual attraction was one thing. But this was something else. Something…*more.* Certainly more than the physical. She possessed a magnetism in the aura she gave off and the way people gravitated towards her. Especially—and Kaspar gritted his teeth at the thought—the other men on the dance floor. Was he the only one to notice how she danced and twirled, shaking and shimmying quite mesmerisingly, and yet all the while deftly kept her friend between herself and any would-be suitors?

As if the intensity of his stare had finally reached her, she lifted her head, met his gaze and froze. Even from this distance, in this light, he could see the sweetest bloom staining her cheeks and down the elegant line of her neck, her chest rising and falling rapidly in a way that had nothing to do with the fact she'd been dancing. Or perhaps it was just the vividness of his imagination. Remembering the way she'd flushed in the plane the other day.

Either way, he was certain she was consumed by the same greedy fire as he was. The fire that had brought him here tonight, against every shred of logic.

And then she moved, heading off the floor and away from him. His stomach lurched in a way that was all too alien to him and before Kaspar knew what he was doing, he had set his untouched drink down on the bar behind him and was shifting his feet, ready to move. Not prepared to lose her.

Abruptly, her friend caught her and pulled her back. He kept waiting for them to glance in his direction, maybe share a giggle, which he'd seen from women time and again. A part of him almost welcomed it. It might help to topple her from whatever invisible pedestal on which he'd set her, help remind him that she was a woman like any other.

But it didn't happen. If anything, Archie studiously avoided meeting his gaze again, and had clearly omitted to mention him to her friend, and her dignified discretion only seemed to add to her allure. Especially when she resumed dancing, only to be a little more self-conscious, a fraction stiffer than she had been before. It was the tell he needed, knowing now she was indeed equally attracted to him.

It should concern him more that it felt like such a victory.

Alarm bells were sounding but too faint, too distant to have the impact he suspected they should have had. To jolt him back to reality. To warn him that she didn't look like the kind of woman who did one-night stands. She looked like the kind of woman who did walks along beaches, and romantic meals, and talking until dawn. Relationships. *Love*. It was such bull.

He'd seen first-hand the toxic depths to which such emotions could plunge. His parents' explosive marriage had been equalled only by their acrimonious divorce. And him, in the middle of it all his life. Their pawn. The tool they'd used to goad and taunt each other. The burden they'd each tried to make the other one bear.

And not just his parents. What about his own explosiveness? That out-of-control side of him that had only had to emerge once to completely ruin someone's life. He'd sworn it would never happen again, and it hadn't. Some might call him emotionally detached, or unavailable. He wasn't. Where his patients were concerned he felt as much empathy as he could, for patient and family, without it impairing his ability to do his job. It was only in his personal life where he exerted such emotional…*discipline.*

So he did sex. He did fun. He did mutual gratification.

He didn't do intimacy and he didn't do complications.

Something told him that this Archie woman was both, and the best thing he could do, for both of them, would be to stay away.

Turning back to the bar, Kaspar picked up his drink and tried not to be irritated by the group of preening, simpering women who had begun to cluster around his part of the bar. It was about as easy as pretending he wasn't searching out blonde hair and a metallic shimmer in the reflection of the mirror behind the glasses.

Apparently, his skydiving butterfly was now edging her way off the opposite side of the dance floor. About as far away from him as she could get.

He didn't give himself time for second-guessing. For the second time that evening, he set his untouched drink down and gave in to temptation.

CHAPTER THREE

'ARCHIE, WAIT. SLOW DOWN. Where are you going this time?'

'Relax,' Archie cast over her shoulder, a bright smile plastered to her lips at her friend's typically bossy tone. 'I'm just going for a drink.'

Still, she didn't slow down in her quest to get off the dance floor and around to the other side of an enormous pillar that would shield her from Kaspar's view. No easy feat in the ridiculously high heels Katie had insisted on lending her to go with the seriously sexy metallic number her friend had also talked her into buying this afternoon.

It was years since she'd been out so called *clubbing it*—not that she'd ever had the time or inclination to go out all that often, neither was this charity wrap party exactly *clubbing it*—but, still, she hoped she hadn't looked too awkward and robotic out there on the dance floor. She'd felt fine…right up until she'd seen him watching her.

The minute she'd spotted him, her body hadn't quite felt her own. As though it wasn't completely under her control. Even now the memory of his eyes scanning over her left her blood feeling as though it was effervescing through her veins, making her entire body hum.

It was an unfamiliar, but not altogether unpleasant sensation.

Ducking behind the pillar, Archie pressed her back

against the cool, smooth concrete and rested her hand underneath her breastbone. She could feel the tattoo her heart was drumming out, leaving her unable to even catch her breath. And it had nothing to do with the dancing. Oh, she'd tried to ignore him, especially when his usual harem had draped themselves around him and he'd barely had the decency to offer any of them the time of day.

But who could ignore Kaspar Athari?

'So, if you're getting a drink why are we the other side of the room from the bar?' Katie bobbed under her nose, her brow knitted.

'Hmm? Oh. I just…needed to catch my breath.'

It wasn't exactly a lie, but she might have known her old friend would see through it.

'Archie, you're about as jittery as a beachgoer trying to get across hot sand.'

'No, I'm not.'

Katie's eyes narrowed sharply.

'Is this about "the Surgeon Prince of Persia"?'

'I don't know what you're talking about,' she managed loftily, only for Katie to snort in derision.

'Yeah, sure you don't. He's been devouring you with his eyes all night and you've been lapping it up.'

'I have not,' Archie spluttered, her knotted stomach twisting and flipping. 'And it hasn't been all night. It has been half an hour at most.'

'Aha!' Katie declared triumphantly. 'So it *is* about the perennially sexy Kaspar Athari.'

'No…not at all…well, not really. That is… Why are you frowning? Aren't you the one who said I needed to get back out there and have fun, like we used to in uni? Like I did before my dad…died? Before I married Joe?'

She tailed off awkwardly as Katie pulled a face.

'I've said it before and I'll say it again, I always hated

the way you changed when you married Joe. You went right into yourself. Nothing like the fun, sassy Archie I'd come to know.'

'It wasn't Joe who did that.' Archie wrinkled her nose. She'd tried a hundred times to explain it to Katie, but her friend had never quite understood. Still, she couldn't help feeling she owed it to Joe to try again. 'He was exactly what I needed at that time in my life.'

'I disagree.'

'I know you do. You remind me often enough.'

Still, there was no rancour in Archie's tone. In many respects it was buoying that her friend cared enough to do so. And Katie's wry smile of response revealed that she knew it, too.

'I just feel that, while he may not have intended to, Joe took advantage of the fact that you were young and naïve. You were grieving for your dad, and your brother and his new wife were half a world away.'

They were falling into a conversation they'd had a hundred times before, but it was impossible to stop.

'He didn't take advantage. It was mutually beneficial.'

Katie's eyebrows were practically lost in her hairline, but at least she had the tact not to bring up any painful reminders of more than three years of failed pregnancy attempts. The miscarriage at eighteen weeks.

Agony seared through her. Black, almost debilitating.

Faith.

As though it didn't lacerate her from the inside out just *thinking* her unborn daughter's name.

She swayed dangerously.

Had it not been for the silent, supportive hand at her elbow, Archie was afraid she was about to tumble to the floor. She blinked at Katie gratefully. Unspoken, unequivocal support shone back at Archie. Bolstering her. Making her want to forget the fact that, barely a year after she'd lost her unborn daughter, Joe was expecting a baby with his new wife.

It hurt.

Though not, perhaps, in precisely the way Archie might have thought it would. She couldn't pinpoint it, but neither could she help suspecting that it had less to do with Joe than it ought to, and more to do with the simple pain that another woman seemed to find it so easy to have a baby while her own traitorous body hadn't been able to do the one thing she felt it had surely been designed to do.

'Fine, let's say it was mutually beneficial…' Katie conceded at length, though Archie could hear by her friend's tone that she didn't remotely believe that.

'You look like you've swallowed a bee.'

She couldn't help a chuckle, even it did sound half laugh, half choked-back sob. Katie valiantly attempted to ignore her.

'Mutually beneficial,' she repeated firmly. 'And you're right. Now is your time to get back the Archie I used to know. The one I admired so much that I used to wish I was more like you. The Archie who threw herself out of a plane today, for her father, for Faith, for a new start.'

'You make it sound so easy.' Archie smiled softly, the sadness she tried so hard to shake but couldn't still tiptoeing around inside her.

But she wanted to. And the jump today was the first time she'd felt she might actually be ready to do so.

Because of the jump? Or because of Kaspar?

Archie slammed away the unbidden thought in an instant but it was too late. It couldn't be *un*-thought. Instinctively, her eyes were drawn back to where Kaspar had been standing, staring at the pillar as though they could bore a path straight through it to see him.

It was pathetic.

But it was also the biggest vaguely positive reaction she'd had to anything or anyone in a very long time. And that felt strangely compelling.

Kaspar Athari, back in her life after all these years. He'd been her first, only crush. Except back then he hadn't even noticed her and so she hadn't had the guts to do anything about it. Suddenly, here he was again and this time he had certainly noticed her. It was as though she was being offered a second chance. It couldn't be just a coincidence, surely? It had to be *fate*. Either way, it was making her want to…*do* something. Anything.

She turned to Katie with as firm a nod as she could manage.

'Fake it till you make it, right?'

'Absolutely.'

It was easier said than done, but what the heck.

'Fine.' Archie sucked in a deep, steadying breath. 'Then if I'm going to…what did you say earlier this evening? Get back on the horse? Then why not go all out with the infamous "Surgeon Prince of Persia"?'

Why did it feel easier to call him by his ridiculous nickname? Was it because it felt too close to home to call him Kaspar?

'Yes.' Katie didn't look remotely abashed. 'I did say that. But not with him. He'd gobble you up and spit you out. The man is pure danger.'

Seriously, how difficult could it be to dredge up a casual grin while simultaneously trying to stop her stomach from executing a perfect nose-dive?

'Maybe that's what I need?' she tried hopefully. 'A bit of danger.'

'Absolutely not.' Katie shook her head so vigorously her shiny halo of curls bobbed perfectly around her pretty face. 'No chance. There's absolutely no way I'm letting a guy like that get anywhere near you. Over my dead body. You can count on me for that.'

Archie frowned, confused.

'I've heard you drool over the Surgeon Prince a hundred times. Are you really saying you wouldn't go there after all?'

'Of course I would,' Katie scoffed loudly. 'Trust me, I'd be in there like a shot if the guy so much as squinted in my direction.'

'So he's okay for you, but not okay for me?'

Archie didn't know whether to feel insulted or honoured.

'He's not okay for you *right now.* If you were the old, fearsome Archie from back in uni, then I'd say go for it. *That* Archie could have handled a man like Athari.'

This was it. She could either go along with what her friend was saying, proving Katie right. Or she could show a little spirit. Like she had on that skydive. Not that she'd told Katie, who'd been occupied with her own charity water-polo match, about the tandem jump.

Archie blew out sharply.

'You know, I think I can handle one little prince.'

Katie opened her mouth, eyed her and closed her mouth again. A crooked smile that Archie knew so well hovered on her friend's lips.

'I do believe you mean it.'

'I do.'

Katie paused, considering.

'Then far be it from me to stop you. Okay, you know that sexy, dangerous scar across his jawline?' Archie nodded silently. 'Apparently it was the result of some big fight when he was younger.' Katie hugged her arm tightly and whispered in conspiratorial tones. 'You remember those massive Hollywood kung-fu, karate-style blockbusters he did as a seven- and eight-year-old?'

The Hollywood life he'd been only too desperate to run away from, Archie remembered. Not that she could say anything.

'Yes, I think so,' she hedged instead.

'Of course you have to know them. They were *huge*, until his mother apparently demanded too much money or riders or whatever and he got kicked out and replaced.'

The rumours didn't come close to the damage his volatile mother had caused. But she couldn't say that either.

'So you heard he got the scar on those films?' Archie tactfully changed subject.

Katie's eyes sparkled with excitement.

'No, the rumour I actually read somewhere was that the fight was down some back alley when he was about seventeen or something, and wasted after a drinking session. Apparently he was outnumbered five to one but he still beat their collective backsides. Juicy, isn't it?'

'Juicy,' Archie agreed half-heartedly.

The idea of the quiet, controlled Kaspar of back then drinking, let alone fighting, was a complete anathema to her. No doubt a lie the press had spun to help them with their paper-shifting image of the playboy Kaspar. Not that he hadn't played his own stupid part to a T.

But the man in the media bore little resemblance to the boy she'd once known. And it was the latter who had stolen her adolescent heart.

Besides, she'd been there when he'd really got that scar, climbing the forty-foot oak tree outside Shady Sadie's house when he'd been fifteen. Or at least she'd been in the living room with her father when Robbie had raced back to say that a damaged limb had given way and Kaspar had fallen to the ground. He'd been carted off to the hospital with a few superficial cuts and bruises and that one deep gash. He'd worn it with all the pride of a battle scar, of course. Trust the media to come up with something far more dark and exotic to explain it.

But they couldn't have made up *everything*, could they? The playboy lifestyle? The dangerous reputation? It had been fifteen years since she'd last seen him so of course he wasn't going to be the same boy she'd known. As Katie gabbled on, Archie let her head drop back, the cool concrete of the pillar seeping into her brain, and tried to think a little more clearly. Maybe opening the Kaspar Athari can of worms really wasn't the best idea she'd ever had.

As Katie's hands grabbed her shoulders and hauled her off the pillar, Archie was tugged back to the present.

'This is your chance, here comes your Surgeon Prince.'

Before she could stop it, she was being swung around and thrust out around the column. The breath whooshed from her body. She didn't need to turn to know that Katie would have already gone.

'And there I was thinking you were hiding from me, Archie.'

The rich, slow drawl was laced with a kind of lazy amusement as every inch of Archie's skin prickled and got goosebumps. Not least the fact that he knew who she was after all. Her stomach spiralled like a helter-skelter in reverse.

Archie. He rolled her name on his tongue as though sampling it, tasting it. She imagined he was measuring it against the woman she was now, compared to the 'Little Ant' he'd always known her as.

She opened her mouth to speak just as Kaspar stepped closer to her. Everything in her head shut down as her body shifted into overdrive. Heady, and electrifying, and like nothing she'd ever known before.

He was dressed smart-casual, a vaguely lemony, leathery scent toying with her nostrils, and he practically *oozed* masculinity. Enough to eclipse every other male in the room most probably. Even every other male in the county. The world.

Even her childhood crush on him didn't compare. It made her feel physically winded and adrenalin-pumped all at once.

The indolent crook of his mouth, so sinful and enticing, gave the distinct impression that he could read her thoughts. Feed into her darkest desires. It made her very blood seem to slow in her veins. A sluggish trickle, which her thundering heart seemed to be working harder and harder to process.

He was simply intoxicating. She cast around for something, anything, that wouldn't betray how at sea she felt.

'How is the patient? Rick, wasn't it?'

Not exactly ideal, but it would have to do. Kaspar only hesitated for a moment.

'He's in pretty bad shape.'

'But you can help him?'

'Possibly.'

He didn't want to talk shop, she could understand that, but it was buying her some much-needed time. She had to settle down. Katie was right, she was like a beachgoer on hot sand.

'I think I read last year that you had a patient who'd had a firework go off in his face and you used some kind of layering technique?'

'You're in the medical profession?' Kaspar's stare intensified.

Archie swallowed. Hard.

'No, actually I'm in the construction industry. I build the hospitals, you work in them.'

'You build them?'

'Well, I work out layout, ease of movement so it isn't a rabbit warren; service routes such as for heating, lighting and medical gases especially for the operating rooms; whether to connect to the existing back-up generators, or build new ones; medical incinerators, that sort of thing.'

There was a lot more to it, and given how much she loved her job she could probably go on about it all night. Which would be a problem. It was hardly the most seductive of conversations.

'Are you part of the team building the new women's and children's wing for our hospital?'

Pride outweighed her need to change the subject.

'Yes.'

'I'm impressed. It's looking really good and I believe you're pretty much on time and on budget.'

She was powerless to prevent a grin so wide it might well crack her face in two.

'Thanks. It isn't going too badly. There are a few niggles but I built decent float into the programme so it shouldn't be too much of an issue. Once we've finished on the new wing we'll start on the new hospice facility across the site. We should be done within ten months, hopefully.'

'Even more impressive.'

'Dad always loved what I did,' she added suddenly.

Waiting, *hoping*, for Kaspar to add something he also remembered about her father. Then fighting the sense of discouragement when he barely even reacted.

'I can imagine.'

'Anyway,' she caught herself, 'we were talking about your firework patient.'

She didn't know why it felt so important that he should answer her. Perhaps because her dad had once told her and Robbie that getting Kaspar to open up about the things he loved was the key to knowing the boy. He kept everything that mattered to him so closely guarded, as though he feared the pleasure could be snatched from him at any time. The way his mother had often cruelly snatched away anything he'd shown an interest in as a kid, from toys, to hobbies, to his only decent stepfather.

According to her dad, Kaspar had never been a kid in the strictest sense of the word. His parents' volatile relationship had caused him to grow up quickly, to distance himself from people, to distrust easily. But her own father had brought him round, treating him exactly as he'd treated Robbie, encouraging when he could, laying down the ground rules at other times. And she'd treated him like a brother while Robbie, of course, had just been Robbie, sweet, funny and easygoing.

Did Kaspar remember all that? If he did, did he care? Enough to answer her?

He hesitated and, for a moment, she thought he was going to sidestep it.

'The boy's jaw was shattered. He'd lost a chunk of it along with the teeth on the right side. He couldn't eat, couldn't even speak, so I needed to build a new jaw and simultaneously implant teeth. We layered pieces of titanium and then used a laser to harden the material. The lattice structure allowed us to really bend and form it so that it was the right size and shape for the kid, fitting perfectly and looking natural.'

Archie didn't realise she'd been holding her breath until he stopped speaking. He was looking directly at her, his eyes were dark, intense, like a moment of understanding. Of connection.

She didn't know whether it was a good or a bad thing that at that moment the music cranked up a notch and whatever else he was saying was lost, swallowed up by the thumping bass line.

'Say that again?' she shouted, but he shook his head.

The moment of opening up to her about his career was clearly over. She leaned in to speak into his ear, swaying slightly on her friend's heels, her body lurching against his as he put his arm around her to steady her. Her lips grazed his skin and she smelled the tantalising citrus scent.

It hit her again, that wall of primal need, stealing her breath away as his touch seared every inch of her flesh. It was almost a relief when the music kicked down again and he released her.

'You want to get out of here?' she asked instead.

'Together?'

'Is that a problem?'

The words were out before she had even thought about them. Seductive, teasing, another flash of the old, adult Archie. Yet the way she could never have dreamed of being as a thirteen-year-old with a crush. It was exhilarating.

'Not for me,' he growled. 'But, then, I'm sure you've heard the endless scandals that seem synonymous with my name. This isn't a high-profile charity event, but it isn't a small gathering either. If any press spot us, your photo will be on the internet before we even get to my hotel.'

'Is that your attempt to warn me?' She deliberately rolled her eyes. 'Only I make it a point never to believe idle gossip. I don't think they know the old Kaspar.'

'The *old* Kaspar?' His brow furrowed and as two light indentations peeked out from between his eyebrows a wave of familiarity unexpectedly coursed through Archie, making her clench her fingers into a fist just to keep from reaching out and lightly skimming them even as her stomach executed another downward dive.

So he *didn't* know who she was. No wonder he hadn't

reacted to her mention of her father. Sick disappointment welled in her, but instead of backing away, as she might have done, a flash of the daredevil Archie Katie had been talking about suddenly flared within her.

Maybe, just maybe she could jog his cobwebbed memory. She would rather he piece it together himself than simply hit him over the head with it. She didn't want to risk anything that might make him back away from her.

'You know, the pre-"Surgeon Prince of Persia" reputation,' she prompted. 'The kid who climbed trees, and built dens, and fought with his best friend.'

Another beat. Imperceptible to perhaps anyone else. She felt rather than saw the shift.

'There is no pre-"Surgeon Prince of Persia".' He winked.

It should have irritated her, being altogether too seductive, suggestive and downright overconfident. It didn't. She'd seen the façade sliding back into place as though he regretted his moment of perceived weakness. That *tell* she recognised from long ago. More polished now, but there nonetheless. Kaspar the playboy might be standing in front of her, but she'd seen the Kaspar she'd known, the one she'd wanted, was still in there. She could still unearth him. For a moment back there she had succeeded.

A thrill coursed its way through her, lending her the confidence she'd been lacking.

'I don't know whether to admire your confidence or deplore your arrogance.' She cocked her head to one side as if genuinely giving it serious consideration. 'I rather fear it's the latter.'

'Oh, I seriously doubt that.'

His wolfish smile did little to soothe her jangling nerves. It was as though he was enjoying the banter. Relishing the challenge. Maybe if she dropped the right prompts, he would finally realise who she was. Finally remember.

'Are you really the blasé Lothario the press paint you as? Bedding a different woman every other night?' she challenged.

'Well, if it's in the press, then it must be true.'

Which wasn't really, she couldn't help but notice, an answer at all. It begged the question of why, if he was more like the Kaspar she remembered than the Kaspar the media seemed to describe, he would ever have allowed this unfavourable reputation of his to slide?

'So you haven't slept with any of the hundreds of women you've been linked with over the years?'

'I didn't say that either.' His teeth almost gleamed and Archie shivered as she felt their sharp edges as surely as if he had them against her skin.

Grazing her. Nipping her. An intimacy she'd read in books or experienced in her fantasies. Never in real life. Certainly not with Joe. She held his gaze, steady and sure, until eventually—incredibly—he broke his gaze.

Archie wasn't sure who was more surprised, her or Kaspar himself.

'I confess that I'm always impressed how I have the time to date quite so many women. Although I won't deny that when I get chance I do enjoy the company of the fairer sex.'

Something kicked hard, low in her stomach.

'Of course you do.'

'I am, after all, a man.' He took a step closer to her and she found herself backing up to the pillar, her entire body fizzing with anticipation. 'Or are you going to pretend that you haven't noticed?'

'And if I said I hadn't?'

'I'd say that, public perceptions and exaggerations aside, I know women well enough to read that such an assertion would be a lie.'

'Is that so?' She barely recognised the husky voice coming out of her mouth. And Kaspar only cranked that sinful smile up all the higher.

'That's so. You noticed me. What's more, you want me. Almost as much as I want you.'

'There's that hubris again.'

'Perhaps it is hubris.' He took another step closer, not looking remotely remorseful. 'But it doesn't make it any less true. Shall we put it to the test?'

Suddenly, she was caged. The pillar at her back and Kaspar on the other three sides. Huge, and powerful, and heady. He wasn't actually touching her, and yet she felt the weight of him pressing in on her. Holding her immobile.

Not that she felt remotely like trying to escape.

'You really are altogether too sure of yourself.' She had no idea how she managed to sound so breezy.

Especially considering the frenzy into which her body currently seemed hell-bent on working itself. Lust and longing stabbed through her.

'Imagine how disappointing it would be if you fell short.'

He actually looked affronted just for a split second, before his eyes crinkled and a warm laugh escaped his lips. It was as though all the air in the room—in the world—went into that laugh. As though she didn't need it to breathe and could exist on that laugh alone. As though there was nothing else but Kaspar.

'I can assure you, Archie, I do not...*fall short.* In any respect.'

Her name on his lips again. If only she had the guts to reach up and kiss him, to discover whether his mouth tasted just as good as she imagined. She tried to but her body wouldn't move, probably due to this overriding need for him to recognise her properly. So in the end she simply stared back into eyes, which were all too familiar. In colour if not in expression.

'Well, of course, you would think that.'

'It isn't a matter of what I think.' His dark, indolent tone spiralled through her. Every inch of her body felt it wrapping around her. Pulling tighter. Drawing her closer. 'It's a matter of what I know.'

It was all she could do to offer a nonchalant eye-roll.

'Let me guess. A hundred women hailing you as a deity in the throes of passion?'

She didn't want to think of those stories the papers loved to run with. The fact that his sexual prowess was lauded quite as much by quite so many. Although, now he'd mentioned it, it didn't add up that he should be quite such a driven, dedicated surgeon and yet have so much time for personal indulgences.

'Bit of an exaggeration. Although, frankly, I wasn't thinking of a single other woman. I was only interested in one. And she's standing right in front of me.'

'Oh, you *are* good,' she conceded, hoping against hope she didn't look half as flushed as she felt.

Hoping he couldn't hear the drumming of her heart or the roaring of blood in her ears. Hoping he couldn't read the lust pouring through her and making her nipples ache they were so tight. Hoping he couldn't feel the heavy heat pooling at the apex of her legs the way no man had ever made her feel before. At least not quite so wantonly.

She had a terrible fear that perhaps no other man would make her feel that ever again.

'Care to confirm that conclusion?' he murmured, his voice pouring over her just the way she would imagine warm, melted chocolate would do.

If she'd ever been that sexually adventurous, of course. Which she never had been. She imagined this version of

Kaspar was, though, and the thought made her pulse leap in her wrists, at her throat.

What was the matter with her?

Kaspar didn't miss a thing. His eyes dropped to watch the accelerated beat, his face so close she could almost draw her breath as he exhaled his. His eyes never left hers, their intentions unmistakeable.

What wouldn't she have given for Kaspar to look at her like this when they'd been kids and she'd been besotted with him? And now he was.

Before she could stop herself, she reached out to trace the scar Katie had mentioned earlier.

'Is this really the result of some drunken bar brawl?'

'What else could it be?' His voice rasped over her as though his very fingers were inching down her spine. It was all she could do not to give in to a delicious shiver.

'I don't know, something more banal.' Archie had no idea how she managed to execute such an atypically graceful and nonchalant shrug. 'Like a childhood accident. Falling off a bike? Charging into a table? Tumbling from a tree?'

His eyes sharpened for a moment.

Something hanging there. Teetering between them.

'You have brothers?'

Her breath caught in her chest. A tight ball of air. Was Kaspar finally remembering?

A slew of emotions rushed her. Feelings she'd thought long since dead and buried. Idealistic, romantic, intense fantasies she'd cherished as an adolescent fancying herself in love with the oblivious Kaspar.

He'd ruined her, without ever touching her. Archie was sure of it. His mother had hauled him back to America right at the peak of her crush on him. If that hadn't happened, no doubt the infatuation would have run its course, as it did with most young girls. Instead, for years, she'd imagined she and Kaspar to be some kind of modern-day star-crossed Romeo and Juliet, torn away from each other before Kaspar had even had a chance to open his eyes and see what had been in front of him all along. She'd carried the ridiculous dream with her long after she should have let it die.

It was the reason she'd never had a serious boyfriend, always holding a part of herself back in her relationships. Until Joe, of course. But that had been tainted with other issues.

Now, suddenly, she had the chance to be with Kaspar. Only for one night, perhaps, but why not? They were both adults. She might never have imagined herself having a one-night stand before—she probably wouldn't with anyone else in the world—but Kaspar wasn't just anybody. Forget the wicked playboy everyone else knew. She wanted one night with the first and only boy she'd ever had a crush on. It might not be who Kaspar was any more, but at least it would help her to finally let go of her unrealistic, romantic, adolescent ideals.

Too late, she realised that his last words hadn't been a question as he'd pieced together who she was but more about explaining her accuracy away as if she was any girl with a brother.

'Nice guess. Most boys have fallen out of tree at one time or another,' he muttered. 'Still, it's refreshing to meet someone who would prefer to see the good in someone rather than simply believe all the media scandal.'

'No one can be quite as two-dimensional as the press seem to like to paint your Surgeon Prince alter-ego,' she breathed, willing the shutters to stop rolling down over his eyes.

'You'd think,' he offered flatly. 'But they're right about

me. The bar brawl, the women, the flashy lifestyle. All things a girl like you would be best staying away from.'

It was impossible not to bristle, even as her entire body lamented the way he was pulling back from her.

'I'm twenty-eight, hardly a mere *girl*.'

'But too nice to get chewed up and spat out by the press, which, I can assure you, would happen if I kissed you the way I want to.'

It purred through her, starting at her toes and gaining speed and strength, until by the time it reached her head the roar was so loud in her ears that Archie was almost shocked the entire party couldn't hear it.

He wanted to kiss her. *Kaspar* wanted *her*.

'Let me get this straight.' She had no idea how her vocal cords even remembered how to speak. 'On one hand the infamous playboy Kaspar Athari is telling me that he lives up to his depraved reputation and on the other he's trying to protect mine by not sleeping with me?'

'Call it a Christmas miracle.'

'You're quite a few months out,' she pointed out shakily. 'What *would* people say if I told them you weren't quite the bad boy they think you are?'

'They wouldn't believe you,' he answered simply.

It felt like a sad fact.

Worse was the fact that he was pulling away from her. Ironic that she'd been right about him being the old, good Kaspar deep down, and that it was exactly *that* Kaspar who was trying to protect her now. Even though he still didn't recognise her.

She couldn't let that happen.

She couldn't allow this one opportunity to slip away from her because she'd let the last few years beat her down. She'd promised Katie she was getting back to her old self. She'd sworn to herself on that skydive that it was the moment she finally stepped away from the mess of the last five years or so.

If she wanted Kaspar, she was going to have to prove it. And she was going to have to tell him who she really was.

Leaning forward before she could second-guess herself, Archie fitted her mouth to Kaspar's. And she kissed him.

CHAPTER FOUR

It was one of the most extreme, adrenalin-fuelled rushes of Kaspar's life. Like nothing he'd experienced before. Ever.

And it was only a kiss.

What would it be like to touch every millimetre of her? Taste her? Bury himself inside her? He'd never wanted a woman with such fierce intensity. Fighting the need to possess her with his body in exactly the way he was now possessing her with his mouth. Claiming her and stamping her as his.

He angled his head, the fit becoming tighter, snugger, and when his tongue scraped against hers, she answered it so perfectly that he felt it through every inch of his being. Her body surged against his as though she couldn't get close enough and her arms looped around his neck as though she couldn't trust her legs to stand up on their own.

Kaspar wasn't sure that his own could.

What was it about this woman?

A few minutes ago he'd been priding himself—not to mention surprising himself—on the urge to protect her by staying the hell away from her. Then she'd kissed him and he'd lost the tight sense of self-control he'd honed to perfection over the last fifteen years. Despite what the press said about him.

The urge to press her to the pillar and shut out the rest

of the partygoers was almost overwhelming. But if he did that, he was afraid he would lose himself completely. Here, in a dark corner of a club. He couldn't even think straight. He would never know how he found the strength to pull away.

She looked startled, then embarrassed, but before he could say anything she was already pulling herself together.

'Tell me that wasn't all you've got?' Teasing him again. But he didn't miss the undertone, the hint of uncertainty.

Somehow it only made him want her more.

Ignoring the alarm bells going off in his head, Kaspar forced himself to step away from her. The sense of loss was as shocking as it was nonsensical. He placed his hand at her elbow, telling himself it was only to guide her away from their current position, but he knew that wasn't entirely true. It was an excuse to touch her again.

'You mentioned getting out of here?' he muttered. A statement disguised as a question.

'Yes. *Hell, yes*.' She started forward, then stopped abruptly and placed her hand on his chest, the shake of her fingers betraying how much effort it was taking her. 'Before we do, there's something I need to tell you.'

Kaspar fought the bizarre urge to throw her over his shoulder and carry her out.

'Can it wait?'

Talking was pretty much the last thing on his mind right now.

'I guess.'

He couldn't decipher her expression. Guilt? Or relief?

In that instant, it didn't matter to him. His fingers closed around hers and he couldn't seem to lead her away fast enough. Anticipation made him feel drunk even though he hadn't touched a drop all night—rarely did, despite what the press loved to report—but no alcohol had ever made him feel like this. Like Archie made him feel. He made a brief call to his chauffeur to bring the car around. He just wanted to be alone with her. He *needed* to be, like the hormone-ravaged teen he'd never been.

Ducking down the stairs and past the few photographers milling around was easier than he'd expected, and his car was waiting right outside the door, Still, it was all he could do not to bundle her inside.

'Mine or yours?' he asked, wanting her to feel in control.

'Mine.' She didn't hesitate. 'I don't want to run another gauntlet of photographers.'

She probably wouldn't, but he didn't intend to argue.

'Come here.' His voice was raw, aching.

Obediently, she shuffled across the back seat towards him, having given the driver her address, but he could see her mind still whirring, and knew she was going to try that *talking* stuff again. It was a complication he could do without. Scooping her up, he hauled her into the air before settling her on his lap. His body tautened with approval.

'Much better.'

'Much,' she managed.

And then his mouth was claiming hers again, his hands roaming her body as she straddled him, the way he'd so urgently wanted to do in the club. From the exquisite curve of her calves to toy at the back of her knees, and then up those impossibly long thighs. But instead of going higher, he toyed with the hem of her short dress, then traced a path up her body instead, over the top of the metallic tassels. The material remained a barrier between them, the halter neck almost taunting him as it concealed her breasts from his gaze.

He cupped her chin with one hand, allowing the other to slide into her mass of blonde hair and cradle the back of her head. And for her part Archie met him stroke for stroke, making an exploratory journey of her own over his shoulders, his arms, his torso. She traced every curve and muscle and sinew, and let her head fall back as he scorched a trail of kisses from her mouth, down the elegant line of her neck and to the hollow by her clavicle. Her intoxicating scent filled his nostrils and heightened his senses.

With every sweep of her tongue and graze of her nails, she was driving him wilder and wilder. The fact that her fingers trembled as they undid the buttons of his dress shirt only added to the delicious tension. He yearned to know every inch of her. Intimately and completely. Reaching up, he unhooked the clasp at the back of her neck and allowed the two sides to fall down, exposing the most incredible breasts and hard, pinkish-brown nipples, which seemed to call out to him.

Kaspar couldn't resist. He bent his head and took one perfect bud in his mouth, his tongue swirling around it before he tugged on it. Just the right side of rough.

Her sharp gasp was like a caress against the hottest, hardest part of him. And then she offered the other breast for the same and as he obliged he couldn't stop a groan of desire slipping from his lips. He liked this bold, demanding side of her. He didn't know why, but he got the impression it wasn't a side of her that everyone got to see.

The idea appealed to him far more than it should have.

Lifting his hand, Kaspar lavished attention on one breast as he lowered his mouth to the other. Sucking on the nipple and then drawing back to watch her shiver as the cool air did the rest. He tried it again. And then again as he swapped sides. Until she wriggled on his lap, unmistakeable heat against the most sensitive part of his body. He reacted. Already hard, he was now so solid it was almost painful. Aching to touch her wet heat, to slide inside her.

But not here. Not in the car. With anyone else maybe he wouldn't have cared, but no one else had ever turned him on with quite the feverish quality that Archie had. He only knew he wanted more with her, and not on the back seat of a car.

'What's wrong?' she asked, sensing his change of attitude immediately.

Moving his hands to her hips, Kaspar shifted her backwards slightly. Enough so that every tiny movement of her hips didn't make his body throb quite so tightly.

It damn near killed him.

'Not here. Not the first time,' he managed hoarsely.

'The first time?' She arched one eyebrow as though that would distract him from the way her body quivered on his lap. Her pent-up tension equal to his. 'You're optimistic.'

'Once isn't going to be enough,' he bit out, the rawness in his own voice catching even himself by surprise. When had *that* become a fact? 'You must know that.'

The distinct hitch of her breath didn't help. But whatever answer she might or might not have been about to give was cut short when the driver pressed the intercom to let them know they'd arrived, moments before the car pulled up.

He could barely believe the ridiculous way he couldn't seem to think straight with this woman. She made him lose his head.

Worse, a part of him *liked* it.

Archie opened the door to her apartment and reached for the lights.

Her skin still sizzled at the mere memory of his touch. It was impossible to shake the presentiment that she would never again be able to quash this shiver that ran so deep inside her. She had absolutely no idea how she managed to keep her voice so calm.

'So here we are.' She licked her lips anxiously. This was the first time she'd ever had a man back to *her* home. In fact, this was the first home she'd ever had by herself. 'In my apartment.'

Kaspar looked around.

'Nice place. Been here long?'

She shifted her weight from one leg to the other. This was her chance to tell him.

'Ten months. Since my marriage fell apart.' She shrugged, as though it hadn't felt like yet another catastrophic failure on her part, in her litany of mistakes over the last five years.

'You were married?' He made no attempt to hide his shock.

'For almost four years.'

'What happened?'

'I thought I loved him. I thought he loved me.' Another shrug as she desperately tried to keep the evening light. 'In hindsight, we rushed into it. My father had just died and my brother had emigrated. I was looking for something to fill a void, and Joe was it. He was kind and he cared for me. It was a mistake.'

She couldn't tell him about Faith. She wouldn't be able to dismiss that loss as lightly. Besides, he was still processing the bombshell she had just dropped.

But what choice had she had? He'd rebuffed her attempts to talk to him. To tell him.

'Your father had died, and your brother had emigrated?'

He raked his hand through his hair. A nostalgia-inducing young-boy action she hadn't seen in any press photograph of him for years. Perhaps ever.

She swallowed, her tongue feeling too thick for her shrinking mouth. Then she raised a shaking hand to a small cluster of photos on the wall. They could say all the things she couldn't.

He peered at them. Stepped closer. Stared harder.

She imagined she could see his eyes moving from one to the other. Photos of Robbie, of her father, of herself. And even the one with Kaspar himself.

The growing look of shock on his face twisted in her gut. He honestly hadn't had any idea. The knowledge clawed at her insides. The silence crowded in on them. Sucking every bit of air from the room, making it impossible for her to breathe. It was an eternity before Kaspar spoke, the words hissing out of his mouth like some kind of accusation.

'Little Ant?'

Despite his incredulity there was also a tenderness in the way he said her old nickname that pulled at her in a way she hadn't been prepared for. And he'd addressed her as an individual in her own right, not simply as *Robbie's sister*, which had to mean something, didn't it?

Even so, he was already physically backing away, heading towards the door. And she hated it. Now, more than ever, she wanted that connection with him. The moment they had never had.

Abruptly, desperation lent her an outward strength. Her voice carried an easy quality that she hadn't felt for years, even though her internal organs were working as hard as if they were completing some marathon or other.

'It's Archie now,' she offered redundantly. Awkwardly.

'God! I kissed you.'

Whether he was more disgusted at himself or at the kiss, she couldn't be sure. Either way, it was everything she'd feared.

'We kissed each other,' she corrected, madly trying to

slow her thundering pulse. 'Oh, don't tell me you're suddenly getting all funny about it.'

'Of course I am,' he snarled, his eyes glittering. Dark, and hard, and cold…and something else. Something she couldn't identify. 'You used to be the closest thing to a little sister.'

He headed for the door, unable to sound more disgusted if he'd tried.

'Exactly. *Used* to be,' Archie echoed, refusing to cow at his tone, however it might claw at her. 'It has been fifteen years, Kaspar, and you didn't even recognise me. To all intents and purposes I'm no different from many other women at that party.'

'You aren't any other woman at that party. You're Little Ant. You're far more innocent than any of them.' He reached for the door, opened it, and she'd never felt more powerless. 'Certainly for someone like me. I have to get out of here. Now.'

And suddenly everything slowed down for Archie. She could read the anger and anguish at war on his face, and she realised what was going on. It bolstered her. A rush of confidence warmed her.

'You're not angry with me for not telling you so much as being angry at yourself that you still want me.' Her voice held wonder. 'You *really* want me.'

He didn't stop, didn't even falter. He just continued walking right out of the door.

'I'm exactly the kind of guy you should stay away from, Little Ant.'

'I'm not Little Ant, Kaspar. I haven't been that girl for over ten years. I'm a woman now, with a career, and my own home, and a failed marriage.'

He hesitated in the hallway, just as she'd hoped he would, and turned to face her. He was still fighting temptation, she could tell, but he knew his arguments were holding less and less sway. Deliberately she swept her tongue over her lips, as if to wet them.

His eyes slid down and watched the movement with a darkening expression. A thrill coursed through her. He wanted to do what he thought was the morally right thing, he was *trying* to do it. But things had gone too far in the car. They'd been too intimate. And now he was having a difficult time turning the attraction off just like that.

'I thought you were in Australia.'

He was stalling, she realised incredulously. No one would ever believe it. Not the press, not the public, certainly not the broken-hearted women who flailed in his wake.

'Robbie went after Dad died because his then girlfriend, now wife, was from there. My life was here. I'd just finished my degree, I had a new job…'

'You'd met your husband.'

She couldn't place the edge to his tone, but she did know the moment she'd been imagining was slipping away from her. Too fast.

She needed to salvage the evening, convince Kaspar that she wasn't that kid any more. She was the woman he'd been kissing, holding, touching in the car.

'As nice as this little catch-up might be, we didn't come back here to my flat to shoot the breeze, did we, Kaspar?'

She couldn't decide whether he admired her forthrightness, or if it merely caught him off guard. Either way, she didn't care. She had a small window in which to press her advantage. If she missed it, that would be it.

She stepped forward boldly and flashed him a cheeky grin, disarming him.

'Good, so now we've aired our concerns, can we get back to the fun we were having in the car?'

'Archie, are you listening to me?' he bit out, but he didn't move away.

She stepped forward again.

'I'm trying not to. It's hardly the greatest foreplay conversation. Certainly not worthy of the great Surgeon Prince of Persia.'

'This isn't going to happen,' he warned, his voice gritty. Not entirely as forceful as she imagined he could be.

'I'm pretty sure it already has. Or have you forgotten just how intimate we were on the car journey here?'

She heard the low growl, which reverberated around her. She knew the image of his mouth on her nipples, making her moan and writhe on his knee, was as imprinted in his head as it was in hers. He was close to giving in to her. To this attraction. She just needed to give him that nudge over the edge.

'I'm leaving now, Archie.' He reached his hand out to grab the door handle and close the door behind him.

She had one last chance to stop him.

'Are you sure?' she asked evenly, even as she reached up to the back of her neck, undid the clasp and let the dress drop to the floor, past the flimsy scrap of electric-blue lace, to pool around the skyscraper heels, which she suddenly didn't remotely feel silly wearing.

She felt sexy and powerful and wicked.

But Kaspar wasn't moving. And she had absolutely no idea what he was thinking.

He couldn't move.

Frozen to the spot, his eyes riveted to the vision in front of him, for the first time in his life Kaspar felt powerless. He should leave. Turn around and walk away. But he couldn't bear to.

She was sublime. So completely and utterly perfect.

The tasselled Latin-dance-style dress might have looked good on her, but they hadn't flattered the sexy, voluptuous curves of her body anywhere near as generously as they should have. They should have worshipped her…the way he ached to do right at this moment.

The pictures were still on the wall, a mere few feet away, but he couldn't reconcile the kid in those photos with the woman standing in front him. This one was a *siren*.

From the long line of her neck, down to glorious breasts, which he hungered to cup, caress, kiss, down to the indent of her waist and the belly button around which he could imagine swirling patterns with his tongue. His eyes dropped lower, appreciative and unhurried, to take in the soft swell of her belly and the sensational flare of her hips, and then the incredible V of her legs where the scrap of blue lace, barely concealing her modesty, only seemed all the more titillating.

'Tell me you don't want me, Kasper,' she murmured. The faintest hint of a quiver in her voice, a moment of uncertainty, only making her all the more irresistible.

His entire body pulled taut. Unequivocal male approbation. God, how he wanted to be where that lace was. With his fingers, his mouth, his sex. He couldn't recall ever having ached to be with a woman before. Not like this.

'You know I want you,' he rasped, unable to keep the admission from spilling from his lips.

'Then claim me,' she breathed, offering herself to him.

But now it was about more than just sex. Perhaps it always had been. Perhaps a part of him had known he knew her, even if he hadn't recognised her. It certainly explained the connection he felt.

And that in itself posed the greatest threat. Archie knew him in a way no one else did. Not the press, and not his previous lovers. And that made her dangerous. Hadn't she already told him that she knew the playboy image wasn't really him?

She saw too much. She knew him too well. And that enabled her to slip under his skin every time he wasn't paying full attention. He certainly couldn't afford to spend the night with her.

He hadn't turned himself into the press's idea of the Surgeon Prince of Persia because he'd wanted to be a playboy. He'd turned himself into that two-dimensional version of himself because, ultimately, it was all he deserved. Because his bad-boy image was the only thing that stopped them painting him out as some kind of surgeon hero. And he wasn't a hero.

Just ask the family of that kid whose life he'd changed that night in the bar. But the press had never run with that story. They, like the judge, had vindicated him, Kaspar, of all blame. No matter that he had been the one able to walk out of the hospital that night while the other kid hadn't.

It was why he'd deserved his bad-boy reputation all these years. It was why Archie should stay away from him. And it was why he should walk out of her door now.

But, then, who in their right mind could walk away from someone like her?

Not just because she looked quite like...*that.* But because there was something more than just the physical, more than the undeniable sexual attraction that crackled between them. There was a connection. He'd felt it on the plane, although it had taken him until now to recognise it for what it was.

Archie knew him in a way that no one else did.

Despite the media's potted history of his less-than-enviable childhood, pushed and pulled between two parents who had seen him more as a pawn in their sick game than as a flesh-and-blood boy who either of them loved or wanted, it had nevertheless always been somewhat sanitised and glamorised. Entertainment channels ran specials on his actress mother and himself but they had never, ever even come close to how miserable it had actually been.

In many ways he was grateful for that. But Archie wouldn't be fooled by it. Her father had been the one to save him. She had been there through enough of his childhood to know the truth. Not all of it. No one but him knew all of it. But certainly closer to the truth than anyone else ever could. Or would.

And that was the problem.

He allowed people to paint him as the cad, the womaniser, because that ensured that no one really knew him, understood him, could get close to him. And if they couldn't do that then they couldn't get under his skin. He couldn't bear the idea that anyone could break through his mental armour and make him feel…something…*anything* because then he'd have to feel all those terrible childhood emotions all over again.

It wasn't just that he was a danger to Archie…she was a danger to *him*. To his sanity. And yet he still stood motionless. Powerless to resist her.

'Come and claim me, Kaspar,' she repeated, her voice cracking through the command.

He was sure it was the sexiest sound he'd ever heard.

Logic and sense flooded from his brain, something far more base and primal flooding the rest of his body.

'This can't lead anywhere, Archie. I fly back to the States next week. I don't know when I'll be back.'

'So you'd better make this the best night of your stay, hadn't you?'

So damn sassy. So damn sexy.

He heard the deep growl that seemed to come from the vicinity of his throat, was barely conscious of kicking the door closed behind him with an accurate jab of his foot, and found himself striding across the room towards her.

Towards Archie.

Some madness had taken hold of him, he was sure of it. And then Kaspar wasn't thinking of anything any more. He was dragging her into his arms, moulding her mouth-watering, practically naked body to his, and plundering her too temptingly carnal mouth. And his seductive siren wasn't remotely shy in her sudden state of undress.

Archie wound her arms around his neck, pressing herself so tightly against him he could almost imagine there wasn't a barrier of clothes between them at all, and lifted her legs to wrap around his body as he willingly cupped her firm, neat backside.

He kissed her mouth, her neck, every trembling inch of her collarbone, and she matched him. Kissing his jaw, tugging at his ear lobe and rocking her body against his sex until he feared he might not be able to hold on much longer.

'Which way?' he managed gruffly, scarcely ripping his mouth from hers.

Her reply wasn't much clearer.

'Behind me.'

Obligingly, Kaspar navigated his way to the door, shouldering it open and carrying Archie into the room, smiling at the queen-size bed with its overabundance of scatter cushions.

He lowered her down, less gently than he might have liked, holding himself still while she reached for the buttons on his shirt, undoing them with painstaking care, kissing her way over his chest and abdomen with each new section of bare flesh she exposed. It felt like an eternity before she finally undid the last button and he could shuck off the shirt, but it seemed Archie wasn't done. She reached for his belt, the crack of leather reverberating around the room as she unbuckled the clasp, followed by the unmistakeable sound of the zip opening.

Kaspar circled her wrist with his fingers and pulled away from her as she protested. He couldn't afford to let this go any further. He'd never felt such a lack of control, as if he might explode like a hormone-ravaged teenager. This was as much about Archie's pleasure as his.

He pressed her lightly back onto the bed and covered her body with his, bracing himself as he looked down at her, drinking her in. Marvelling. Every inch of his skin was on fire as Archie ran her fingertips over him, tracing the muscles on his shoulders and down his body.

Heady, and exhilarating, and addictive.

When he cupped her breast, his thumb grazing deliberately against one straining nipple, she gasped, her back arching slightly. Repeating it offered the same glorious result. Then Kaspar lowered his mouth and tasted her as he had in the car, his tongue tracing out an intricate whorl as Archie slid her fingers in his hair and gave herself over to pleasure. He took his time learning every last contour of her breasts, then her abdomen and her hips. Slowly. Thoroughly. Ignoring the almost painful, needy ache of his sex.

Finally, when her soft moans became more urgent, he laid a trail of hot kisses from her navel straight down over her belly and over the top of the flimsiest blue lace panties, which he pulled off in one swift movement. Then he dropped back down to press his mouth to the hottest, slickest, sweetest part of her, making her cry out.

She tasted of fire, and honey, and *need*. Her hips were moving, dancing with him, as he licked his way into her. Her hands cradled his head, the most beautiful, wanton sounds escaping her mouth almost against her will. It spoke to something utterly primal inside Kaspar. As if he would never get enough.

He kissed, licked, sucked until her hands slid from his hair to clutch the cover of the bed, her hips moving erratically, trying to jerk away.

'Please, Kaspar…' She reached for him, but despite the hunger in her voice he had no intention of taking his pleasure yet. This was about Archie.

'There's no rush,' he murmured. 'We've got all night.'

Then, slipping one hand underneath her to hold her in place, he lowered his mouth back down to her intoxicating heat and slid his finger inside her, deep and sure.

Archie shattered, crying out his name as she arched her back and fragmented all around him like some victory he couldn't identify. He kept it going long after she would have pulled away, making her shudder over and over, murmuring against her and making her come apart again.

And when she finally begged him to release her, he let her go, a satisfaction he couldn't explain seeping through to his very bones. As well as a slow, deep ache.

'That was…' She floundered for the words to describe the incredible way she felt. Like nothing she'd ever experienced before. Not even close. 'I feel… You were…'

'We're not done yet.'

His voice was gravelly, raw, and still it felt to Archie as though she was taking a lifetime to refocus. Her body felt exhausted, contented. She struggled to lift herself up onto her elbows.

'We aren't?'

'Not by a long stretch.'

She wasn't sure if it was an avowal or a warning, but the sight of Kaspar standing up, shedding himself of the rest of his clothes until he was naked before her, stole her breath away all over again. His solid physique and utterly male beauty, waiting there just for her, went beyond even her wildest fantasies. Archie let her eyes drop to take in his length, straight and flat against his lower abdomen, as taut and unyielding as a steel blade. Though she would have thought it impossible a moment before, her body gave a fresh kick of lust.

How could it be, after all that, that she wanted him again so instantly?

'That's a relief,' she tried to tease him, but the quake in her voice betrayed her. 'I was beginning to think that was all you had. After talking yourself up earlier tonight, I was expecting a lot more.'

'Is that so?' He arched one eyebrow and she couldn't contain the gurgle of laughter that rumbled in her chest.

'It was a…concern.'

Then he was moving back over her, nestling himself between her legs as his hands moved under her shoulders and he rested on his forearms above her.

'Then let me put your mind at ease. We have a long, long night ahead of us.'

Whatever witty response she might have come out with was chased from her head as he nudged against her hot, wet core. It was too much, and at the same time not enough. She sucked in a deep breath, her legs parting slightly further as his amused eyes caught hers.

'You were saying?'

She shook her head and bit her lip, unable to speak. And then he thrust into her. Hard and strong and deep, stretching her in a way that felt more delicious than uncomfortable. As though she'd been made for him; they'd been made for each other. She shifted instinctively and he groaned, making her feel sexy and powerful all over again. Archie watched him in fascination, his face pulled tight as though he was trying to control himself, as though *she* made him feel unrestrained.

She couldn't help it, this wanton side of her that seemed to be taking over tonight. Lifting her legs, she wrapped them around his waist, locking her heels at his back, drawing him even deeper into her slick, welcoming heat. He groaned again and it pulled at something low in her, and then his eyes caught hers, smoky and strong, the colour of richest brandy, his intent undisguised. Archie's breath hitched somewhere in her chest. All she could do was dig into his arms, his shoulders, as he began to move. A dance as old as time and a pace equally as steady. Her body was helpless to do anything but match it, stroke after stroke, thrust after thrust, his eyes never leaving hers.

She had no idea how long they moved together. A lifetime. Maybe longer. As though she had never been meant to be anywhere else but here. With Kaspar. Better than any of her dreams if only for the simple fact that this was real.

At some point he swept his hand down her side, her already sensitive body shivering at the feather-light touch, and then he was touching her at the centre of her need and there was nothing *feather-light* about it at all. He knew exactly what he was doing. And how much pressure he needed to exert.

Archie gasped and arched her back, her hips, her neck. She wanted to tell him to slow down, not because she didn't want this but because a tiny part of her couldn't stand the thought that he might leave as soon as this was all over, but her tongue refused to work. At least as far as talking was concerned. Instead, she slid her hands down his back, her nails leaving their own exquisite trail, and he shuddered and growled, plunging into her more deeply. So desperate and demanding and *right.* It threw her straight back over the cliff edge until she was tumbling and tumbling, and she didn't care where she landed so long as it was with Kaspar.

And as she called out his name, surrendering herself completely to him, this time Kaspar followed.

CHAPTER FIVE

'FOURTEEN HOURS OF surgery and it all comes down to this.' Kaspar grinned with satisfaction at his team. A reconstruction and rehabilitation procedure on a patient who had lost almost all of his upper jaw and teeth almost a decade earlier, following oral cancer surgery.

'Yeah, rebuilding a man's jaw and bone palate using advanced osteointegration and three-dimensional computerised design. It's awesome.'

Kaspar glanced at the young surgeon. Rich, arrogant, the son of a renowned surgeon, he came across entitled and lacking in empathy, but he was a solid surgeon, if only Kaspar could find a way to steer him.

'More than the medical kudos, it's going to be life-changing for our patient. He'd become almost hermit-like, unable to venture out without people pointing and staring.'

'I guess. But, still, we're, like, in ground-breaking territory here.'

Normally, today's surgery was exactly the kind of challenge on which Kaspar thrived. Had always thrived.

But despite his triumph, Kaspar was preoccupied. He had been ever since that stolen time with Archie almost five months ago.

Five months in which he hadn't been able to get her out of his head. The way she sounded, smelt, tasted. Night after night his body ached for her, in a way it never had for any other woman. He told himself it was just the sex, that he didn't recall the walks, the laughter, the shared memories with such clarity. He refused to admit to whatever alchemy went on in his hollow, astringent chest. Even so, one night hadn't been enough. He'd had to eke out the weekend, then an extra day. Even that hadn't sated the yearning he had for her.

Yearning.

Him.

Every day had been a battle not to contact her. Even whether or not to send her flowers when he'd seen the date a couple of months earlier and had realised it was her birthday. Every day he'd prayed for challenges like this one to walk into his consultation room, if only to have somewhere else to pin his focus.

But it always came back to Archie. And whether, if he took up the offer to return to the UK next month, he should contact her or not.

'I mean, think of it this way,' the younger man enthused, pulling Kaspar back to the present, 'using implant bone to live and grow around a titanium plate, being able to create the bone and tissue to support an implant of a whole new set of teeth. Traditionally we'd have had to use plates and grafts and cadavers.'

'And our patient,' Kaspar continued firmly. 'Being able to speak and be understood, or to eat food or have a drink without fluid spilling from his sinuses and mouth.'

But the young surgeon was only interested in the surgery, and Kaspar didn't have the inclination to lecture as he might otherwise have done. His head was too full of Archie.

He'd told himself he was too damaged. Too selfish. Too destructive. Especially for someone as bright and vibrant as Archie Coates was. He'd kept an ocean between them with the excuse that he was protecting her. But the truth was that he was concerned about her. The longer they'd spent together, the more he'd noticed that she'd seemed to have lost a little of the special lustre he remembered about her. As though life had somehow scratched at her when it shouldn't have. Her father's death, the idiot husband she'd mentioned, maybe even Robbie emigrating.

Whatever it was, something in him ached to be the one to take her pain away.

Ridiculous.

He was the last person to take *anyone's* pain away. It was better to keep his distance.

She was going to be sick.

Archie let her hand fall from the door for the third time in as many minutes, her legs threatening to collapse beneath her. Around six hours ago she'd still been somewhere across the Atlantic. And twelve hours before that she'd been to have a twenty-week ultrasound to determine that her baby was all right.

Their baby.

Hers and Kasper's.

She'd had months to get used to this but it had made little difference, it still felt utterly surreal to her. So how was it going to feel for Kaspar?

Perhaps she should have thought this through better. Yesterday she'd only been grateful that her work and her life to date meant she had three years remaining on her visa which allowed her multiple visits to the States, for up to six months.

Foolishly, she'd taken it as some kind of sign.

The push she'd needed to go and find Kaspar. To tell him about their baby.

Now Archie stopped, one hand reaching out to lean on the wall, the other hand running tenderly over the slight swelling in her abdomen. It was incredible. A miracle. At least to her. Nothing would ever make up for losing her first baby, Faith, at eighteen weeks gestation, and no baby could ever replace her, but in some ways this new tiny human growing inside her went some way to healing those still-raw wounds.

She hovered outside the door, the small cabin bag and work laptop at her feet, trying to summon the courage to knock. It had to be the last thing he would want to hear. Might even prefer not to know. The Surgeon Prince of Persia a father? The press would have a field day.

Nevertheless, deep down she knew she owed it to this baby, and to herself, to at least tell him. To let him make that decision for herself. Still, it was turning out to be a lot harder than she'd hoped it would be.

The old Archie would probably have blurted it out, however awkwardly or untimely. The Archie of the last few years might have shamefully buried her head for as long as she could.

But which Archie was she now? She was more confused than ever. Swinging wildly from the daredevil Archie of old, right over to the reticent woman of recent years, and then back again.

The skydive, then that night with Kaspar when she'd stripped—*stripped*—to seduce him, emboldened in a way she hadn't been for years. For weeks afterwards she'd strutted around feeling ten feet tall and even her friend, Katie, had been forced to admit Kaspar hadn't been such a bad influence after all.

When she'd discovered she was pregnant, it had been a moment of sheer joy and disbelief that her body had effortlessly achieved the one thing it had been struggling to do throughout her entire marriage to Joe. And then she'd been catapulted right back into the dark, cold prison of her mind.

The fear of losing this baby the way she'd lost Faith overrode everything else. With it, the uncertainty, the confusion, the regression to the hesitant Archie of the previous five years. And so she'd spent the past few months bouncing between the two polar opposite versions of herself.

It was how she'd had the confidence to fly halfway around the world to confront Kaspar, and yet now she was here she couldn't bring herself to lift her arm and knock on that door. She could make that final move or she could turn around, head straight back to the airport and be on a plane, with him none the wiser. The most shocking part about it was that Archie had absolutely no idea which way she was going to jump.

Who was she? Really?

And then the decision was taken out of her hands. The door suddenly opened and he was striding out. Stopping dead the instant he saw her.

'Archie.'

'Kaspar.'

There was a beat as his eyes seemed to take her in. Scanning her face, then dropping down. Another beat as they hovered around the evident swell of her belly.

Her whole world pinpointed around him, her breath seeming to slow and then stop in her chest. Time had done little to diminish the impact he had on her. Maybe it had even amplified it. She had the oddest sensation of falling. Plummeting.

The question was, *How painful was the landing going to be?*

'You'd better come in,' he managed at last. The unusually hoarse tone to his voice only made her nerves jangle all the more.

Then he picked up her bags and was gone. Walking back into his office with as little surprise, as little emotion as if she'd been his next patient he'd been waiting to see.

Still, it took her several long moments before she was able to follow him.

She was barely through the door before he was speaking.

'You're pregnant.'

His voice seemed palpably colder now. More forbidding. Or perhaps it was just her nerves. Behind her the door closed with a soft *click*. It might as well have been the clang of prison gates but somehow it offered her the strength she needed.

'*Clearly* pregnant,' he added.

Had her hand wandered to the obvious swell of her abdomen before or after his observation? Lifting her head, Archie met his eyes, not allowing her voice to falter for a second. Though how she managed it, she would never know.

'Yes.'

'We used protection,' he stated flatly.

A statement but not a defence. As though he didn't exactly disbelieve her. She was grateful for that much, at least. It allowed her to soften her voice somewhat.

'Not that first time.'

'So he or she really is mine?'

It felt like a slap across her face, although she supposed it was a reasonable enough question. Still, she couldn't seem to prise her jaws apart, answering him through gritted teeth.

'Who else's would it be, Kaspar? The invisible man's? I'm not in the habit of picking up random men or sleeping around. Yes, it's your baby. *Our* baby.'

It was impossible to follow the flurry of emotions that

passed across his face. But, then, he had always been the poster-boy for denial. Pretending that he was happy, that his family life was fine, to his friends, his school, the world, when her family had seen first-hand how broken he'd been inside. How he'd spent every school holiday with them, along with his nanny, Maggie, just to avoid being dragged into yet another of his parents' twisted games against each other.

'He or she,' he bit out flatly.

'Sorry?'

'Say *he* or say *she.* Don't call the baby an *it.*'

She frowned, confused.

'I don't know whether it's a boy or a girl. I didn't find out. I didn't want to.'

'I don't care,' he growled, the unexpectedly menacing quality to his tone making her skin prickle. 'This baby is not an *it*. Pick *he* or *she*, interchange them, or I'll call her a *she* while you call him a *he*, for all I care. Just don't ever use the term *it* again.'

Fury swirled in his words, but it was the look of torment behind his eyes that really clutched at her, squeezing at her heart. A torment that made her wonder about the childhood she'd pieced together from things she remembered, things her father had said, things she'd read.

'Okay.' She dipped her head. 'I'll say *he*, you can say *she*.'

He didn't reply, but his lips curled in what she took to be a silent thank you.

'So you're…'

'Twenty weeks,' she cut in, barely able to help herself. Although he wouldn't have any idea how significant that was to her.

'You should have told me,' Kaspar bit out, and she had to protect herself against the kick of emotion. The irrational fear that by talking about it she was somehow jinxing things.

'Would you really have wanted to know?'

'That has nothing to do with it,' he almost snarled. 'You've had five months to tell me.'

He hadn't denied it. And even though she'd known the answer before she'd even asked the question, it still hurt.

But she couldn't let him see that. It took everything she had to keep her voice even.

'I'm telling you now.'

'That isn't good enough.'

'It will have to be.' She jutted her chin out, trying not to let him intimidate her.

He narrowed his eyes as if he could see straight through her. As if he knew there was something she was hiding.

'Why not?' he demanded abruptly.

Archie flinched.

'It's…irrelevant.'

'I don't believe that for a moment,' Kaspar barked, folding his arms across his chest.

She tried not to notice how it made his already wide shoulders seem all the bigger, his strong chest all the more unyielding. And she tried not to notice the long fingers that had done such…*things* to her. Over and over that night. That weekend.

When they'd made a baby.

What was she playing at? They were kids and this wasn't a game. She owed him an explanation.

'I didn't tell you because I was scared. I was pregnant once before.' She heard her voice crack but she pushed on, pretending it hadn't. A part of her had known this subject would come up. That it was inevitable. She was ready for it. 'Eighteen months ago. But I lost that baby at eighteen weeks.'

She stopped abruptly, pain ripping through her. Lacerating her from the inside out. Dizzying and unforgiving.

'I'm sorry,' he said simply.

'Her name was Faith.'

She didn't even realise she'd spoken until she heard the words. The agony that had haunted her ever since with *what ifs* and *if onlys*. The self-recriminations. She'd thought she'd been mentally prepared. She'd been dealing with the pain every single day, and each day it had felt just that tiny, minuscule bit easier. But hearing the words aloud, for the first time since it had happened…nothing could have prepared her for that.

She only realised he'd caught her from crumpling on the spot as she found herself in a seat she didn't recall moving to, and Kaspar coming back into the room, a steaming plastic cup in hand.

'Sweet tea.' He thrust it at her. 'Drink it. All of it.'

She didn't dare disobey.

Bit by bit, she sipped at the cup until it was empty. And Kaspar just sat opposite her. Waiting. Wordlessly. While the minutes ticked by. As if he had nowhere else to be but right here. With her.

Tears pricked her eyes and she blinked them back. She shouldn't read anything into that. It didn't mean anything. She couldn't afford to think it did.

'I…needed to get past that point…the eighteen weeks. And then I thought that when I had my twenty-week scan, if it…' What had they agreed, that she would call the baby *he*, and Kaspar would say *she*? 'If *he* was okay, I would tell you. So…here I am.'

She trailed off. Not quite sure how to articulate the storm that roiled around her entire body, constantly upending everything.

His eyes never moved from her. Clear and unblinking.

'So the scan was fine?'

'Yes. But these things are always fine until...until they're suddenly not.'

It was all she could do to keep her voice even and sound calm. There was no point in letting the dark fear that lurked deep inside her take a hold. No point in imagining scenarios that might never happen. The doctors didn't think there was anything they needed to worry about or do, so she had to trust them. They were the medical professionals. Not her.

'What are you doing?' She frowned as Kaspar stalked around his desk, snatched up the phone and stabbed a couple of numbers on the pad.

He didn't answer her, too intent on the call.

'Dr Jarvis, please, it's Dr Athari.' There was a brief pause. 'Catherine? It's Kaspar. I have a patient I need you to examine. It's urgent. Archana Coates, twenty-nine-year-old, approximately twenty weeks pregnant.'

Too shocked to speak, Archie listened as he described her in completely dispassionate terms. Like a third person. *Like a patient.*

'She has a past history of spontaneous second-trimester abortion.' Archie flinched. It was the same terminology the doctors had used around her and she'd never hated a medical term so much in her life. It sounded so wrong, as if she'd had any choice in the matter whatsoever. Kaspar continued, oblivious. 'No, not a referral. It's personal.'

Within moments he had replaced the handset.

'What...what are you doing?'

'Catherine Jarvis is one of the best perinatologists in the world.' He paused as Archie stared at him in confusion, then clarified. 'Maternal-foetal specialist. She has a patient with her now but she'll see you in half an hour.'

'I don't... *No!*' Archie shook her head at the implications of what he was saying, the suggestion that the pregnancy wasn't as low-risk as she'd believed hitting her altogether too hard. 'I've had a scan. I've been checked. They know my history. If something was wrong, if it was going to happen again, they would have known.'

'Shh,' he soothed. 'I'm not saying they're wrong. I'm just… I want to be sure.'

But the expression in his eyes didn't exactly fit.

'Is the loss of the baby…of Faith why your marriage fell apart?'

She knew he was distracting her, but the very fact that he'd remembered her daughter's name cut through everything else. It was more than Joe had done. He hadn't even cared enough to want to name her.

'Yes,' she managed quietly. 'And no.'

'Meaning?' There was a slight curl to his lip, as though he couldn't help but sneer. As though he knew what kind a man Joe had been.

But he didn't know anything at all.

'He got the job opportunity of a lifetime in Switzerland. I didn't want to go with him.'

'Why not? He was your husband.'

'My life was in the UK, plus I'd just lost my baby, and I didn't love him,' she began hesitantly.

'You married a man you didn't love?' His censure made her bristle.

'I thought I loved him. I told him I loved him. But, with hindsight, I don't know if I ever did or if I was more grateful to him. He was there after Dad died. I was falling apart and Joe looked after me. He was kind to me. He took care of me. He loved me. I thought I loved him, too.'

'Enough to marry him?' Kaspar didn't even try to keep the scorn from his voice.

'He was twelve years older than me. He was like a rock.

Stable, emotionally secure, knew what he wanted, including a family. That all appealed to me. Now I know I was just trying to fill the void left by Dad's death and Robbie going to Australia.'

'It sounds like this bloke took advantage of you.'

'No.' She shook her head. 'At least, not like you're thinking.'

'He knew you were grieving and vulnerable and he seduced you into marriage by pretending to love you,' Kaspar accused.

'No, it wasn't like that.'

Archie shifted on her seat, splaying her hands out as though that could somehow help her articulate the words that were in her head but which she couldn't seem to get out.

'I think it was. You were lost and grieving while he should have known better. I think when you finally see it for what it is, you'll stop making excuses for him.'

'I think the sooner you get your head out of your backside the sooner you'll stop trying to tell me exactly what I do or don't feel,' Archie snapped suddenly, taking both herself and Kaspar by surprise. A welcome flash of the vibrant, no-nonsense side of herself.

Still, she didn't expect Kaspar to drop his head back and let out a laugh.

'What's so funny?' she demanded coldly.

'You are. Welcome back, Little Ant.'

A small smile played on her lips, despite herself. He was right, and it felt good to see the re-emergence of her old feisty self.

Every time she was around him, it seemed.

Hastily, she bit her tongue before she could utter *that* particular nonsense aloud.

'I'm sorry for judging. For criticising.'

Kaspar's tone was surprisingly tender. Even…nostalgic? It elicited another smile from her, albeit this time a wry one.

'You and Robbie may have called me Little Ant, but Dad used to call me his Little Tardigrade.'

The throaty laugh rippled through her, doing things to her it had no business doing. Rushing straight through her body and to her very core, where she was, shamefully, in danger of melting all over again.

'I think I remember that. You always were little but hardy.'

'Yet also, sometimes, more fragile than people thought,' she heard herself replying, too late to clamp down on her words, to swallow them back.

She'd never admitted that to anyone but her father before. Why on earth would she say it now? And to Kaspar, of all people.

'I never realised.' His face sharpened. Hard, angular lines that signified his disapproval. 'I always thought you were such a tough little thing. So strong.'

Archie took in his almost contemptuous expression. It left her feeling as though she'd let him down, let herself down, and she told herself that her heart wasn't being squeezed, right there, in her splintering chest. She gritted her teeth.

'Kaspar, I didn't come here to talk about my ex-husband or my historical mistakes. I just felt I owed it to you to tell you I was expecting a baby, *your* baby, and I didn't think it was something that I should do over the telephone.'

'And then what? You expected me to fall on one knee and propose? To play happy families?'

Actually, she hadn't thought past this awful meeting. But now he looked so dark, so forbidding, so cold, it was like being plunged into an icy, glacial milk flow. She got the sense that no amount of shivering would ever be able to warm her up while his eyes bored into her like this.

It occurred to her that her best form of defence right now was attack. She folded her arms, tilting her chin up and out as she forced herself to stare him down. Refusing to cower, however he might make her feel.

'No, Kaspar. I've been there, I've done that. Marriage isn't a mistake I intend to make again.'

'So then what? You thought you'd drop the bombshell and then hop on the next plane back to the UK?'

He was goading her, his scepticism unmistakeable. It was a struggle not to bristle. She had no idea how she forced herself to her feet. Took her first few steps across the room as though she was in complete control of herself.

'I don't know what I expected you to do. Any more than, I suspect, you know what to do right now. But I just felt I owed it to you to at least tell you I was pregnant.' It was a hauteur she hadn't even known she possessed. 'Now that I have, I think it's time for me to leave.'

Kaspar, apparently, wasn't as impressed as she was.

'Sit back down, Archie,' he ground out furiously. 'You're mad if you think I'm letting you go anywhere with my baby.'

CHAPTER SIX

WHAT THE HELL was he playing at?

Pacing silently on the other side of the curtain as Catherine conducted a thorough examination of Archie, he struggled to quell the out-of-control fear that was spiralling inside him.

He wasn't ready to be a father. He'd never thought he ever would be. And that was another of the reasons why he'd always avoided romantic entanglements. He could never, ever risk being the kind of parent his father had been. Worse, being the kind of parent his mother had been. He remembered how it had felt to feel insignificant, unworthy, not...*enough.* Pain and grief poured through him, like the boilermakers he'd drunk as an unhappy, lost, late-teen; a shot of whisky chased down by a strong beer.

But now his life and Archie's were bound together. For ever. He'd known that after the first few moments of blind panic had cleared, back in his office. He would never allow a child to grow up the way he had, feeling unwanted or unloved.

He had to be the kind of father to his child that Archie's father had been to his own kids. The closest thing Kaspar had ever had to a father himself. He owed it to Archie. The woman whose door he suspected he would have been banging down months ago had he not kept the expanse of the Atlantic between them.

Which made no sense. Because that absolutely wasn't him. He didn't know what had come over him. The ghosts she had been resurrecting ever since that first night together when he'd realised who she was. When he hadn't been able to help himself from claiming her anyway.

It was all he could do to stay this side of the screen and not march around that blue curtain and demand to know exactly what was going on. But staying here was as much about trying not to crowd or frighten Archie as it was about stopping himself from trying to tell Catherine Jarvis how to do her job. As much as she might like and respect him, Catherine wouldn't think twice about calling him out for interfering where one of her patients was concerned.

'Right,' Catherine addressed Archie. 'Let's clean you up and then you can sort yourself out. When you're ready, come back around and we can all have a bit of a chat.'

His stomach lurched. It was exactly the professional, calm tone he used when he suspected a serious issue but didn't want to worry anyone. Or perhaps it was his imagination.

It was strange, being this side of the proverbial table. He felt ill at ease, *lost*, and he didn't like it at all.

So how must Archie feel?

An unexpected wave of...*something* flooded through him. He'd told her that he wasn't about to play happy families. And that was true, he didn't want that. But there was something else there, too.

Had any other woman walked back into his life and declared herself pregnant with his child he might have expected to feel anger, resentment, and maybe there was a little of that with Archie. But there was something more. Like it was his duty to look after her. *To protect her?*

It was like a physical blow. For a moment all he could do was fight to maintain his balance, rocking on the balls of his feet. His whole career he'd fought for his patients. To the last moment and without exception. Because it was his duty, and because they mattered.

He'd felt a kind of protectiveness towards her as a kid, but that had been completely different. Certainly never in his entire adult life had he felt the urge to protect someone because he cared about *them*, on some…emotional level. He hadn't even thought he was capable of such an impulse.

What was he even to do with such sentimentality?

Unnerved, Kaspar thrust the plethora of questions from his head. He would concentrate on the medicine. That, at least, would make more sense. Sitting down, he forced himself to engage in polite conversation with his colleague, none of which he could recall even a minute later, and waited for Archie to appear.

The sight of her wan, nervous face twisted inside him. Instantly, he switched into cool surgeon mode.

'What did you find, Catherine?'

'Right. So, I did a full examination of you, Archana, and I would concur that you are approximately twenty weeks pregnant.'

'What is the issue?' Kaspar prompted sharply. This might not be his field of expertise but he wasn't considered a top surgeon for being oblivious to other fields. The way his colleague's examination had progressed, and the comments and questions she'd been asking didn't fit with a smooth, non-complicated pregnancy. Sure enough, she turned to him with an almost imperceptible nod. One colleague to another.

'I did see faint evidence of funnelling but I stress it *is* faint. I could send you for an MRI but I'd prefer to concentrate on the cervix length before making any firm decisions.' She turned back to Archie. 'However, I don't have a baseline length without calling your doctors and requesting your notes.'

Kaspar nodded, turning expectantly to Archie, whose expression was even more pinched and white. Instinctively, he reached out to take her icy-cold hand in his.

'Archie,' he prompted gently.

Slowly, so slowly, she turned her head to him, her eyes taking a little longer to focus.

'Archie, we need your doctors' details so that Catherine can contact them.'

'No one told me there was a problem.' Her voice was so quiet they had to strain to hear her.

'Archana.' Catherine's voice was gentle, coaxing. The way his usually was with other patients. But this wasn't *other patients*, this was Archie. 'Would you like me to explain this in more detail?'

Archie nodded stiffly. She didn't look at him but her fingers gripped his surprisingly tightly. Something shot through him, a powerful but fleeting sensation. He couldn't identify it. He wasn't even sure he wanted to.

'All right, during pregnancy the cervix, or the neck of your womb, normally remains closed and long, rather like a tube. As the pregnancy progresses and you get ready to give birth, the cervix begins to soften, shortening in length and opening up.'

Catherine paused, waiting for confirmation as Archie jerked her head in a semblance of a nod.

He bit back his own questions. He couldn't take over, he had to let Archie go at her own pace.

'However,' Catherine continued gently as Archie mumbled a vague acknowledgement, 'in your instance, there is evidence to suggest that the neck of your womb might be shortening. It's very faint and without knowing what the measurements were at the start of your pregnancy I can't be sure. It isn't, at this point in time, less than twenty-five millimetres, which is the point at which I would usually advise having an emergency, or rescue, cervical suture. However, with your past history of miscarriage I would suggest that there is a high enough risk of premature delivery for me to consider performing the suture on you.'

'So…? We…wait?' Archie managed, frowning as if she was having trouble processing it all.

'For right now, yes. But we don't want to wait too much longer.' Catherine shook her head. 'After twenty-four weeks we don't usually perform cervical sutures either here in the US or back at your home in the UK. The standard of care for preemies is of such a high standard that it's generally considered that the risks of being born early is less than the risk to the baby of attempting to delay labour with an emergency suture.'

'So there are risks?'

For the first time, Archie's head snapped up, as though she was hauling herself back to reality by her very fingernails.

Kaspar felt a sliver of pride slip through him, and he clasped her hand tighter as if that could somehow lend her strength.

'There are risks with any procedure,' his colleague answered, 'but particularly in an emergency procedure where the cervix has already shortened and is partly dilated. There's a risk of waters breaking and of infection developing. In your case, there's only faint evidence of effacement and no dilation.'

'But if I'm going to have it, it has to be now?' Archie asked tightly.

'As I said, I'd like a baseline measurement first, and we'll go from there.'

'Why didn't my doctor pick up on it?'

Her pained expression tugged and twisted at something inside him. He wasn't prepared for it. It was a strange, inner tussle not to jump in and grill Catherine on a much more detailed, medical level. Instead, he forced himself to continue sitting quietly, allowing Archie to go at her pace. The kind of questions he wanted to ask would only frighten her unnecessarily. They would deal with any other issues if and when they had to. Still, he would be calling Catherine as soon as he got a moment alone.

'As I said, it's very faint. This is my area of expertise...'

'They're supposed to be experts too...' Archie cut in, panicked, and, with an instinct he hadn't known he possessed, Kaspar found himself drawing her to him, making her meet his gaze. His voice quiet, level, as one might use to a frightened, cornered animal.

'Catherine is a highly specialised, world-class neonatal and maternal-foetal surgeon,' he soothed. 'We will deal with this. *She* will deal with it.'

'But if we miss it. If I don't have the...the...'

'Cervical suture,' he supplied evenly, wondering if this raging storm inside him was how every patient felt when they were sitting opposite him and *he* was the one delivering their diagnoses or prognoses.

'Right. If I don't have that then I lose this baby like I did before?'

'There's no way to know,' continued Catherine. 'You're past the point at which the previous miscarriage occurred. However, there is some evidence that your cervix *might* be beginning to efface. It's possible you could go to term like this, without any intervention. I can't be sure. I need more information. In cases like yours, where it isn't clear, the suture is usually only put in if there's a history of two or more late miscarriages or premature births.'

'Lose two babies?' Archie gasped, horrified. 'Before they will do anything? No. No, I can't lose another baby. I can't.'

'I know it's hard, I'm sorry. But sometimes we have to be sure,' Catherine was saying, but he couldn't sit quietly any longer.

'If Archie doesn't have the cervical suture and then after that twenty-four-week mark begins to go into labour, you'll do what?' he asked his colleague sharply. 'Pessaries?'

'Yes.' She nodded, turning her focus back to Archie. 'If that is the case, then we would probably offer you progesterone or pessaries instead. As you mentioned during the examination, they tried an Arabin pessary with your first baby.'

'Which didn't work,' Archie choked out as Catherine bobbed her head, again softly.

'And that's why I'd like to request your medical records from your doctor to determine whether a cervical suture might be a sensible precaution.'

'And it will stop me from losing my baby?'

'There's no guarantee. Research into how well cervical sutures stop preterm birth is always ongoing, but it is thought to reduce the risk of early delivery by significant percentages. Once I have more information, I'll bring you back for a further examination and we'll discuss things in greater depth if we feel we might go ahead.'

'But…'

The pleading in her tone twisted at Kapar's gut, but he couldn't indulge it. He had to be the strong one.

'Archie, give Catherine your doctors' contact details. Once she has your full notes she can make a more informed decision and, I promise you, we'll answer every single one of your questions then.'

'Right.' Catherine shot him a grateful look. 'You have full insurance?'

'No…' She froze, as if she hadn't really thought that far ahead.

'The medical expenses will be covered,' Kaspar cut in firmly.

He'd pay for it out of his own pocket if necessary.

'And she's staying with you?'

'Yes.'

He ignored Archie as she glowered at him.

'Good.' Catherine nodded, holding out a form for Archie's medical contact details.

Grimly he took it, coaxing the information out of Archie, line by line. And when it was finally done, he helped her up, sorted out her scant belongings, and led her out of his colleague's office with a word of thanks.

She looked dazed, thrown. The exact way he felt. But he refused to give in to it. He couldn't afford to. If it sucked him in, he'd be no use to Archie, and right now he knew she needed him more than ever.

'I didn't come here for your money,' Archie muttered as she found herself being ushered out of the office. Her mind was grappling for some diversion, however banal, from the bone-gripping terror that she might lose this baby the way she'd lost Faith.

'Or for you to house me,' she added absently.

She had given Dr Jarvis the right name, hadn't she? The right address for her doctor's surgery?

'What should I have said, Archie? That you jumped on a plane and came out here wholly unprepared?'

She pursed her lips, his tone exactly what she'd feared when she'd been halfway across the Atlantic. The accusation out before she could stop it.

'You'd rather I hadn't told you about the baby.'

'That isn't what I said.' He blew out an angry breath and, for one moment, if she hadn't known it to be impossible she would have thought he was as confused as she was.

'I'll stay in a hotel.' It was hard to summon some semblance of pride when all she wanted to do was break down on his shoulder and howl.

Kaspar let out a scornful snort.

'You're pregnant. With my baby. You will remain with me. For the duration. It isn't up for debate, Archana.'

'There is no *duration*. What you and Catherine seem to be forgetting is that I don't come from here, and besides I can't afford medical care. I need to go back home and I need to speak to my own doctors.'

'You can't just run away,' Kaspar snapped. 'And as for medical costs, I will deal with that. You won't be going back to the UK while you're pregnant. In fact, you won't be going back at all.'

'Sorry? What?' she asked. Very calmly. Very deliberately.

She couldn't possibly have heard that correctly.

Did it make it better, or worse, that he looked equally stupefied?

'You won't be returning to the UK,' he said slowly, as if he wasn't really sure of the words coming out of his own mouth.

It was disconcerting to see the famously focussed Kaspar Athari uncertain about anything.

'I… I…' Archie was aware that, for a moment, she opened and closed her mouth feeling much like the fish in the calming tank in the luxurious waiting area outside. Finally, her voice came back. 'I can assure you that is *exactly* what I'll be doing. It's where my flat is, my career, my *life*.'

'Except that now you're carrying my baby.'

'I had noticed.' Her heart pounded so loudly she was afraid it was ready to slam its way right out of her chest. 'But you told me we wouldn't be playing happy families.'

'That was before.'

The conversation was all too similar to the one she'd had when her ex-husband had told her about his job opportunity in Zurich. She'd known then that there was no way she wanted to leave the UK, that her life *was* there. This time she heard the words but she didn't feel the same passion.

She told herself the difference was the baby. Not Kaspar.

It couldn't be him. She couldn't afford to let it be. She turned on him.

'Before what?'

'Just...before,' he ground out. 'I don't know, Archie. You need to give me time. You've had months to get your head around this pregnancy. I've barely had a couple of hours. You'll stay here until I have a plan.'

She could see what it cost him to admit to her that he, Kaspar Athari, had no idea what to do right at this moment. She could more than relate. But she couldn't afford to crumble right now, much as she might want to. Much as the weaker Archie wanted to lean on him, even cling to him. She forced her head up.

'I can't stay here forever. I think Immigration might have something to say about that.'

Far from throwing Kaspar, her words seemed to galvanise him. The powerful, authoritative man the world knew was coming back. Shutting out once and for all that tiny glimpse she'd seen of a remotely vulnerable side to him.

'We'll sort that out.' His disdainful rebuttal was aggravating. 'We'll have to. You're carrying my baby. My blood. Which means, whether I like it or not, you're now my family. And I'll do whatever I need to in order to keep my family with me. I won't allow this baby to grow up thinking she wasn't wanted. Feeling she doesn't have a home.'

'It...*he* will have a home,' she bit out, remembering at the last moment their agreement not to call the baby *it*. Surely there was no doubt that Kaspar's current autocratic attitude stemmed as much from whatever horrors lay in his childhood as that *it* label had been?

'His home is with me. The mother.'

'And with me. The father,' he said, narrowing his eyes at her. 'I will not be an absent father. You can't push me out of this, Archie.'

'I'm not.' Her voice was too loud, too fractured, but at least she now knew she was right about Kaspar's past dictating his actions now. 'You're the father. I wanted you to know. I felt I owed it to you, to the baby, to give you the choice of being part of its life. But...I can't give up my whole life just to stay in the States with you. I can't even work out here, for one thing.'

'I can take care of you.'

'Out of what? A sense of duty?' she challenged. 'Not because you *want* me. Or our baby.'

'What difference does it make?' And it was only at that instant that she realised just how desperately she wished he could tell her otherwise. 'I *will* take care of you. Both of you.'

'I don't want to be taken care of.'

'Make your mind up, Archie.' His barbed tone pierced its way through her, lodging inside her, twisting painfully. 'An hour or so ago when I said you'd always been a strong kid, you were telling me how fragile you were. Now you're telling me you can handle everything yourself?'

'That isn't what I said.' Archie threw her hands up. He was distorting things, confusing her. Or was he right? Was *she* confusing things? She tried again. 'I want to be…cared for. Not cosseted.'

'And I will be a part of my child's life.'

'I'm not saying you can't be…'

It was infuriating. And yet, somehow, it was also reassuring. The fact that he was planning for the baby's—*their* baby's—future. As though it had one. As though the fact that she might lose it the way she'd lost Faith wasn't even a possibility for him. It was what she'd needed. He made her feel strong again. Just like he had a hundred—a thousand—times before. As a kid. Even if he didn't remember it.

Suddenly she was tired of fighting. And scared. And it was making it harder and harder for her to think straight. Words began floating around her head. The risks she hadn't even known about a few hours ago were now threatening to overwhelm her.

She really could lose this baby the way she'd lost *Faith.* Having her suspicions had been one thing, but to hear it so unequivocally was another.

She longed for him to fold his strong arms around her and pull her to his huge chest, comforting her and caring for her, as though he really wanted to. Not just out of some sense of moral decency. But he didn't. They simply stood there, pretending they weren't squaring off against each other.

'I want you to be a part of our baby's life, Kaspar,' she said softly. 'A big part. But I can't stay here. Your life is here and that's fine. But mine isn't. And for what it's worth, I don't see you offering to give up *your* life and *your* work to follow me permanently to the UK, where you could also be with your child on a daily basis.'

Kaspar sighed. 'We both know that your work is more

relocatable than mine is. I have teams here that depend on me, patients that trust me to be there throughout their care.'

Archie scowled, though she knew he had a point. As much as she loved her job, it was fairly flexible, and unlike his it wasn't a matter of life or death. 'You just think your life is more important than mine,' she finished petulantly, in spite of herself.

His dismissive shrug didn't help.

'There is no *your* life and *my* life. Not now. You're carrying my baby so whatever our individual lives were like in the past, that's all gone now. Like it or not, it's *our* lives. I will not be apart from my child.' Misery was etched into every line, every contour on his unfairly handsome face. 'I won't have her growing up the way I did, pulled between one parent and the other.'

His unexpectedly searing admission ate at her.

Archie began to speak, then hesitated. She had to choose her words very, very carefully. She reached out to touch his chest, steeling herself for the jolt of awareness that charged through her even before she made contact. Even prepared for it, even now, she couldn't make herself immune to him.

That was another thing she was going to work on.

'We're not your parents. If we both want to be with this baby, we'll find a solution. It…*he*…will know he's wanted. We don't have to be in the same country but we do have to work it out carefully and fairly.'

'I want to be in my child's life. Every day.' He covered her hand with his, but didn't even seem to notice what he was doing. Still, it stole her breath away.

'It doesn't have to be that way,' she began, but he cut her off.

'You'll move in with me, Archie. For all intents and purposes, this child will have a proper family.'

Without warning, her heart flip-flopped in her chest. It was worrying how much the notion appealed to her. How close she was to agreeing to such a ridiculous idea. But as much as she tried to back up both physically and mentally, she could no more remove her hand from the compelling heat of his body than she could refuse outright.

'But we won't be a proper family, will we?' It was meant to be a demand, but her voice was far breathier than she would have liked. Sadness and regret still lined his face.

'Of course not,' he scoffed, oblivious to the fact that he found it so easy to slam all her pitiable dreams away with those three words. 'But our child will at least have a mother and father around who don't want to kill each other on a daily basis. And that's more than I ever had.'

'I don't want to settle for that.' She barely recognised her own shaky voice. 'I want so much more. I want love. I want to be cherished. I want what my father always told me he and my mother had before she died, but which I was too young to remember.'

He shut her down, clearly not listening to her.

'This subject isn't up for discussion, Archana. You're coming home with me and we'll work out the rest from there.'

And before she could respond any further Kaspar was gone and she was alone. In the middle of an empty corridor.

CHAPTER SEVEN

KASPAR'S HOME WAS everything she should have expected and so much…well, *less*.

It was stunning. Modern glass, sleek design and cool granite perched atop a slight hillside overlooking a private, tantalising beach. As if he was showing her all he could offer their child that she never could.

Archie stared up into the double-height ceiling space of the main living area. All gleaming white and black metal, framing enormous windows that offered breathtaking views across the sea and off into the horizon.

Gorgeous.

It was also completely and utterly soulless. As if no one lived here at all. The perfect show home. Which only proved to her that it wasn't all about money. She cradled her belly protectively. It was about love, and stability, both of which she could provide.

Strong foundations. Dependable.

Could Kaspar?

She doubted it. Or perhaps that was just her own bias since everything he did left her wound too tightly to even think straight. It hadn't escaped her that ever since he had walked out into that corridor when she'd been trying to pluck up the courage to knock on the door, her body had filled with a low, faint humming. Desire. Need.

One afternoon with the man was all it had taken to convince her that she wasn't over anything. That a part of her still hankered for him. Even now. That realisation alone should have told her that she needed to stay as far away from Kaspar as possible. Certainly not spend even one night at his home.

But he'd terrified her by taking her to see Dr Jarvis. Reinforcing every last fear she'd spent five months telling herself was simply in her head. That what had happened with Faith wouldn't happen again.

For all her earlier arguing, the car journey home had given her time to calm down. Time to acknowledge that she would stay with Kaspar as long as she needed to if it meant her baby would be all right. In many ways she was more grateful to Kaspar than she could ever have anticipated. He didn't have to help her, there'd been nothing compelling him to get her in to see his colleague. He'd always made it clear to the media that he didn't have any intention of settling down or having a family. He could have thanked her for telling him and let her return to the UK.

But that wasn't Kaspar.

It was reassuring to know she hadn't misjudged him five months ago.

'There's a guest suite through those doors over there.' Kaspar cut across her thoughts as he headed back down across the hallway to a different set of doors. 'I'll be through that way.'

She gripped the large, rather masculine-looking, leather wingback chair in front of her.

'You're going?'

'I have to get showered and changed.' He frowned. 'I've got a charity dinner event tonight. I'm a guest speaker.'

'Okay.'

'Do you need me to stay?'

A part of her wanted to say yes. A bigger part of her knew the time to herself would be welcome. She forced a bright smile.

'No. I could do with the evening to myself. Besides, you can't let people down.'

He nodded, unsmiling.

'I would prefer not to. But if I wasn't speaking, I wouldn't go.'

'Should I…? Do I…come with you?'

He looked entirely unimpressed. She tried not to let it get to her.

'I hardly think that's the best idea. Aside from the fact that you're meant to be resting, tonight is a high-profile event and being photographed out with me—especially looking like…*that*…' he gestured to her baby bump '…is the quickest way to get people nosing into every single facet of our lives. I can't imagine you want to see yourself splashed across the entertainment news headlines tomorrow morning, do you?'

'No, of course not.' Archie blinked, attempting to command her faithless heart not to read so much into the way he'd said *our lives*.

As if it implied some form of…togetherness.

'Good.' He nodded, satisfied, although she thought he might have had the decency not to look quite so smug. 'Then you'll stay here, keeping a low profile.'

He was gone before she could answer, leaving Archie alone to explore her new surroundings at her apparent leisure. Instead, she could only stare at the closed door and wonder where they were supposed to go from here.

She needed a distraction. Something to take her fears off the idea of losing this baby, something to ground her and remind her of the strong woman she was in other arenas of her life.

Like in the workplace. Yes, that was it. She could work, she'd brought her laptop. She was lucky that the nature of her job meant she could work from any number of sites or offices—emails and video conferencing were practically *de rigueur*. Certainly at this stage of the project. And she was lucky that she'd worked with the commercial manager on so many projects before over the years that he knew how reliable and fastidious she'd always been. Still, hopping on a plane to different country wasn't exactly usual practice. If she was going to keep her job then she would need to do some work for as long as she was out here.

And she would need a job to get back to once the baby was born. How else was she supposed to keep a roof over their heads? Because no matter what Kaspar had said back in the hospital, it wasn't practical for them to live together and pretend to be some kind of family, even for the sake of their baby.

She booted up her laptop, the waiting emails a welcome diversion as she fired off a handful of easy responses before working on a couple of more carefully worded letters to contractors and the client. But after a few hours the words began to swim before her eyes, the grid patterns of the spreadsheets all merging into each other. And, instead, Kaspar's face began to creep back into her head.

It couldn't be a good thing that all she could think about was him. And their baby. He was insisting on taking control, the way he always had seemed to do, but what kind of a *real* father would he allow himself to be?

The realisation clung to her mind.

She'd never appreciated, growing up, just how badly his parents' volatile relationship had damaged Kaspar. What if he couldn't get past that? What if he carried it into any relationship with their own baby? With her?

It was as though in asking herself that first question,

she'd opened the floodgates for a hundred more to rush into her brain.

She'd never realised just how deeply his parents had influenced him before. She'd known a bit, growing up, but her father had shielded her from a lot. Had she been completely naïve in clinging to her memory of the sweet, sensitive young boy she had once known, who had looked to her own father as more of a role model than anyone else?

She couldn't bear the idea that, in time, Kaspar might come to resent her if she and the baby impacted too heavily on his life.

What if he dated other women?

Something spiked inside her, like the stinging slice of a razor-sharp blade, even as she told herself that it didn't matter to her either way. She told herself that what he did in his personal life was no more her business now than it ever had been. It wouldn't make any difference to her. She would have him to thank for the most precious gift he could ever have given her.

Archie slammed the laptop lid down without even thinking about what she was doing. She could tell herself she didn't care all she liked. She didn't buy a word of it. Not even for a second.

What Kaspar did mattered to her. It shouldn't, but it did. And the longer she stayed in his company the more hurt she was going to wind up getting. It was inevitable. Inexorable.

And yet there was no way she could leave. Not to go to a hotel, and certainly not to return to the UK. Not after what she'd discovered today. The very life of her unborn baby now depended on Kaspar, and how he could help her, and she'd walk over coals searing enough to melt the soles of her feet if it meant not going through the agony of another hateful miscarriage.

She'd just have to find a way to seal her heart, her mind off from Kaspar. Think of him as a business deal. The father of her baby but, ultimately, nothing to do with her.

That couldn't be too hard. Could it?

Kaspar dodged yet another nameless woman—he'd lost count of how many had tried to corner him this evening—and glowered at the auctioneer who was delighting the crowd as he chaired the charity auction.

It was a successful evening, even pleasant, but he couldn't enjoy a moment of it. His thoughts were centred around Archie, their baby and the unwelcome news Catherine had delivered.

He wondered what Archie was doing now. Still working on her laptop, as she'd been when he'd left her? So focussed and wrapped up in her work that she hadn't even noticed him leaving. It was ironic, the one thing he strived for in himself, admired in others, was the thing he was already beginning to resent in Archie.

Because he didn't need her to tell him what that driven expression on her face meant. He recognised it. It told him she was determined to maintain her job, and therefore her life, back in the UK. That she intended to return with his baby as soon as she could, despite everything he'd said to her about not wanting to be an absent father.

He hadn't even realised how strongly he'd felt when he'd first uttered those words. But the fact of it was that it was true. The idea of losing them was unimaginable. *No.* Kaspar pulled himself up short. It was *unacceptable.*

The temptation to go home and tell Archie exactly that was almost overwhelming. There was only one thing stopping him. He needed something more compelling than words. He needed to prove to her that he would do anything for this baby. He needed to prove to her that he *wanted* this baby.

No easy feat when, if anyone had asked him twelve hours ago how he felt about having a baby, he would have laughed in their face. He'd never wanted children, or a family, or a wife. He'd been content to play the genius surgeon, perennial bad boy, who would never inflict himself on anyone the way his parents had inflicted their distasteful, damaging vitriol on either their son or themselves.

For decades he'd told himself that the best thing he could ever do for any child was to ensure that he wasn't their father. No child should ever have to endure the upbringing of his own youth. Pushed from one volatile parent to the other, a pawn in their explosive games. Unwanted and in the way, even when his mother had suddenly realised that it might help his father's career, and hurt hers, if she didn't drag her unhappy fifteen-year-old with her.

And then Archie had knocked on his door and his whole world had shifted on its axis.

He was going to be a father.

Possibly.

Without warning a terrible tightness coiled through him, as unfamiliar as it was uncomfortable. For a moment he couldn't identify it at all, and then it dawned on him. It was fear. And powerlessness.

Everything that Catherine had said this afternoon had made sense to him *medically.* But now that the initial shock was wearing off, his brain was finally locking onto the fact that this wasn't any baby they were discussing, this was *his* baby. His and Archie's.

He wanted this baby to be safe and he wanted to provide the loving family he had never had.

The fact that Archie had made it abundantly clear that she would rather cross the Atlantic, swimming the entire way if she had to, than have him be a daily part of her baby's life cut him deeper than he would prefer to acknowledge. It scraped at him like nothing else ever had.

He'd thought he'd long since got over the pain of not being wanted. By his mother, his father and, to some extent, his best friend Robbie when they'd fallen out over some girl whose name he couldn't even remember any more. *Sarah* perhaps? *Suki? Sadie?* Not that it even mattered.

But Archie's rejection of him ate into him far, far deeper. She'd done her duty by telling him she was pregnant, but she evidently now wanted to be as far away from him as she possibly could get. And he didn't want to let her go. Not just, he suspected, as an image of her breathtaking smile and dancing eyes filled his head while his insides hitched, for the health of their baby. The restlessness he felt whenever he was around her was like an ache of desire.

It made no sense. He was losing his mind and Archie was the one making him lose it. She threatened the order he had created around himself, blurred his clearly set-out parameters, and blasted away his peace of mind.

He could pretend he had been strong all afternoon for Archie's sake, but he was terribly suspicious that the truth was that he needed to stay strong for himself just as much. What he really needed was a plan. Something that would keep his unexpected family around him, allow him to be the father his baby deserved.

Something with which Archie couldn't possibly argue.

'Do you promise to love, honour, cherish and protect…?'

Archie stared at the registrar as though her soul was wholly disconnected from her body. As though she was one of the witnesses, who she didn't even know but apparently Kaspar did, watching the brief ceremony, rather than the not-so-blushing bride standing opposite a grim-faced Kaspar and clutching a small bouquet that was so jaunty and bright it seemed to mock her.

She felt numb. As numb as she'd felt when Kaspar had returned home from the fundraiser early the other night and issued his edict.

Even now she could recall exactly how her body had felt, as though it had been too small to contain her, squeezing her until every last breath had been crushed out of her. And yet Kaspar had looked, for all the world, as though he was relaying something as banal as the weather.

'Marriage?' she had whispered, a lump of something that was halfway between desolation and fury, or perhaps a combination of the two, lodged in her throat. 'We'll never get a license.'

'This is California, there's no waiting time. A long line could mean a two hour wait, but that's about it.' He brushed her concern aside with a sweep of his arm. 'Then we have ninety days to actually get married before the license expires, so unless you're planning on some elaborate ceremony somewhere, I know a couple of ministers who can perform marriages. Either one of them would be happy to step in at such short notice for us. I'm sure we can even go to the beach if you'd prefer something more…romantic.'

He pulled a face which wasn't exactly encouraging. She tried again.

'I'm not Californian. I'm not even American.'

'You don't have to be a resident.' Again, he dismissed her with apparent ease. 'And there's no restriction against foreigners marrying here either. You just need the correct documentation which you have. I've already checked. '

'Kaspar…'

'There's no other way.' His crisp response had been damning. 'But if you need another reason, then how about this; you need to be here where you can be seen by Catherine and my health insurance will cover you only if you are my wife.'

She had savings. Money she'd set aside year in and year out as her rainy-day fund. But nothing that might cover something like this. She'd hated to put it to Kaspar, but she'd had little choice.

'What if you paid?' She could actually remember running her tongue over her teeth in an effort to free them from her top lip. 'I would pay you back. Every penny…or at least every cent…in time, of course.'

'No.'

'Please, Kaspar?' It wasn't like he wasn't wealthy enough to afford it. Although she hadn't been able to say that, it would have sounded so cold-blooded, and that wasn't how she would have intended it. Her voice had dropped to a whisper. 'Why not?'

'Why should I pay out of my pocket just so you can run back to England and take my child away from me at the first chance you get?' he had ground out, and if she hadn't known better she might have thought he sounded almost urgent. But then his commanding tone had come back and she'd known she'd just imagined it. 'I told you, this baby will be brought up knowing her father.'

Archie blinked as she realised that, back in the present, the minister was looking at her expectantly. She clutched the flowers tighter and prayed her subconscious was paying enough attention to know what stage of the ceremony they were up to.

'I do,' she choked out, relieved when he bobbed his head, turning back to Kaspar. 'Repeat after me. I, Kaspar Athari…'

She tried to concentrate, but it was too much. Her head still swam with memories of that night. She had assured him that their baby would know him. Promised him. But he had been intransigent, his cool, level responses only heightening her agitation.

She hadn't known why the idea of marriage had disconcerted her so much. She'd told herself it was because the idea was ludicrous, but feared it was more because a part of her actually longed to say yes. To take the easy solution that he was offering. To accept the safe stability of a marriage. A unit.

But how long would that safe stability last? Especially with a man like Kaspar, who had spent his life vigorously avoiding ties of any kind.

As if he could read her thoughts, he had thrust his hands into his pockets, looking, for all the world, like the conversation bored him.

'I don't work on promises, Archie. I never promise my patients or their families anything that I can't one hundred percent guarantee. I prefer to put in place assurances.'

'And marrying me is an assurance?'

'The closest I can get, yes.' He'd given a light shrug. 'You can't deny me, or the baby, that way.'

She'd told herself that it couldn't be happening. That it wasn't fair. She'd resisted the urge to run from the room, knowing that it might offer her relief for a moment or two but that ultimately she couldn't escape Kaspar. Or the conversation.

'Please. I'll give you any other assurances you want. Sign any contract you put in front of me.'

'Of course you will. It will be called a marriage contract.'

'No.' Her vehemence had turned Kaspar's eyes to hard, opal gleams. As though she'd hurt him. But such a notion was ludicrous.

'If the idea of marrying me is that abhorrent to you,

Archana, then surely you can see how I might think you'd leave with our baby the first chance you get.'

But wasn't that exactly what the problem was? That she *didn't* find the idea of marriage to Kaspar so abhorrent. Or at least she only abhorred the idea of a loveless marriage to him. She could tell herself it was because she'd been there and done that. She'd made the mistake of thinking the way she and Joe had cared for each other had been enough. But it hadn't, and she didn't want to go through that again. Certainly not with Kaspar.

Because the truth, as much as she'd tried to deny it until now, was that a part of her—a small, childish remnant from her youth, no doubt—was in love with him. And being married to him, without him loving her back in any way, would be too much to bear. How could she stand the fact that he would never be *hers*? Even if she married him?

Kaspar Athari was his own man. He would never belong to any one. And she wanted so much more than that from him.

Archie paused as the celebrant turned to her now. Her turn to repeat the vows. She didn't even recognise her own voice. The ceremony could have been happening to someone else. She was still stuck there, in her own head, stuck back in that night.

In her urgency, she'd even asked him exactly what marriage to him would look like. She didn't know what she'd hoped he would say. It certainly hadn't been the casual shoulder hunch he'd offered. The nonchalant, *'Why don't we cross that bridge when we come to it?'*

There certainly hadn't been any words of love, or even affection. There and then she'd promised herself that she would never settle for half-measures, with Kaspar or with anyone else. If she couldn't have all of him, she wanted none. She'd done half-measures before and look where that had got her. She refused to do it again.

In her mind's eye, Archie could see herself heading resolutely across the room. But it was no good. By the time she'd reached the door she'd stopped, her hand on the handle but still not turning around.

'I can't marry you, Kaspar. I've made that mistake before. And I can't make you help me,' she'd whispered again, desperately summoning the strength to turn the door handle. 'But I'm begging you to do so.'

He had crossed the room, the heat of his body like a wall behind her, searing her as his hand had covered hers and drawn it from the cold metal.

'Are you so sure it would be a mistake?' The rawness in his voice had been like a rasp against her heart.

Archie had wanted to tell him that of course it would be a mistake. She'd known she shouldn't cave. But his question had sounded so skinned, like an exposed wound, his hand had still been holding hers and she could still *feel* his body so close to her. She remembered dropping her head, then in defiance of all logic she'd turned and faced him.

The pinched expression on his face had taken her aback. As though she'd wounded him. As though he actually cared. She'd wondered if she could be wrong about him. If he could really want her in his life. As his wife.

She'd averted her eyes but his other hand had slid instantly beneath her chin, his fingers had tilted her head up and forced her to look at him.

'My baby will want for nothing,' he'd stated firmly, fiercely. 'I'll make sure of that. Neither will you, but your lives are here now. With me. I'm not your idiot ex-husband who let you walk away from him. I suggest you don't make the blunder of mistaking me for him.'

She hadn't been about to tell him that was hardly likely.

That no one could mistake Kaspar for anyone but himself. His utter certainty had been mesmerising. No wonder people rarely refused him. Including her. *Especially* her.

'Love should be the core of your marriage.' The registrar smiled benevolently now. 'Love is the reason you are here. But it also will take trust to know in your hearts that you want the best for each other.'

She tuned out again. Joe might never have been enough to compel her to leave her life for Zurich. But Kaspar was so much she wondered if she might even leave her life to follow him to the very bowels of hell.

The notion had terrified her. Kaspar didn't love her or want her, he only wanted their baby. Abruptly she'd heard herself lashing out. Wanting to wind Kaspar the way he had done to her.

'I should never have come here,' she'd blurted out, hugging her laptop in front of her chest like it had been some form of body armour against Kaspar's words. 'I should never have told you about the baby. You ruin everything.'

She hadn't been even remotely prepared for the look of absolute pain and devastation that had tugged at his features. She'd opened her mouth to apologise, to find some way to take it back, but then it was as though he'd sucked all the misery back in and instead a wave of fury had smashed over her, emanating from him like a thick, black, lethal cloud.

'You won't take my baby away, Archie.' His ferocity had been unmistakeable. 'You won't shut me out of my child's life, or leave her thinking for a single moment that I didn't want to be there for her. This is my baby, too. I will be a part of every aspect of things. Not some weekend or holiday father but a proper dad, who is there for the first word, the first step, the first dry night.'

She'd tried to take it back. Guilt and regret had almost

overwhelmed her. She'd opened her mouth to tell him she had never meant those words that had tumbled, so cruelly, out of her mouth. But the apology hadn't come, and anyway Kaspar wouldn't have let her.

'This isn't about you or me, it's about the life of this baby,' he'd hissed out, his voice lethal. 'You need medical supervision, which is here, with me. This is non-negotiable.'

And that had been the end of it. Those words, uttered in what felt like a lifetime ago.

Now, a few days later, they were here, and Archie was gazing at a grim Kaspar. She gaped as the registrar beamed his widest smile yet.

'I now declare you to be husband and wife.'

The worst thing was that a part of her was only too eager to comply.

CHAPTER EIGHT

'DID YOU CALL that a kiss?' Kaspar demanded as they stepped back into his…*their* home a scant few hours later.

He didn't know why he was trying to tease her. Perhaps because now they were married he knew they finally needed to get past the animosity that had settled on them. Black, heavy and cold. They had to move on from it.

It was one of the reasons he'd arranged for them to have their wedding breakfast at a private, fine dining experience in one of LA's most exclusive restaurants. It was his attempt at an olive branch, but he hadn't accounted for how entrenched they had become.

The silence at their table, the scrape of metal against fine china, the hollow clink of crystal wine glasses, both filled with water, had only emphasised the emptiness of the day, until finally Kaspar was able to bear it no more.

'I know you're not sure about this marriage,' he sighed, covering her hand lightly with his across the table, 'and I'm sorry if you feel I pushed you into it. Seeing you in front of the minister looking so sad…well, that isn't what I want. Please,' he implored her, and in his eyes she saw an unexpected flash of the vulnerable, proud boy she had once known. 'Let's try to make this thing work, let's try to make our home a pleasant one, if nothing else. The baby deserves that much.'

Archie's heart sank a little. Of course it was the baby he was really worried about, but she nodded anyway, and in a small, tight voice agreed. 'I can be pleasant.'

'Thank you.'

Now, though, as they walked down the hallway of the beach house, Kaspar tried for a little more levity. 'I know you can kiss far better than you showed me today.'

Archie tilted her chin up at him, utterly elegant and poised. It gave him an unmistakeable kick to realise that he could see straight through her. He could read her in a way he'd never expected to be able to.

'It may shock you to know this, Kaspar, but I don't want to kiss you again. I certainly don't want to sleep with you.'

He grinned unexpectedly. The first in days.

'I was talking about a kiss. Who said anything about sleeping together?'

'I surmised it was where you were going with the conversation.' She flushed, struggling hard not to sound so prim. Too hard.

'I hadn't been. Interesting it was where *your* mind went, though.'

'My mind went nowhere untoward, I can assure you.'

Something like relief skittered across her face and Kaspar realised it was a game. One designed to speak to his basest instincts. She was wriggling under his skin, the way she'd always been able to as a kid. Only there was nothing childlike about the attraction that now fizzed between them.

'Is that so?'

'That's so,' she confirmed, but her voice quivered.

'Are you sure?'

She didn't answer and his gaze held hers, missing nothing. Not her quick, shallow breathing, or the flush creeping up her neck, or the way she tried to swallow so discreetly. For a moment there was nothing. No sound, no movement. Then, suddenly, without even thinking, he closed the gap between them and hauled her body to his and wrapped his hand around her hair to tip her head backwards until she was staring up at him.

She didn't speak. He suspected she couldn't, and that send a shot of pure triumph jolting through him. And then he was crushing her mouth to his and a thousand glorious, dazzling fireworks were going off in his head all at once. Greedy and demanding, he feasted on her and she responded willingly. Wantonly. Her body, bump and all, pressed to him, her tongue dancing to his tune, her hands reaching for his powerful shoulders. And when she moaned against his lips his whole body tightened in response, everything shining that much brighter in his mind.

If he didn't stop this now, he feared he would never be able to do so. She was too damned intoxicating. Still, he didn't know how he succeeded to drop his arm or move away from her. He had no idea how he managed to hold his ground as she stood there, swaying and confused. It was a battle to talk as though he wasn't every bit as affected by the kiss as she clearly was.

'You're right, your disinclination to have sex with me again is abundantly clear,' he taunted softly, feeling bizarrely exhilarated as the oddest sense of calm seemed to permeate his body.

It didn't matter that Archie was staring at him as though he had lost his mind, and it didn't matter that even though he could see the jumble of thoughts that were barging through her head, he felt oddly detached. Confident. *Right.* A whisper of euphoria curled inexplicably through him.

'You had no right to do that,' she choked out eventually. 'I don't want you to do that.'

'Then you shouldn't kiss me back so willingly,' he responded, offering no room for argument.

Not another. Not when he was already feeling so rattled. And yet so triumphant. He felt another chunk of ice fall away.

'Marriage isn't what you wanted when you came here,' he told her quietly. 'I know that. Just as I know you gave me a thousand reasons why it was insane. But we're married now and those reasons don't matter. *You* don't matter. I don't matter. All that matters is our baby. And that he or she has the childhood, the life that you had. Not the one that I had.'

'How would I know that much about your childhood?' she bit back. 'I saw a little but my father kept his confidences. Mostly, I know the rumours from the press. Now I'm your wife. But how can I begin to really understand?'

He had no intention of answering, certainly not in a way that invited investigation of his life, but suddenly he heard himself speaking.

'What do you want to know?'

'You would tell me?' Wide, round eyes pinned him down. It was all he could to get a response out.

'Ask.'

She visibly deflated. Her anger seeped out of her and into the ether so suddenly it was though it had never existed. Still, he wasn't prepared for her fingers to suddenly reach out and skim his cheek.

'What happened, Kaspar?' she murmured. 'I know your mother was volatile, selfish. I know both your parents were. But what is it that I *don't* know?'

She was asking him to trust her enough to open up with the one thing he'd never told anyone. Not ever. His entire life.

He drew in one deep, steadying breath. Then another.

And all the while she stood there, her eyes locked with his and her fingers resting on his cheek, so lightly that he wasn't sure if he could feel them or merely sense them.

Everything in him railed at the mere thought of revisiting those hateful memories, let alone voicing them aloud, reliving them. But he'd offered. He couldn't renege now.

Wordlessly, he led her into the living room. It took an eternity for them both to settle. And then she sat, staring at him. Half expectant, half just waiting for him to shut her out instead.

He wasn't sure where to even start. As if she could read his mind, Archie tried to prompt him.

'Robbie met your parents once. Or at least saw them dropping you off once at boarding school. He…said they wasn't exactly…loving.'

He swallowed a bark of bitter laughter. Let it burn the back of his throat. Used it to propel him forward the way he always had done.

'They wouldn't have been remotely loving.' His voice was more clipped than he might have liked, but that couldn't be helped. 'Love didn't exist in our home. At least not towards me. Which I think was a step up from my parents' twisted version of *love*.'

'But you were their son.' She looked dazed.

'I wasn't wanted. Not like you and Robbie. I was a mistake.'

'That's how you felt?'

'That's what they called me.' He let out a humourless laugh. 'It was one of their more restrained names for me. The only time they really referred to me was to call me names or to fight about whose turn it was to take responsibility for me. I was rarely a *he*, I was most often an *it*.'

Cold realisation flowed through her.

'Which is why you got so mad when I called our baby *it*.'

'I couldn't stand it,' he admitted. 'The memories were so strong when you did that, that a sense of worthlessness that ran through me, even all these years later.'

'Were they…as volatile as the press makes out?' she pressed cautiously.

How could she already have grown to hate that expression that clouded his face? To detest his parents for putting it there? It occurred to her that she'd seen it once before. The first summer Robbie had invited him to stay at their house. Too late, she remembered the introverted, awkward seven-year-old he'd been back then.

'You don't have to answer that,' she blurted out suddenly.

Her entire body felt like it was combusting as he cupped her chin gently as if to reassure her.

'You know when Hollywood make films and they're horrific and poignant and the world says how it makes them think, and yet the truth is that it doesn't even come close to how appalling the real truth actually was? Well, that's what the media have reported my life and parents' marriage to be versus the reality.'

'They've always called it explosive.' She frowned.

'And then they've dressed it up to be something sensationalist and implied that such uncontrolled passion was somehow romantic and dramatic,' he ground out. 'But the truth was that there was nothing romantic or sensational about it. It was ugly and twisted and destructive. What's your first memory, Archie?'

It was a fight to keep his voice even, not to let the bitterness creep in. Nonetheless, Archie bit her lip as she slowly bobbed her head.

'It's probably not a real memory, just a memory I've cobbled together from photos and the stories my father told me. But it's of my mother helping me to paint a wooden race cart my father had made for me. It was just before she died so I was probably about six. Then we went out onto the dirt track behind our house and Robbie and I raced each other while my mother refereed and my father pushed me to help me keep up with Robbie.'

His chest cracked even as he knew that such special memories were exactly what he wanted for his child. For the baby Archie was now carrying.

'Mine is of my parents screaming at each other as my mother accused my father of not wanting her to succeed in Hollywood because he wouldn't give her another tummy tuck. I was standing in the kitchen doorway as they went at it the way they always did. She was throwing pots and pans and he was grabbing her and pushing her. I think I shouted out because my parents turned to the door and my mother roared at me to get out because her sagging figure was all my fault anyway. Only her words weren't that restrained. Neither was their fight.'

But he didn't want to scare Archie away. To make her fear that he was *too* damaged.

'Kaspar!' Her cry tugged at something he couldn't identify. 'How old were you?'

'Who knows?' He shrugged. 'It wouldn't have been a unique occurrence. I ran for the phone, I don't know who I was going to call. Anybody, I guess. Then I recall his footsteps thundering behind me, cuffing me across the back of the head and telling me to mind my own business. Then he picked me up, opened the front door and threw me outside, telling me to go and play in the garden or the sandpit or something. Only no one was as polite as that.'

He had a hundred memories like that locked away in some dark, deep pit of his mind. In many of them he'd copped a lot more of the blame, verbally and physically.

'Didn't anybody know?'

'There was a woman who lived down the road. Her husband was some high-flying guy in the city. She'd been the stay-at-home wife, and also his punch-bag. Her kids had grown up and moved out and she took me in often enough, gave me milk and a cookie. Somewhere to lick my wounds. She made me feel cared for. Like I wasn't alone.' He shrugged again, not able to put into words how much she had helped him, in her own way.

'That's appalling,' Archie uttered in disbelief. 'I never really understood.'

'Why would you? Your childhood was so different. And that can only be a good thing.'

She shook her head at him.

'How can you be so blasé?'

Kaspar wasn't sure how to answer that. 'I don't know. It was just…how things were. It was normal to me. It could have been worse, I guess. A lot of the time they didn't really take much notice of me at all. If I stayed out of their way I could pretend the shouting and screaming and fighting was some bad movie on a TV in another room. I used to pretend I was somewhere else. Someone else.'

'Is that why you used to love school so much? Because it made it easier to pretend?'

'I guess. I never really thought about it.' Actually, that wasn't true. He'd thought about it from time to time. 'I don't think it was personal, Archie, as odd as you might think that sounds. I don't think it was ever about me. It was always about them. That was the point.'

'Is that what you think?' She shook her head.

'I guess. It's what your father once said to me.'

'I remember Dad used to take us into his workshop and help us make a wooden toy, or later a metal one on his lathe, and weave long stories that you couldn't help but find yourself caught up in.' Archie laughed softly. 'The next thing you'd be pouring your heart out to him about whatever was wrong. At least, *I* would be.'

He smiled, bowing his head so that she couldn't read his expression. He suspected it was suddenly a fraction too wistful. Of all the people he'd felt he'd let down when he'd lost his cool that night in the bar, it was Archie's father. To this day, he had no idea whether the man ever knew about the monumental mistake he'd made that night.

Suddenly Kaspar felt too full of sorrow for all he had lost over the years but never previously allowed himself to mourn. He swallowed, breathed, waiting until he felt less emotional.

Him. Emotional?

'Your father helped me to realise that it wasn't my fault. Whatever they said there was nothing that I did or didn't do that influenced them. I was an easy target, but they would have followed the same path with each other whether I'd been around or not.'

'You sound so…rational about it all.' A hint of wonderment coloured her tone. 'So logical. I can't imagine how I could handle it the way you do.'

A laugh escaped him. A hollow, empty sound that seemed to bounce off every hard, flat surface.

'You have no idea. I don't handle it, Archie. I never have. I ignore it, hiding it away somewhere and pretending it doesn't exist. I did it successfully for years, but in the end it all bubbled over. I physically hurt someone, Archie. Why do you think I've let the press portray me as this ridiculous "Surgeon Prince of Persia"? Because it's what I deserve.'

'You don't deserve anything of the sort.'

'Yes. I do. Why do you think I avoid relationships? Why do you think I avoid emotional connections of any kind? Why do you think that until you came along I didn't want to settle down and have a family of my own? I couldn't bear the idea that I might do to them even a fraction of what was done to me.'

'You could never do that,' Archie asserted fiercely, the certainty in her voice surprising him as much as it warmed him. 'You aren't them. You're nothing like them.'

'I was never sure of that before. Not until you turned up, carrying my child. Not until that moment when I knew I *would* be a part of my baby's life. A full, complete part, not some part-time dad. I won't accept that, Archie. And I won't let you relegate me to that. That's why we had to marry.'

He couldn't tell her that he was becoming more and more suspicious that it was only part of it.

She watched him intently, her eyes never leaving his face.

'And what about love?' she challenged, so quietly he had to strain to hear her.

There was no reason for his heart to suddenly hang a beat. He didn't like what it might mean. What it might be trying to tell him. Kaspar forced himself to regain control.

'I can't tell you about love,' he informed her steadily. 'But I can tell you about chemistry.'

'Five months ago?' She let out a nervous laugh.

'It wasn't just that night, Archie. You know it as well as I do. That kiss before proves it.'

She wanted to argue. But she didn't. She couldn't. And he felt that was a good start.

She was still riding on the unexpected high of Kaspar opening up to her the following day when they were back in Dr Jarvis's office. Wondering if marriage to Kaspar would be so bad after all. Her marriage to Joe might have gone wrong, but they hadn't had a fraction of the chemistry Kaspar had mentioned. Not to mention the fact that she was carrying Kaspar's baby.

Could it really be that easy? Fitting together so neatly? It almost felt too good to be true.

'Right.' Dr Jarvis strode across the room to them, snagging Archie's attention as she advanced.

The woman's expression was too careful. Something dark, and terrifying, churned inside her.

'So I've spoken to your doctor and got your records, as you know, and I've carried out another examination today. I believe that there is funnelling taking place. However, it's no more advanced than when I examined you last week.'

Kaspar's arm unexpectedly moved around her back, and instinctively she leaned into it, drawing strength from his solid body.

'So what happens next?' he asked clearly, calmly, like he knew her vocal cords were too paralysed to even try to speak.

He probably knew already, of course. He was asking for her benefit. But that only made her all the more grateful.

'It means it's your call, Archana. There's no need to become alarmed but, given your history I would be prepared to do a cerclage in the expectation that it might help to ensure this baby stays in there where it needs to be.'

'What would that entail?' She swallowed a wave of nausea, trying to focus, to understand.

'I would place a band of strong thread around the neck of your womb, under spinal anaesthetic. I could do it this afternoon and it should take around twenty-five minutes. Antibiotics will help to reduce the risk of infection but I would want to keep you in for at least twenty-four hours anyway to ensure that the procedure hadn't induced labour. After that you should be able to go home provided you take things very easy.'

'Bed rest?' Kaspar sounded gravelly compared to his usual voice, but Archie couldn't process it. She didn't know what it meant.

'For a few days if possible.' Dr Jarvis nodded. 'Then you can slowly start to resume light movements, graduating to normal. With some emergency cerclage, we recommend no sexual intercourse for the duration of the pregnancy, but with Archana the funnelling is so faint that I'm anticipating you can resume sex in a week or two as long as it's light and infrequent, say once or twice a week.'

Later, much later, she would flush at the memory at the rather one-way conversation, and the fact that neither she nor Kaspar had refuted the idea that they were enjoying a healthy sexual relationship.

Later. Not now.

'But you should wear a condom, Kaspar,' Dr Jarvis was continuing blithely. 'Obviously that's more about reducing the risk of infection rather than concern about conception.'

On some vague level Archie was aware that the woman had been making a joke. No doubt one she made to all her patients to try to elevate the mood a fraction. But Archie couldn't laugh, she barely even cracked a smile. She wasn't sure if Kaspar did any better.

'We won't be having sex,' came Kaspar's tight, rasping admission eventually. But when Dr Jarvis continued, it wasn't clear if she had misunderstood or was simply being discreet.

'That's probably wise until I have chance to do a two-week post-op check-up. Then I'll have a better idea of how your body is reacting to the cerclage, Archana. Often orgasms can soften the already compromised cervix, which can also lead to premature birth. Although, again, in your case, I don't believe that will be the case. This is more a precaution due to your history along with the fact that there is faint funnelling. If it was just one of those factors then I wouldn't be considering the procedure.'

And if Kaspar hadn't been the one pulling the strings, would anyone have done anything at all? Her doctors had dismissed it, if they'd even noticed it, just as they had done when she'd been carrying Faith.

She couldn't lose another baby. She *wouldn't*.

She didn't need to look at Kaspar to know what she wanted to do. Somehow, him just being here, his arm around her, gave her the confidence she needed to make her own decision.

'Schedule the procedure, please.' Her voice cracked but she didn't care. 'I'll have it done as soon as possible.'

CHAPTER NINE

THE SUN BEAT DOWN, seeping into Archie's skin and melting into her very bones, its warmth heating the poolside paving slabs under her feet. Archie relaxed in the shade and tried not to stare too obviously at the sight of Kaspar cutting through the water as he executed perfect length after perfect length.

The past few weeks since the cerclage had seemed surreal. Like she'd woken up in a parallel life where she lived in pleasant domesticity with Kaspar. He'd been attentive, and patient, and easy company.

But they'd never mentioned his childhood again. Or their marriage.

They never really talked about anything of substance. Not even the cerclage. Their conversations were light, sometimes funny, always friendly, but they verged on the superficial, and it galled Archie more than she cared to admit. As though their moment of breakthrough had never happened.

Even when Dr Jarvis had expressed her satisfaction that Archie's body seemed to have accepted the intervention well with bed rest slipping into house rest then into gentle activities, but not yet sexual activity.

Archie had no doubt that her searing cheeks had raised the temperature of the consultation room by several degrees, mortified that she'd instantly thought back to that weekend together and had not been able to get the incredible X-rated images from her head. Yet Kaspar had schooled his features as though the conversation hadn't bothered him in the least.

It had somehow felt demoralising, making her wonder why he hadn't even touched her since the kiss that wedding night. Had it simply been about proving a point? Why did it even bother her?

Archie stood up abruptly. The need to get away from the house—something she hadn't been able to do in the last few days—more overwhelming than ever.

That one moment of openness, of almost vulnerability on Kaspar's part those weeks ago had been gone even by the following morning when she'd awoken. She could remember it as vividly as if it had only been hours ago.

Not even a trace of their temporary connection had remained as he'd presented her with a freshly squeezed orange juice courtesy of the juice-maker on his sparkling kitchen island, scrambled eggs with asparagus on wholemeal toast courtesy of the pan on the pristine cooker, and rich herbal tea courtesy of the instant hot-water tap at the plush sink.

She had plastered a beatific smile to her lips and pretended not to notice that the vulnerable Kaspar had disappeared as abruptly as he'd appeared. Pretended not to care that he hadn't dipped his head and kissed her the way she'd so ardently wished he would as they'd stood in that room, her hand over his heart, trying to feel whether it was beating as loudly and as quickly as hers had been.

But he'd remained as shut off to her as he always had been. A closed book.

'So you do actually use this kitchen for cooking?' It had

been an effort to keep her tone upbeat at first. To tease him. 'I'm impressed.'

'You should be. It was your father who taught me how.'

'His only real signature was all-day breakfasts,' Archie had corrected him, this time striving for a laugh. Surprised when it was actually more genuine than she'd expected. 'He was useless at most other cooking.'

'You're right.' Kaspar had nodded after a moment's consideration. 'I've been making his famous all-day breakfast since I was fourteen.'

'Ah, yes. You and Robbie would cook it every single Sunday of every single holiday.'

'I seem to remember you wolfing it down as fast as anybody.'

'I had to.' Archie had feigned indignation. 'I had to keep up with you two. You didn't exactly want a twelve-year-old following you around. You both always tried to ditch me.'

'Yeah.' Kaspar had chuckled. 'And you've no idea the rollicking your father gave us whenever we were successful.'

They'd laughed and, for a moment, it had felt good again. Until she'd realised that all Kaspar's light-hearted banter was a way of keeping her at arm's length. Even as she lived in his home as his wife, carrying his child.

Shaking off her thoughts as she reached the expansive glass sliders that led from the poolside to the cool lounge, Archie sensed, rather than saw, Kaspar coming up behind her as she entered the house.

'Archie? Is everything okay?'

She wanted to shout and rail and vent all her frustrations. Instead, she simply turned to greet him with a pleasant, if rather flat smile plastered onto her lips.

She should be grateful he cared.

She should be.

'I'm fine. The baby's fine. I just wanted to head in for a while.'

He didn't believe her for a moment. His gaze pierced through her, making her blood fizz in her veins in a way that even the hot sun hadn't managed.

Dammit, when was she ever going to get a grip of herself around this man?

'What's wrong?' he demanded. 'You've been more and more jittery with each passing day.'

Fear that he could read her so easily, that he might guess the embarrassing truth, lent her voice a frustration she hadn't intended.

'I'm sick of being cooped up in this house, unable to even go out, when you refuse to talk to me about anything remotely important. I can't take it any more. I'm getting my trainers and I'm going for a walk along the beach.'

He eyed her again, the same intensity, the same knowing expression in those unfathomable depths. How was it that he seemed to find it so easy to read her while she had no idea what he was thinking, most of the time? It was hardly fair.

And now shc sounded like the kind of petulant teen she liked to pride herself that she'd never been.

'Have I upset you in some way, Archie?' Evenly. A little too calmly.

'No.' She gritted her teeth.

'Have I treated you badly and not been aware of it?'

'Of course not.'

'Then perhaps you would care to tell me why I suddenly seem to have become your enemy.' His eyebrows shot up. 'Only here was I thinking I was looking after you.'

He had been. That was the problem. He was looking after her for the baby, which was right and proper, but not because he also wanted to look after *her.* The difference was subtle, but it was there. And it hurt.

Logic, it seemed, stood little chance against a heart that yearned for something else. Especially when that something else was Kaspar Athari's love.

Archie balked at the realisation.

Surely she wasn't still imagining herself *in love* with Kaspar? No, that had to be the baby mushing up her head.

'You're right.' She backed down abruptly. 'Sorry. Maybe I just need to get out of the sun.'

The last thing she needed right now was to engage in a bit of verbal back and forth with him. Or stir up more emotions in her that her hormone-riddled head might mistake for *love.* It was all she could manage not to squirm beneath his unrelenting gaze. Assessing her, as he always did.

'Get changed,' he bit out unexpectedly. 'I'm taking you out for the afternoon.'

Flitting around the city, playing the tourist with Archie and doing the sightseeing thing was certainly not the way he'd been expecting this day to turn out. Yet here they were in downtown Los Angeles, soaking up the atmosphere.

To his surprise, he found himself enjoying it, even forgetting his concerns for Archie, and for their baby, for a while.

Over the last week he'd become more and more aware of the beatific yet simultaneously false smile that she'd flashed him from time to time. He was aware that, to a greater extent, it was his own fault. After opening up to her that one night he'd not so much regretted it but, more, had had his misgivings. At loading something like that onto Archie when she already had enough to worry about. And, yes, about opening up so easily, so naturally. As if it hadn't been the greatest secret he'd lugged around for his entire life, which had defined him, driven him, moulded him. And as though it didn't even matter any more. Not when he had Archie.

Because the truth was, he didn't have Archie. She may have married him, but only because she'd been pregnant with his baby and he'd insisted on it. He would do well to remember that before he risked letting himself get carried away with this sham marriage of theirs. The marriage he was altogether too happy to accept. So he'd managed to shut himself off to her as he always had. A closed book.

But always aware that Archie could so easily take him off the shelf, blow the cobwebs away and open him up if she took it into her head. Encouraging him to give up his stories, his secrets when they were better left unread.

Unseen.

'The Walt Disney Concert Hall?' she breathed, a look of quiet awe on her face as she dragged him back to the present.

'Yeah, well, I figured with your background in construction this might be of particular interest.'

'It is.' Archie nodded, taking in the iconic structure in front of them. 'The way it looks and, I believe, the sound are incredible.'

He dipped his head in confirmation.

'The LA Philharmonic are performing next month. I have tickets. Accompany me.'

It was meant to be an invitation but he knew it sounded more like a command. Even more unexpectedly, however, Archie merely looked up at him in surprise and then smiled. A genuine, sweet smile that he felt everywhere, as if she were running her hands over his bare flesh the way he knew her eyes had been doing—albeit against her will—earlier in the afternoon at the pool.

She made him feel so good. Perhaps too good. He didn't

have any right to still want her the way he did. As wrong as he knew it was—she was the mother of his child, after all, and he was supposed to be caring for her, protecting her—he couldn't seem to stop it. She preyed on his waking thoughts. And most definitely his sleeping thoughts.

'Come on.' He forced one leg in front of the other, but his hand still reached for hers as he led her around the building he'd somehow *known* she would love to see.

The tour should have been a welcome distraction, allowing him to clear his head, but Kaspar was too preoccupied to enjoy it. He was just grateful that Archie seemed happy, throwing herself into the history and the story as though nothing was more important to her.

After that, they toured the MAK Center for Art and Architecture, the gardens at the exposition centre and another museum whose name he couldn't remember afterwards. Yet each time she barely seemed to notice he was even accompanying her while, for Kaspar, the drive in the back of the chauffeured car was becoming a little harder with each journey. He couldn't shake an irrational urge to jolt her, to remind her that he wasn't just the guy who'd got her pregnant, he was her husband. Whatever that meant.

'Where now?' Archie asked as she glanced out the window as if she had any idea where they were.

'Home.'

It was ridiculous how those words rippled through him, but it was only when Archie shivered that he realised she wasn't quite as immune to him as he'd let himself believe. With mounting curiosity he watched her force herself not to react, grasping instead at the first thing to come into her head.

'You mean that incredible house you own with the stunning views? Though I couldn't describe it as a *home*.'

'By which you mean…?' he prompted when she stopped talking with a strangled sound.

'Forget I said anything.'

He knew he should do precisely that. Let it go. It wouldn't do any good to encourage the kind of conversation they'd had the other night. Yet he couldn't just stay silent. He wanted to know what she thought. It *mattered* to him.

He didn't care how dangerous that sounded. At least it was something more than the trivial conversations they'd been having recently. He told himself he was being foolish. But *that* didn't seem to matter at all.

For her part, despite all the biting of her lip, which he was fast recalling meant that Archie was trying to bite back words she knew she shouldn't say, Archie swivelled her head to look at him.

'It's hardly a home, Kaspar. It doesn't have an ounce of heart. It doesn't tell a visitor the slightest thing about the person who owns it. It's a beautiful building but it's soulless. There's nothing of *you* in it.'

She was right, of course. Because that was exactly how he'd wanted it. At some point he'd come to equate being unreadable with being invulnerable. Not that he would ever have admitted that before now, of course.

'So change it.' He shrugged as though it was no big deal but his eyes never left hers.

As if somehow that way he could convey all the thing he couldn't, *shouldn't*, say. He told himself it was part of the plan. A necessity. To break down the barriers in order that they could grow close enough to be the kind of parents their child would need. It wasn't about *wanting* to break down barriers with Archie.

He wasn't sure even he believed himself.

What the hell was wrong with him?

'Sorry? Change what?' she pushed tentatively.

'Change the house.' He waved a hand that he was glad to see didn't look as leaden as it felt. 'We're married and we're having a baby. That place is your house too now, so make it a home. The family home of your dreams.'

'What, to match the marriage of my dreams? I can change anything, but without your input it will just be *my* home in *your* house. It still won't reflect you at all.'

The tone verged on hysterical. Out of nowhere, or so it felt. The words cracked out like a whip slicing through the air. He had to fight not to flinch.

'So?' he replied coldly, not trusting himself to say any more.

The silence was so stark that he could hear the almost silent hum of tyres on tarmac. Archie blew out a deep breath.

'I just don't understand you, Kaspar.' She splayed her hands out on her knees. 'It's like we take one step forward only to take a giant leap back.'

'I disagree.'

'Really? One minute you're telling me we won't be playing happy families, the next you're hauling me off to the registrar. You kiss me like we're in some kind of epic movie, but then you don't even look sideways at me. You open up to me finally about something that actually *matters*, and then you shut me out as though I have no right to know anything about you. Now you're telling me we can redecorate your house like a real couple but you barely react when I challenge you about this not being a real marriage. Which version of *Kaspar* should I believe in?'

'The movie version sounds good. This is Hollywood after all.' He didn't know how he managed to sound appropriately dry. Even amused. 'This place loves a good "Girl Next Door Tames Playboy" love story after all.'

'This isn't a movie,' she snapped, a little shakily. 'This is my life.'

'Now it's both.'

She exhaled again. Even deeper this time, and more forcefully.

'If this really were a movie, Kaspar, you wouldn't be shutting me out.'

He really didn't like the way his blood suddenly rushed through his body at her accusation.

'I haven't shut you out,' he managed, although even on his lips the words sounded hollow. 'I opened up to you.'

'One conversation? One night?' She was incredulous. 'That's your idea of opening up? You cracked the portcullis a fraction and then the next morning you'd not only slammed it back down but you'd dug a moat, filled it and set me squarely on the other side.'

His jaw locked so tightly he thought his bones might crack, but he couldn't refute her accusation. More to the point, *why did he find he even wanted to*?

'What did you expect me to do?' he demanded. 'Rage and roar and gnash my teeth? That isn't who I am, Archie. I thought you knew that.'

She flinched, just as he'd expected she would. But then she rallied. Quickly.

'I didn't expect you to treat me like the enemy because you regretted even that tiny show of vulnerability from yourself. I didn't expect you to push me even further away. I didn't expect you to shoot down any conversations that involved anything real.'

'You saw a bike with stabilisers in a shop and asked what colour we would for buy our baby,' he stated in disbelief. 'The baby isn't even born yet.'

'It was hypothetical. And it wasn't just that. It was about

getting an opinion from you on anything at all. You know exactly what I mean. Every conversation. Every time.'

He shot her a deliberately disparaging look.

'I don't know anything of the sort. You're being overly dramatic.'

He did know, though. That was the issue. For a moment she didn't answer, but when she did it wasn't to say what he might have expected.

'Please, Kaspar. I know you *do* understand.'

Her soft plea scraped away inside him. Raw. Guilt-inducing. He tried to ignore it. Turned his head to watch the LA landscape as it sped past the window, the sights and smells as clear to him as if he'd been able to taste then, feel them, without the thick glass and metal in the way.

Abruptly he hit the intercom, instructing his driver to change direction.

'What's Hector's?' Archie asked, despite herself, and, incredibly, a smile began toying with his lips.

How did she change the mood so easily? Bring him around when he'd thought things too dour?

'You'll see,' he replied, only half-surprised when the hint of teasing didn't satisfy her. 'Fine, it's a crazy golf course. I used to go there all the time when we first moved out here and I was sixteen.'

She eyed him, a little too knowingly.

'Do you remember the course we used to sneak onto as kids? When it was closed for the day and the guy who ran it knew we didn't have enough pocket money to pay full price but he let us give him whatever money we could scrape together?'

'And then he'd leave us whatever pastries hadn't been sold that day and were going to get chucked out anyway?' Kaspar added.

Archie laughed, her face flushing with pleasure.

'You were really good at crazy golf. Robbie used to hate it because sometimes you'd hit the shots backwards just to give him a chance.'

'Considering how co-ordinated he was at other sports, he really was remarkably bad at the game. So were you, for that matter. The athletic Coates kids, foiled by a crazy golf course.'

'I wasn't that bad,' she objected.

'You weren't that good either.'

'Now wait a minute…' She paused, then jabbed her finger at the tinted glass with barely disguised delight. 'There. Is that Hector's?'

He knew the drive without even looking.

'That's Hector's.'

'Come on, then.' She was out of the door the minute the car pulled up. 'I reckon today might be the day for a little payback.'

He vaulted after her.

'Payback, huh? Care to wager?'

'How much?'

'Not money. A forfeit.'

She wrinkled her nose.

'What kind of forfeit?'

'Winner gets to choose.' He shrugged, striding ahead and slapping the money on the counter of a rather disinterested-looking young man.

'Surely that's not Hector?' Archie whispered as they ducked through the paint-chipped turnstile.

He wasn't fooled.

'Changing the subject, Coates. Are you that doubtful about your crazy golf abilities?'

'I am not.' She selected her club and thrust her chin in the air. 'Fine. A forfeit. Winner's choice.'

In the event, the game was more fun than he had anticipated. Light relief after the tension. He'd never thought that revisiting any element of his past could ever be anything but painful, but he was beginning to understand that in his need to bury his childhood he had lost many happier times. Almost always concerning the Coates family, the way her father had taught him to be a man, or the way Robbie had shared everything with him, or the way Archie had treated him like another annoying big brother. They had made him feel like any other normal boy. A person, not an *it*.

All too soon, they were at the final obstacle, their game almost over, and Archie hadn't been quite as appalling as he'd remembered.

Still, Kasper knew it was a mistake the moment he moved behind her, her back against his chest, his arms skating down the length of hers, her delicate hands under his, all under the pretext of holding the golf club with her and allowing her to help him make his winning shot.

Until that moment it had been a good game. Simple, uncomplicated fun, a round of crazy golf on a balmy afternoon. They had exchanged banter and laughed and she had teased him, coughing and doing funny dances to try to put him off his shots, like a grown-up version of the Little Ant he had known. Her ploy hadn't worked, his shots had been true each time. But occasionally he'd pretended her antics had put him off, making some melodramatic mishit that had only made her laugh all the more.

A genuine, throw-her-head-back laugh, which was surpassed only by the vivid sparkle in her glorious eyes. The more she did so, the more he yearned to make her do it more. The intense pleasure it gave him to be the person making her so outwardly happy had taken him back, made him forget who or where he was. It seduced him into focussing on Archie and himself together, simply playing crazy golf. Like when they'd been young, carefree, their whole lives ahead of them.

She'd played well but he'd played better. Of course he had. Because everything in life was a competition for him. And yet, right at that moment, he'd wanted them both to take that winning shot. He'd invited her to join him and she, without even thinking about it, had skipped almost girlishly to comply.

The moment his body had touched hers everything changed. The innocence of the moment was gone, replaced instead by something far more charged. Far more sensual. Only then did Kaspar admit it had been there all afternoon. Simmering quietly. Just waiting to catch them unawares.

He should move back. But he couldn't. He could barely even breathe. His head was over her shoulder, his cheek brushing her ear as they both stared at the ball. Archie's own breathing was shallow, fast, although he knew she was trying to fight it, desperately struggling to control it. He could take the shot, pretend he didn't feel what she felt. But he was powerless to move. Rooted where he stood.

He turned his head, so very, very slightly it should have been imperceptible. But Archie noticed. She knew. Her head mirrored his, and now their mouths were an inch apart and the beast inside him was roaring with the compulsion to close the gap. His body wanting her with the same ferocity it had all those months ago.

He had to walk away.

Now.

CHAPTER TEN

KASPAR DROPPED HIS head but misjudged it. Or rather he judged it perfectly, his lips skimming the bare skin just above the neckline of her T-shirt. Archie shivered and he was lost.

Before he could think once, let alone twice, Kaspar tilted his head and then they were kissing as she pressed her back into him, their hands still holding the grip of the golf club and his feet still positioned on either side of hers.

He drank her in, her taste, her feel, her scent every bit as perfect as the recollection imprinted on his brain, and yet also a hundred times better. He remembered kissing every inch of her skin, tracing it with his fingertip, his mouth, his tongue, and as his body tightened against Archie's perfect bottom, she pushed back against him, then gentlest of moans reaching his ears.

He almost lost it, there and then. A lifetime of being in complete control gone because no one else had ever got under his skin like this. No one but Archie. He would never know how he managed to pull his brain into focus, to remember where they were, or that he was meant to be easing Archie's stress, not adding to it.

It took everything he had to wrench his mouth away. This was pure physical desire, nothing more. *Nothing more.* But if that was true then why was he still behind her, why were his arms still around hers, her hands still held under his?

If he didn't stop now, he wasn't sure he ever would. Somehow he found the strength to pull away.

The loss of contact was almost painful.

'What was that for?' Archie whispered, turning slowly to face him, her fingers hovering over her lips.

He wondered if her mouth burned for him as his did for her.

'Call it my victory kiss.' His attempt to sound casual fell far short of the mark. 'Your forfeit.'

'You didn't win.'

Half teasing, half shaky, and entirely shocked. He knew exactly how she felt.

'You'd better finish the game to prove it.'

'I don't give a damn about the game.'

He just gave a damn about her.

'The game, Athari.' She emitted a delicious growl.

All he really wanted was to haul her back into his arms and finish kissing her, thoroughly and completely. Even though it made absolutely no sense.

'Right,' he muttered eventually, stepping forward and taking the proffered club.

Stepping to the mark, he swung and hit. He barely even waited to see if it reached its mark. He knew it would.

'Let's go.' He spun around and begun walking away, but he couldn't help extending his arm behind him. Felt triumphant when she took his hand without a word.

He told himself it meant nothing, the way his chest constricted as her fingers entwined with his. He promised himself he'd let go as soon as they were back in the car.

But now they were back in the vehicle and he still hadn't let go of her hand. He still couldn't take his gaze off her sparkling eyes as he instructed his driver to finally take them home. He couldn't shake the fact that the word *home* sounded somehow right, and natural, and easy, and perfect.

Archie stared right back at him, her gaze never leaving his for a moment, but he saw the hesitation on her face. Watched the way her tongue flicked out nervously to wet her lips.

'Why are you looking at me like that?'

Uncertainty in her tone mingled with raw need. Kaspar gritted his teeth. It was a heady combination.

'You realise that we kissed out there. Like a proper married couple.'

'Imagine that,' she tried to tease him, but her breathy tone belied her confidence.

Another Archie quality that he apparently found sexy as hell. Especially after the overly cocky women of his past. *What had he ever seen in them?* The answer was clear now. He hadn't. They'd been the perfect choice for a man looking to keep himself emotionally unavailable because they'd never threatened to unravel his carefully crafted design. The construct that Archie had picked apart in a matter of months. Or, indeed, one heady weekend.

'If people see us, recognise me with a woman looking as unambiguously pregnant as you look, your photo will be all over the papers. The internet. We might have kept things out of the media for now, but they will find out eventually and it *will* fire up their interest.'

'So you'll control it.' She schooled her features. But it was too late, he'd seen that flash of contempt in her eyes. 'You control anything you want to. You're Kaspar Athari.'

Until a few months ago he might have believed her.

'Not anything,' he muttered. 'I can't control how I am when I'm with you.'

The words were out before he could swallow them back. Archie paused, as though momentarily unable to answer.

Then her hand reached out, slowly, tentatively, giving him plenty of time to draw away. Had he wanted to. Her fingertips brushed his jaw. Gentle. Careful. But it fired him up nonetheless.

Before he could stop himself, he was lifting her through the air to settle her on his lap and her soft, startled cry even as she leaned instinctively into him, her arms slipping around his neck and her bottom nudging against the hottest, hardest part of him, only acted as an accelerant to the fire.

He closed the gap and allowed himself to taste her all over again, light and deep, languid and demanding. Indulging in the feel, the scent, the breathy sounds of pleasure that were so essentially Archie when he plundered her mouth and pressed kisses into the creases at either corner. She quivered deliciously as he scorched a trail down her neck to the sensitive hollow where his lips, his tongue, his teeth all worked in harmony until she was breathing hard and wriggling on his lap. And he was aching, *physically* aching, for her.

His hands found their way to the hem of her T-shirt, hauling it over her head in one fluid movement, and as her hair tumbled back down and over her shoulders, he couldn't help lifting one hand to wind it around his fist, pulling just the wrong side of gently to tilt her mouth back up to his and claim her all over again.

Archie pressed her chest to him. Hard nipples scraped urgently against him, even through his own thin shirt. She fumbled with the buttons, tugging them open and rubbing against him as though the skin-to-skin contact might somehow alleviate her longing. And Kaspar loved it. The way she acted out of pure desire. The feel and the taste, and what she wanted. The kind of women he'd been with before her had been too busy trying to show him how good they were and too hung up on the aesthetics of it.

He let his thumb graze one swollen peak with deliberate nonchalance, moving quickly away when she arched her back in order to repeat the action. She groaned softly.

'Kaspar…'

'What is it, Archie?'

He was amazed that he could managed to sound even a fraction as in control as he did.

'You know what,' she whispered, pushing her chest to his again.

'Tell me,' he rasped. 'I want to hear it.'

She flushed slightly, but met his eyes boldly.

'Touch me.'

It was like some exquisite torture, keeping his hands to himself. But he wanted to hear her say it. He thirsted to hear the longing in her tone, knowing that it was a need only he could sate for her.

For both of them.

'Where?' he demanded.

'Anywhere,' she whispered. 'Everywhere.'

He couldn't stand it any longer. Dropping his head back to the hollow, he kissed and teased.

'Here?'

'There,' she agreed, tilting her head to one side to allow him better access. Taking his time, he made his way down her body, his fingertips hooking down the lace of her bra to free one perfect nipple.

'Here?'

She gasped, and nodded, her head falling back slightly as he licked, sucked. And with every stroke of his tongue he stoked the fire and revelled in the way the flames roared within him. It was all he could do to stay where he was, lavishing attention on first one rosy peak and then the other. Then back again, as her breathing grew ever more shallow, catching in her throat.

And then he was sliding his hand up the bare skin of her thigh, the summery skirt puddling around her bottom as though only too happy to fall away for him. Archie moaned, a low, soft, long sound that seemed to wind its way through him and coil around his sex as potently as if it were her delicate hand. He reached the top of one thigh and then, his knuckles barely brushing her hot, molten core, he skimmed his way slowly down the other thigh.

'You're teasing me again,' she moaned, burying her head in his shoulder.

Half a gasp, half a growl, but wholly frustration. Another shot fired through him.

'I am,' he managed, shocked at how difficult it suddenly seemed to speak.

Kaspar could stand it no longer. He ached for her. Physically *ached.* He wanted her. And she was his. He lifted his hand and slid it beneath the silky triangle of material.

Hot. Wet. So very ready for him.

He had never wanted anything more than he wanted her right now. It was time to claim her. Brand her as his. He would never want anyone the way he wanted Archie.

She froze at exactly the same moment he did.

What the hell was he thinking? She was pregnant. With his baby. And Catherine had said there could potentially be an issue. They couldn't risk it. They couldn't take that chance. Allowing himself to be driven by his desire, his emotion was exactly the kind of selfishness that his parents had exhibited time and again. He would not repeat their mistakes.

He would not let the fact that he shared their DNA make him like them.

'This can't happen,' he growled, lifting her bodily of his

lap and placing her as far across the back seat as he possibly could. Never more grateful for the privacy glass which concealed them from both the driver and the outside world.

She made a sound. It might have been a mutter of agreement but he didn't care. He busied himself locating her clothes. Fastening his shirt.

'That should never have started.' He was aware that he was directing the fury he felt at himself towards Archie, but he couldn't seem to stop himself. 'You have the baby to consider.'

What the hell was wrong with him?

'Dr Jarvis said occasional light sex is acceptable,' she parroted. 'It's not as if we're going at it every day.'

A flush raced up her cheek as though she could scarcely believe her own audacity. It was more of a turn-on than he was prepared to admit.

'This can never happen again.' Determined, Kaspar cut her off. 'This *will* never happen again.'

But she was becoming emboldened.

'Really? Because it seems that the more time we spend together, the more it's inevitable.'

For a moment she actually sounded like it wasn't such a bad thing. And he wanted too much to believe her. If he stayed, he was sure that he'd wind up letting her talk him into things when he ought to know better.

'Then it seems clear to me that the only solution is to spend *less* time together.'

'You're going to stay at the hospital,' she guessed, cutting in.

'One of us has to take responsibility for this…*thing* between us.'

To his shock, she swung around, her eyes flashing with a fury he hadn't seen in her since she'd been a little kid shut out of the more daring exploits he and Robbie had egged each other onto.

'That's not taking responsibility, Kaspar. That's running away. It's not something I thought I'd ever see you do.'

It was only when the car pulled into the drive of Kaspar's oceanside home that Archie felt she could finally breathe again, let alone speak. Ever since her uncontrolled outburst the atmosphere in the car had pulsed with barely suppressed fury, but Kaspar hadn't uttered a word to her.

If he had, she feared she might have melted from their molten ire. The urge to run inside and bolt the door was almost overwhelming, but if she did that then Kaspar would leave. She didn't want him to.

So instead she folded her arms across her chest and summoned one last ounce of strength.

'Don't go, Kaspar. Not tonight.'

For a moment she thought he was going to ignore her, but then he turned his head, his eyes pinning her to the seat.

'I have to.'

'Please.' She couldn't say what passed between them, or what it meant, but she knew instinctively that he was going to stay. 'Take me for a walk along the beach?'

Carefully, with his arm under her elbow, she made her way down the hillside to the beach, slipping her sandals off and spreading her toes in the soft sand. She tilted her face towards the warm setting sun and realised that in spite of everything she wasn't unhappy, or lonely, or wishing she'd never got on that damned plane to America.

To Kaspar.

Because if she hadn't got on that plane then she wouldn't be here now, walking along the beach and realising that even if he never loved her the way she wanted him to, he would always love their child. Always fight for him or her.

'Why are you so determined to fight your feelings for me, Kaspar? Whatever they amount to. This isn't just about the risk to the baby, is it? You're scared to let go with me. Why?'

'It's for your benefit,' he bit out.

'What is it you think I need protecting from? You? In case you've forgotten, I know the other side of you. That kid who I think is more of the real you than you've ever allowed anyone else to see. A good, kind kid.'

'Then your memory isn't what you think it is,' he mocked derisively.

'It's exactly what I think it is. Why haven't you met someone before now, Kaspar? Had a family? You really will make a strong, good, supportive father.'

It took a little while for him to answer and, for several long moments, she wondered if he was ever going to answer her.

'My mother is, in polite terms, an oxygen thief,' he stated. 'She always has been. My father was no better. So what does that make me? Their son. Their blood. The lethal mix of the worst of the both of them.'

'I've said it before—you aren't like them, Kaspar.'

'You don't know what I really am like.'

'Maybe, but I don't think you do either.'

It was a silent challenge and he could either ignore her or talk to her. She knew what she wanted him to do, but she tried not to let herself get too carried away.

'I...don't *do* emotion, Archie,' he managed, at length. 'I don't connect with people. I'm not built that way. I know how destructive so-called relationships might be. How intense and violent and toxic. You say I'm not like them, but I'm still a product of them. I share their DNA and even if it wasn't about nature, I was certainly around them long enough for it to be nurture.'

'Is that why you've made a point, all these years, of never allowing yourself to get caught up with any one woman?'

'It's easier that way.'

'It's lonely,' she refuted. 'And it doesn't suit you. You're a decent guy, underneath all the playboy rubbish.'

'Did you know that as a teenager I stole a girl from under Robbie's nose? Not because I liked her or particularly wanted to date her but because Robbie did and I didn't want him ditching me to spend time to with her. That was when I realised I wasn't rounded and *normal*. I wasn't the decent human being your father tried to teach me to be. I was a product of my own parents, already on the way to becoming damaged and twisted.'

'You can't be serious.' Archie swing around to gawk at him. '*That's* what you're basing part of your argument on? *Shady Sadie?* Because I can tell you plenty of mean things my brother and I did to each other and so-called friends as we were growing up. It's called a part of being a kid. And a teenager who thinks the world revolves around them.'

'No, Archie. It's not just that. You don't want to know the things I did when I came out here. They weren't part of growing up, they were out of control. Harmful.'

His face twisted painfully but she couldn't believe it. Not of Kaspar.

'You mean after your mother dragged you out here? Ripped you away from the tiniest bit of security you'd ever had? You played up? But look at you now. You turned your back on the Hollywood scene she'd mapped out for you and instead became a skilled surgeon, a decent person. You volunteer your time to make surgical trips to war zones to help people who really need you.'

He looked frustrated, and angry, and drained. But most of all he looked torn. She'd never seen him look that way before. Her whole body ached for him.

'It's not as altruistic as you think. Did you ever stop to wonder why I went from acting to surgery? Did you think that out of nowhere I developed a driving need to take after my volatile, unpredictable plastic surgeon father?'

'Becoming a surgeon like him doesn't also make you as…unhinged as him,' she cried.

'That's where you're wrong. I'm every bit as out of control as he was. That's *exactly* why I turned my back on acting and suddenly worked to get into a good school, gain a good degree, get into med school.'

'You got into top universities, Kaspar. Not just good schools.'

'You're missing the point. I wasn't doing it because I was a good person, I did it because it was the only way I could think of to make amends for…something I did. So bad that even you couldn't make excuses for me if you knew, Archie.'

'Isn't that the definition of *good*? How long are you going to punish yourself, though?' she whispered. 'What did you do that was so bad?'

The quiet was almost oppressive.

'I fought someone, Archie. I put them in hospital because they looked at me the wrong way in a bar one night.'

Her chest stretched and ached. So that was how that story Katie had told her that night at the charity wrap party had got started. Still, she knew there had to be more to it than that.

'How old were you?'

'Old enough to know better.'

'How old?' she demanded.

'Seventeen.'

'And the other guy?'

'Twenty-five, though I didn't know that at the time. I saw them in court.'

Her stomach lifted and dropped.

'Them?'

'There was another lad.' Kaspar lifted his shoulders. 'But he was almost too drunk to walk. He'd just been swinging a piece of wood around.'

'A piece of wood in a bar? And no one did anything?'

'We were outside by then, in a back alley.'

'And all because they looked at you the wrong way? I don't understand.'

Kaspar gritted his teeth, obviously hating every moment of the story but determined to tell her, to make her understand why he was so *damaged*.

'We were in a bar, a bit of a dive. As they passed me, one of them tripped over my bar stool. He pushed me off it and told me to apologise. I refused and they suggested taking it outside and I didn't have the sense to say no.'

'So there were two of them and one of them was wielding a plank of wood. My God, Kaspar, you could have been killed. Surely you were just defending yourself?'

'No, I wasn't drunk. They were. I could have walked away. I should have.'

'You were seventeen,' she cried. 'It was a mistake.'

'I hospitalised the guy. They were both swinging at me and I saw red. I made a kick—*one* kick, Archie—and I broke his jaw. He needed reconstructive surgery.'

'God, Kaspar.' Her fingers were pressed to her mouth.

'In one stupid, drunken, angry moment I'd changed some stranger's life.'

'It…it was one kick, Kaspar.'

'Exactly. What if I'd really lost control and not been able to stop even there?'

For a moment she couldn't respond and then, suddenly, it was easy.

'But you *didn't* lose control. You stopped. One kick, unfortunately well placed but hardly premeditated or unprovoked. What did the judge say?'

'It doesn't matter what he said. It's what I know that counts.'

'So he said it was self-defence?' she guessed.

'The guy was wasted, he probably couldn't have hurt me, but still the judge dismissed the case,' Kaspar said contemptuously.

'Because even a drunken guy could get lucky if he'd, say, picked up a bar stool, or a glass ashtray, or who knows what else,' she argued. 'What did the judge say?'

He eyed her reluctantly.

'That there were too many witnesses who had told him how those men were acting up all night, were always in there, acting that way. He said *I* was the innocent party and he let me walk away scot-free.'

'Only you didn't walk away scot-free, did you? You changed your whole life because of that one incident. Your whole new career choice was based on that moment, wasn't it? Because of the surgeons who repaired that lad's face? They're who you wanted to become?'

'It was a hell of a lot better than the out-of-touch, diva-like actor that I was becoming.'

'It was self-sacrificing.'

'Hardly,' he snorted. 'I knew if I turned my back on the lucrative deal my mother had just made with a major studio, she'd never forgive me. Two birds, one stone.'

It was pointless arguing. She knew the truth and she felt sure Kaspar did, too, deep down. Instead, she reached her hand out, placing her palm on his chest, feeling the heat and thrumming of his heartbeat.

Drawing strength from it.

'You didn't just become an average doctor, Kaspar, you became one of the top surgeons in the world. A pioneer in your field. You're even more famous than some of Hollywood's best A-listers. And what's more, you save lives. Do you really believe you're still damaged? Out of control? Just like your parents?'

'It isn't what I believe, Archie,' he bit out, remorse etched into every contour of his face. 'It's what I know.'

'You're wrong.' She shook her head vigorously but she already knew Kaspar wasn't listening.

She'd lost him. Again.

CHAPTER ELEVEN

'THIRTY-TWO WEEKS.' CATHERINE, as Archie had finally come to know her, smiled as she finished up the examination. 'And you're doing really well.'

'The cerclage is okay?'

'It's fine. If anything, it appears to have lengthened the cervix and reversed the funnelling that we were seeing before. It's a great sign but it can be temporary so don't think it's a green light to start running marathons or anything.'

'So I keep limiting the physical activity.' Archie nodded. 'Got it.'

'And I understand it must be difficult, but you're keeping the sexual activity gentle and less frequent? No more than a couple of times a week?'

She nodded, but couldn't bring herself to look at Kaspar, her face feeling like it probably resembled some kid's rosy-cheeked doll. They'd both agreed it would raise fewer questions if they didn't try to explain the situtation.

'Again, use protection,' Catherine continued blithely. 'More to reduce risk of infection than as contraception.'

Archie forced a laugh. The same joke as last time and just as awkward.

'So now that we're getting closer to the due date—' it felt incredible good saying that '—what can I expect?'

Catherine glanced at Kaspar as if assessing how much

he might have told the concerned mum-to-be, then continued professionally as if Archie were any other patient and not one with a renowned OMS sitting next to her.

'If your baby was born right now, barring any health troubles in the womb, it would have a very good chance of surviving and of continuing life with no long-term health problems. One of the most common concerns would be under-development of the respiratory system.'

'Which is one of the reasons we previously considered steroid injections?' Archie prompted.

'Right. However, your body seemed to have been adjusting well to the cerclage so we decided not to go ahead. I think that decision has proved correct given how good it all looks now.'

'So if I go into labour now?'

'If you go into labour now we would still try progesterone or pessaries to try to delay the birth. Every additional day the baby is in there now, he or she is gaining that all-important weight and strengthening internal systems. But as I say, birth at thirty-two weeks has a very good survival rate. Depending on the baby, he or she may spend as little as a week in NICU if feeding and breathing are going OK.'

'And if he can't?'

'If he or she can't—' Catherine's continued care not to give the gender away continued to delight Archie '—then he or she will remain in the NICU with a feeding tube and a respirator for as many weeks or even months as might be necessary. But we'll cross that bridge if and when we come to it.'

'Right.' Archie nodded, her eyes sliding across to Kaspar, who looked remarkably stiff in his chair. She couldn't stop a smile. *Expectant father* mode, not *skilled surgeon* mode. It was so very endearing. She might even say he looked...*content.*

'There's a medical charity event this weekend…' she began, as Catherine nodded in recognition.

'Kaspar's the patron, I know. You want to know if I recommend going?'

'Yes.'

'I don't see why not, depending on how you feel on the day. As long as you take it easy, aren't planning on running around madly getting ready or dancing a jive.'

'Definitely not.' Archie laughed, although maybe it was time for her to show Kaspar a flash of the old, confident Archie.

The one she'd felt returning over recent months. Thanks, ironically, to Kaspar. She'd spent so many years putting him on a pedestal and thinking, somehow, that his lack of interest in her had been because she wasn't pretty, feminine, sexy enough. Especially given Shady Sadie's maturing fifteen-year-old body compared to her thirteen-year-old one. But from that first charity wrap party when he'd homed in on her to the golf course the other day when he hadn't been able to keep from kissing her, Archie was beginning to realise that she had more allure, more dynamism, more *power* than she'd realised.

If Kaspar could resist her then perhaps it was simply because she wasn't trying hard enough to be his undoing. And that sounded like the kind of fun challenge she was more than willing to take up. Perhaps tonight she could remind him what he was missing. That she wasn't just the mother of his baby but a woman in her own right, too.

'Then I'll probably see you there,' said Catherine with a smile.

Archie adopted her most beatific smile, not willing to give Kaspar any forewarning of what was to come.

'I look forward to it.'

* * *

Leaning on the bar, an untouched tumbler of some of the most expensive brandy money could buy in hand, Kaspar leaned back against the bar and watched Archie from across the room.

It was a scene that seemed all too familiar to him. An echo of the charity wrap party that had started all of this.

Only this time, instead of having to watch her fend off a couple of admirers on the dance floor and being able to glower in peace, he was forced to pin a smile on his face as she sparkled and floated, as though she was on some kind of mission.

She charmed every single person who stopped to talk to her, particularly the men despite, or perhaps because of, her pregnancy radiance.

And all the while she made sure she was absolutely anywhere but by his side.

It was his own fault, of course. He had no idea what had happened the other day in Catherine's office but Archie had walked out a very different woman. And yet, in many ways, altogether too familiar. More confident, more vivacious, a grown-up version of the Little Ant he'd known. She'd been adamant about accompanying him to this party, and hadn't let any of his, albeit half-hearted, objections deter her.

He was letting her dictate to him. Worse, he was comfortable with it.

To a degree anyway.

Kaspar refused to accept it was because a part of him secretly wanted the world to know the truth. That he was about to become a father. That he, the feckless Surgeon Prince, was quietly content being married to the mother of his baby.

It made no sense.

Archie had even begun to tease him and galled by his constant inability to master his desire around her, he'd determined that tonight he would keep his distance. Allow her to weave her magic of the people in his social circle and the press alike, without his physical presence, which inevitably meant him placing a guarding hand on her here and there. And he knew exactly where that always led to.

Perhaps a part of him had expected her to fail, even hoped she would. Just so that he could finally have a reason to tell himself that this perfect image he'd had of Archie was flawed. That she couldn't possibly be as perfect for him as his mind—and body—seemed to want to believe, and thus she might stop invading his dreams every night. Stop making his body react in ways it had no business reacting when he saw her.

So there she was, working the room and channelling more and more the spirit and boldness he'd begun to remember. And he, for his part, was standing here staring at her like some lovesick puppy.

It would not do.

In a minute he would turn around. He would find a decent medical conversation and he would throw himself into it, as he always did.

In a minute.

The only thing tempering his immense frustration was that at least the distance afforded him the pleasure of observing, and appreciating, Archie at his leisure. And there was certainly plenty to appreciate in her stunning blue, floor-length ballgown with silver straps that hooked over silky smooth shoulders to cross over beneath her breasts and frame her burgeoning baby bump. Radiant and beautiful. And his.

But she couldn't be.

He could only bring her trouble. His parents' miserable marriage wasn't something he ever wanted to risk inflicting on any woman, but certainly not Archie. And not their child. He had spent too many years terrified, lonely, numb, before he'd met Robbie. Before the Coates family had welcomed him into their safe fold.

They could have seen him as an unwanted entanglement. Yet they had welcomed him. Because he'd wanted to be there. Because he'd craved that life, that stability. And now Archie had returned to him. The fact that she was pregnant with his baby after a one-night stand should have been the greatest unwanted complication of all. Instead, he'd welcomed her. Wanted to be with her. Craved her.

Another man had crossed the room now to greet her, her obvious state of pregnancy apparently not putting him off in the slightest as he leaned in a little too closely to whisper in Archie's ear. *As though the guy didn't care for the fact that Archie was his.* And Archie tipped back her head so that the glorious long line of her elegant neck was exposed, and laughed unashamedly.

Kaspar didn't recall moving from the bar, but suddenly he was across the room in an instant, the blood bubbling and *popping* in his veins. The man didn't even stay long enough to introduce himself, although Kaspar supposed the baring of his teeth in what wouldn't have passed for a smile might have had something to do with it.

'Shall we dance?'

'Are you intending to chase off any male who dares to talk to me, as though you're some dog peeing on a post to mark its territory?' she enquired archly.

He shrugged, unrepentant.

'If I need to.'

'I see.'

Half amusement, half chastisement. Still, Kaspar merely held out his hand. A command rather than a request.

She eyed him, a touch incredulously.

'I'm pregnant.'

'Funnily enough, I hadn't forgotten.'

'Don't be facetious.' She bit her lip. 'I have a bump. The press will photograph us. It will look silly.'

His bump. *His* baby.

'It would never look silly,' he ground out fiercely. 'Besides, isn't this why you insisted we come here tonight? Why else put yourself through this ordeal if not to show the world?'

Without waiting for her to agree, he took her hand and led her to the dance floor. People moved out of their way, one pair of curious eyes after another locking onto them, wondering if this was where he was going to make his unspoken statement to the world. Necks craning to see how his Hollywood royalty mother was taking it.

But he ignored them. No one else mattered anyway. It all simply fell away until there was nothing but the feel of Archie in his arms. At last. Her fingers curled into his, her delicate scent filling his nostrils, their baby cradled in her belly and pressed against him.

They moved together so sinuously, so harmoniously that it felt as though they were melding, just as they had done before. It felt comfortable, and good, and *right.* They danced until the meal was served, a sumptuous feast, which he couldn't remember tasting a morsel of, and some polite, inane conversation that flowed out of his head instantly. He could only remember the feel of Archie's bare skin as his hand rested on her back, or the way she leaned slightly against him, or her hand within his.

And then something changed, so quickly, so suddenly that there was no chance to pre-empt it.

Photographers were crowding in on them, their manner not quite that of the ball's official photographers and

Kaspar tensed instinctively. He glanced around, but the security team seemed relaxed and comfortable, and not wanting to make a scene he forced himself to stand down. Ordered himself not to let his imagination, or his worst fears, run riot.

Kaspar had no doubt a hundred cellphones had been capturing them all night, in order to post on the various crude forms of social media so many of the so-called charity supporters favoured. But it didn't bother him.

He only cared about Archie.

And then...

He thrust her back, gently but firmly, shock pulsing through him.

'Was that...?'

'The baby kicking,' she whispered, nodding, her eyes locked onto his as though, like him, she could barely register the other people in around them, the music, the noise.

Tentatively, he reached his arm out and then stopped. Only for Archie to take his hand and place it over her stomach. The kick bounced against him almost immediately. Hard, strong, playful.

Until this point, he'd appreciated everything in the abstract. Whatever other buttons being with Archie had pressed, the baby had always been something he'd known within context. Logically.

Suddenly, there was nothing reasoned or logical about it. Emotions coursed through him and he had absolutely no control over them. But instead of terrifying him, or worrying him, it was almost...*freeing.*

Right up until the throng crowded around them, jostling as they vied for position. Kaspar looked up and saw Archie's face turn from elation to panic. Watched helplessly as she stumbled back a step, a hair's breadth out of his reach so that he couldn't catch her.

And he lost it.

He didn't know what happened next but he had a vague recollection of trying to protect Archie, of grabbing a camera that was so close to her face she squealed and fell back, of it somehow smashing. Not what he'd intended but he didn't care right now. At some point he managed to haul Archie into the safety of his arms. The way her hands clutched at him as though she trusted him, and only him, to protect her, only heightened the wild, savage possessiveness with which he was already fighting a losing battle.

She was his. No one else's. *His.*

He had no idea how he didn't just scoop her into his arms and carry her out of the room. Probably because he knew that might have made her feel undermined and overly fragile, but, still, he recalled bundling her out of the ball and into his car. Throwing himself to the other side of the back seat just so that he didn't give in to this rushing, roaring urge to claim her as his, right there and then in the back of the car.

It was a lethal combination of anger, and fear, and that flicker of helplessness when he'd seen her stumbling and had been unable to get to her in time. Watching it all happen in sickening slow motion. Just like that night when he'd lost control in that back alley fight, doing the only thing that had come into his mind to save himself. Realising too late that if he hadn't been who he was—Kaspar Athari—the thug would probably never have bothered to have a go in the first place.

And if Archie was any other pregnant woman, would the press have crowded in on her like they had? Or was it because of him? Because she was carrying his child?

Kaspar already knew the answer. Of course he did. He should have known better than to risk Archie like this. He should have kept her well away from here.

The car ride couldn't end soon enough. He was out of the door before the vehicle had even come to a stop. Racing around, he snatched open Archie's door and, this time he didn't fight the impulse to lift her into his arms and carry her, still trembling, through the house and to her rooms. Only once he was sure she was settled and okay did he leave, stalking through the corridors until he came to his suite, hauling his clothes over his head, slamming the shower on and stepping inside.

Icy-cold water spilled over his body, biting and unforgiving. But it still couldn't assuage the fire inside him that raged so fiercely it felt as though it was devouring him from the inside out. As it had been all evening, when they'd been so close, so intimate on that dance floor, oblivious to anyone and everyone around them.

There had only been Archie. In perfect, crystal-clear, vibrant detail. Her hand folded into his, her fragile body standing side by side with him. All night. And he had beaten back every single urge to drag her off somewhere more private and haul her onto his lap. Had intended to when he finally got her home.

And then the incident with the photographers had occurred. He'd lost control. Smashed a camera, though he couldn't even remember how. It was all such a blur but it rammed home, in no uncertain terms, that Archie was much better off without him.

And still Kaspar could barely restrain himself from slamming the shower off and pounding down that corridor to Archie's room. Every fibre of his being wanted to drag her back into his arms, lower her onto that bed and drive so deep inside her than he didn't know where he ended and she began.

Pressing his hands to the travertine tiles, Kaspar forced

himself to stay where he was, rooting himself to the huge porcelain shower tray. Chill water still coursed off his shoulders, down his chest, his back.

He didn't hear the click of the door but instantly he knew she was in the room. His entire body knew.

Slowly, very slowly, he lifted his head and turned.

She didn't speak but she actually braced herself. The move was almost imperceptible but for the fact that it caused the lapels of her silken nightgown to fall open, exposing the creamy valley of exposed skin and a tantalising glimpse of her breasts, which he'd been imagining kissing, tasting only a few minutes earlier.

It was more than his body could take and as though he was some kind of adolescent kid all over again, Kaspar found his body reacting in the most primitive way it could. He could turn away or he could stand there and ride it out.

His muscles spasmed and clenched as she let her eyes drop down over his body, as surely as if it were her fingers scorching a trail over his skin instead. And then the slight widening of her gaze, the way she sucked in a deep breath, the way her chest swelled that little bit more.

He tightened, so hard it was almost painful. The way only Archie seemed to be able to do to him.

'Stop pushing me away,' she whispered, the longing in her tone twisting inside him worse than any knife or scalpel could have.

'You saw what happened tonight. It's better for you if I keep my distance.'

His voice rasped, raw and unfamiliar.

'Why? Because you protected me from the kind of gutter photographers who, unlike their welcome, wanted, respectful, carefully selected press colleagues, had never been invited in the first instance? Who had snuck in for the very purpose of causing trouble; pushing me and shoving their cameras into my face and against my stomach? They acted like animals.'

'Exactly like I acted.'

'Nothing like you acted,' she exploded. 'You were defending me. Anyone could see that. I was scared and you saved me. Besides, it was nothing compared to the way the security guards rough-housed them out of there, or didn't you see that?'

'I know what happened,' he lied. All he could recall was Archie's pinched expression, the fear in her eyes. 'I smashed that guy's camera. I lost control. Just like I lost control in the alley with that kid that night.'

She looked at him like he was crazy. It almost made him want to laugh. Almost.

'Firstly, that *man* in the alley was eight years older than you and looking for trouble. Secondly, you did not break any camera.'

'I grabbed it, it smashed.'

'You took it out of my face. That's all. The photographer tried to snatch it back and some security guy punched it out of his hands and into the post behind him. So forget that one, tainted moment, and remember the rest of the evening,' she whispered. 'Remember how good it was. And don't pull away from me now.'

He wanted so much to believe her. To take what she was offering him. But he couldn't.

If he stood here, enduring the icy waterfall still on his body, then maybe he could withstand the unfamiliar sensations that zipped around his chest. Which made him… feel. And wonder. And yearn.

'I have to. Because if I don't, if we start things, I don't know if I can stop myself around you. And we have to think of the baby.'

'That's an excuse. It might be a factor, even though I've

told you I feel ready, and even though you've heard what the doctor has said in every check-up I've had, but it isn't the real reason you push me away.'

'Then what is?'

'That's the part I don't know.' She bit her lip. 'I don't think even you know for sure.'

He just about managed not to flinch. Her words cut closer to the bone than he ever could have imagined. She knew him so well. Maybe too well.

'So,' he bit out, his tongue feeling too big for his mouth, 'if we're done here, perhaps you'd care to leave me to have the rest of my shower in peace?'

The pause stretched out between them.

'Not a chance,' she eventually muttered thickly.

Before he could move, Archie had untied the satin belt and let the dressing gown slide off her shoulders and down over her bump in one easy movement. Far from detracting from the moment, the fact that she was swollen with their baby—with *his* baby—only made her all the sexier.

Still, he should stop this, stop *her*, but she was walking into the shower enclosure with the air of a woman who knew exactly what she was doing and he found it utterly mesmerising.

Worse, though, was that gleam in her eyes. As though she saw a man the rest of the world had missed. As though she saw him the way no one else ever had—a better man. And when she looked at him that way, he so desperately wanted to *be* that man.

Suddenly, she was there, and Kaspar barely had time to turn the temperature up as she closed the last bit of distance separating them. The tips of her fingers grazed over his torso so feather-light he couldn't be sure it she'd actually touched him or if it was just the movement of air, and the wickedest of smiles toyed at the corners of her ridiculously carnal mouth.

What the hell was he meant to do with this woman?

And then her lustrous eyes not leaving his for even a second, Archie dropped to her knees, curled her fingers around his sex, and licked the droplet on the tip, which had nothing to do with the water cascading over him.

He was so nearly lost it took him a moment to move. He tried to step backwards but she was still holding onto him and, honestly, he didn't try very hard.

'Let go, Kaspar,' she murmured. 'Stop trying to control everything and let me take the reins. Just for once.'

And then she took him into her mouth, hot and libidinous. So good it might well have also been immoral. He'd had this done to him before. Many times. A perfect sexual release.

But it had never, ever felt like this. Watching Archie move over him, feeling her hands, her tongue, even the graze of her teeth on him, and also experiencing these complicated emotions swirling around his chest.

Nothing had ever felt so like...*this.*

He gave up trying to think and finally tried to do what she'd instructed. Leaning back on the tiles, because his legs suddenly felt absurdly weak, he buried his hands into her hair and allowed her to take charge.

He wanted her. *Needed* her, even. And whatever he tried to tell himself, he knew it wasn't just the sex. It wasn't just the way she sucked on his head and then slowly drew his thick, solid length deep into her mouth.

It was *her.*

He wanted everything with her. No one else could ever possibly have convinced him to give up the reins like Archie had. And yet here he was, completely at her command. And a part of him thrilled in it.

She started slowly. Deliberately. Setting an unhurried pace as though she was intent on savouring every last moment. She licked him, and sucked him, swirling her tongue over him and using her fingers to apply just the right amount of pressure exactly where he needed it.

He heard himself groan, but he was no more in command of his voice than he was of his body. Instead he was completely and utterly at Archie's mercy and, as though she understood just how much she held the power at this second, she teased him until he thought he was going to die.

And then, suddenly, he was all too shamefully close. As though he was the kind of overexcited adolescent he'd never actually been.

Wrenching himself from her touch, Kaspar ignored her cry of protestation and scooped her up into his arms even as he shut the water off with a flick of his wrist.

'I wasn't finished.'

'I nearly was,' he growled, which only seemed to elicit an exceptionally cheeky grin from Archie.

'That's why I wasn't done. So where are we going instead?'

'Where do you think?' Kaspar demanded, carrying her through to his bedroom and depositing her carefully on the enormous bed.

He'd never wanted anyone the way he wanted Archie. In some dark recess, a voice asked whether he thought he'd ever get enough of her, and alarm bells jangled so loudly there might as well have been a belfry in there.

But he refused to heed them. Instead he muffled the sound.

Still, even as he moved over the bed next to Archie, his hands cradling the beautiful swell to her body, he couldn't help checking.

'Are you sure about this?'

'I've been ready for months,' she groaned, but it was softened with a smile.

The tremble of her body almost sent him over the edge again.

Dropping his head, his lips sought hers, demanding, claiming her as if her mouth was his to take, tilting his head until the fit was perfection itself. As though he could kiss her for ever and never tire of it. Archie looped her arms around his neck, pressing her body, her bump, against him. Not too tight, just enough, as his hands caressed her belly. The fire between them was hotter than ever, threatening to burn out of control at any moment.

Ignoring the deep, heavy throb still clutching at his sex, Kaspar lavished attention on her. When he'd finished kissing her mouth, he moved to her jaw, her ear, her neck, inching his way down her body until she was arching into him and wordlessly begging him for more. When his lips finally alighted on her breast, pulling one exquisite nipple into his mouth as she gasped in pleasure, he at last allowed his hand to wander lower.

She groaned again, her voice an insubstantial whisper.

'Kaspar, I need you to…'

'To what?' he demanded mercilessly, his mouth still full of her soft flesh, his fingers tracing an intricate pattern over her hips.

'To…touch me.'

'I am touching you.' He switched his attentions to her other breast, half enjoying himself, half fighting the urge to pull her on top of him and slide inside her. Finally branding her as his.

Just like he had that first night.

'Not there,' she managed hoarsely.

'Ah.' He allowed his fingers to wander to the top of her thigh, repeating the pattern on the outer side. 'Here?'

'Kaspar,' she moaned, shifting on the bed, subconsciously parting her legs for him, drawing him in.

'Here?' he teased, moving his hand back up until it was stroking her abdomen again.

He lifted his head and she caught his gaze. But this time, instead of the needy sound that threatened to undo him, she pursed her lips into a sinful grin, her hooded eyes were loaded with wanton need.

'Perhaps *you* need a little reminder,' she murmured, moving her own hand down to flutter over him, his body reacting instantly.

He heard the guttural sound, but it took a moment to realise it was him. Her touch was like some exquisite torture. He'd never known it was possible to ache quite like this. Too incredible to be bad yet too painful to be good.

He sought out her core. So slick, and hot, and ready. His fingers played with her, moving over her at a pace that was faster than he would have liked but he couldn't seem to stop himself, especially at Archie's soft, urgent moans. And then he didn't know who moved first, him or her, but Archie was astride him, one of his hands on her belly and one cupping a heavy, perfect breast.

'Condoms?' she muttered.

'Top drawer.' He jerked his head towards the nightstand, before adding unnecessarily, 'The pack Catherine gave you.'

As though he needed her to know he hadn't bought them for anyone else. In actual fact, he had never brought anyone else into this space.

He watched her open the foil packet, fumbling slightly with her shaking fingers, rolling it down his length with excruciating care. And then Archie was moving over him, guiding him inside as he watched her face for any sign of discomfort. When he finally, *finally* slid inside her wet heat, felt her stretching around him, gripping him tightly despite the slightly shallower depth, he wasn't sure he would last at all. Experimentally, she began to move.

'Okay?' he checked.

She nodded, tentatively increasing the pace, and it was all Kaspar could do not to move inside her the way his body longed to do. He wanted to move faster, thrust into her deeper and harder until she shattered around him. But he couldn't. Not yet. He tensed with the effort, only realising it when she stroked his jawline, a soft laugh escaping her lips.

'Relax, I'm fine.'

'Sure?'

She nodded again and Kaspar let his hands trail over her body until his thumbs were circling in the soft hair between her legs, her head slumping slightly forward, her breath coming shallow and quick. He dipped lower, playing with her even as he moved inside her, her body thrilling to his touch, tightening around him, moving faster on top of him.

He was so close. So incredibly close. Everything about Archie turned him on in a way he hadn't previously known was possible. And as they moved together in flawless harmony, the initial soft shudders of her body giving way to something far more urgent, and unrelenting, he imagined that this, here now, her, would be all he would ever need.

It was the last thought he had as she finally came apart around him. Her body arched as she surrendered to him, crying out, rocking over him and against his fingers and her hands braced against his chest as though she thought she might otherwise collapse. And just as Archie seemed to start coming down, he changed his rhythm and hurled her over the edge all over again.

This time, when she cried his name, Kaspar couldn't contain himself any longer. He tumbled off the cliff edge with her, better than leaping out of any plane. He released himself into her, and the flames roared and surged through him and he feared they could never be quenched.

Dangerous, even lethal. Yet blissful perfection.

He might have known it could never last.

CHAPTER TWELVE

ARCHIE AWOKE THE next morning to the sun streaming through the curtains, the call of early morning seabirds. And the fact that she was alone. Again.

But this time she didn't worry. Instead she stretched languorously as rarely used muscles lazily grunted their objections, and recalled an hour earlier when she'd awoken to the feel of a warm, solid body behind her.

Kaspar, pressed to her back and his hand cradling her bump. She'd snuggled back, his reaction even in sleep unmistakeable, and tried to drift back off into slumber. As much as they might want to make love again and again, they couldn't. Light and infrequent, that was what Catherine had advised.

At some point, she could just about remember him mentioning going for a run. His attempt to distract his urgent body. And now here she was finally awake, what had to be several hours later. Her ears strained for the sound of the shower or for him in the kitchen, but she heard nothing.

Then again, marathons weren't unusual for Kaspar.

Abruptly she realised what had woken her.

The low, insistent humming of her phone tumbled through the room and though there was no reason at all for the sense of foreboding that flooded through her, she nevertheless shivered under the sheets, despite the warmth of the sunlit room. At this hour, what were the chances it would be the press? Especially after last night's little scene? Kaspar had wordlessly unplugged the phone last night and turned his own cell off, but it wouldn't have taken them much to get her number. She knew what they were like.

So Archie sat, her knees hugged tightly under her chest, waiting. Only breathing again once the drumming finally fell silent.

In.

Out.

In.

Out.

Throwing off the sheets, she crossed the room to look out of the window, seeing the golden beach spread out below her like the most luxurious picnic mat in the world. The sight of Kaspar racing powerfully along the sand, the only figure on the private beach, an unexpected but welcome sight.

Her fingers pressed against the glass as her eyes drank him in, from his muscled thighs to the wide, bare, olive chest that glistened from the exertion, all sending images of last night hurtling around her feverish mind.

But then she caught sight of the expression on his face. Dark, brooding, even angry. And her stomach flip-flopped.

Slowly she backed up, across the room, so that by the time he had powered up the hillside to vault over the small balcony and to the picture-height glass doors, she was already edging to the door. As though, somehow, the distance could silence whatever words he was about to utter. Words, she already knew, she didn't want to hear.

And then he was in the room, stopping dead as he saw her. For one moment she thought she could read frustration, regret in those chocolate depths. And then they were cold, and dark, and forbidding, shutting her out as effectively as anything he could say.

'Kaspar...'

'Have you seen the papers?'

He cut across her and it was almost too much to bear, the way his tone devastated her so easily. So completely.

'How could I have?' She swallowed hard, as if it could buy her more time. 'I've only just woken up.'

'Then allow me to show you.'

His harsh voice sliced her like a hundred scalpel blades, the barely contained fury in no doubt as he stalked past her, flinging the door open and striding down the hallway with all the ire that could have parted the ocean behind them had he changed direction.

It was all Archie could do to scurry behind him, her mind racing too fast for the rest of her thoughts to catch up. Later, she would wonder how she'd had the presence of mind to grab a dressing gown as she left. Short and flimsy as it was, she had no idea at that point how grateful she would be to pull it around her near-naked form in some semblance of self-pride.

'They're emblazoned with ugly photos of the scene from last night,' he continued bitingly, as he entered the study and powered up the laptop, which still sat quietly on the side from his latest round of research. 'Headlines detailing exactly what kind of a volatile, out-of-control man I am. Screaming it for the world to know.'

'They don't know you.' Her breath came out in a whoosh as she moved, actually took a step towards him. 'I do.'

She didn't realise how foolish it was until he snatched his arm away from her outstretched fingers, his eyes darkening with a dangerous glint, the spat-out word a Persian curse that she only now recalled from her youth.

'I do not want your sympathy, Archana.'

She flinched but he barely seemed to notice.

Or perhaps he was deliberately trying to hurt her. To push her away.

'This is exactly who I told you I was; who I told you I wanted to spare our baby from seeing. But you wouldn't listen. You, in your arrogance, thought you could change me.'

'This isn't who you are,' she faltered, but he shot her down.

'This is exactly who I am. I knew it before. It was only my own ego that let me believe your naïve, rose-tinted view of me. You insisted on making us a spectacle, but I was the one who should have known better. Now they have uncovered the story from my past. And so we must both pay the penalty.'

Archie opened her mouth to speak, but then she caught sight of some of the photos he'd been talking about and her lips became too dry, her throat too cracked to form any kind of coherent words. Even if she could have, her heart was clattering in her chest so wildly that she couldn't hope to think straight, couldn't organise the words that jumbled in her head.

One thing leaped out of her more than anything else. One sad, shameful, truth. The expression in her eyes as she stared at Kaspar. The pathetic, unadulterated adoration in her expression.

He was right. She was naïve, and a fool. Nothing more than the silly little girl she'd always been. She'd fallen in love with him. It was there on her face, mocking her, just as Kaspar was mocking her. Once again, she'd fooled herself into believing he'd let her in and here he was reminding her that he never truly would. Perhaps he simply wasn't capable of it.

Kaspar could never be hers. He could never be anyone's. She was a fool for even considering for a moment that he could be.

I deserve better, she chanted desperately, as if repeating it wildly in her head would be enough to convince her. *I deserve someone who truly* loves *me.*

And one day, maybe, she might believe that.

So much for the bold, sophisticated Archie she'd tried to kid herself that she was. It was time to grow up and take responsibility. And that meant putting Kaspar Athari into her past once and for all. Or at least the idea of any relationship with him. The truth was that he was her baby's father, she could never truly escape him for the rest of her life.

It was embarrassing how much that thought gave as much comfort as it did torment.

But she didn't have to show it. Lifting her head, Archie forced herself to look him directly in the eyes, her voice conveying a breeziness she hadn't known she possessed.

'You're right.' *Where did that hint of a tight, cold smile come from?* 'I see that now. This marriage was a foolish idea and I apologise for anything I did to make you feel you had little choice but to suggest it.'

Her entire chest wrenched at the words, splitting her apart from her insides out with such force that she had no idea how she managed to stay standing, let alone talking. It was torture not to be able to read a single expression on his face, not that any expression even flickered over Kaspar's unrelenting features. The only reaction at all was the clenched jaw and steady, clear pulse. But even that told her nothing of what was running through his head.

How had she failed to realise before how little she knew him?

'It's the most logical solution.' He offered a curt nod. 'Once the baby is born, we'll get divorced. Blame it on my playboy reputation. The press will be expecting that anyway. You can return to the UK. I'll make the financial arrangements to provide for my child. Once all the furore has died down, which I'm sure won't take too long, we'll decide how I can have contact without turning your life, or our baby's, into a circus.'

She wanted to answer him but she couldn't speak. Her tongue, like her body, was going numb. She could feel herself shutting down.

'I'm going for a run,' he bit out, as if her silence was answer enough. Neither of them mentioned the fact that he'd only just returned from his last one. 'You should pack. I'll let my driver know to pick you up and take you to a hotel near the hospital. It's five-star, and you'll have my suite.'

'No…' she blurted out, but he silenced her with a brief wave of his arm.

'I'll cover the costs.'

As if that was her only objection. Still, it was enough to silence her. Clearly he thought so little of her, what was the point in trying to defend herself?

'Understood.' Her tone sounded nothing like herself.

For a start it didn't betray any of the howling pain that raged inside her.

But then she clutched the flimsy dressing gown around her and was grateful she didn't have nakedness to add to her tearing sense of vulnerability right now.

Too late, Archie realised her mistake. Her action pulled Kaspar up sharply and he raked his hand uncomfortably through his hair.

'Archie…' His voice faltered, something so unfamiliar that for a moment she didn't recognise it for what it was.

And then suddenly she did.

It was *pity*.

Pride slammed into her. He could reject her, and distance himself, that was his right and there was nothing she could do about it.

But she *could* make damned sure that, on top of everything else, he didn't pity her for her pain.

'What about the press?' she asked.

'What? Does it matter?' He blew out a deep breath. 'Fine, we'll tell them it was the safest option. Closer to hospital, and people would always be around if anything… happened while I was away at work.'

So that was it, she realised as her heart actually seemed to slump inside her drooping ribcage. He had an answer for everything, and she had no more excuses.

She had to be strong. She had a baby to consider now. A future in which someone else was counting on her to make the responsible decisions, and she couldn't ignore that fact. Especially with the way the atmosphere had changed within the room. Heavy. Strained. Foreboding. Even the sunlight getting in on the act since it didn't quite reach this part of the house, and so the shadow left her standing, quite literally, in the cold.

It took more than she could have imagined to shake off the ridiculous notion.

'You're right.' The words sounded thick, heavy, gungy. She forced herself to say them anyway. 'It's best if you go.'

'Then you agree?' he bit out, his gaze boring into her until every fibre of her being trembled under its onslaught.

No, I don't agree, a part of her wanted to scream. But what was the use in arguing?

None of this was enough for her any more. Kaspar was right. Their marriage was a pointless sham. She'd almost convinced herself that if she'd married Joe for practical reasons, then she could certainly stay married to Kaspar. For the sake of their baby. Yet deep down she'd always known it was an entirely different scenario. She'd never *craved* Joe the way she craved Kaspar. Why spend her life watching him, yearning for more, aching for something that could never be?

'I agree.' She thought the words might choke her.

She didn't know whether it was a relief or a disappointment that they didn't. Then, with an offhand dip of his head, Kaspar dismissed her. And she let him. She backed out of the door and walked down the hallway on legs that had no business holding her upright.

Just like that, she'd walked out of another marriage. Or Kaspar had pushed her out. Either way, there was no doubt in her mind that *this* time there would be no getting over it.

He was doing the right thing.

Pounding down the beach, his legs burning from their fight against the soft sand, Kaspar wondered if any amount of beating his body could ever assuage this agony that ripped through his chest.

The sense of failure. Of treachery. Of absolute loss. And it was all his own doing.

The moment he'd seen that photo, the murderous look in his eyes as he'd slammed away that photographer's camera, he'd realised that as much as he might pretend to be a different man—one worthy of someone as innocent and delicate as Archie, one who deserved the way she looked at him, as though he was something special, someone good—he wasn't.

He wasn't special and he wasn't good. He wasn't at all the man she seemed to have convinced herself that he was. He was still the arrogant, out-of-control, emotionally bankrupt teenager he'd been who'd destroyed a man's life all those years ago. All for the sake of a row over an upturned bar stool.

He should have known better that night, just as he

should have known better with the photographer at the ball. The press were animals. They'd had no right to jostle Archie as they had, especially not when she was so clearly pregnant. But that didn't mean he could be equally savage and uncontrolled.

And Archie had agreed.

The whole thing only proved that he was as toxic and dangerous as his father had been.

And, for that matter, as manipulative as his mother. Hadn't he pretty much blackmailed Archie into marrying him in the first instance? What kind of a man did that? What sort of an example could that ever set for their child?

Letting her walk away from their marriage was the only honourable thing he could do right now. Set her free. It was shameful that he was having to will himself so hard to keep running. Not turn around and race back up that beach, back to the house, and tell her that she couldn't leave after all.

All the while, a voice inside him grew. A whisper at first. Kaspar could barely hear it even as he pretended not to know what it was saying. It grew in volume, more insistent, more triumphant. He thundered along the beach as though he could outrun it, but the faster he moved the louder it grew. Until, at last, it was a bellow. A roar. It stopped him in his tracks, and it made him swing back round until the only thing he could see—the only thing his eyes would look at—was his beach house, in the distance.

Or, more accurately, the house that had become a *home* ever since Archie had set foot inside. He planted his feet firmly, as though willing himself to ground himself into the sand the way a tree bedded itself into soil. Anything to stop him racing back there and charging in. Telling Archie she couldn't leave. She could never leave. And not just because she was carrying his child. For a long, self-indulgent moment he allowed himself to imagine what she might say. What she might do.

And then he wasn't indulging himself any more because he knew exactly what she would say. She would ask if he loved her. The way she'd wanted to do so many times before, whether she realised it or not. He'd seen it for the first time one morning a few weeks ago. She'd been hovering by the pool, waiting for something, although he suspected she hadn't even realised it herself. It had taken him days to figure out she'd been waiting for him to tell her that he loved her.

And he did.

Unconditionally. Irrevocably.

It was the reason he needed her to leave now. From the instant he'd discovered she was pregnant he'd known he would be there for his child the way his parents had never been there for him. He wanted to give his baby the childhood the Coates family had given to him.

But there had always been something more to it than that. There'd had to be. He would never have proposed such a marriage to any other woman. Only Archie.

Because he wanted her. He wanted *to be with* her.

And if it hadn't been for his ruinous behaviour last night, he might have told her so. Now he knew he owed it to her to let her go. Before the press tainted her with the same poisonous brush with which they were so clearly intending to paint him.

It was only what he deserved.

Just as Archie deserved better. If he really loved her, as he claimed to, then he would let her go, no matter how painful it was to him. Wasn't that what love was supposed to be about? Selfless acts for another person?

All of which ensured that him returning to the house to declare his love for her was the one thing he absolutely *couldn't* do. Kaspar snarled, but only the crashing sea and the squawking gulls bore the brunt of his frustration. And then, with what felt like a superhuman effort, he whirled around and ran, sinking furiously into the sand as though he might leave his footprints there for ever.

He had no idea how long he kept running, or how far he went. But when he finally lifted his head he was no longer on the beach, he wasn't even anywhere near the ocean, and the morning sun was on the other side of the sky as people began to emerge for their early evening revelries.

He'd been running all day. Around in circles. Just as his head was doing.

Only then did Kaspar finally turn back and head for the house which would no longer ever be a home to him.

CHAPTER THIRTEEN

FOR THREE DAYS she had stayed cooped up in the hotel room, wallowing in her misery, which wasn't easy as she wasn't a person generally accustomed to self-pity. She hadn't wallowed when her marriage to Joe had ended, or when she'd lost the baby, or even when her father had died. She'd tried to be strong, and stoic, and soldier on.

And look where that had got her.

She hadn't actually pushed through all the grief and the heartache, at all. She'd simply been sucked even deeper down into it. The more she'd struggled to pretend she was fine, the faster she'd sunk, a little like trying to fight when the quicksand already had an unbreakable hold.

So Archie had decided that maybe if she wallowed this time, gave in to the wealth of misery that swirled around her, she could exhaust all her sorrow and make it out the other side.

It wasn't working. Because the more she indulged her sadness, the more her brain started whirring again, wondering if she wasn't perhaps missing something. Second-guessing herself.

Her mobile phone rang for the umpteenth time. An unknown number every time. She'd learned not to answer it after the first few times, when the media's questions had been fired at her before she'd even finished saying hello. But this number had a Swiss code in front of it.

'Archana?'

Archie stopped, any response lodged in her throat.

'It's me,' he faltered uncertainly. 'Joe?'

'Yes.' She bit back the additional, *I know who you are.*

'I just thought I should…' He cleared his throat and she could imagine him, rigid and upright.

A neat shirt and tie under a round-necked wool jumper. She couldn't imagine why he was calling. She couldn't imagine it was to revel in her public humiliation. Of all her cx-husband's flaws, taking delight in someone else's misfortune had never been one of them.

Archie sucked in a breath, waiting for him to continue. Not wanting to reveal her confusion.

'I saw your photo in the paper. I…wanted to call and congratulate you.'

'Sorry?' The word escaped before she could stop it. A squeak of shock.

'The baby. And that you look…happy,' he continued awkwardly, clearly mistaking her response. 'In love.'

The words didn't come easily to him. They never had. But she knew him well enough to know the sentiment was genuine.

'No…' she managed, her tongue struggling to wrap itself around any form of coherent response. 'You've got it wrong.'

'Archana.' He silenced her quickly, and she could hear the rueful smile in his voice. 'Please don't do me the disservice of trying to spare my feelings, however well intentioned.'

'I—'

'You love him. That's plain to see from the photos. Had you once, ever, looked at me in that way…' He tailed off, clearing his throat again. 'Well, perhaps if I had treated you to the same…passion as Kaspar Athari does, maybe you *would* have looked at me in that way. It's clear that he loves you in a way that I never did. Or could. The way you deserve to be loved.'

Archie wasn't sure what he said after that. She heard him speaking, as far from his usual reserved manner as she thought she'd probably ever heard him, but she was too busy hurrying across the suite to retrieve her laptop, to fire it up and find those images she'd refused to look at since that morning in Kaspar's study.

By the time Joe ended the short conversation, she was sinking down on the dining chair, staring at the truth, which had been there all along—only she'd been too caught up in the puppy-dog expression on her own face to see it.

Only this time that wasn't what she saw. It was as though all the scales had dropped from her eyes, taking with them all the preconceived notions she'd been carrying around. Suddenly, she could see what Joe could see. What he'd been trying, in his typically restrained way, to say. What the rest of the world could see.

A couple so patently in love with each other that it shone out from the page.

She didn't look like a pathetic, lost puppy. She looked like a woman—an expectant mother—very much in control of her feelings. And it showed a man who, even as he dealt efficiently and necessarily with the unmistakeable threat to her well-being, never once let his hot, possessive gaze leave her. As though she was the only important thing in the room. In the entire world.

How had she failed to see it before?

It was time to go and claim her husband. The father of her unborn baby. She wanted a life with him, as a proper family. It was the reason why she'd jumped on that plane to the States those brief few months before, whether she'd realised it or not.

Archie stood with more purpose than she'd felt in a long time, striding across the expansive space to snatch up the phone and call Reception.

'It's Archana Athari, from the Princess Suite,' she began unnecessarily. 'I would like a taxi, please. To take me to me…home.'

It was done. In that instant she felt lighter, and more optimistic.

She could call Kaspar's driver, of course, but he might call Kaspar, and she didn't want to alert her husband to her change of plans.

He loved her. She knew that with a bone-deep certainty that she'd never realised existed in her before now. But she also knew that Kaspar was proud, and stubborn. He had pushed her away because he truly, incredibly, believed that her life was better without him in it. He couldn't be more wrong, which was exactly what she intended to tell him. He wouldn't want to hear it at first, but she didn't care. She could convince him, however long it took. Still, it wouldn't hurt to stack the deck in her favour as much as possible, and that included giving herself the element of surprise. If he knew she was at his house, he might suddenly decide he had more pressing matters and stay at the hospital, but if he got home to find her already there, he could hardly just walk out.

She threw everything into her suitcases with lightning speed. It wasn't really difficult since she hadn't unpacked the bags Kaspar had sent over that first day. Possibly that should tell her everything she needed to know. And then she opened the door to the hallway ready for the bellhop.

As Archie checked the room over for anything she

might have forgotten, she wasn't prepared for the first contraction that gripped her with almost no warning. Neither was she prepared for her husband to walk through the door as though she'd summoned him by her very thoughts.

'Kaspar...?' She gaped, her mind struggling to work.

Thirty-five weeks? She still had a month to go. They had to be Braxton-Hicks, right?

'There are probably a million ways I could do this that would make the moment romantic, and meaningful, and everything you could want,' Kaspar plunged on, oblivious. 'But right now I can't think of a single one of them. So I'll just say it as simply and as clearly as I can. I love you, Archie. Not as the mother of my child, but for *you*. I love, and I'm in love with, you.

'I thought I was broken, and beyond repair, but you found a way to put me back together, and although I may not always show it in the right way, I promise you that I'm learning and if you give me another chance I'll ensure you never regret it. Not for the rest of time.'

The pain was spreading through her abdomen even as her heart felt as though it was sprouting wings ready to take flight. Whoever knew it was possible to feel so frightened and yet so elated all in the same moment?

'Archie...'

'I love you too, you idiot,' she managed. A combination of clenched teeth and a joyful sob. 'But do you...do you think we could do this later? Only... I think the baby is on his way.'

One day, she knew, she would remember the look of marvel on his face. She would remember this feeling that she was ready for anything, and she would remember this moment as the perfect start to the new chapter of her life.

'Of course our baby is on its way.' The smile was wide, his eyes gleaming, and a look of almost triumph was in his gaze, making her feel very powerful. 'She clearly approves of the moment and can't wait another few weeks to join us in our new future.'

EPILOGUE

SHUFFLING FORWARD ON her bottom, Archana Athari took the hook from the front of her harness and fitted her static line through the eye on the floor of the tiny light aircraft, pulling hard to ensure it was locked securely in place before Kaspar double-checked the line for her.

'Are you ready?' Kaspar called over the roar of the engines and the wind. 'Remember, aside from our one tandem jump together four years ago, you haven't jumped in a decade. And a three-year-old and a one-year-old make the most critical audiences ever.'

'I know.' She grinned at the thought of her son and daughter down on the ground, waiting for them both. 'According to your eldest, those go-carts you made them last week are ruined because you put pictures of the wrong animated films on the side.'

She had no idea whether Kasper heard her or not but it didn't matter. He understood anyway, and his lazy, sexy grin of response sent a wave of adrenalin coursing through her, just like it always did.

Sliding forward, still on her bottom, to the door of the plane, Archie stuck her feet out and leaned forward. The blur of the ground rushing by a few thousand feet below snatched her breath away. For a moment she froze.

'Go!' he bellowed.

And then she offered Kaspar a cheeky wink, yelling against the rushing wind, 'Race you to the bottom!'

Grasping the doorframe with one hand and the metal spar with the other, Archie pulled herself out of the aircraft, twisted and let go. Gravity took over.

Every single thought went from her head.

Spread-eagled in the air, her back arched as she fought for stability, the plane seemed to disappear in seconds, its increasing height above her the only indication that she was falling. And then the jolt of the ripcord opened her chute and reminded her of where she was and what she was supposed to be doing.

One-one-thousand.

Two-one-thousand.

Three-one-thousand.

Archie looked up and her heart slammed into her chest. The canopy hadn't fully deployed.

I probably counted too quickly. I hope I counted too quickly. What did they say about cutting away? I don't want to have to do that. I'll count again and then I'll act.

Her mouth parched and her chest hammering, Archie reached up for the guides that would help her steer for landing. And when she looked again, even before she had chance to count a second time, the parachute opened fully with an ear-splitting *crack!*

And then the complete, utter silence.

She felt weightless. Perhaps not *being in space* weightlessness, but certainly as though she was just floating down, the sky going on for ever around her.

She'd finally done it. Not just for her young son, and younger daughter—who were waiting down on the ground with a very pregnant Katie, and who had been going on about wanting to see her skydive ever since they'd seen the photo of that first tandem jump of their mummy and daddy—but also for herself and for her father.

'Here's to you, Dad,' she whispered. 'I finally got everything I ever dreamed of.'

Peace flowed through her. Her life was so very different from the last time she'd tried this and it was all thanks to Kaspar, and Darius and baby Yasmin. She felt more complete than she had ever imagined possible.

For what felt like an eternity she simply drank it in.

Without warning, a figure dropped in front of her, arms and legs outstretched to slow their fall but, without an open chute, they were still dropping considerably faster than her. He might be too far away to impede her jump but she didn't need to see his face to know who it was.

Kaspar.

And, by his thumbs-up gestures, he was clearly taking her challenge seriously. Her stomach knotted with a kind of anticipation, a thrill, then he was gone, his legs straightening back and his arms pinned to his sides as he tipped his body to dive lower.

But he knew what he was doing and Archie knew he would be safe. The adrenalin junkie at his extreme was long gone. Replaced instead by a fun-loving, proud husband and father, although still—always—her Surgeon Prince of Persia.

Archie laughed into the silence. A rich, happy sound. Then she let the wind carry her gently down to earth.

She should have known that Kaspar would beat her. By the time she'd gathered up her parachute and made her way across the field, he was already heading back with a feverishly clapping three-year-old on his shoulders and a one-year-old glued to his chest.

'Wow, Mummy.' The awestruck voice carried easily with its childish lilt. 'It was good? Yes or no?'

'Yes, baby. It was very good. But being back here with you is even better.'

And it was true. Her little family was perfect. Everything she could have ever dreamed of having.

Her past, her present and her future, all rolled into one.

* * * * *

THE NURSE'S PREGNANCY MIRACLE

ANN McINTOSH

MILLS & BOON

This book is dedicated to my late mother, Helen Delvaillé,
a voracious Harlequin/Mills & Boon reader.
I think she'd be happy to see my book
printed by her favourite publisher,
although she'd probably just deadpan, 'Oh, good.'
Not all romantics are effusive!

CHAPTER ONE

WALKING BRISKLY THROUGH the waiting area of the Lauderlakes Family Medical Center, Nychelle Cory scanned the room, once more noting the contrast between the opulent surroundings and the rather squalid interior of the inner-city clinic she'd worked at up until just a couple of years before.

The marble flooring and the crystal chandelier, hung precisely beneath the domed skylight, wouldn't be out of place in a grand home. Instead of the standard faux leather seating typical of medical clinics, comfortable upholstered chairs and love seats were arranged in small clusters around antique side tables. Every inch of the place was designed to give the illusion of being a luxurious hotel lobby, perhaps in the hope of helping people forget they were waiting to see a doctor.

Few people would understand but, oh, how she missed the hustle and near chaos of working at the low-cost clinic. So rewarding, helping those that others often forgot. But she'd known from the moment she took the job there that, financially, it wouldn't be enough to advance *The Plan*.

Funny to realize that was how she always thought of it—not as Plan A, or as a prospective life plan. Just *The Plan*, with caps and italics, the way she'd written it in her diary when she was just thirteen years old. Below that she'd listed what she wanted, and the list was pretty short.

Children. Three or four.
A job that lets me spend lots of time with them.
A nice husband who wants to spend time with the kids too.

Looking back on it, number three had been tacked on at the end, as if she'd already made up her mind that the husband wasn't exactly a necessary part of the process.

That thought made her suppress a little snort of laughter. *The Plan* definitely hadn't come about the way she'd initially thought it would, but she wasn't complaining. In fact she'd go so far as to claim she had the best of all worlds.

Getting a plum job at Fort Lauderdale's premier general care clinic was helping bring her dreams to fruition, yet money alone wouldn't have lured her to Lauderlakes. Her need to help the less fortunate was strong, and luckily Dr. Hamatty, Lauderlakes' founder, believed in giving back too, working with local charities to put on free clinics three times a year.

Not the same as being in the trenches all the time, but it helped give her altruistic nature much-needed satisfaction.

There were a handful of people scattered around the waiting area. Sitting close together on a love seat, phones in hand, were a young couple who looked as though they'd just stepped out from between the pages of a high-end travel magazine. In the play area, just visible behind a floor-to-ceiling, glass-paneled waterfall, a toddler laughed, the sound muted by the tinkle of water.

Nodding hello to her next patient—a stylish older lady seated in a club chair—Nychelle paused for a moment in front of the intake desk and transferred her attention to Gina, the receptionist, who gave one of her usual tight-lipped smiles.

"Glad to see you back." Gina raised one perfectly groomed brow as she spoke quietly, the way they were all instructed to, so as to maintain the atmosphere. "Did you have a good vacation?"

"I wouldn't call it a vacation." Nychelle gave a quick shrug, even as her heart did that trip-hammer thing it kept doing every time she thought about her days off and what they could mean. "Just took some time to get some things done."

Like undergo intrauterine insemination and then keep quiet for a few days to give my body the best chance to make a baby.

Thankfully her complexion was too dark to show the blush as heat rushed up from the neck of her silk shirt and the stylish lab coat covering it into her face. Keeping her expression neutral was so hard, but imperative. Despite Gina's chic, cool appearance, the receptionist was a Class A gossip, highly effective in ferreting out any and all information others tried to keep from her. With just the slightest hint of anything out of the ordinary going on Gina would be off and running.

"Boring." Gina drew the softly spoken word out until it was half a mile long, flipping a long curl of black hair over her shoulder for emphasis. "I was at the very least hoping to hear you'd gone to Jamaica." The smile was a little more relaxed, a little more interrogatory. "The stories I've heard about your homeland and the men there..."

Nychelle couldn't hold back a little gurgle of laughter as she took another look at the information on the tablet in her hand.

Katalina Ivanenko.
Sixty-two years old.
Routine wellness check, including follow-up on previous bone density test.
History of arthritis...

"The rumors of my countrymen's decadence are highly exaggerated." Then she couldn't resist winking and adding a whispered, "Most of the time."

When Gina hid a giggle behind her hand, a little spurt of relief at pulling the wool over the other woman's eyes made Nychellc's smile widen.

No one, with the exception of her cousin and best friend, Aliya, would know about the IUI before her pregnancy was a *fait accompli*. Most people wouldn't get why, at just twenty-eight, she was going this route. They'd expect her to be dating, looking for a long-term relationship, as though she should and would want that. *Nope.* Not in the cards. The relationship she'd gotten out of two years before had shattered both her faith in her own instincts and her ability to trust any man's intentions.

Then there were her medical issues, which would only make conception harder the longer she waited to try. This was the optimal time for her to get pregnant, while leaving herself room to try a few more times if she needed to, and she was grabbing the opportunity with both hands. It was what she'd planned and worked toward since Nick had dumped her, and she knew she was extremely lucky to be able, both emotionally and financially, to make this huge step alone.

The reception phone rang, distracting Gina, and Nychelle took the opportunity to turn away toward her patient.

"Oh!"

The sound was so unexpectedly loud in the hushed environment, so rife with pain and surprise, Nychelle instinctively turned toward its source.

The young woman on the love seat was bent over, in obvious distress, her hands pressed to her lower abdomen.

"Call Dr. Leeson." Nychelle was already moving across the waiting area toward the couple as she threw the demand back over her shoulder to Gina.

"It's okay, Gina. I've got it."

The deep voice came from near the door leading to the clinic, and by the time Nychelle had stooped down beside the young woman Dr. David Warmington was coming up behind her.

Great.

No time to dwell on how unsettled Dr. Warmington made her, or to wonder if he was the right physician for the situation. The other nurses said his bedside manner was exemplary, in between singing his praises and panting over the man's incredible good looks.

"He's not bringing the warm," Nancy, the nursing coordinator, had said with a laugh before he'd started. "He's packing heat."

Among the nurses the name stuck, and to hear them talk you'd think "Dr. Heat" was more enticing than free chocolate and a bottle of Chablis.

Secretly Nychelle agreed, but nothing would get her to admit it. She knew all too well the danger of handsome men—especially those able to somehow charm even the most hardened of nurses. They weren't to be trusted, and were apt to use their looks to their own advantage and the disadvantage of others.

No doubt if he wanted to he could make a lot of money modeling, showcasing expensive sunglasses on that chiseled face, with the wind blowing through his toffee-colored hair. Or making women run out to buy cologne in the hopes of suddenly transforming their hubbies into a six-foot, two-inch wall of muscle, with linebacker shoulders and a bootie made for nipping.

One glance from his intent blue eyes, reminiscent of the most gorgeous of Florida skies, could make the coldest heart quicken—even hers. But, while Nychelle admired his looks, she viewed him with suspicion—as she now did most, if not all, men.

Pushing all those thoughts aside, she said to the young woman, "Hi, I'm Nychelle. Tell me what's going on."

She took the other woman's wrist firmly between her fingers, finding a strong but rapid pulse, and noting the patient's pallor and the perspiration dotting her hairline despite the clamminess of her skin.

"I… I'm pregnant. I just realized a day ago. I was going to see my doctor after I got home."

A visitor to the area, then, with perfect but accented English. Wide brown eyes, gleaming with tears, looked beseechingly into Nychelle's, as though hoping for an instant end to fear and pain. Then she doubled over with a little shriek, arms crossed protectively over her abdomen.

Hugging her, the man beside her interjected, "She did a home test, but we knew she was not far along. When my wife saw a little blood and was worried, my *tio* told us to come here—"

The young woman turned toward her husband and unleashed a spate of angry, rapid-fire words. Working in Florida, Nychelle had made sure to keep up with her Spanish, but now she caught only the occasional familiar-sounding word. Something about a boat trip, his uncle, and losing her baby, in what Nychelle assumed was Portuguese.

"No, no. Don't worry about any of that now." Sympathetic but firm, the doctor's voice cut through the young woman's tirade and drew the couple's attention. "I'm Dr. Warmington. Come with me and let's find out what's happening, okay?"

Nychelle was watching the patient and saw the moment when, even through her pain, the woman registered how handsome the doctor was. The young woman's eyes widened and her lips parted on a silent *Oh*.

Under different circumstances it would have made Nychelle want to giggle, but they were already moving, the patient supported by her husband on one side, the doctor on the other, through Reception toward the examination rooms.

Nychelle simultaneously held doors open and pulled up the young woman's information on her tablet, in preparation for handing it to Dr. Warmington on arrival at their destination.

Not a miscarriage. Please, not a miscarriage.

The thought caught her by surprise, made her stomach clench and roll, and as she began helping Mrs. Cardozo undress, she realized her hands were shaky.

Steady. Steady.

She was projecting. She knew she was. Imagining herself in Mrs. Cardozo's position, feeling the other woman's emotions as if they were her own, instead of putting her mind where it needed to be—on the equipment Dr. Warmington would need, the tests he'd want her to run.

It was the first time in her career she'd ever felt this way while in the midst of an emergency. Usually if she fell apart it was afterward, when she was alone and could release her emotions in private.

Taking a deep breath, and then another, she forced back all the fears building in her mind, and by the time she'd helped Mrs. Cardozo onto the examination table she'd gotten herself together.

"We're ready for you, Dr. Warmington."

Habitual efficiency took over then, and the well-remembered routine of working with a doctor kicked in—although since qualifying as an Advanced Practice Registered Nurse she usually worked alone, or with her own nurse assistant.

Yet her emotions seemed perilously close to the surface, and it was only Dr. Warmington's soothing presence that kept her on an even keel. On the few occasions she'd witnessed him with patients before she'd been impressed by his professional demeanor, but this was different. Even though his understanding and reassurance were aimed at the patient, Nychelle found herself reacting to it too, letting it wash over her in calming waves.

"I can confirm you're pregnant."

Nychelle noted that he spoke to Mrs. Cardozo, rather than to her husband the way some other male physicians would be inclined to—another point in the doctor's favor.

"But," he continued, "I can see no apparent reason for the symptoms you're experiencing."

He glanced at Mr. Cardozo for a moment, and Nychelle thought his gaze briefly dropped to where the young couple's fingers were tightly intertwined.

"It could be something as simple as dehydration, or a complication that will only become apparent with further testing, so I recommend you go to Broward Medical and have an obstetrician take a look at you there. While we have our own specialists here, at the hospital they'd be able to deal with any eventuality."

As he gave them the information for the hospital, Nychelle slipped into the adjoining office to call ahead and make arrangements. The entire situation had taken maybe thirty minutes, but she felt as though it had been an emotionally grueling marathon. She didn't even realize her eyes were damp until she reached up to swipe at a tear.

Hanging up the phone, she stiffened her spine and turned to find Dr. Warmington watching her from the doorway. Perhaps it was the set of his lips, or the way he seemed to be watching her, with a hint of the gentleness he'd lavished on Mrs. Cardozo, but whatever it was made Nychelle's heart rate escalate and warmth bloom in her chest.

Once more thankful for the cocoa-toned skin that made her blushes unnoticeable, she said the first thing that came to her mind. "You speak Portuguese?"

He laughed quietly as he stepped into his office and moved toward the desk. "I'm lucky to have an ear for languages. I speak a few and understand a few more."

"Lucky indeed."

She should go. Although another nurse practitioner would have seen the patient she'd left waiting in the reception area, the day's schedule was full. No doubt there was another patient for her to see. And she had details to iron out regarding the free child wellness clinic she was helping coordinate, scheduled for the coming weekend. Yet she lingered, watching as Dr. Warmington sat down and pulled his chair up to the desk.

"I'm pretty good with Spanish," she said, after a moment, "but never got past that. Out of curiosity, what was Mrs. Cardozo saying to her husband?"

When he looked up, Nychelle's breath caught in her throat. For an infinitesimal moment she read excruciating hurt in his eyes, but then he blinked and it was gone.

"They're here from Sao Paulo, visiting his uncle, and when she realized she was pregnant she didn't want to go on the boat trip they'd planned. But her husband talked her into it. She was saying if she lost the baby she'd never forgive him."

He was still looking at her, seemingly waiting for her to reply, and suddenly—desperately—she wanted to say the right thing; wished she knew what the right response was. Wished she could smile and soothe the hurt she was sure she'd seen in his eyes.

"Well," she said slowly. "That was patently unfair, but pregnant women—especially those expecting their first child—aren't always known for their rationality."

She risked a little smile, and was relieved and unreasonably happy when those stern lips relaxed into an answering tilt: not quite a smile, but enough.

"Hormones running rampant, as you men are quick to point out."

That brought a wider smile, and Nychelle laughed quietly, before turning away from the magnetic pull of his grin.

"I won't tell anyone you said something so blatantly sexist, Nurse Cory. It'll be our secret."

The laughter in his voice lightened her mood more, even as the rich baritone trickled like liquid sin down her spine. Suddenly she was glad she didn't have to work with him too often. Now she understood what the other nurses were talking about, why they gazed at him like lost puppies whenever he passed by.

"I appreciate your tact, Dr. Warmington."

She said it briskly and, her face still warmer than she'd like, she beat a hasty retreat before her own hormones went from simply gadding happily about in her system to having an actual full-on dance party.

He was too sexy for his own good—and hers.

Still smiling, David swiped a hand through his hair as the door closed behind Nychelle Cory. If anyone had told him he would smile after attending to a patient who might be losing her first child to miscarriage—especially one who seemed determined to blame her husband if it happened—he'd have said they were demented. It cut too close to home, brought the pain and regret that still haunted him after all these years into sharp focus.

If he closed his eyes he knew he'd instantly be able to bring Kitty's face to mind, see the anger and near hatred glittering in her eyes, hear the blame she'd spewed at him before walking out of their home and his life.

That wasn't something he dwelled on often; he knew she'd been devastated by the loss of their child, had lashed out at him as the only available target. But to have a patient come in at this time of the year, when the memories were so close to the surface anyway… Usually he'd be hard-pressed not to be overwhelmed by them, but now, instead, he clung to Nychelle's warmth and kept smiling.

Just seeing the nurse practitioner buzzing around the clinic, dispensing that wide, sunny grin like instant relief medication, always gave him pleasure. This was one of the few times they'd interacted directly, but that was his own fault. When they'd first met, looking into those dark, gleaming eyes, seeing her gorgeous smile, had sent a sensation like an electric shock through his body, and he'd known immediately she was a woman to stay away from.

Agonizing memories were overshadowed by more enjoyable ones, and he closed his eyes, pictured Nychelle as he'd first seen her. Her hair had been pulled back into a simple bun, which had only emphasized the beauty of her oval face, her wide-set eyes and sweet, full mouth. Her smooth dark skin had been set off to perfection by a silky sunshine-yellow top that had done nothing to camouflage the high, rounded breasts beneath it, and her smart linen pants had showcased the rest of her glorious curves.

As far as he'd come from his rural roots, and as many

lovely women as he'd met, something about Nychelle Cory had regressed him to the stuttering idiot he'd been in junior high school. She was intelligent and beautiful: the kind of woman men fantasized about finding and cherishing forever.

Making a family with.

But going down that road again wasn't an option he wanted even to contemplate. Having children was a dream that had died for him, and he didn't dare reawaken it. So, even if he was feeling that instinctive pull toward her, the smartest thing to do was to stay far away.

Painful memories threatened once more, the agony almost as sharp as it had been all those years ago. With a curse, David pulled his thoughts back from that precipice and reached for the tablet on his desk. He had notes to finish and an appointment due to begin any moment.

Yet his eyes strayed one more time to the door, and he remembered seeing Nychelle wiping away a tear as he came into the office. Apparently he wasn't the only one affected by their shared patient, and the knowledge of her tenderheartedness tugged at something deep in his chest.

Cursing again, he turned his attention to the digital device in his hand, determinedly putting all thoughts of the delectable nurse practitioner out of his head.

CHAPTER TWO

"THIS COUNTRY HAS been so good to me, and it is my pleasure to be able to give back in some small way."

Crowded around the raised stage at the front of the school auditorium, the assembled doctors, nurse practitioners, RNs, medical and nursing students listened respectfully to Dr. Hamatty's pep talk.

It was a great turn-out, and Nychelle was cautiously confident that they were fully prepared for the influx of children who, brought by their parents, would soon be streaming in for the pediatric clinic. It had taken months of intense work by all the committee members to pull it together, but with Dr. Hamatty's connections they had assembled all the equipment and personnel they needed.

She'd been on site the evening before, helping to supervise the setting up of field hospital cubicles and examination tables, and directing the placement of diagnostic machines and dispensary. The Lauderlakes free clinics were famous for their quality of care—a point of pride for Dr. Hamatty, his staff and associates. Even the older, more established doctors turned out to lend their talents when time permitted.

In the middle of the group, Nychelle split her attention between the familiar speech and the conversation scrolling across her phone.

How much longer before you know for sure?

Aliya had added an excited face emoji for emphasis, making Nychelle smile. Anyone meeting her cousin in her guise as a rising young oncology researcher would never guess the depth of Aliya's silly side.

Already told you, another week and a half. Asking every day isn't going to speed up the process!

Are you going to cheat?

Nychelle smiled, shaking her head at how well her cousin knew her. The thought of buying one of those early detection pregnancy tests and taking it a couple of days before her next appointment *had* crossed her mind.

No. It would be like tempting fate.

A quick check found that Dr. Hamatty was at the point where he spoke about coming to the States as a child. His family had been poor, unable to speak proper English, and suffering the effects of the war-torn situation they'd left behind. After telling the story of how he'd got to where he was, he'd wrap it up and they'd all take their places, ready for the deluge of patients. He'd be another five, maybe seven minutes, she estimated.

Just enough time to finish her conversation with Aliya.

Without more than a glance at her phone, she typed her message.

Have you told your mom you won't be at the gala?

Yes. She's not amused, but agreed work had to come first.

Pursing her lips, Nychelle replied.

Not surprising at all.

To Dr. Monique Girvan work always came first. There had been a time when Nychelle had resented her mother for rarely being around, for putting her career advancement before everything else, up to and including her children. Now, although it still rankled, she'd learned to accept her mother for who she was.

It didn't mean her daughter had to walk in her footsteps, though. In fact, if anything, it made Nychelle determined not to. *Her* children wouldn't want for love, affection, and understanding.

Dr. Hamatty was getting close to winding up his speech, so Nychelle typed, Okay, almost go time. TTYL, then stuffed her phone into the pocket of her lab coat.

The crowd shifted, and muffled apologies following their movement as people bumped into one another. The nurse standing just in front of Nychelle turned to frown at the source of the disturbance, but her disapproving expression immediately faded and she lifted a hand to smooth her hair.

Following the other woman's gaze, Nychelle found herself face to face with David Warmington.

As usual his expression was serious, but there was a glint of a smile in his eyes and Nychelle was suddenly breathless, her heart stumbling as she drowned in the bright blue gaze.

He inched a little closer, surrounding her with the clean, fresh scent of utter maleness and, her legs suddenly wobbly, she turned back toward the stage, feigning the greatest of interest in the wrap-up of Dr. Hamatty's speech.

Keeping her head steadfastly trained forward, she contemplated with some annoyance the fact that the darn man was suddenly everywhere she looked. Over the last week it had felt as though she couldn't go two steps without seeing him. Worse, she'd found herself paying him far more attention than was warranted.

She had to admit, though, that what she'd seen was surprising, considering her previous assessment of his character. What she'd thought of as smooth charm seemed instead to be simply politeness. He never crossed the line into familiarity, and even seemed to display, on occasion, a touch of shyness.

He was unfailingly courteous, had a sly sense of humor, and he spoke to everyone from the janitorial staff to the senior partners in exactly the same way. Professionally, everyone agreed he was an excellent diagnostician and a thorough, diligent doctor.

Anyone hearing the nurses talk would believe him to be a paragon of every virtue, and Nychelle was beginning to understand why. He knew all their names, and she'd even overheard him asking one of the nurse aides about her son, who'd been ill the week before.

Once you got past his amazing looks, David Warmington seemed to be just a thoroughly nice person—but she knew better than to trust her own assessment of a man's character. She'd thought the same of Nick, and had been horribly wrong. She just wished she could get her hormones to remember how painful disappointment was, especially when it left you feeling used, so that they'd stop reacting to the man standing at her side.

"And now it's just about time to open the door and let our patients in." Dr. Hamatty beamed as he rubbed his hands together in what looked like anticipation. "Have a great, productive day, and on behalf of everyone involved in planning this I once more thank you for giving up your Saturday to help those in need."

There was a short round of applause as Dr. H. stepped away from the microphone and the clinic committee chairperson stepped forward.

"Any latecomers who haven't received their instruction packages, please report to the intake table. Everyone else—please go to your assigned cubicle." She glanced at her watch. "We have fifteen minutes, folks."

Her smile was slightly strained, and Nychelle felt a pang of sympathy. It was no wonder almost every free clinic had a different coordinator. The stress of getting it all arranged was immense.

Clapping her hands together, like a schoolteacher trying to rally her students, and injecting a strident enthusiasm into her voice, the chairperson concluded, "Let's do this!"

As the crowd dispersed, Nychelle hesitated. She should acknowledge Dr. Warmington in some way, but was reluctant. Ridiculous as it might be, just thinking of meeting his intent gaze made goose bumps fire down her spine and had her nipples tightening to tingling peaks.

"This is quite some set-up. I wasn't sure what to expect."

His words were obviously directed at her, since she was the only one left standing in the immediate vicinity.

Silently admonishing herself to stay cool, Nychelle made the half turn necessary to face him. Thankfully he was taking in the room, his gaze on the dispensary across the gymnasium.

Before she could answer, he continued, "I don't think I've ever seen a pharmacy at a free clinic."

Okay, this was a safe topic to talk about, and since she wasn't skewered by that intense gaze Nychelle relaxed.

"Dr. Hamatty had to work really hard to get a special license for it. Apparently he realized, after the first few clinics he arranged, that it didn't help the patients if they were given prescriptions they couldn't afford to fill. All the medications are donated and, with a few exceptions, they're limited to mostly over-the-counter drugs, so eventually he was allowed to have it."

Nychelle couldn't help chuckling softly, before continuing, "Dr. H. has a lot of clout in the medical community, and beyond. It was inconceivable they'd be able to hold out against him forever."

As though drawn by the sound of her laughter, David looked at her, and immediately she was snared. Really, was it fair for a man to have eyes like that? So gorgeous they made a girl's heart stop for a second and then had it galloping like an out-of-control horse?

No, Nychelle decided. No, it wasn't in the slightest bit fair.

David's lips quirked at the corners and amusement lit his eyes again. "Somehow I'm not surprised. Dr. H. is a powerhouse. I doubt anyone says no to him. Not more than once anyway." He waved his hand in an abbreviated arc, gesturing to the room at large. "The number of us here is testimony to that."

Had he *wanted* to say no? Wasn't being charitable a part of his nature?

Unaccountably disappointed at the thought, she asked, "You weren't at the last one? I would have thought you'd be roped in from the start."

David briefly lifted one shoulder in what she'd come to realize was a characteristic shrug. "I had already committed to going to Los Angeles to finish a course on genetic counseling for oncology patients. Dr. H. knew about it when he hired me, so knew I wouldn't be at the free clinic. I assured him I'd happily participate going forward."

He looked down at the information package in his hand.

"I should try to find my spot." Glancing up at the alphabetically arranged banners hanging from the ceiling, he continued, "I'm in D section, cubicle five."

"I'm just two cubicles down from you, so I can show you where it is."

"Oh, good."

He gave her a full, beaming smile, and the breath seized in her throat.

"So I can run to you if I have any questions?"

"Um..." Nychelle swallowed to make sure her voice wasn't breathy and ridiculous before she attempted to answer. "Somehow I doubt you'll need my help. I, on the other hand, am glad to know I'm in close proximity to the polyglot doctor."

Wanting to lighten her emotional response to his smile, she narrowed her eyes, giving him a mock glare.

"You *do* speak several languages, right? You weren't just pulling my leg?"

With a touch on her arm, which even through her lab coat caused a burst of heat over her skin, David guided her around to face their section and began to walk. Nychelle fell in beside him, keeping her attention on where she was going rather than looking up at the stunning profile of the man beside her.

"Spanish and Portuguese, French, Italian and some German—enough to get by anyway. A little Arabic and a smattering of Hindi. I can understand a bit of Mandarin, but just the basics. I've been told my Cantonese is a disgrace, but once the person I'm talking to stops laughing I can carry on a conversation..."

That last bit was said in such a disgruntled tone Nychelle couldn't help giggling. "Okay, okay—I believe you."

"Oh." David paused abruptly, just before they got to their assigned areas. "I actually sought you out to let you know that Mrs. Cardozo and her baby are in no danger, and she's been cleared by Dr. Tza to fly back home next week."

Nychelle was about to ask for more details when the coordinator's voice boomed through the auditorium. "Ten minutes, people. Ten minutes."

"Oops, better get going." Nychelle smiled up at David, was rewarded by an answering grin. Then she asked, "Did Dr. Tza's office call with the update?"

"No, I called to follow up. See you."

He strode toward his assigned examination area and warmth flooded Nychelle's chest. Checking on a patient he'd only seen once and likely wouldn't see again was beyond his purview, but knowing he'd done so made her unreasonably happy.

Get a grip on yourself. You're getting as bad as the other nurses!

But the admonishment couldn't wipe away the smile on her lips.

"I'm going to suggest going back to your old detergent. The location of the rash seems to indicate contact dermatitis, and the recent change to a different brand of laundry soap seems the obvious culprit."

As the elderly man and preteen boy David was escorting out paused at the entrance to the examination area David continued. "The hydrocortisone cream will help with the itching, but if you go back to the old detergent and the rash doesn't clear up in about a month, you'll need to have him examined again."

The old man nodded, then held out a gnarled and wrinkled hand to shake.

"Thanks, Doctor." He shook his head and grumbled, "Darn kids. That new brand is cheaper than the old one. Wouldn't you know one of them would be allergic?"

But, despite his grousing, he slung his arm around the boy's shoulders as they walked away, and the youngster looped his own arm around the waist of the man he'd called "Grandpa." Clearly there was genuine affection between the pair.

It was funny, David mused, how freely people talked about their lives in the short period of time they had with him in this clinic setting. Already today he'd heard myriad stories about difficult circumstances—like Mr. Jones and Tyrell, the pair now making their way to the dispensary. Mr. Jones wasn't even the boy's blood relative, but was married to Tyrell's great-aunt, who'd taken Tyrell and his two sisters in after their mother went to jail. A sad story in a way, and yet a testament to people's innate goodness.

David could relate to many of the stories of poverty. After all, he'd lived it, and it really wasn't that long since he'd broken away from the grinding cycle of just trying to survive.

Sometimes it felt as if it were yesterday he'd been patching his shoes with newspaper and wearing clothes donated to the family by charitable organizations. Often he caught himself reverting to type—hesitating to buy something he could definitely afford because the price was still shocking to him on an almost visceral level, or rinsing a jar to save instead of putting it into the recycling. Some habits were definitely harder to break than others when they'd been acquired at a really young age.

About to call for the next patient in line, he glanced toward where Nychelle was working, just in time to see her trying to get his attention. He stayed where he was for a moment, allowing himself to enjoy the sight of her hurrying toward him. Even in a pair of pink scrubs printed with pictures of bunnies and teddy bears under a generic white lab coat, her face bare of makeup except for a slick of lip gloss, Nychelle was beautiful.

The only thing missing was her habitual smile. Instead her mouth was set in a firm line, and noticing that had him moving to meet her in front of the examination area that separated their assigned areas.

"Dr. Warmington, if you're free I'd appreciate your assistance."

Her voice was level, without inflection, but David searched her eyes, saw the hint of deep emotion she was trying hard to subdue.

"Of course. What's the problem?"

"I have a toddler—male, three years old, underweight—with jaundice and an elevated temperature, and a Haitian mother who doesn't speak much English, so I can't get an accurate history."

She turned to lead the way to her area.

"What are you thinking?"

Nychelle sent him a worried glance over her shoulder. "I don't know how long they've been in the country, so until I do I can't rule out malaria or Hep A—although it would be unusual for a toddler to show symptoms of hepatitis."

Children that young, he knew, were usually asymptomatic when they contracted Hep A, and quickly recovered without treatment. The real danger would be the chance of the child passing Hepatitis A on to others around him, especially if they were living in less than hygienic conditions.

"Without a history I can't rule out sickle cell anemia or Gilbert's syndrome either."

She paused outside the curtain surrounding her examination area, and David could hear the little boy fussing and the sounds of his mother hushing him without success.

Nychelle shook her head, her frustration patently clear for an instant. "I'm pretty much dead in the water without knowing more." Then she squeezed his wrist—just a quick, strong clasp of her long fingers—and said, "I'm so glad I have you to call on."

Then she slipped between the curtains, leaving him there trying to catch his breath and get a grip on his suddenly wayward libido.

Who knew that one little touch could be as effective as a striptease?

Cursing himself, he ruthlessly pushed away all imaginings of what it would be like to have Nychelle Cory's fingers on other parts of his body, and then followed her through the curtain.

The mother looked harried, and instinctively David held out his arms to the little boy. Big brown eyes widening, the toddler stopped crying and gave David a considering look. Then, after a hiccup, he smiled and tipped forward right into David's grasp.

As he caught the little boy, and then settled the slight weight against his chest, David took a quick inventory. The little fellow was definitely warm, and the sclera of both eyes had a distinctive yellow tint. Time to figure out what was going on.

So, putting on his most calming smile, he turned to the little boy's mother. *"Bonjour, madame. Puis-je vous poser quelques questions?"*

CHAPTER THREE

NYCHELLE SIGHED AS she stepped into the kitchen of her South Fort Lauderdale bungalow and pulled the door closed. Putting down her tote bag, she toed off her shoes, appreciating the cool air indoors, so different from the heat of her garage. Twisting her head first one way and then the other, she tried to work out the tension tightening her neck muscles.

Although each of the medical personnel were only asked to work a three-hour shift at the free clinic, she knew extra hands were always needed at the patient intake booth, or as troubleshooters for the other medical practitioners, and she'd offered her services.

The afternoon had flown by, and before she'd even realized it the clinic had been winding down, so she'd stayed until it ended at five. She was tired—maybe even more so than she'd usually be—but as she yawned widely a feeling of accomplishment made the weariness bearable.

Barefoot, she wandered into the kitchen to retrieve a bottle of water from her fridge, grabbing a handful of grapes at the same time.

The day had been a resounding success, as usual, yet a nagging sense of discontent dogged her every move, and she wasn't able to put her finger on the source. Stifling another yawn behind the water bottle in her hand, she considered having a nice soak and an evening of watching some of the myriad TV shows she'd recorded.

Usually there would be some wine thrown into the mix for good measure but, of course, that wasn't in the cards right now. Hopefully wouldn't be for another thirty-nine weeks.

There was no stopping the grin stretching her lips to the maximum, nor the little thrill trickling down her spine. No matter what else was bothering her, the prospect of a baby—*her* baby—made it all okay.

She was still smiling as she put the grapes in a bowl and then headed across the living room toward her bedroom to prepare her bath.

When her cell phone rang, the distinctive sound of Beethoven's *Fifth* made her good humor all but evaporate. A little groan escaped before she could stop it, and the immediate wave of guilt that brought had her shaking her head.

Reversing course, she strode back toward the kitchen, hurrying so as not to miss the call. Dumping the water bottle and bowl on the console table, she launched a frantic rummage in her bag to find her phone. Locating it under her wadded-up lab coat, she swiped the screen and brought it up to her ear.

"Hi, Mom."

"Nychelle. How did the clinic go?"

Not *How are you?* or *What are you up to?* Nope—straight to work. Sometimes Nychelle wondered if that was all herself and her mother had in common. The thought irritated her more than usual tonight, and she had to temper her annoyance so it wouldn't show in her voice.

"It went very well. We had approximately two thousand patients come through."

"When will you be taking on the chairperson position? Haven't you been asked?"

Nychelle took a deep breath, willing herself not to react to the obvious implication of her mother's last question.

"I was asked, but I didn't accept."

Before her mother could launch into another lecture about ambition and the necessity of taking on hard tasks so as to be able to advance in the workplace, Nychelle continued.

"I was in the middle of those skill improvement courses Dr. Hamatty requested we all take. To be honest, I wanted to make sure I didn't just complete them, but aced them."

"Hmph."

Nychelle knew her mother still wanted to take her to task for not accepting the position anyway, but really couldn't, since her reason for not doing so was also work-related.

"Well, I suggest taking it on if it's offered to you again. But don't be surprised if it isn't. Many of the best opportunities come along only once. Rarely are there second chances in life."

Nychelle bit her lip, holding back a snort of laughter. Her mother would have a fit if she knew Nychelle had already gotten another chance to chair the committee and had once again asked to defer to one of the other committee members.

"Also, I want you to make sure you're on time for the pre-gala reception next Saturday."

Having said her piece on one subject, her mother had swiftly moved on to the next. She probably had a list of points to touch on written out in front of her.

"I know it's embarrassing to come to these functions by yourself, but please endeavor to arrive early. If you lived closer to Martin, he and Jennifer could pick you up, but your house is too out of the way to be convenient."

Another one of her mother's thinly veiled criticisms. While her parents and her cousin Martin all lived in the northern end of the city, in far more expensive neighborhoods, Nychelle had chosen to live in the trendier and more affordable South Fort Lauderdale. It was a nice area, but the way her parents talked about it anyone would be forgiven for thinking it a slum.

"No problem, Mom. The hotel isn't that far from here, so it wouldn't make sense to have someone pick me up anyway. And, yes, I'll be there early enough for the reception."

"Do you have something appropriate to wear?"

Nychelle allowed the chuckle she'd been holding in to escape.

"Not yet, Mom." Her mother didn't wear the same formal dress twice, and expected the same from her daughters. "I plan to go and buy something this week."

She actually didn't plan to buy a new dress. For her, the outfit she'd worn to a friend's wedding would be suitable—but she wouldn't be telling her mother that. No. She'd avoid the lecture until later, then just say she'd been too busy with work to get something.

"Leaving it a little late, aren't you?"

Shaking her head, Nychelle picked up the water bottle from where she'd put it on the console table and, juggling it, her phone and the bowl of grapes, started back across the living room.

Suddenly exhausted, all she wanted was that longed-for bath and a chance to relax: impossible to do with her mother on the other end of the phone.

"I haven't had a chance before. You know how it is. Work must come first."

Unfair, perhaps, to quote her mother's words back at her, but it should be an effective topic-closer.

Yet it wasn't.

"The annual Medical Association charity gala is where you'll find all the movers and shakers of the Florida medical community assembled in one place. You need to make a good impression."

"Yes, Mom. I know." If there was one thing her parents had drummed into their daughters, it was that connections were important when it came to building a career. "One day I might be applying to one of them for a job."

If she'd had more energy she'd have pointed out that Dr. Hamatty, arguably one of the most influential doctors in the city, had hired her without knowing anything about her other than her credentials. Tonight she just felt as if she'd be battering her head against a wall.

"Exactly. Well, I'll let you go. See you next Saturday."

And just like that, without waiting for Nychelle to reply, her mother hung up.

"Wow, Mom. Bye to you too," she said to the dial tone, before throwing her phone onto the bed.

While she undressed, she carried on the imaginary conversation. "And how's Dad? Oh, I'm glad to hear his shoulder is better. How was the surgical conference? Will his latest paper be published?"

Still grumbling to herself, she filled the bathtub and added a sprinkle of bath salts, hoping to soak out the aches of the long, busy day. Sinking into the warm water, she released a long sigh and willed herself to relax.

There was no changing her parents at this late stage, so it didn't make sense to let their attitude toward her life and her career stress her out. Especially now. When she told them she was pregnant there'd be no excitement or joy, just more disapproval, so best she prepare for it.

Realizing she was grinding her teeth, she sank a little deeper into the tub and, forcibly dismissing old hurts, turned her thoughts to the day just past.

Immediately David Warmington came to mind, and she smiled as she remembered little Etienne, the Haitian toddler, throwing himself out of his mother's arms into David's. Children of that age were notorious for clinging to their parents, especially if they weren't feeling well, but Etienne had hardly hesitated before happily going to the doctor.

Not that Nychelle blamed the little boy in the slightest. She'd found herself wanting to throw herself into Dr. Warmington's arms too. Which was ridiculous—and no doubt caused by some strange chemical reaction that all the IUI drugs had created in her brain. Yes, he was gorgeous, seemed nice, and was sexy as hell—but those weren't good excuses to be panting after him. In fact they were all great reasons to avoid him like the plague.

Besides, even if she had been tempted, now she knew for sure David Warmington would never be the man for her even if the circumstances had been different.

Suddenly wanting to move, to be active, even though the whole point of the bath was to relax, she sat up and reached for her body wash, shivering slightly as the cooler air touched her shoulders and breasts when they rose out of the water.

It wasn't a conversation she should even have been privy to, but it wasn't as though she'd eavesdropped on purpose. She'd just happened to be sitting at the table behind David and Dr. Tomkins, one of the other doctors from Lauderlakes, in the cafeteria during her lunch break. Besides, neither had made any effort to keep their voice down, so they obviously hadn't had any expectation of privacy. Mind you,

Dr. Tomkins had a voice like a cannon, his words booming out in ear-shocking volleys.

"Dr. H. mentioned to me that the parents are very impressed by you, David. Saying how well you handle their kids. Maybe you should have gone into pediatrics."

When David had replied he'd sounded neither gratified nor amused. "No…no pediatrics for me. It was never an option."

Dr. Tomkins had chuckled. "Well, at least when you have children of your own you should have a good rapport with them, if today was any indication."

"That's something else I don't consider an option."

Had it been her imagination, or had his voice been cold—not like his usual mellow tones? Without being able to see his face she hadn't been sure, but the alacrity with which Dr. Tomkins had changed the subject had Nychelle suspecting she was right.

Shaking her head, she sank back into the water and frowned. Another man who professed not to want kids—probably for some damned selfish reason too. Nick had said he'd consider children once his career was more settled, although he was already well on his way. Now Nychelle couldn't help wondering what David's reason was. He didn't strike her as the selfish type.

Charm, which Nick had exhibited in abundance, was something she'd learned could be easily feigned, and it differed markedly from good character and genuine caring. Even her father, normally coolly distant, had the ability to turn on the charm when he thought it worthwhile.

Nychelle couldn't help wondering if the real David was hiding behind a thin veneer of charisma, like the one Nick had. Not that it mattered to her. She couldn't care less. Wouldn't allow herself to care.

What truly irked her, though, was her physical reaction

to David, since she should know better than to be attracted to another charmer.

As she lay back in the water, it wasn't the popping of the soap bubbles floating away from her skin that raised goose bumps on her arms and chest and made her nipples tighten and tingle. It was the memory of watching David's hands as he'd worked, hearing the warm cadence of his voice as he'd soothed the patient and his mother, and the breathlessness she'd felt each time his gaze caught hers or she looked at his lips.

With a little groan of surrender Nychelle swept a palm over one breast, succumbing to the lure of a fantasy in which David Warmington pulled her close to his strong body and kissed her until she turned to putty in those gorgeous hands.

And somehow she knew those hands, lips and body could bring her more pleasure than she'd ever known before.

"Cut it out, Nychelle."

Saying it out loud didn't stop the ache building in her core, and with a growl of frustration she slapped both palms down on the surface of the water, inadvertently splashing herself in the face.

"Oh, for crying out loud!"

Spluttering, she wiped the soapy water from her cheeks, then laughed as she reached for a towel to dry her eyes. It was the kind of silly thing she'd usually share with Aliya, but in this case probably wouldn't. The last thing she needed was to get in the habit of talking to her cousin about David. Aliya would definitely pick up on hearing his name over and over again.

Despite claiming to understand why Nychelle was undergoing IUI, her cousin had tried to convince her to wait a little longer before having a baby.

"There's a man out there for you," Aliya had said over lunch the last time she'd come to Florida for a visit. "I know Nick broke your heart, and you're probably not ready to trust yet, but give it a little more time."

Just the sound of her ex-fiancé's name had made a sour taste rise into the back of her throat, and Nychelle had shaken her head. "It's not about Nick."

When Aliya's eyebrows had gone up, Nychelle had known her cousin didn't believe her.

"It's not *all* about Nick," she'd qualified. "Yes, he broke my heart, but that was a couple of years ago, and I'm over it."

"Are you really?" Aliya had pressed the point. "You were with him for years, and he used our family connections to advance his career. Then he cheated on you and got some other girl pregnant after telling you he wasn't ready to have a child yet. I'd have a hard time getting over that. And the fact you won't even consider waiting to find someone else tells me you're anything but over it."

"I don't need a relationship to get what I want." She raised her hand to stop her cousin launching into a rebuttal. "And I don't have time to build one, to learn to trust again, before I start trying to conceive."

"But..."

"No. You know that with the scarring on my uterus the longer I wait to try to start a family the harder it will be. Realistically, I'm almost thirty, and at the optimal time in my life—physically, financially and emotionally—to start a family. I don't want to wait, hoping I'll meet someone, and miss this chance."

Aliya's expression had softened, and she'd said, "From when you were little you said you wanted a big family. I guess that's never changed."

"Exactly. So I'm going to do the IUI and let the rest

of it take care of itself." Then she'd added, just so Aliya wouldn't figure out she wasn't planning even to consider another relationship and get on her case, "If there's someone out there for me he'll find me, or I'll find him. If not, it's not a big deal."

"Huh." Disgruntlement had radiated from Aliya's snort. "I still think waiting a couple years more wouldn't hurt."

Now, as Nychelle stepped out of the tub, she reached down to touch her belly, skimming her fingertips over the place where, hopefully, her baby was growing and thriving. "It's okay that it's just you and me, sweetie. We really don't need anyone else."

Funny how suddenly the words had a bittersweet quality—but she didn't want to consider why that might be. Instead, she gave her reflection a bracing nod, then turned away to reach for her towel. This was the best time of her life and nothing would make her regret trying for a baby.

Nothing.

CHAPTER FOUR

THERE WAS SOMETHING a little off about David Warmington today, but Nychelle couldn't put her finger on it. Perhaps it was that for the first time she sensed he was growing ever more irritated with a patient.

Not that she could blame him. Douglas Comstock, a sports agent referred to the clinic by one of his star clients, was being willfully difficult. He'd come in complaining of persistent leg pain, and after examining him she'd sent him for X-rays and a MRI. He had requested pain medication, because over-the-counter painkillers were no longer working, and since nurse practitioners weren't allowed to prescribe medication Nychelle had requested one of the GPs see him. David had been available.

Now she was being treated to a battle of wills, her head swiveling back and forth between the two men as though she were at a debate. It would be entertaining if it weren't for the fact she was sure David was having a hard time dealing with this patient.

As she watched, it seemed David took a deeper than necessary breath before saying, "Mr. Comstock—"

"Doug." The man grinned, totally at ease. Almost seeming to be enjoying himself. "Call me Doug, Doc."

"Doug. I'm going to refer you to Dr. Napoli, who is one of the best orthopedic surgeons in Florida. But, I'm telling you, she's not going to be able to help you until you lose some weight."

Doug Comstock was still smiling, even as he shook his head. "Don't bother sending me to anyone else. Just give me some meds, Doc, and I'll be on my way. As I was telling Nychelle, that losing weight thing's probably just not going to happen. I'm on the road for most of the year, traveling with the athletes I manage, and I don't have time to add anything else to my schedule, you know?"

He made the argument sound reasonable, but David was having none of it.

"No," he countered. "I don't know. Explain to me how eating healthier and getting exercise are going to disrupt your schedule."

"Sure, Doc."

Doug kept right on smiling, and Nychelle realized it was probably part of the reason he was successful. It was an effective way to rebuff almost any dissent.

"I'm at sporting events most nights, or out scouting new talent. Then there are after-parties or press conferences. Even if there are no events there are dinners, where I'm schmoozing prospective clients or dealing with owners. I'm up with the birds, on the phone making connections, setting things up, talking to people on the other side of the world. Then I'm taking people to lunch, or sitting around in meetings most of the day. My day is long, and as full as you can get, and it involves a lot of eating and drinking to boot. Add one more thing into that and I have to drop something else. What do you suggest? The three or four hours of sleep I get a night?"

While his pleasant expression hadn't changed, there was a steely tone in his voice. He obviously wasn't used to being lectured or opposed, but once more David didn't back down.

"I see from the chart Nurse Cory tried to schedule you for some tests, but you told her not to set them up."

"Yup." Doug shifted on the table, lifting one beefy leg and then the other, obviously uncomfortable although his smile remained in place. "I'm heading to Taiwan in three days, so it doesn't make sense for her to bother. I won't make the appointments anyway."

David glanced at Nychelle and she gave him a quick upward quirk of her eyebrows. A silent *good luck*. Then David gave Doug a thoughtful look. Normally by now he should be telling the patient to put on his clothes and come into the adjacent office, where they could sit and discuss the situation in comfort. Instead, perhaps to underscore the importance of what he had to say, David launched right in.

"Okay, Mr. Comstock. I know I should probably be more tactful, but I don't think you'll take me seriously. So I'm going to give this to you straight."

Was that a slight wavering of the smile on their patient's face? Nychelle couldn't be sure, but she hoped so. It might mean the other man was really listening.

"You're at least a hundred pounds over the optimal weight for your height and bone structure. I suspect, from the X-rays and MRI results, that you may have a herniated disc, which accounts for the leg pain, and the numbness and weakness you're experiencing. While there are treatments that could help with the pain, those are best explored with a specialist like Dr. Napoli. Realistically, though, the treatment is probably going to be ineffective if you don't address the root causes of the problem. And pain medication on its own will only mask the symptoms."

"But—"

David gave the man a stern look and held up one hand. "Wait, please. Let me finish."

Smile totally gone, Doug gave a little huff of clear annoyance, but subsided.

"Perhaps even more important, even at your age, your weight puts you at risk for so many other diseases. Ones that can halt you right in your busy tracks."

He glanced down at the tablet in his hand, maybe to give his words a chance to sink in, then continued.

"Your blood pressure is elevated, and although you're on the appropriate medication you say you haven't been to a doctor in a few years, so I suspect your management of that hasn't been tracked, nor your medication adjusted. Uncontrolled blood pressure can lead to a stroke."

Doug's eyes widened slightly, but David pressed on, relentless in a way she suspected he normally wouldn't be. Seeing him like this was a little surreal.

And surprisingly attractive.

She shook that thought away, but not before a little tingle had tiptoed down her spine.

"You're also at an elevated risk for diabetes—which, should you develop it, would definitely add new tasks to your daily routine, such as taking your blood sugar levels three times a day and giving yourself injections of insulin to ensure you don't go into a diabetic coma."

Doug Comstock paled. His lips parted, but then he looked down and closed them again. David waited and then, assured the other man wouldn't interrupt, he continued.

"Nurse Cory has noted you've had some breathing issues, which could be something as simple as a reaction to air quality or as serious as imminent congestive heart failure. I'm also concerned about your cholesterol levels, considering your lifestyle, but there is no way to know whether you should be worried about either of those matters without further tests. Furthermore, your excess weight, as well as putting undue pressure on your back, is also putting immense pressure on your other joints, so you can expect to begin experiencing knee, hip and/or ankle problems. Also, with all the traveling you do, you are definitely at risk for deep vein thrombosis. Do you know what that is?"

A now somber Doug shook his head. David definitely had his attention now, thank goodness.

"That is when blood clots form in your legs, which can then travel through the veins and cause a pulmonary embolism—a blockage in your lungs. You have two of the major risk factors—you sit down a lot, and you're overweight."

Sensing the patient's rising anxiety, Nychelle stepped closer, and said, "Mr. Comstock, I know it seems like a real inconvenience to try to lose weight, or to concentrate on your health when you have so much going on, and so many people depending on you, but we can help. Make it achievable without adding too much fuss to your day."

She smiled, hoping to soften the words. It was like playing "good cop, bad cop," and if it would help to get the patient on the right track, she was willing to go with it.

"I..." Doug Comstock frowned, then looked down again at his hands, where they lay on his thighs. "I guess I can at least try. I haven't been feeling so good lately, and I'm not sleeping well, but I just put it down to the pain."

David opened his mouth, and Nychelle hoped he wouldn't bring up any of the other myriad conditions obesity might be causing the patient, like sleep apnea. There was no point in overloading Doug with *what ifs* and risk him shutting down. Not now, when he seemed amenable to letting them guide him to a healthier way of life.

But instead David said, "Why don't you put on your clothes and come through to the office? We'll get you scheduled for some blood tests—many of which we can do right now, before you leave—and Nurse Cory and I will set you up with a plan to get you on the right track."

"Okay. Okay." Doug heaved himself off the table. "I've only gotten this big in the last six years, since my management business took off, believe it or not."

"That's actually good," David said. "It's not the habits of a lifetime you're trying to break, just those you've developed over a short space of time. I think, for a man of your drive and character, this will be a breeze."

And Doug, thankfully, was smiling again as David and Nychelle left the room.

David was hard pressed to remember when last he'd been so annoyed with a patient and, given the thoughtful look Nychelle sent him as they entered her office, he guessed he hadn't hidden it very well.

"Whew," Nychelle said quietly, after making sure the door to the examination room was firmly closed. David was already on the defensive, even before she said, "I'm glad you got through to Mr. Comstock, but you were pretty hard on him."

"He needed me to be."

He realized how much of a growl that had been when Nychelle glanced at him again, her eyebrows raised.

But all she said was, "Apparently. I said a lot of the same things to him and all he did was brush me off. I was a little worried he was prescription shopping, when he kept insisting all he needed were painkillers."

As she crossed to the credenza where she kept various informational brochures, David went to sit at her desk and blew out a long breath.

"At least we cleared up that misapprehension, but I honestly have no idea whether he'll actually listen to us and try to make the changes we suggest." He pulled the laptop closer to bring up the necessary records. "Sometimes I wonder why we bother."

Pausing in the midst of pulling pamphlets from a drawer, Nychelle sent him a steady look over her shoulder. "It can frustrating at times, I know." Turning back to her chore, she asked, quietly, "Everything okay?"

"Yes." Yet, he could hear the lie in his voice—feel it in the jagged ache that fired through his chest. "I'm fine."

Thankfully she didn't reply immediately, allowing him to continue selecting the tests he wanted the patient to undergo on the electronic form. It was easier to concentrate on that than to think about what today meant, or let Nychelle's instinctive kindness undo all the emotional barriers he'd marshaled to get him through the day.

He didn't look up from the computer screen when she came across to the desk, not even when she said, "Well, if you need anything—an ear, or a hand—just let me know."

Her compassion was almost his undoing, and he was thankful when the door to the exam room opened and Douglas Comstock came in to join them.

After Nychelle had taken their rather subdued patient off to have some of the tests run, David made his way back to his own office. Dropping into his chair, he scrubbed both hands over his face, as though to awaken himself from the aching sorrow wrapped around him like a pall. He should have taken the day off, but the thought of being at home without anything to do had had zero appeal, and there was nowhere he could think of going that would have been any better. Work seemed the best way to deal with the pain.

How tempted he'd been to tell Nychelle what today was. Something in her empathetic gentle gaze, the timbre of her voice, had made him want to share with her that which he never shared. Had never been tempted to share, neither wanting to worsen the wound nor, conversely, diminish the loss. As if saying the words *Today was the day my baby girl, my Natalie, was born way too early and didn't survive* would be a betrayal of the love he still felt ten years later.

She had been born at just shy of twenty weeks. As a doctor he would call it a miscarriage or, worse, a spontaneous abortion. As a man, Natalie's father, he couldn't bring himself to think of it that way. It was simply her birthday, the day he'd truly learned, for the first time, what love was. And it was also the day he'd learned the immensity of the agony love could cause. The irrevocable, heartbreaking loss hadn't become easier to bear over time. Probably never would.

Taking a breath, he held it for a moment and then blew it out. Leaning back in his chair, he wished he were still in Chicago so he could visit her grave, the way he had every other year. When he'd been offered the job in Florida he'd thought about moving away from her and almost refused. Yet he'd known it was time to move on—not from her, but in his professional life. He'd reassured himself he didn't need to be there to remember her, to miss her, but he hadn't realized how bad today would be, the pain magnified by distance and the strangeness of his new life.

What he needed was something that would center him, pull him back from the dark clouds threatening to overtake his spirit. It was at times like this he wished he could call Kitty. As Natalie's mother, he knew she would share his grief, but Kitty had a new life, a husband who could comfort her, and two other children to think about. A few years after the divorce their contact had dwindled away to Christmas cards only—the last acknowledgment of what they'd shared and always would. His struggle to cope with this anniversary was no reason for him to encroach on her life and perhaps make it worse for her too.

No, he had to accept that nothing would take away his pain today, but there was one person who could at least dull it.

So he picked up the phone and dialed.

After a couple of rings, the receiver on the other end was picked up and his mother said, "Davie. I wondered if you'd call today."

Just hearing her voice eased the band of heartache around his chest. Leaning back in his office chair and rocking slightly back and forth, he listened to his mother's melodic voice coming through on speakerphone. He knew she wouldn't mention Natalie—that wasn't her way—but just hearing her voice as she spoke about the family and doings in the tiny town he was born in leeched more of the tension from his body.

His computer pinged, and he leaned forward to look at the message his receptionist had sent.

Nurse Cory is asking for a few moments of your time when you're finished on the phone.

Stress—different from what he'd felt before when thinking about Natalie, but just as potent—tightened his shoulders and neck. She probably wanted to bring him up to speed on Doug Comstock, and he was tempted to ask her to leave a note for him rather than have to see her again. Being around her unsettled something deep inside him, stirred feelings he didn't want to examine. Yet, he found himself typing…

Send her in, Trina.

CHAPTER FIVE

A FEW SECONDS later the door opened just far enough for Nychelle's face to appear in the crack between it and the jamb. When she hesitated, raising an eyebrow, he waved her in. She glanced at the phone before slipping into the room and closing the door behind her, and he suddenly realized she looked tired. There were little bags under her eyes which, in the midst of his own self-absorption, he hadn't noticed earlier and now wondered about.

He'd lost track of the conversation with his mother and now, not taking his gaze off Nychelle, tried to catch up with what Momma was saying.

"Then Ms. Lattimore refused to contribute to the bake sale, because she felt slighted, and I had to give her a firm talking-to." Momma gave a huff of annoyance. "Told her that's no way for a grown lady and a parishioner to behave. In the end she made a dozen of her pecan pies, after saying she'd never do a thing for the church again if Janie Carruthers was running the charity committee."

Nychelle's lips twitched, then spread into a smile as she settled into the chair across the desk from him. If it were anyone else David would have hesitated to allow them to be privy to his conversation, but for some reason he didn't mind Nychelle hearing his mother ramble on.

"You're a born peacemaker, Momma. Should have been a police officer."

"Go on with you."

Her laughter trickled through the office, and David smiled to hear it.

"You're so silly, Davie."

Nychelle covered her mouth with one hand, but not before a little burst of laughter escaped.

"Someone there with you, Davie?"

The gleam of laughter in Nychelle's eyes increased at hearing his nickname again, and David sent her a mock glare as he replied, "One of the nurse practitioners, Nurse Cory, just came in, Momma."

"Oh, you're busy. I should let you go."

"Wait, Momma." He'd almost forgotten to mention one of the reasons he'd called. "Have you and Poppa given any more thought about coming down for a visit? I have the spare room all ready for you."

He knew what she was going to say before she said it, just from the few moments of silence before she replied.

"You know what your poppa is like, Davie. Always working…never wanting to take a break. Besides—*Florida*?"

She said it as though it were outer space, rather than just a couple states away. Not that strange, since the farthest his parents had traveled before they'd reluctantly flown to Maryland for his graduation from medical school was to Charleston, about an hour away from their home. The reluctance in her voice was clear, when she said, "I don't know…"

"Well, think about it, okay? Now that Jessa is out of school I'm sure she and Little Bub could help Mary-Liz for a little while at the shop." He well knew his sister could probably manage their dad's business by herself, but her kids would probably be glad to earn some pocket money over the summer.

"I'll ask him, Davie."

Skepticism was rife in her voice, and he knew her agreeing to ask his father again was the best he could hope for.

"Now, I'll let you get back to work."

"Okay, Momma. Love—"

But, with a click, she was gone before he could finish. Shaking his head, David reached over to disconnect the speaker, cutting off the buzz of the dial tone.

"Ah. Your mom belongs to the Dr. Monique Girvan school of telephone conversations." Nychelle was still smiling, but the laughter had faded from her eyes. "As soon as she's finished talking she hangs up."

Leaning back, he asked, "Dr. Monique Girvan?" Why was that name so familiar?

"My mother."

"Ah..." He still wasn't sure where he'd heard the name before, but gave Nychelle a half smile. "I'd suggest it's a mom thing, but I think my mom was just a little flustered to think I was supposed to be working. What I do for a living is a bit of a mystery to her. Her experience of doctors is limited to what she's seen on TV and the old family practitioner in our little town, who's always rushing around, busier than a one-armed coat hanger."

"Busier than...?" Nychelle started to giggle. "Where did you get an expression like that?"

Her laughter was contagious and, inexplicably lighthearted, he chuckled before replying. "My roommate in college was from Canada, and he used that expression all the time. I like it."

He moved an invitation he'd left on his desk from side to side, wanting something to do with his hands. The sudden urge to put them on Nychelle Cory—trace the sweet, smooth lines of her cheeks and neck, rub his thumb across the soft pillow of her lower lip—was shocking, and he quickly squelched it.

"I can see why." She was still giggling a little. Then she added, *"Davie,"* in a credible facsimile of his mother's accent, and they both dissolved into full-blown laughter.

Strangely, he didn't feel the least abashed at her teasing, although he knew himself to be touchy about his poor, Low Country roots. Even stranger was how their shared laughter lightened the darkness still swirling in his soul, pushing it and his lingering grief back just a bit more.

"South Carolina?" she asked, after she could talk again. "I've been trying to figure your accent out, but it really only became pronounced when I heard you talking to your mom."

"I've moved around a lot in the last twelve years, and lost most of my accent. It seems to come back when I'm talking to my family."

"Mine does too. I've lived in the States since I was ten, but if you hear me on the phone with my cousin Aliya you'd think I just got off the plane from Jamaica."

She reached up to tuck an errant strand of hair back into her bun, causing her blouse to tighten across her breasts, and David forced his gaze away from the alluring sight. What on earth was wrong with him, ogling her every chance he got? Hopefully she hadn't noticed what he was doing.

As she straightened in her chair, her gaze fell to the invitation he was still shifting from hand to hand across the surface of his desk. "Is that an invitation to the FMA charity gala?"

Surprised by the change in the conversation, David glanced down at the card before replying, "Yes. Will you be there?"

Curiosity swept him as he realized he knew nothing about Nychelle Cory other than the fact she was intelligent, beautiful and a wonderful nurse. Was she married? He didn't think so. But he'd avoided asking too many questions about his colleagues and the staff, preferring them to volunteer whatever information they wanted him to have.

"Couldn't miss it." Her lips twisted briefly. "My life wouldn't be worth living if I did."

She must have seen the confusion in his eyes, because she waggled an index finger toward the invitation.

"My mother is chairperson this year. She'd have my guts for garters if I didn't turn up."

"Ah…"

Now he remembered where he'd heard Dr. Girvan's name before. Dr. H had advised him not to miss the gala, and had given him a rundown on some of the people he'd meet there. Dr. Girvan—Head of Psychiatry at the prestigious Brevard University Medical School—had definitely come up as a force to be reckoned with both in the medical and the wider communities.

"I've been dreading it a little, to be honest," he said, giving the card a flick of his finger. "I haven't been in Florida long enough to get to know many people and, frankly, any event where I have to wear a tuxedo is almost guaranteed to make me break out in hives."

Nychelle's laugh told him she didn't believe him for a moment. "I bet you'll fit right in. And there'll be a number of doctors from the clinic there, including Dr. H, so you'll know some people."

"Including you."

She dropped her gaze for a moment and he wondered what she was thinking. Then she looked up again, and he still had no idea what was going on in her head. It was as though she'd intentionally wiped her face clean of all expression.

"Including me."

"Do you have a date?"

As the impulsive words left his mouth David felt himself go still, waiting for her response.

"Um…no. I don't." She was rubbing her left wrist with her right hand, and then abruptly stopped, both hands going still in her lap.

Why was that a relief? He didn't want to know, really—was still wondering in the back of his mind exactly what the heck he was doing. Of all the people to ask to accompany him anywhere, Nychelle Cory was the worst possible choice.

Yet, as though from a distance, he heard himself ask, "Would you go with me?"

Surprise had her blinking at David as he continued, "I'd appreciate not having to walk into the gala by myself."

The one question that immediately reverberated in her head was, *Why?*

Why was he asking her to go with him when he could have his pick of women? Was it because he'd found out her mother was chairing the prestigious function? Perhaps he had even heard of her father who, as head of a world-renowned cardiac institute, also wielded considerable clout in the medical world? She knew what it felt like to have someone use her in an attempt to advance their medical career, and it was a situation she'd promised herself never to get into again.

Not wanting him to see how conflicted she was, Nychelle looked back down at the invitation, avoiding his gaze. How easy it was to remember Nick sucking up to her parents. She'd thought it was because he wanted to make a good impression. It was only later she'd realized he was only with her to get close to them—especially her father—hoping to worm his way into a position at the institute. There was no way she could trust David not to try something similar.

And, even without the fact she didn't want to be used that way again, going with David to the gala would be stupid. There was something about him that drew her, excited her, and in her heart she knew staying away from him was definitely the best course of action. Being coolly professional over the last few days had been difficult enough, and just today, in the face of his obvious unhappiness, she'd so easily lost that clinical distance. Spending the evening with him seemed like pushing her luck too far.

No, she couldn't take the chance on any of it, so she replied in as expressionless a tone as she could manage. "I'm not sure that would be a good idea. It might lead to gossip here at the clinic."

David seemed to consider that for a moment, and when the silence had lasted longer than she'd expected, she finally looked up.

Meeting her gaze, he shook his head and held up one finger. "First, we're colleagues. Colleagues go to functions together all the time. It'll be more like carpooling." Another finger went up to emphasize his next point. "Second, I'd be happy to tell anyone who asks that you're doing me a good turn since I don't know that many people here yet." One last finger. "Third, if anyone comes to me trying to stir up trouble I'll tear a strip off them." Dropping his hand, he concluded, "I don't think it'll be a problem."

Damn him, those eyes made her just melt. About to press her palm to an overwarm cheek, she arrested the motion and lowered her hand back to her lap.

Maybe it wasn't such a bad idea after all. Perhaps seeing him currying favor with her parents would put an end to this silly attraction she felt. While her mother would take any deference as her due, her father, for all his status, seemed to thrive on being fawned on. Nychelle couldn't think of anything worse than watching David Warmington stroke their egos. It would immediately make him *persona non grata* in her book.

Tightening her lips, she gave in to the determined look in his eyes and nodded. It seemed wise, though, to qualify what they were doing. Make sure he knew it wasn't a date.

"Okay. Since you put it that way, I'll go with you. I don't like going to these functions solo either, so really you're doing me as much of a favor as I'm doing you."

"Great."

The corners of his lips twitched in one of his abbreviated smiles and Nychelle had to look away. Every time he did that she—ridiculously—just wanted to kiss him. Going with him seemed a worse and worse idea with each passing minute.

"Let me have your address and I'll pick you up," he added.

Without looking back up at him, she reached into the pocket of her lab coat and pulled out a pad. "I have to be there in time for the reception, so pick me up by six at the latest." She quickly scribbled down her address. "Do you know South Fort Lauderdale at all, or do you need directions?"

"I'll use my GPS. I'm sure I'll find it. But give me your phone number too, just in case."

Jotting down her home and cell phone numbers, she realized her heart rate was through the roof, as though from a shot of epinephrine. She tore the sheet off the pad and took a deep breath.

Then, reaching out to give him the paper, she forced her mind back to work and said, "I'm just following up on Mr. Comstock—letting you know he left here telling everyone what a brilliant doctor you are and promising to do his best…"

Yet, despite her carrying on a perfectly professional conversation regarding their mutual patient, one thought was paramount in her mind.

I'm going to have *to get a new dress!*

CHAPTER SIX

SEATED IN THE passenger seat of David's sedan, waiting for him to come around and open the door for her, Nychelle tried not to fidget with her hair or smooth down her dress.

Her wildly expensive, extravagant dress.

The kind of dress she usually never, ever bought but in this case hadn't been able to resist.

Nothing at any of the shops she usually patronized—most of which sold designer garments at reduced prices—had seemed appropriate. Finally she'd given in and gone to a boutique Aliya had once taken her to, where price sticker shock had almost caused her to have a heart attack. Right in the middle of the store, displayed in pride of place, she'd found *the dress* and, despite wanting to cry when she heard the price, she'd known it was perfect. After all, she was going to the gala with a man who just might be the best-looking one there. The last thing she wanted was to feel frumpy in comparison—especially in front of her parents.

Made of luxurious silk, with an intricate side-pleated, strapless bodice that fit her like a glove, and from which flowed a swirling, clingy skirt, the dress was two shades lighter than David's eyes. Looking at herself in the mirror, she'd felt beautiful, even sophisticated, and the appreciation in David's gaze when she'd opened her front door to him had been the icing on the cake. Having a gorgeous man solemnly tell you how beautiful you looked was an ego-booster, although she sternly cautioned herself not to take it to heart.

Now, as he swung the car door open and held out his hand, she steeled herself for the night ahead.

"Have I told you how lovely you look?" he asked, keeping hold of her hand although she was already out of the car.

"This makes three times." Slanting him a look, she reminded herself they weren't on a date one more time, and wriggled her fingers to try to make him let them go.

Instead of releasing her hand, David simply slid it up into the crook of his elbow, holding it there.

"Only three?" The corner of his mouth quirked, as he started leading her into the hotel. "I'm lagging behind… need to up my game. It should be at least a dozen times by now."

She had never thought she'd laugh while about to be subjected to her family in a formal professional setting, but somehow David managed it with his dry delivery.

"So, what am I in for tonight?"

They were crossing the lobby toward the banquet hall as he leaned in close to ask the question, his breath warm against her cheek.

"Will the food be good, or will I need to take you to a burger joint afterward?"

That made her giggle again, and it wasn't until they were right at the door that she realized her stomach wasn't tied in knots the way it usually was before one of these events.

"Nychelle—glad you could make it on time." Her mother gave her a perfunctory hug and the obligatory air-kiss near one cheek, before adding, "And you took time to find something suitable to wear."

"Yes, Mom."

Ugh. That lukewarm reception knocked a lot of the wind out of her sails, leaving Nychelle caught somewhere between annoyance and disappointment. And, even though she wanted to see David's demeanor as she introduced him, she was too embarrassed by her mother's greeting to look at his face.

"Mom, I don't think you've met Dr. David Warmington? David, this is my mother, Dr. Monique Girvan."

The look of quickly disguised shock on her mother's face when she realized Nychelle had a date should have made Nychelle want to laugh, but it only served to make her feel that much worse.

"A pleasure to meet you, Dr. Warmington." Back to her usual urbane self, her mom gave David one of her piercing, interrogatory looks. "Dr. Hamatty has mentioned you. So nice of you to come—and to give Nychelle a ride."

"The pleasure is all mine, Dr. Girvan. On all fronts."

Nychelle thought there was a hint of coolness in his greeting and glanced up. Although he was smiling, the expression didn't reach his eyes.

"Your daughter was kind enough to agree to accompany me, and my appreciation for that knows no bounds."

Then they were moving forward, and Nychelle was greeting the next person in the receiving line, and whatever her mother said in reply to David was lost in the murmur of voices.

Once they'd cleared the line Nychelle glanced around, still stung by her mother's attitude, looking everywhere but at David.

"They've really outdone themselves with the decor this year. Those arrangements of calla lilies and orchids are amazing." She was babbling, and she knew it, but somehow couldn't stop. "Did you get a chance to check out the items up for auction? They should have sent you a list with the invitation. There are some gorgeous paintings, and a sculpture I absolutely covet…"

Warm fingers closed around her wrist, stemming the flow of words spilling from her mouth, and when she glanced up David's intent expression made her breath hitch. Then he was leaning close, his cheek almost resting against hers, and the scent of expensive cologne and heated male caused a cascade of goose bumps over her arms and back.

"I don't care how old you are. If you were my daughter the last thing I'd call that dress is *'appropriate.'*"

His fingers, somehow both firm and gentle at the same time, skimmed up her arm to her shoulder, stopping just shy of her collarbone, and a sweet shiver traveled up her spine.

"It's alluring. Decadent. Deliciously sensual. It'll make every red-blooded man in this room want to take it off."

His hand fell away. That simple touch had left her far more aroused than it should have been able to. Made her want to grab his hand and pull it back, guide it lower, to where her breast swelled over the bodice of the dress in question.

"Highly inappropriate from a parental point of view, I would have thought."

The right response would be to laugh, make light of what he was saying, but her insides were at war. She was dry-mouthed, her heartbeat threatening to go completely out of control. Taking a deep breath made it worse, because David was still leaning close and that scent, which she found excessively sexy, filled her already swimming head.

Then he straightened. "I'm going to have to beat the men off you tonight, aren't I?" He said it in a wry, conversational tone, but his lips twitched, revealing his amusement. "Good thing I've been going to the gym."

Trust him to make her smile, even when it was the last thing she felt like doing. Gathering her composure, she slanted him a glance, then quickly looked away again, because the warmth in his eyes was threatening to undo all her hard-won poise.

"Oh, I think we'll be okay. Everyone tends to be on their best behavior at these galas."

Tucking her fingers into the crook of his arm again, David muttered, "Darn it. I suppose I'll have be too, then. Just my luck." Then, before she could do more than chuckle, he continued, "Come on—let's take a stroll around and look at the auction items. I want to see this sculpture you like so much."

And she was happy to comply, knowing the night probably wouldn't get any better.

Dinner had been delicious—far better than he'd expected from past experience—and the after-dinner speeches hadn't droned on and on, as they so often did at these affairs. And being seated at a table with four other doctors from the Lauderlakes clinic, along with their accompanying spouses and significant others, had ensured pleasant dinner conversation, without any of the awkwardness that would have come with sitting with strangers.

And, of course, there was Nychelle—who had taken his breath away when she'd opened her front door earlier, and continued to do so every time he looked at her. At least here he had the opportunity to watch her openly, instead of surreptitiously as he often found himself doing at the clinic. Truth be told, tonight he'd had to tear his gaze away periodically, since the temptation was to hang on to her every word and gesture like a doofus.

Or some kind of creepy stalker.

He really wasn't sure which one was accurate, but at least he was able to acknowledge it was one or the other and rein himself in. It shouldn't be this difficult. They weren't on a date, and he didn't want it to be one.

At the time, asking her to come with him had seemed like a great idea. He liked her, found her good company, and got the impression she wasn't particularly interested in him other than as a colleague and perhaps a casual friend. That last fact made her the perfect companion, so any problems he had were squarely on him.

Despite his fascination with Nychelle, and the spurt of annoyance he'd felt with the way her mother greeted her, from David's point of view it had been a great evening.

Until now, when they were mingling with the other attendees. In particular, standing and chatting with Nychelle's father.

When first introduced to the older man, David had been struck by the similarities in looks and deportment between father and daughter, and had been inclined to like the man just on that basis. Now he was wondering how such a cool and pompous man could have produced the warm and friendly Nychelle.

"Nychelle would have made a competent doctor if she'd had the ambition." Dr. Herman Cory paused to take a sip from the glass in his hand. "Unfortunately she refused to listen to career advice from her mother and me. Luckily her sister makes up for it."

Annoyed, David lifted his glass to his lips just so he wouldn't have to reply to Dr. Cory's comment. Glancing at Nychelle, he saw a half smile tipping her lips, but zero amusement in her eyes. However, she didn't look surprised at the fact her father was singing her sister's praises and had been for the last five minutes straight. Apparently it wasn't anything new.

"Olivia was in the top five percentile in all her courses,

and before she even graduated she was being headhunted by the Mayo Clinic and John Hopkins."

Unable to stand it a moment longer, David replied, "It must be very satisfying to have two such intelligent and talented daughters."

Dr. Cory waved his hand—somewhat dismissively, David thought. "Of course. It's just a shame Nychelle isn't living up to her full potential."

"I disagree."

If the circumstances had been different, he'd have been amused at the older man's obvious surprise at being so clearly contradicted. As it was, Dr. Cory's arched eyebrows just added to David's annoyance.

"I have no doubt Nychelle would make an excellent doctor, in any specialty she chose, but as a nurse practitioner she's fulfilling a vital role at our clinic, and she is one of the very best diagnosticians I've come across, whether doctor or nurse."

The noise Dr. Cory made in the back of his throat didn't bode well for the direction the conversation was about to take, and David braced himself.

"Being a nurse practitioner is all well and good, but it certainly isn't the same as being a doctor."

"Of course it isn't." David tried to smile, but it probably looked more like a snarl. "In many ways it's better. The move we've made away from the 'cradle to grave' style of medicine, where a family doctor knows his patients over the long term, necessitates people like Nychelle. She can and does take the time to get to know the patients and their histories, without costing the same amount as a doctor would. Without her, and others like her, many more patients would fall through the cracks, or be diagnosed with diseases too late for the doctors to do anything for them."

Dr. Cory drew himself up to his full height. "It doesn't

change the fact that Nychelle has wasted the opportunity she had to excel in the medical field. If she wanted to be a clinician, then she should have gone to medical school and become a general practitioner. As a father, I find her choices untenable."

Taking a deep breath and a sip of his drink bought David enough time to control his close to boiling temper.

Once he was assured he wasn't about to say something he'd regret later, he replied, "Not to put too fine a point on it, sir, but it seems to me your daughter *has* excelled in the medical field. If she weren't the best of the best in her specialty I doubt Dr. Hamatty would have hired her, or given her the level of responsibility she has. I think most fathers would be ecstatic to have her as a daughter."

Silence fell between the three of them, leaving David to wonder if he'd totally overstepped the bounds of politeness the way he feared. Didn't the man know how lucky he was to have Nychelle? It was infuriating to see that Dr. Cory was so focused on his own wishes he couldn't even appreciate the joy of fatherhood, much less be proud of the wonderful woman Nychelle had grown into.

What David wouldn't give for the opportunity to see his daughter growing into a woman. He wouldn't care what career she chose, as long as she was a good and decent person like Nychelle.

He had the urge to look at Nychelle, to see if she was angry with him, but instead he kept his gaze fixed on her father, willing the stubborn man to concede at least that to his daughter.

"Hey, Nychelle. How are you?"

The interruption, caused by a tall, handsome, dark-skinned man, who bent to hug and kiss Nychelle before turning to shake Dr. Cory's hand, was welcomed—by David at least. Also by Nychelle, if her smile was any indication.

"Martin. I was wondering where you and Jennifer were." She turned to hug the short blonde woman who'd been a step behind the man. "Jennifer. Good to see you." Then she waved a hand in David's direction. "Have you two met Dr. David Warmington? David, this is my cousin, Dr. Martin Girvan, and his wife, Dr. Jennifer Howard."

"I do believe I have."

When Martin Girvan turned to shake David's hand, a big smile on his thin face, his eyes twinkling from behind thick glasses, David felt a trickle of recognition.

"The New York conference on the international transmission of vector-borne diseases."

"Yes, of course." David felt some of the tension ease from the back of his neck at the other man's warm reception and at the knowledge that, hopefully, the conversation he'd just been engaged in was now over. "Nice to see you again."

"And you." Martin threw an arm over his diminutive wife's shoulders and pulled her closer. "Jen, this is the doctor I told you about—the one who saved me from an uncomfortable situation with a rather tipsy gentleman in the hotel bar."

David laughed, remembering the incident in question. "I was just glad we were both able to get away unscathed."

"Are you working in Florida now? I remember you being elsewhere at the time…"

"I was in Chicago. Now I'm at the Lauderlakes clinic."

"Ah." Martin smiled. "Snapped up by Dr. Hamatty, eh? And I assume that's where you met Nychelle?"

All three of them—David, Martin and Jennifer—turned toward where Nychelle had been standing, but she was gone.

Looking over her cousin's shoulder, David saw her slipping out of the ballroom and with a quick, "Excuse me," went after her.

CHAPTER SEVEN

SHE SHOULD BE used to it by now, and in many ways she was, yet tonight her parents' attitude toward her and her work—her life—stung worse than ever.

For them to speak to and about her like that, in front of a man who not only was a stranger to them but also her colleague, had Nychelle seething in a maelstrom of anger and embarrassment.

As she made her way quickly through the hotel lobby toward the open terrace doors on the other side, she tried to unclench her fists and keep a pleasant expression on her face.

It was so hard.

Her father denigrated her so casually, as though nothing she'd worked for and achieved had any value. Oh, she knew it was what he thought—he'd made it known *ad nauseam*. But somehow tonight it had sounded worse than usual. Made her *feel* worse than usual. Not even reminding herself why she'd made the choices she had, and how close she was to fulfilling one of her most dearly held dreams, took away the hurt and sense of isolation.

Nychelle had long ago recognized her parents' seeming inability to offer any kind of affection, knowing their every thought regarding their children was focused solely on career paths and advancement. She wasn't built that way. Never had been. Oh, as a child she'd tried desperately to be what they wanted, constantly striving for perfection in the hope of getting positive attention from them. It had been soul-destroying—especially as she'd grown older and realized what they wanted her to be was vastly different from who she wanted to be.

Everything had changed when she was thirteen, and had been diagnosed with dysfunctional uterine bleeding. A D&C had been her final course of treatment, and the doctor had warned that conception might prove difficult later on, because of the scarring left on her uterus.

But it wasn't the diagnosis that had caused her change of perspective; it had been her mother's response to hearing it. Coldly and clinically, she'd expressed a kind of satisfaction. It was the perfect reason for Nychelle to concentrate completely on a career in medicine. There would be none of the potential stumbling blocks or distractions children often caused.

Nychelle shook her head, still unable to comprehend how such a well-regarded psychiatrist could have so little understanding of her own offspring. It was one of the universe's great mysteries.

Maneuvering around a cluster of people near the doors, she slipped past and out into the warm night air. The long terrace was dotted with folks, many of whom were familiar to Nychelle. Hopefully keeping her gaze distant and her steps brisk, as though she was on her way somewhere important, would deter anyone inclined to speak to her. She really needed a little solitude to get her temper under control.

Near the middle of the terrace, some steps led down to a boardwalk above the sand at the ocean's edge. Reaching them, she swerved to descend toward the beach, quickly leaving the lights of the patio behind as she went.

As soon as she was alone, she tilted her head back and released the sigh of anger and pain she'd been holding inside toward the full moon above, trying to let the sound of the water soothe her.

She'd tried so hard to get to a place of acceptance where her parents were concerned, but it was an ongoing battle—one she feared she'd never win and, as a result, often considered giving up on. They didn't even attempt to understand her—why should she bother trying to understand and be tolerant of them? They might be at the top of their fields professionally, but as parents they were, in her book, dismal failures. They'd let her down and embarrassed her once again.

It all made her want to pound her fists on the wooden railing in front of her, but instead she took a deep breath. As she exhaled she tried to relax, but the memory of her father's words kept digging at her, tightening her muscles.

Yet it also could be taken as another indication that she was doing the right thing. A sign that being married, or even in a long-term relationship before having children, was highly overrated. Her parents might have been married for almost thirty-five years, but they spoke to each other with the coolness of strangers. They treated their children as though they were ongoing work projects, rather than individuals whose particular talents and desires should be nurtured.

Once upon a time Nychelle had hoped to find a soul mate, a partner in every respect of the word, but having given her all to Nick, only to be completely betrayed, she'd given up that dream. No. She knew she had what it took to give her children everything they needed without any help. And if her parents ever tried to embarrass her children the way her father had just done to her, making someone else—virtually a stranger—feel it necessary to come to their defense…

She let out a little growl.

Thank goodness for Martin and Jennifer interrupting before her father had had a chance to answer David. Dr. Herman Cory, head of the world-renowned Maynard Heart Institute, wasn't used to being challenged and didn't like it one little bit. In fact, Nychelle would go so far as to say he hated it. And David had definitely thrown down the gauntlet.

A little smile broke through her anger at the memory. When last had anyone, even herself, stood up in defense of her life like that? She couldn't remember. It showed David wasn't intimidated by her parents, or out to worm his way into their good graces, and it made her like him all the more.

"I like you a lot, Nychelle, and I already think of you as a friend. But I have to be honest. Your dad is a piece of work."

The sound of David's voice was startling. She'd been so wrapped up in her thoughts she hadn't heard him approach, and she was too embarrassed to face him.

"That he is."

Trying to inject even a veneer of amusement into her voice was difficult, and she wasn't sure she'd managed it. Keeping her gaze fixed on the creamy disc of the moon rising over the water, she continued, "My parents are both overachievers and they raised my sister and me to be the same. It irks them that I went my own way rather than follow the path they planned out for me."

David's chuckle was warm, as was the hand he cupped over the curve of her shoulder. "I understand. In a strange way, although our situations are very different, they're also remarkably similar."

Oh, Dr. Heat was living up to his name, if the little licks of flaming awareness tickling over the skin of her arm were anything to go by. The attraction she felt was impossible to ignore, but she had to disregard it. For her own sanity, if nothing else.

Yet she was unable to resist the lure of his voice and, wanting to see his face, tilted her head to look at him over her shoulder. Even with just the glow of moonlight, she was effortlessly trapped by his gaze, and it was a struggle to ask, "How so?"

"I come from a poor family. The town where I grew up was once a thriving mining center, but steadily declined over the years. My parents expected me to learn a trade—preferably become a mechanic so I could eventually take over my father's shop. Imagine their shock when I decided I wanted to study medicine."

There was a flash of his abbreviated smile, but there was genuine sadness behind it.

"I was ten when I first mentioned it, and they were horrified. No one in my family had ever gone to college, much less to med school. I don't think they knew what to make of me. They still don't."

Dragging her gaze from his, she nodded, seeing the correlation—although to her mind it was tenuous. "I guess it all boils down to unmet expectations."

"Exactly."

His fingers tightened on her shoulder, just enough to bring her full awareness of them, and then relaxed.

"Our parents expected us to follow in their footsteps but we decided to forge our own course. None of them is comfortable with that, even though we're successful and, I think, we've both turned out okay."

"And not even, in my case, when they have another child happily following the life plan they laid out."

The spurt of annoyance she experienced as she spoke was swiftly swamped by the sensation of his fingers soothingly tracing along the skin of her upper arm. It was impossible to continue speaking, and she was glad when David replied so she didn't have to say anything more.

"Mine too." David chuckled again.

A shiver of desire raced up her spine, and she barely heard him continue.

"My sister, Mary-Elizabeth, works with my dad now, and my little brother, Donny, is just about to get his master mechanic's ticket. The family business is in good hands. But I want you to understand something..."

She waited for him to go on, trying to control the tremors fluttering in her belly. During the conversation he'd moved closer, and now his scent and heat, and the sheer sexiness of his voice, seemed to envelop her, ramping up the waves of arousal washing through her blood.

"I didn't say what I did to your father for any reason other than I believe every word."

His hand slid back up to her shoulder, and before she realized what he was planning he'd turned her to face him.

"You're an amazing person. You excel at your job and you make the clinic so much more efficient than it could ever be without you. On top of that, you make the entire place brighter just with your personality. Any father would be proud and happy to have such an incredible daughter. If your father can't appreciate how lucky he is, that's his loss."

Gratitude and something deeper, more intense, tightened her chest. His tone, matter-of-fact and sincere, made tears prickle behind her eyelids.

"Thank you."

It was little more than a whisper, and instinctively she

reached up to kiss his cheek, wanting to express in some tangible way how much she valued his words.

When her lips touched his skin, all the sounds of the party, the calling of the nocturnal frogs, even the wash and retreat of the waves faded. As though struck to stone, neither of them moved for a long moment, and then, with what sounded suspiciously like a curse, David turned his head and their mouths met.

A shock like hundreds of volts of electricity jolted through her at the first firm, delicious touch of his lips—and then everything stopped.

Her breath caught somewhere deep in her chest.

The racing of her heart stilled.

The world, the universe, seemed concentrated on that one stunning point of contact between them.

Then David was holding her, one hand on her nape, the other around her waist, pulling her close, and her body shuddered into hyperawareness, her heart galloping, breath rushing. With a light sweep his tongue requested entrance to her mouth and she opened for him instinctively, gladly. A rumble vibrated from his chest, through his lips and into hers, causing a cascade of sensation so intense Nychelle trembled from head to toe. Putting her arms around his neck was not only a way to get closer but also necessary to stop herself from melting into a puddle at his feet.

With each of her rushed inhalations came his scent, excitingly familiar and yet different, more intimate. Beneath her hands his shoulders flexed and, being held so close to his chest, she not only heard but felt the escalation of his breathing.

Need crashed through every cell of her body, bringing her nipples to tight, aching buds and causing yearning to bloom deep in her belly. It was more than mere craving. It was agonizing want, and it tore a gasp from her throat.

As though in response to that telling sound, David deepened the kiss. Nychelle pressed even closer, lost in the power of the desire building between them, which threatened to overwhelm her completely. David shifted, bringing one muscular thigh to rest between her legs, and as she felt his erection against her Nychelle arched into the contact, suddenly desperate for more—more of him, more of these out-of-control yet, oh, so decadent feelings.

His lips slid from hers, tracing a path along her jaw to the sensitive flesh below her ear.

"Nychelle..."

How had she never heard her name said that way before? As though it were the most beautiful word ever created? As though it were the code to unlock the door leading to every fantasy of fulfillment she'd ever had? Just the sound of it made her head fall back, baring her throat for the onslaught of his lips.

"Yes," he growled, before taking advantage of what she offered and kissing down the tendons straining in her neck.

"Ahhh..." A soft, moaning sigh broke from her as those firm, determined lips found her collarbone. Already she was anticipating them on her breasts, imagining the pleasure as he kissed lower, and then lower still.

A burst of laughter came from the terrace above, loud enough to break through the fiery bubble of lust they were cocooned in, and they both stiffened.

"I think the waiter said they only allow smoking at the end of the boardwalk, so if you want to smoke those stinky cigars that's where you'll have to go."

The woman's voice carried clearly through the night air, but it took a moment for Nychelle's befuddled mind to understand what she was saying.

Once she did, reality came crashing down, and she pushed David away as hard as she could.

* * *

Realizing they were about to have company, David cursed under his breath, and he had already started straightening when Nychelle's hands found his chest and gave him a hard shove. Stepping back, he held on to her long enough to make sure she didn't lose her balance, and then let go as though touching her burned his palms.

In truth, Nychelle had brought to life an inferno with her kisses. *Shocked* didn't begin to describe how he felt about the instant devastating arousal just the touch of her lips had created. The intensity of his desire for her had awoken something deep inside him. Awakened needs so long suppressed he'd thought they'd completely died.

And everything about the emotions coursing through his veins told him it was so right as to be completely wrong.

He couldn't afford to chance getting seriously involved again. The pain of losing Natalie and the destruction of his marriage as a result of that loss had left him damaged in a fundamental way. Desire was fine, but what he felt now seemed to go crazily beyond that into the danger zone.

He didn't want to take the chance of losing another child, so he'd long ago decided it was better not to put himself in a position where it might happen. He'd only just gotten to know Nychelle, but somehow, deep inside, he sensed she posed a threat to all the decisions he'd made about his life going forward.

They stared at each other, and she seemed poised to dash away.

Forcing a deep breath into his lungs, he gathered all the calm he could muster. He needed to get her back at arm's length.

"I suppose I should apologize."

He was proud of how cool he sounded, even with his heart still crashing against his ribs.

"It was an impulse—probably brought on by the moonlight."

Nychelle blinked, then looked up at the moon. "No, it was my fault for—"

"Look," he interrupted, not wanting to prolong what might turn into a painful conversation. "I think the best thing is for us to just pretend none of this happened."

He only just stopped a bitter bark of laughter from escaping. He'd suggested it, but in reality it would be easier to stop the moon from orbiting Earth than to forget the sensation of her body and her mouth, hot and eager, pressed to his.

"That's a good idea."

He heard her inhale and then let the air out with a *whoosh.*

"It shouldn't have happened. We work together. Situations like this can cause so many problems, make life difficult at the clinic, even threaten my career."

Her tone was brisk—the one she often used with patients or other members of staff. It wasn't offensive at all, but each time she used it David could hear her putting distance between herself and the person she was talking to.

He tried to tamp down his irritation at her eager acquiescence. Wasn't he the one who'd suggested they forget it?

Gritting his teeth at his own contrariness, he replied, "I completely understand what you mean. Too much of a risk for something as unimportant as one kiss shared in the moonlight."

He thought she tensed for a moment, but then she relaxed again before replying, "Exactly."

Desperate to bring some sort of normality back to their evening, he said the first thing that came into his still muddled head. “Glad to know my lunacy hasn’t chased you away.”

“Ha-ha-ha.” She brushed her hands over the front of her dress, as though making sure it hadn’t become disarrayed during their embrace. “So many studies say the supposed increase in incidents needing police or medical intervention during the full moon is just anecdotal, but when I worked in the ER it sure seemed real.”

“When I was doing my clinical residency in Chicago it seemed real to me too.” Unable to resist, he touched her arm, guiding her back toward the steps leading to the terrace. “There was always an increase in patients being admitted from the emergency room the day after a full moon.”

Near to the steps, and in the pool of light shining down from the terrace above, he paused. It felt wrong to leave things the way they were.

“By the way, I want to thank you again for agreeing to come with me tonight. Functions like this can be pretty awkward when you walk in alone.”

Nychelle glanced at him, and David suddenly wished he had a way to capture how amazing she looked bathed in moonlight, made mysterious and otherworldly by the attendant shadows. Not that he’d ever forget it. No, these moments they’d shared would definitely stick with him, he was sure.

“You’re welcome.” Her brows dipped together for a moment. “I meant it when I said you were doing me as much of a favor as I was you.”

There were shadows in her eyes, sadness in the set of her lips, and the memory of her mother’s lukewarm greeting and her father’s denial of her worth made anger spurt through him once more.

Why couldn’t they see how wonderful Nychelle truly was?

The impulse to see her smile again was irresistible, and without thinking it through he said, "Ha! Let's see if you still feel that way after I step on your toes a few times on the dance floor."

Her delicious giggle eased something in his belly, but he was kicking himself. So much for keeping her at arm's length… At least for tonight.

CHAPTER EIGHT

THE MONDAY AFTER the gala dawned clear and warm, a typically beautiful Florida day, but Nychelle had to drag herself out of bed. Yawning prodigiously, she contemplated whether to forgo her usual yoga workout. She thought she'd slept fairly well, once she'd actually got her brain to shut up long enough for her to doze off, but her bone-deep weariness seemed to indicate otherwise. Pushing herself to exercise seemed the right thing to do, and she felt somewhat revived by the time she got into her car to go to work.

Yet in the back of her mind the events of Saturday night kept swirling, just as they had all Sunday. It seemed as though her brain was caught in a loop, replaying the kiss she'd shared with David over and over. And every time she thought about it waves of hot and cold chased each other through her body.

Oh, she had no doubt he regretted it had happened; he'd made that crystal-clear with his reaction and the cold way he'd told her to forget it. That was good advice. She just wished she could follow it as easily as she'd agreed to do so.

Besides, she must have been crazy, giving in to his kisses like that. There was no room in her life for that kind of nonsense—especially with a man who seemed able to turn off his emotions so easily. Just because he hadn't made any attempt to impress her parents didn't mean she could trust him. Getting burned by Nick was more than enough embarrassment for one lifetime.

As she made the turn off the highway a couple blocks from the office she realized she was grinding her teeth, and forced herself to stop. By the end of the day the entire building would know she had gone to the gala with Dr. Heat. If she wanted to retain any sanity she was going to have to convince everyone they were just friends, even with the memory of his embrace refusing to go away.

After climbing out of the car at the office, she slammed the door closed a little harder than was strictly necessary.

Gina, of course, cornered her almost before Nychelle had a chance to put on her lab coat.

"You sneaky thing, you. I heard you were at the FMA gala with Dr. Heat. Why didn't you mention you were going on a date with him?"

Nychelle pulled her head out of the supply locker to give the other woman a bland look. "It wasn't a date—more of a mutual favor. He didn't have anyone to go with, and neither did I." Then she smiled, which at least came naturally. "You should have seen my mother's face when I walked in with him. That was definitely worth the price of admission."

Gina looked disappointed, but then perked up again almost immediately. "Did he make a pass at you?"

"Nah." Thank goodness she'd gone back to gathering the samples her office was low on, so Gina couldn't see her face. "He was a perfect gentleman."

The sound Gina made was filled with a mixture of disapproval and disappointment, and it made Nychelle snicker. Then the receptionist moved a little closer, and whispered, "That's crazy. Do you think he's gay?"

"What? No!" Nychelle glared at the other woman. "I'm

sure he isn't. It's just that..." She remembered how David had convinced her to go with him, and grabbed onto the words like a lifeline. "We work together. It was more like... um...carpooling than anything else."

"Huh." Gina tossed her head. "Well, I guess it's not a bad thing, really, that he behaved himself. But, *sheesh*, I'd have thought—"

"You're too much for me this morning, girl." Nychelle forced a laughing tone into her voice, thankful there were only a few more minutes before the clinic officially opened. "I've got to get going."

Gina glanced at her watch. "Gosh, yes. Me too."

Nychelle sighed as the receptionist walked away. Hopefully the rest of the day wasn't going to be more of the same.

It wasn't as bad as she'd expected—mainly because the clinic was so busy. Which was why she was so surprised to notice that all the appointments after three o'clock were gone from her schedule. When she buzzed through to the medical office assistant who handled her schedule she was told Dr. Hamatty's assistant had called down and asked for it to be done, and couldn't stop a little spurt of anxiety.

"Did she say why?"

"No, Nurse Cory. She just said there was to be a meeting at three Dr. H. wanted you involved in, and told me to clear you for the rest of the day."

Unusual, but she refused to get herself worked up until she knew there was a good reason for it. "Where's the meeting?"

"In your office."

The woman sounded harried, and Nychelle could hear phones ringing in the background. The questions flying around in her head would just have to wait, apparently.

"Okay, Marion. Has my next patient arrived yet?"

By two-forty-five her last patient had left and Nychelle had entered her notes into the records system, which gave her plenty of time before the meeting. More than enough to have her once more wondering what it was all about.

Encircling her right wrist with the fingers of her left hand, she convulsively twisted it back and forth—a nervous habit she'd had from when she was a young child. Why was she so on edge? Lauderlakes was a busy, vibrant place, and special projects and situations arose all the time. There really was no need to be this tense about an unexpected meeting, but she'd been as jumpy as a flea since the gala.

Telling herself it was because she would know within a few days whether the IUI had been successful or not didn't quell the nervous flutters in her stomach. Maybe because she was honest enough to admit that wasn't the entire reason.

She took a deep breath, trying to ease the rush of sensations firing through her body, but didn't succeed.

Despite not trusting him, she'd found herself building fantasies, both sexual and otherwise, around David when her entire attention should be on the future she was trying to create for herself. All her emotional energy needed to be focused on the life she hoped was growing inside her—not on a man who had clearly stated he wasn't interested in fatherhood.

Perhaps she was using him as a distraction—a way to not have to concentrate on Wednesday and the tests her obstetrician would have run by then. That was hopefully the day she'd start planning her life as a mother. She had no time to waste on David Warmington.

Luckily, she had no reason to see him very much going forward, other than in passing here at the clinic. After the kiss they'd shared, which neither had mentioned again once they'd gone back inside to the gala, he'd been the perfect gentleman. Polite. Polished. Amusing.

And subtly distant.

While she'd appreciated all the former attributes, that last one had stung. Which annoyed her no end. It was what she wanted, right? In fact, what she needed. It should have put her at ease, erased the heightened awareness she felt in his presence—not left her still shivery and aroused, flustered and unhappy. The unreasonableness of her reaction annoyed her even more.

It was definitely time to put all that behind her and concentrate on going forward the way she'd planned—including making sure her work here at the clinic was exemplary. This was a job she intended to keep for a very long time. Stability would be especially important when she became a single mother. In three months there'd be another free clinic, this time for adults, and because of the insane preparations necessary to make it a success the committee meetings started that evening.

Pulling up the list of first steps they'd compiled after much trial and error, Nychelle started going through it, making notes on what should be changed or adjusted. She was so immersed in her chore, it was only when the intercom buzzed that she realized it was already ten minutes past three.

"Yes, Marion?"

"Dr. Warmington is here for you, Nurse Cory."

What? David? Why?

Thankfully, professionalism was so deeply ingrained in her character she didn't say the words aloud, even though they'd risen into her suddenly dry throat.

Knowing her silence was on the verge of becoming ridiculous, she said, "Send him in, please, Marion."

David blew in through the door, giving Nychelle only

a couple of moments to gather her wits and arrange her expression into a mildly surprised one.

"Sorry I'm late," he said, as soon as he was in her office. "I just finished a meeting with Dr. Hamatty."

Her heart rate, which had jumped when she'd heard David's name, ramped up a little more, but she kept her response to, "Oh? What's going on?"

He glanced at his watch and, although she waved a hand toward the visitor's chair on the other side of her desk, stayed on his feet.

"He's requested that you and I handle an off-site intake. The patient flew in today by private jet from New York, and we need to meet with her, receive her records from the medical team who flew in with her, and do an evaluation."

"Okay." It was a little unusual, although not unheard of. Some of the patients Lauderlakes attracted were extremely wealthy, and demanded special attention. "Where are we seeing the patient and what time do we need to get there?"

David gave her the address, while looking at his watch again. "The medical team has to leave by four thirty to get back to the airport, and since I'm not that familiar with the area I think we should leave immediately. I can fill you in on the way there."

The clipped tone and the way he hardly even glanced at her gave her the sense that whatever friendship they might have developed had evaporated. She wasn't sure whether to be angry or relieved—wasn't even sure what the achy feeling growing in her chest could be. So she ignored it, storing it away for later consideration. If he wanted a cool, professional relationship that was exactly what he'd get.

Nychelle turned the address over in her mind. "That's in Las Olas. I know the way, so I may as well drive." Without waiting for his reply, she added, "That way you can concentrate on bringing me up to speed on the patient without having to keep your eyes on the road."

By the time she'd finished speaking she already had her phone in her hand and had dialed. David's lips parted, but she held up one hand to forestall him when she heard Marion answer.

"Hey, I'm heading out for an off-site intake. If anyone asks, let them know I'll be back in time for the committee meeting this evening."

As she hung up the receiver David said, "I can drive and talk at the same time."

At any other time the disgruntled tone would have made her smile. Just now, though, she felt anything but amused by him. She stood up and made tracks for the door, striding right past him without even a sideways look.

"No doubt—but I'm driving anyway."

Then she walked out of the office without another word.

David didn't bother to argue with Nychelle. He knew that expression all too well. It was the same bland, don't-mess-with-me look his mother often got when she put her foot down about something. It was probably wisest not to complain—not even about Nychelle's sedan being so small he was forced to push the passenger seat all the way back to get enough leg room. The atmosphere was frosty enough without risking another layer of ice being added.

It was what he'd aimed for, wasn't it? This impersonal, professional distance? He knew that after that kiss they'd shared, and the erotic dreams he'd had about her since, dialing back their relationship was imperative. So why did he have this intense need to get back on friendly terms?

Nychelle drove the same way she did everything else—with smooth, calm competence. Turning out of the clinic parking lot, she went east for a while, and then turned south on Highway US1. She didn't seem at all perturbed by the silence that had fallen between them, and David rubbed the back of his neck, wondering why it was bothering him so much.

He found himself searching for something to say—something that would make her smile, or at least start talking to him in that easy, cheerful way she had.

"I'm surprised you drive a stick shift."

As the words left his mouth he had to swallow a groan of disgust. His comment bordered on insulting, and Nychelle seemed to think so too, if her response was anything to go by.

"I'm not sure why." There was that cool, uninterested tone again. "Why don't you tell me about the patient?"

The snub was deserved, although it made heat spread uncomfortably across his nape and up into his scalp.

Opening the small laptop, he cleared his throat, hoping to sound normal and professional—not to mention as cool as she did—while he spoke. "Twenty-year-old female, Carmen Fitzpatrick. Hemoglobin SS Sickle Cell Disease."

"In crisis?"

"Had one—" David checked the notes "—four days ago. She's a musician and was just coming off tour when the crisis occurred."

"Ah. Now I realize why her name sounded familiar. That's Carmie-K."

Surprised, he looked over at her. "You know her?"

Nychelle shrugged. "Just her music. She sings a fusion of rap, reggae, blues and soul. It's not bad, actually. And, before you ask why someone my age listens to her, Martin's kids love her music, and, after hearing it first through them, I do too."

He'd just gotten over his first round of embarrassment

for the stick shift comment, and now she'd put him back on the spot.

"I'd never ask something like that."

Good grief, he sounded defensive even to his own ears, and Nychelle just pursed her lips, her gaze firmly on the road and the traffic around them, her expression both skeptical and annoyed.

He was racking his brain for an appropriate follow-up comment—one that would get him out of the doghouse—when she asked, "Did Dr. H mention why she was here in Fort Lauderdale? I got the impression that she lives in New York City."

While he was relieved at this return to business, David had to fight the urge to take the conversation back to a more personal level. He didn't want her thinking of him as some condescending idiot, but keeping the conversation on the patient was probably a good idea.

"She bought a house here a while back and planned to move here after the tour. I get the impression her hematologist in New York wasn't too happy about her making the trip, but she was determined."

Nychelle checked her rearview mirror before changing lanes. "Does she have a hematologist lined up here?"

"Yes. Dr. Yuen at Broward Health."

"And Lauderlakes is to be her primary health provider." It wasn't a question, but a statement. "Will she come in to the clinic after this, when she's feeling better, or will she want house calls going forward?"

"I don't know. That's something we'll have to discuss with her."

Nychelle had turned off US1 onto Las Olas Boulevard a while back. They'd passed a high-end commercial area, then gone over a bridge, and now she navigated a construction zone.

"She's notoriously private," she said in a thoughtful tone. "Leighann, Martin's daughter, is obsessed with Carmie-K but she's never said anything about her having sickle cell disease, so I don't think it's common knowledge. It would explain why she bought a house here, rather than in South Beach or Miami. Less chance of being stalked by the paparazzi."

"I wouldn't know about that." He was watching her profile, enjoying the opportunity to do so without it seeming weird. "Paparazzi are as far outside of my experience as traveling into space."

"Mine too, but I guess Carmie has to think about things like that. Remind me of the address."

She slowed down, and after reading it out to her David turned his attention to where they were going. One of the myriad canals that crisscrossed the city was on their left, and on their right were large houses, just visible behind high fences and verdant vegetation.

"Nice area," he said.

The houses were on what seemed to be a series of manmade peninsulas, separated by canals. Looking along the canals, he could see the backs of mansions with neat lawns flowing down to the water. Berthed behind most of the houses were boats of varying sizes—none of them dinghies, by any means.

"I didn't know this was here, but I haven't spent much time exploring the city."

"My parents live just down there."

She pointed to the road they were going past, and David looked. More mansions.

"Is it just the two of them?" Considering her parents' positions, he shouldn't be surprised, but he was. Part of him still found it difficult to reconcile what people had in comparison to what they needed. "Not to be rude, but

I don't see any small homes around here. Isn't it a lot of house for just two?"

"Yep."

She sent him a sideways glance, and he thought there was a glint of amusement in her eyes. Seeing it made his neck and shoulder muscles suddenly relax, although he hadn't been aware of how tight they'd become.

"It's rather wasted on them—especially since neither of my parents like the sea, so they don't own a boat." She chuckled. "Not that you have to have a boat when you live on the water, but it makes sense. No, that house is a show-place for visitors and a giant, fancy peapod for the two of them to rattle around in."

She'd turned onto one of the roads off Las Olas, and they both started looking at the house numbers to figure out which house they were going to.

"I think it's all the way at the end," she said. "That's where the biggest lots are. They were told we were coming?"

"Yes."

She'd been right about where the house was located. Once there, they were faced with a tall stucco wall with bougainvillea trailing over the top and an ornate metal gate. Pulling up close to a freestanding post with a speaker imbedded into it, Nychelle wound down her window and pressed the intercom button. When she told the man who answered who they were, the gate immediately began opening.

"Please follow the driveway to the right," the disembodied voice instructed. "Someone will meet you at the car park."

"Thank you," Nychelle called out, putting the car back into gear.

It was time to deal with their patient, but David resented the end of the trip. Despite Nychelle's initially cool attitude he'd enjoyed her company, as always, and they'd gotten back on a friendly footing. He didn't want that to fade away.

"By the way, your cousin Martin invited me to go out with him and his family next weekend."

Nychelle flicked him a sideways glance, then veered the car to the right, as instructed, and followed a brick-paved drive around the side of the huge Spanish-style house.

"They're lots of fun," she replied. "You should go."

Rounding the corner, she passed a fountain in the center of a wide paved area. Parking the car next to a high-end SUV, she turned off the ignition.

"Are you invited too?" he asked, trying to keep his voice light, although the tightness was back in his shoulders. "I mean, I hardly know Martin, so I figured he'd ask you to come along as well."

Swinging her legs out of the car, she replied, "Nope—and you'll be fine without me."

As he reached for his bag on the back seat David had to stop himself from arguing. And the fact he was supposed to be keeping his distance did nothing to alleviate his dissatisfaction when he thought about going without her.

CHAPTER NINE

CARMEN FITZPATRICK WAS as petite and pretty as she appeared on her album covers, but her *café au lait* skin was sallow, and a pair of wrinkles marred the spot between her eyebrows.

At first Nychelle thought the young woman was still in pain from her sickle cell crisis, but she soon realized at least part of her scowl was anger.

"I don't know what the fuss is all about," she said, as soon as David and Nychelle had been introduced. "Having you around is just a waste of time and money. I've been dealing with this since I was a child."

"Just stop your squawking." Milo LaMar, the man who'd met them outside and introduced himself as Carmen's manager, lowered himself onto one of the couches in the massive room and gave his artiste a glare. "You wanted to come down here, so we came. Making sure your health doesn't suffer because of the decision isn't a waste of anything."

Carmen snorted, matching his glower with a dagger stare from her dark, flashing eyes. "You're like an old woman, Milo. I'm fine."

They'd already received her medical records from the young doctor who'd flown in with her, and David had scanned them. Nychelle hung back slightly, letting him take the lead.

"Ms. Fitzpatrick, I'm glad you're feeling better, but your manager has a point." The young woman looked set to argue, but David smiled and held up his hand, forestalling her. "Most people recovering from a crisis wouldn't be traveling, much less going someplace where they don't already have a support system. We're here to make sure that whatever happens while you're in Florida will be dealt with as efficiently as it would be had you stayed in New York."

Carmen gave him a defiant look out of the corner of her eye. "I know what to do if a crisis comes on. I'm telling you—this isn't anything new to me."

"But living here is."

Nychelle liked the calm way David spoke: frankly, and not talking down to the patient.

Carmen gave a little head-toss. "I just need some peace and quiet. It's been a long few months. I just want to stay in one place for a while—preferably with no one coming by or wanting anything."

"Okay." David infused a little laughter into his voice. "We can take a hint, can't we, Nurse Cory? We'll get out of your hair as soon as we've given you a quick examination."

"We'll be gone in a flash," Nychelle agreed, handing David the medical bag. "Mr. LaMar, if you'd excuse us?"

Milo heaved his considerable bulk out of the sofa, then pointed a finger at Carmen. "Be nice. They're here to help you."

Carmen's rapid-fire spate of Spanish had Nychelle biting the inside of her lip to suppress slightly shocked laughter. The singer certainly knew how to get her point across in a colorful way, and Nychelle made sure not to look at David, in case his expression set her off.

Milo LaMar had warned them Carmen was feeling out

of sorts—"Just not herself since this last crisis," was the way he'd put it—and Nychelle made sure to pay special attention to the younger woman's sullen mood.

When David started asking her about her condition, Carmen lost control.

"*Yes*, I've been taking my hydroxyurea. And, yes, it's been working fine." She was almost shouting, tears making her eyes gleam. "I *told* you—I've been dealing with this for most of my life. I don't need a pep talk or you going over everything all over again."

"So what's different this time?"

David's quiet question cut through her tirade and Carmen sank back into the corner of the couch, turning her head away.

"Nothing. Nothing's different. It's just the same life-interrupting garbage I've had to deal with all along."

"So why are you so upset this time?"

The silence stretched between them and Nychelle found herself holding her breath, almost afraid to move in case it stopped the young woman from opening up.

"Life was going so well." It was a whisper. "It had been almost two years since I had a crisis. The tour was great. I finally had someone I was interested in…"

Her voice faded, and Nychelle felt her heart contract in sympathy.

"He couldn't handle seeing you in the midst of the crisis?"

"It wasn't that… Oh, forget it. You wouldn't understand."

Nychelle took a chance, and sat down next to Carmen. "Maybe *I* would," she said quietly. "You didn't tell him about the sickle cell, did you?"

Carmen drew in a shuddering breath. "No. I don't tell anyone I don't think has to know. I never wanted anyone to say, *Oh, there's that Carmie-K—the chick with the sickle cell disease*. I never wanted to have people thinking about that instead of my music. Besides, we weren't really serious yet. Just getting to know each other."

"I get it," Nychelle said softly. "I really do."

Carmen whipped her head around to give her a glare. "How could you? You don't have it, do you?"

"No." Nychelle shook her head. "I don't. But I do have a condition I'd need any man I'm thinking of having a long-term serious relationship with to know about. The question becomes when do I tell him? It's not a first date conversation. Not even second or third. It's something I wouldn't want anyone I'm not planning a future with to know. So, then I have to figure out when's the best time? And sometimes it's easier to just forget about it."

"Yeah." Carmen nodded, tears trickling down her cheeks. "Yeah, exactly." She sighed. "I haven't had time for guys or relationships before, so it never came up. Then I was feeling so well that everything else other than the SCD just kind of became more important. I didn't have to think about it—like you said, just take my meds and go on with life. Then…"

Nychelle touched Carmen's hand—just a fleeting contact on the young woman's tightly fisted fingers. "Then the disease butted in, when it was least wanted?"

Finding the right words was difficult, but there was no way to sugarcoat the situation, and she doubted Carmen would appreciate it if she tried.

Drawing on her own experience, she said, "It's never going to be easy—but you know that already, and you have to live your life the way you want to. That includes what you keep private and what you share with others. It's tough for you, because you're in the public eye, and I really don't have any advice on how you should deal with that."

Carmen sighed, then said, "Yeah, it's gotten harder to keep it secret."

"At some point it will probably be in your best interests to go public with it." David shrugged slightly when Carmen threw him a scowl in response to his matter-of-fact statement. "I'm no expert on the press or social media, believe me, but it seems to me they thrive on ferreting out people's secrets and making a big deal out of them. If you choose to put the news out there, then it won't have the same impact."

"That's what Milo's been saying for the last year."

Slumped in the corner of the couch, Carmen looked forlorn. Funny how because of her talent and her poise Nychelle had forgotten just how young she really was.

"I just don't want the stares and the fuss—or to have it overshadow the music."

"It might for a while." David gave one of his abbreviated smiles. "But Nychelle advises me that you have many dedicated fans, and I'm sure they'll just want more music, no matter what."

"You know my music?"

Carmen's expression was skeptical, and Nychelle chuckled. "Yeah, yeah—I know I'm old..."

Carmen's stuttering, embarrassed reply just made her laugh harder, and soon David and then, after a few seconds, Carmen joined in.

By the time they left the mansion Carmen seemed in a better frame of mind. As Nychelle drove back toward the clinic David stretched his legs out as far as possible and said, "I think that went well." Looking at her, he continued, "We make a good team."

"Just about now I should probably tell you I've been trained to work smoothly with every doctor I come in contact with." Her lips quirked in a mischievous smile, and there was a twinkle of laughter in the glance she sent him. "But we both know it doesn't always work out that way."

David chuckled, even as his thumb beat an anxious tattoo on his thigh. "Yes, that's true. I'm just glad we seem to click. I think you did a great job finding out what was going on with Carmen."

Nychelle put on her indicator and checked her mirrors. "You did too. So I guess you're right—we do make a pretty good team." She sighed. "I feel for her. It's hard having a disease that you know shortens your life expectancy as well as periodically completely disrupts your life."

"That's true—but sometimes you have to look at the positives too, right? Less than fifty years ago kids with sickle cell rarely lived past their early teens. That's not the case anymore."

"I know. I know… And the new bone marrow transplant treatment is promising. But not for her. She's an only child, and mixed race, so the chances of her finding a bone marrow match are miniscule."

He knew and admired many dedicated doctors and nurses, but Nychelle's seemingly unending well of knowledge and kindness was touching. Her remark about having a condition of her own had echoed in his head since she'd said it, and although it really was none of his business he had to ask.

Making his voice as casual as possible, he said, "You're a wonderful nurse, but I think your greatest asset is actually your empathy. Getting Carmen to talk by opening up about your own life is a good example of that." When Nychelle didn't say anything, he went on, "Were you telling the truth about having a medical condition?"

The car had stopped at a red light, but she didn't look

at him when she replied, "Yes. I wouldn't make up something like that."

Her long, elegant fingers gripped the gearstick hard enough to make her knuckles pale. He should leave it alone. But, try as he might, he couldn't contain his fascination with the woman beside him, who haunted him even when she wasn't around. He kept telling himself to stay clear, yet he couldn't resist the need to know everything he could ferret out about her.

"So, what kind of condition is it?"

Nychelle pursed her lips slightly as she put the vehicle in gear and started to drive through the intersection. Then she relaxed, and shot him an impish glance. "Are you telling me you want a long-term intimate relationship with me?"

Okay.

The word leaped into his throat and literally froze him to his seat. How easy it would be to say it. And mean it.

Okay.

His temperature rose as fantasies of being with Nychelle wound through his head. He imagined silly things, like sharing the Sunday paper in bed, or laughing at a corny joke with her, and it made his heart rate go through the roof. Visualizing other, more important things sent an exciting, erotically charged ache spreading through his veins. Listening to her. Holding her. Making love to her.

Seeing her grow round with their baby.

He clenched his teeth as fear shot like ice through his chest, banishing the arousing images. Then his heart clenched with a second jolt of terror.

Where had that thought come from? Why had it entered his head? Unless it was to remind him how dangerous it would be to get closer to Nychelle? He'd struggled these last few weeks, with memories of Natalie and the time after he'd lost her stronger than they'd been for a long time. Now guilt ate at him for even *thinking* such a thing.

David turned his head to stare, unseeing, out the side window, swallowing against the sour taste rising in his throat.

Nychelle snickered. "Ha! I didn't think so."

Suddenly tired, he battled competing emotions. Guilt and sorrow sat like molten iron in his belly, reminding him that he couldn't take another chance on love. He'd already had enough pain to last him a lifetime. There was no way he'd chance a repeat of the horrific agony he'd felt after losing Natalie. And yet his chest was tight with fear too.

Still looking out the window, unable to bear facing her, he asked, "Just tell me this then. Is it life-threatening? Your condition?"

"No," she replied, her tone subdued, as though his mood was affecting her. "No, nothing like that."

And for a moment, before he resolutely pulled himself together, relief made him literally weak. "Okay. Good. I'm glad to hear it."

CHAPTER TEN

NYCHELLE LEANED BACK in her office chair, her heart pounding a mile a minute, and pressed the cell phone tighter to her ear. She'd been as jumpy as a mouse at a cat convention all afternoon, waiting for a call from Dr. Miller's office. It had finally come, and now she was waiting for the doctor to pick up on her end. The canned instrumental music was no doubt meant to be soothing, but at that moment it was getting on her last nerve. Perhaps it was just as well the call had come now, when she'd been just about to leave the clinic. She was sure no matter what the news was there'd be tears involved.

These last few days she'd been on an emotional rollercoaster worse than any she'd ever experienced before. Normally she was good at compartmentalizing her life, keeping work, family and her personal business determinedly separate. That hadn't worked worth a damn these last forty-eight hours.

Tuesday morning she'd arrived at Lauderlakes and immediately looked for David's car in the staff parking lot. When she'd spotted the maroon Audi her heart had seemed about to jump straight out of her chest, and for the rest of the day she'd been on high alert.

It had been exhausting.

There was no good reason to be this het-up over him.

None at all. Surely it was her imagination that had her skin tingling every time she was around him?

The frequency of their encounters wasn't helping. From hardly being aware he existed, it seemed she couldn't avoid him, and now they were practically living in each other's pockets. Working together on Doug Comstock's case and then Carmen's, sitting on the planning committee for the next health fair—and, of course, going to the gala together.

Every time she thought about that night, and the kiss they'd shared, she shivered. Yet, there'd been no follow-up to that arousing encounter, so why couldn't she just forget it and move on?

David clearly had.

And she didn't want any follow-up, right? There was no place in her life for anything like that right now—*none*. Even if David was interested, which he obviously wasn't.

After she'd got home on Tuesday night she'd given herself another round of pep talks. She had really wished she could confide in Aliya, whom she knew would give her good advice. Unfortunately her cousin was also prone to saying, *I told you so*, and wouldn't hesitate to do so if Nychelle told her there was a man she was even slightly attracted to. That was the last thing Nychelle needed.

In fact, she'd thought, while putting together a salad she really hadn't wanted to eat, hearing those words at this particular time would no doubt make her burst into tears.

Nope. Didn't need it—any of it.

All she could realistically do was get over this attraction to David, because the alternative scenarios were too horrible to contemplate. If she continued to harbor these ridiculous longings they not only wouldn't be friends anymore, but even working with him would become impossible too. The problem was, she wasn't just in *lust* with him, she was…

Her mind had gone completely blank and she'd stared down at the greens she'd just tossed with sunflower seeds, cucumber and red peppers.

You're what, exactly, Nychelle?

Her brain hadn't been inclined to come up with an answer, shying away and contemplating instead what dressing to put on the salad.

In her mind she'd heard her mother's voice say, *Avoidance*, and she'd snorted with irritation. Bad enough to be in this situation, but imagining her mom analyzing her too was ridiculous. Worse was knowing her diagnosis was probably correct. She was ducking thinking about her growing feelings for David, so as not to take the soul-searching to its logical, and no doubt painful, conclusion.

Sitting at the island, she looked around her home, suddenly lonely in a way she'd never been before within its walls. All the contentment she'd felt just a few short weeks ago seemed to have fled, leaving hollowness behind. Yet she couldn't allow herself to continue this way. She'd made a choice, and it was a good one. *That* was what she needed to remind herself whenever she started thinking about David. *The Plan* was in motion and she had to focus on staying healthy, both physically and emotionally. To do the latter she would just have to keep Dr. Heat discreetly at arm's length. Not rebuff him altogether. That would be too obvious. Just enjoy his friendship and nothing more.

Telling herself that a thousand times had finally had her convinced she was being stupid. It wasn't David causing her emotional upheaval at all. No. Surely these absurd mood swings, the icy dips and somersaults of her stomach, had nothing to do with him. Stressing about him was just a way to escape thinking about whether the IUI had worked. No doubt the uncomfortable physical reactions were actually about waiting for the next round of tests. After all, which was more important? There was no contest. Being pregnant trumped anything David could offer.

Right?

The excitement of knowing today was the day she would find out whether the IUI had been successful had buoyed her up all through Wednesday morning. That and her new determination had even allowed her to smile and wave at David in passing, although she hadn't stopped to talk.

The joy of anticipation had lasted up until her dash to Dr. Miller's office at lunchtime, and then quickly faded as she'd waited, none too patiently, to hear from the doctor. Now her stomach fluttered and rolled with nervous dread.

"Come on. Come *on*," she muttered, her hand aching from the strength of her grip on the cell phone.

As if hearing Nychelle's entreaty, the phone clicked and the music stopped, to be replaced by Dr. Miller's voice.

"Nychelle. Sorry to keep you waiting."

And just from the other woman's tone Nychelle knew what the OB/GYN would say next.

David paused at the corridor leading to Nychelle's office, wondering if she was still at work or had already left for the day.

He really wanted to see her.

Which annoyed the hell out of him.

Equally annoying was knowing there was no way to avoid this encounter. Carmen Fitzpatrick's test results were back and they needed to confer. With them both being tasked with her care, a case conference was inevitable.

He could have sent a message, asking her to come to his office, but he'd put it off all day and finally, when he hadn't been able to avoid it anymore, he'd accessed the staff schedule online to see if she might still be around. According to that, her last patient had been forty-five minutes ago. Hopefully she was finished with the appointment, but maybe was still writing up her notes.

Decision made, he strode down the corridor, refusing to acknowledge the way his heart raced or the tension building at his nape. When he got to the waiting area outside of Nychelle's office he was glad to find just one medical assistant there, packing up her bag.

Lena looked up, and her eyebrows rose briefly in obvious surprise. "Dr. Warmington." She smiled, but it was a questioning smile rather than a friendly one. "What can I do for you?"

"Is Nurse Cory still around, Lena?" He held up the file in his hand.

The medical assistant's eyebrows dipped momentarily and she shot a quick glance at her watch as she replied, "She's still in her office, Doctor. Do you want me to ring through and ask if she's available?"

"That's okay."

At David's words Lena's hand fell back to her side, but not before she'd snuck another peek at her watch. Ah, yes. Lena was getting married in a few weeks. He remembered hearing her telling some of the nurses in the staff cafeteria.

Giving the woman a smile, he said, "You look like you have somewhere to be. Don't let me hold you up. I'll just knock and see if she has time to talk to me."

Lena grinned, her face lighting up as she grabbed her bag. "Thank you, Doctor. Have a good evening."

David watched her walk away, then stepped over to Nychelle's door. Hand poised to knock, he paused and took a deep breath, his heart rate going into overdrive. His reaction to her infuriated him, made him determined to, once and for all, get past it.

They were colleagues—nothing else.

They would never be anything else. He wouldn't let them be.

With another deep breath, he rapped on the door and then, responding to the muffled reply from inside, unlatched it and pushed it open.

Nychelle was looking out of the window when David stepped through the door, and something about her posture arrested his forward momentum. She was so still she hardly seemed to be breathing and, judging from her reflection in the glass, her usually expressive face was blank. The heat of his resolve bled away, was replaced by a cold spike of surprise.

"Nychelle?" He said her name softly as he stepped completely into the room and closed the door behind him.

She turned to look at him, but the movement was stiff and her eyes were blank, slightly glazed, as though with shock. Did she even know he was there?

It only took a couple of strides to get to her side, to reach out and touch her face. Warmth bloomed beneath his fingers as she leaned her cheek into his palm and closed her eyes. Her face relaxed, and the slight tilt of her lips was beatific. She'd never looked more beautiful, and David's heart stuttered.

He'd come into her office wanting to get her off his mind, to get over the crazy attraction he'd felt. Seeing her like that, leaning so trustingly into his hand, he realized it would probably never happen. If anything, his feelings would only deepen.

But giving in to them would lead him back down a path he refused to traverse again. Down that road lay the giving of his heart to another, risking the devastation he'd lived through once before and couldn't imagine surviving again.

The coldness in his belly flooded through him, invading his limbs, making his chest tighten almost sickeningly.

Yet although he wanted to step back, he forced himself to stay where he was, concern for Nychelle somehow still foremost in his mind.

Swallowing, he found the wherewithal to ask, "Nychelle, are you okay? What's happened?"

Her eyelids fluttered and then opened. The glow in her eyes made his heart contract again, but she just shook her head and stepped back. Disappointment making him frown, David let his hand fall back to his side, instead of using it to pull her close the way he wanted to.

"Don't shake your head at me." It was little better than a growl, but he couldn't stop the way annoyance had tightened his throat. "There's something going on. Tell me."

Her eyes widened momentarily, her eyebrows rising, no doubt at his demanding tone. Yet her voice was soft and calm when she replied, "I just got some good news." She lifted her hand, as though to forestall whatever he might say next. "I'm not going to share it. Sorry."

It wasn't his place to demand that she tell him, and he had no reason to believe she would feel inclined to tell him even if he did demand it, but he had to swallow again so as not to do exactly that. He scowled at her, torn, and for some reason that made her laugh.

"Thank you," she said, stepping back, still smiling.

"For what?"

She gave a little shrug. "For being here at this exact moment."

Confused, he shook his head. "Share your news and I'll celebrate with you."

With a chuckle she shook her head again, taking another step back as she did so. "I can't. But I'm happy you were the one I almost spilled the beans to."

The radiance of her face, the memories of the trusting way she'd leaned on him and the softness of her smile overcame all his defenses. Something inside him gave way, collapsed, and then was incinerated in a wave of desire so intense it was irresistible.

With a groan of surrender he stepped forward and drew her unresisting form into his embrace. Looking into her stunning eyes, he tried to pull himself back from the brink, but couldn't get his arms to release her, couldn't back away.

All good intentions fled as yearning for her overwhelmed him completely.

CHAPTER ELEVEN

SHE'D SEEN HIS eyes serious, and seen them smiling. Nychelle even thought she'd seen them hot with passion. But now she knew what she'd experienced the night of the gala had been little more than warmth, since now they blazed.

The joy and gratitude she'd felt on learning the IUI had been successful still swam in her veins, but now it was joined by a new kind of elation. One that sparked and zinged through every synapse, brought on by being held in David's arms.

An almost preternatural stillness fell; Nychelle couldn't move, couldn't breathe, and David seemed similarly afflicted. His face was frozen into an expression of such tender ferocity it caused tears to prickle the backs of her eyes. She'd never suspected how beautiful being looked at like that would make her feel, or how it would make her already powerful arousal spike to incendiary levels.

Which one of them moved first was an immaterial question, lost in the wonder of David's lips on hers, the passion of their kiss. He aligned their bodies so she fit snugly between his legs, and when his arms tightened around her Nychelle melted into him, bones and muscles going liquid with desire and pleasure.

From the hard length of his erection pressing against

her stomach there could be no doubt as to how much he wanted her. It was also in the tangle of their tongues, the way they devoured each other's mouths.

His strong hands slid down her back to grip her bottom and pull her even closer. The heat radiating from their bodies was a physical manifestation of the need flowing like lava between them. The want.

There was no hesitation in their embrace. The way he held her was masterful, compelling, and she loved it. She'd never felt delicate or treasured in a man's arms before, but somehow in David's she did.

A sound of passion broke from his throat, and the ache that had been building in her nipples, between her legs, intensified and became almost unbearable. And when his mouth left hers to slide down to her throat she gasped, echoing his delight. Finding the hem of her tunic top, he slid his hands beneath to find the bare skin of her back, causing her to arch, to rub against him, wanton under the spell of his lovemaking.

"Nychelle…"

It was a growl against her neck, causing a delicious shiver to climb her spine and bringing a little spasm of pleasure.

"So beautiful. So sexy."

She'd have said the same about him, but words deserted her as his lips kissed and sucked with glorious effect along her skin. When his hands slid to her sides, his thumbs lightly caressing the curves of her breasts, she was already trembling, longing for even deeper contact. His mouth moved lower, to the sensitive curve where neck met shoulder, and she whispered a plea, arching to offer him her breasts, almost sobbing with relief when his palm brushed one nipple through her bra.

Strong, tender fingers closed around her breast, caressing it, and his thumb rubbed back and forth across the straining peak. She worked at pulling his shirt from his pants then opening it, wanting skin-to-skin contact. He followed her lead, unbuttoning her tunic and pushing the edges aside. When he undid the front closure of her bra it crossed her mind that she'd never felt this aroused, especially this quickly, but the thought was lost in a burst of ecstasy when his lips closed around one oversensitized nipple. The draw of his mouth and the damp sweep of his tongue had her crying out softly, the pleasure almost too much to bear.

"David!"

"Yes," he replied, causing cool air to rush over her flesh, bringing another, stronger tremor between her legs.

Had she ever been this close to orgasm without a touch there? She didn't think so. The craving grew, had her pressing against him, ready and willing for whatever came next, wanting more and more.

He knew. How could he not know when she was being so blatant? Somehow one of his legs had made its way between hers and she rocked against it, getting closer and closer to coming with each undulation of her hips.

"God..." It was a groan against her skin, and the vibrations traveled from his lips into her, driving her higher. "I have to—"

David picked her up as though she weighed nothing at all. With a few long strides they were at the desk, and when he lowered her to sit on it Nychelle wrapped her legs around his waist.

The opening notes of a nineties rap song reverberated through the room, the sound so jarring they both jumped.

They froze as the cellphone ring tone stopped for an instant. When it started again David stepped back so quickly Nychelle rocked in place, almost sliding from the desk.

Their gazes collided, and in his expression Nychelle read the same shock she knew was mirrored on her face.

Tugging her tunic closed with one hand, she reached unthinkingly for the phone with the other. When David turned away and began buttoning his shirt she went cold with remorse—and something deeper. Sadder. The ringing phone had broken a beautiful erotic spell. One that should never have been cast.

Taking a shuddering inhalation, she looked away, so he wouldn't see the threatening tears.

"Hey, Nychelle, what's going on?"

Martin's voice made her realize she'd actually answered the phone, but it took her a moment to gather herself and reply. "N…nothing much."

"Is this a bad time? You sound like you're busy."

Probably because she was holding the phone between her shoulder and chin while fumbling to refasten her bra. "No, it's fine. What's up?"

"I just texted David Warmington, reminding him about my invitation to go out with the family this coming weekend, and I want you to come too. After all, he and I only met briefly once, before the gala. It'll be good for him to have someone there he knows a little better."

Hearing his name made her automatically look toward David. Luckily he still had his back to her, but watching him straighten his clothing made her icy veins heat through.

She quickly looked away. "I… I don't think…"

"Aw, come on, cuz." Martin was using his wheedling voice—the one he knew she found hard to resist. "We've hardly seen you over the last few months. Leighann and MJ keep asking when you'll be by."

"Let me get back to you on that, okay?"

She'd finally got her tunic buttoned, but felt as if her

bra was crooked. Even being fully dressed didn't mitigate her deep discomfort. What the heck were they thinking, making out like teenagers on her desk? What the heck was *she* thinking, especially after the news she'd just received about her pregnancy?

"I have some things I have to take care of before I can make a decision."

Things like making sure David Warmington agreed that what had just happened had been a huge mistake and wouldn't happen again.

No matter how much she wished it would.

His insides swirling with a mixture of arousal, surprise and self-recrimination, David moved over to the window in Nychelle's office and stood looking out, trying to ignore the soft murmur of her voice.

He wanted to leave—just take off without saying anything—but that would be the coward's way out. Nychelle deserved better.

And that was the whole truth of it. Nychelle deserved the very best life had to offer—everything a man had to give—and he didn't have everything to give anymore. There was an important part of his heart and soul that was dead, killed by grief and fear. Or at the very least was locked away where no one could ever reach. Not even someone as amazing as Nychelle.

And there was no way to explain that without exposing his pain, ripping away the thin scab over his wounds. As much as he wanted to crush whatever it was building between them once and for all, he wanted her sympathy even less. No. Best to simply pretend, once more, that it didn't matter, and then make himself believe it didn't.

But, either way, he had to put a stop to this…this…

His brain stumbled, unable or unwilling to find the appropriate word for the emotions and impulses that overcame him whenever Nychelle was near. All he knew was that they had to stop.

The room was silent, and he realized she must have finished her call and hung up. He made his expression as stoic as he could, then turned to face her. Before he could speak she held up her hands, as though ready to push anything he said back at him.

"Don't." She shook her head, her lips wavering into something that he figured was supposed to be a smile. "There's no need to say it."

Perversely, now it appeared she was thinking along the same lines as he was, he had the sudden urge not to just let it go.

"Say what?"

"That what just happened was a mistake. Believe me, I agree wholeheartedly." She straightened, taking on an air of dignity and resolve. "I'm not in the habit of leading men on. I'm also not in the habit of having casual sex." She shrugged slightly before she added, "And that's all I could offer you—sex that, even casual, could have unwanted repercussions for us both."

He wasn't sure what "repercussions" she was worried about for herself, but knew what he needed to avoid. It would be so easy to fall for Nychelle, to begin craving her love…

Spinning on his heel, he bent down to retrieve the folder, which he'd dropped in his eagerness to get closer to Nychelle. He really needed to get away—to think about what had happened. Being around Nychelle twisted his emotions into crazy knots and he needed to unravel them, to figure out exactly what to do. Yet it felt wrong. As though there was more that should be said.

Before he could figure it out she slid off the desk and

glanced down at the file in his hand. "So, did you want to talk to me about a patient?"

Just like that the sensation of sharing something special vanished, leaving him strangely flat. When she circled her desk, staying as far away as possible, the small act of avoidance made his chest ache.

"Yes." He opened the file, gathering his composure. "Carmen's tests are back."

"Anything unusual?"

"Her iron levels are elevated. Not unusual in someone who just underwent a transfusion, but something I'd suggest we keep an eye on."

Nychelle sat in her chair and pulled it close to the desk, as though to put a physical barrier between them. "If you leave the results with me, I'll forward them to the hematologist and make sure our notes are up to date."

She was rubbing her right wrist, and he took an impulsive step forward. "Are you hurt? Did I hurt you?" Just the thought made him angry.

"What? No. Why do you ask?"

"You're rubbing your wrist." He remembered seeing her do it before, but this time it worried him. Reaching the desk, he held out his hand to her. "Let me see."

Immediately she stopped, dropping her hands to her lap. "It's fine, David."

The snappish reply brought him up short. He wasn't used to that from her.

"It's just a nervous habit from when I was a child. I broke my wrist one summer, and got used to rubbing it after the cast came off, when it ached. Nothing to worry about."

Somehow hearing her admit to her own disquiet made his dissipate slightly, and he nodded. "Fair enough."

Their eyes met, and the confusion in her gaze made

that stupid ache in his chest expand. He wanted to comfort her, even as he acknowledged that it was the worst thing he could possibly do.

She looked away, down at the file in his hand, and nodded toward the desk. "Leave it with me and I'll deal with it."

"Thank you." He set the file on her desk and without another word made his feet take him toward the door, even though they were inclined to stay exactly where they were.

"David?"

The soft sound of his name on her lips froze him in place, his hand grasping the door handle but not unlatching it. He didn't turn, fearing looking at her, and felt the desire still thrumming through his veins despite it all. "Yes?"

"That was Martin on the phone. He's invited me to come along this weekend."

"I haven't had a chance to say yes or no myself," he replied. His knuckles were turning white from his tight grip on the handle. "If you don't want to go, or don't want *me* to go—"

"No, it's not that. It's just…"

"You want to make sure it won't be awkward?" Risking a glance back at her, he forced a small smile. "I can handle it. Can you?"

"Yes. Of course." She neither looked nor sounded convinced. "It'll be…fun."

"Okay." He opened the door and lifted his hand in farewell, eager to leave before he gave in to the impulse to ask her what she'd *really* wanted to say. "See you then, if not before."

But he hoped it wasn't before. He wanted as much time as possible to exorcize his growing need and the agonizing desire he felt for Nychelle. Time to figure out how he could keep her friendship without losing his heart in the process.

CHAPTER TWELVE

"PINK EYE?" NYCHELLE plopped down onto her kitchen stool. "MJ has pink eye?"

"Can you dig it?" Martin sounded harassed and annoyed. "Woke up with it this morning—on the first day of summer vacation, to boot."

"Oh, no. What about Leighann?"

"So far, so good, and we're doing everything we can to stop her from contracting it. Jennifer's been running around with antiseptic wipes all morning. Martin Tremaine Girvan Junior!" Martin suddenly shouted, the bellow only slightly muffled by what Nychelle suspected was him pointing the phone at his son. "Do. Not. Scratch. Your. Eye. Mom will be back in a minute with some drops to make it stop itching."

Nychelle chuckled, suppressing it when he said, "He's driving us crazy—alternately whining, rubbing his eye, and threatening to infect his sister. We're supposed to be going on vacation in ten days, but if Leighann gets it we may have to cancel."

"Hopefully that won't happen."

"From your lips to God's ear," Martin grumbled. "Just coordinating a vacation with our schedules is hard enough. And, speaking of canceling, I was planning to take you and David out on the boat today, but I can't risk taking

MJ anywhere. Not fair to leave Jen here to suffer by herself either."

Nychelle stared out the window, biting her lip as a combination of disappointment and relief swirled through her. "Well, it can't be helped. Taking care of your family is the most important thing. We'll go out another time."

"I don't want to disappoint David."

There were a few more moments of muffled shouting, and Nychelle figured the phone was clasped to her cousin's chest this time, so she wouldn't hear the threats he was making to his son.

"Sorry about that. This boy is a menace."

"He's eight. What do you expect? At that age you were a pain too."

"I was not."

Nychelle chuckled at his lofty tone.

"I was a perfect little paragon. All right. All *right*." He interrupted her laughter to get back to what he was saying. "We can't go out on the boat, but I went ahead and bought two tickets for you guys to take the river taxi. It'll be a good way for you to show David more of the city without having to think about parking."

"I'm sure he won't mind if you have to cancel—"

"I already talked to him and told him you were willing to go."

"What? Without talking to me first?"

Martin obviously wasn't listening to her. If he had been he surely would have heard the outrage in her voice and put even a hint of remorse into his reply. Instead, he just said, "I knew you wouldn't mind. I'll email you the tickets, and he'll come to pick you up at ten."

Nychelle clenched her teeth to hold back her instinctive refusal. Would she never get away from this man? Well, maybe that was too harsh. David was the one man she both craved and was afraid to be around. How many times had she decided it would be best to avoid him, only to end up in his presence almost immediately thereafter?

"It'll be fun." Ironic to have Martin quoting her own words back at her. "He seems like a nice guy. Don't you think so?"

"Yes, he's a nice guy." Resigned to her fate, she sighed. "It's fine. Take care of the family."

"Awesome. Thanks, Nych. Call me later and let me know how it goes."

"Okay. Will do."

Almost before she'd finished speaking Martin was hollering at MJ again as he hung up.

Putting the phone down on the counter, Nychelle rubbed her suddenly aching temple.

Two days before, she'd finally given in to the need to speak to someone about David and told Aliya what had happened between them.

"The timing isn't optimal," her cousin had said. "But I guess the real question is, what do you want to do about it?"

"I don't know," Nychelle had confessed, tears welling. "I'm confused."

For two people who claimed to want to be friends, David and she constantly seemed willing—no, determined to put strain on their relationship. Making out like teenagers. Blowing hot and cold. Hiding from each other instead of coming clean.

Well, okay, that last one was all her. And, while she'd agreed that it would be wise for them both to forget what had happened in her office, she found herself thinking and dreaming about making love with David all the time. Then getting angry with herself.

Since meeting him she'd been a mass of contradictions and seesawing emotions.

Which was why she knew she had to stop seeing him.

"You have feelings for him." Aliya hadn't asked, simply stated it as a fact. "I know you, and you wouldn't have been making out with him if you didn't."

"I—" She'd wanted to disagree, but the lie wouldn't pass her lips. Instead she'd concentrated on not sniffling, hoping Aliya wouldn't realize she was crying.

"Don't tell me you don't. I won't believe you." Then her cousin's voice had softened. "Listen, best-case scenario is he has feelings for you too, and won't care that you're pregnant. Worst-case is that he does care, and his feelings aren't strong enough for him to see past it. But the only way you're going to know what will happen…"

"Is for me to tell him." Abandoning her attempt to hide her tears from her cousin, Nychelle had blown her nose. "I know I should—but it's all happened so suddenly. It feels as though I'm making more out of the situation than I should."

"Have the conversation, Nych. Whichever way it goes, at least you'll know."

Aliya was right, of course.

Now restless, Nychelle got up and wandered over to the sliding glass door. Looking out at the verdant greenery in her backyard usually calmed her, but today it didn't. In less than half an hour she'd be thrown into David's company again. Just thinking about it made her body tighten and heat. No other man had ever had this effect on her—not even Nick, who she'd thought was her forever guy. Despite telling herself it was hormones, deep down she knew it wasn't. This attraction was too intense, too multifaceted to dismiss.

If it had just been the physical attraction, she probably

could have ignored it, but what she couldn't disregard was how deeply she liked and admired him too. Long gone were her fears about his character. Everything she'd seen about him told her he was trustworthy, and a genuinely wonderful man. It wouldn't take much to push her over into falling for him completely.

So, yes, she was going to have to deal with it…

But not today.

This chance to spend time with him was, in a way, a gift. She was going to take advantage of the opportunity to simply take pleasure in his company without strings or overanalyzing.

It'll be a last hurrah.

The decision was calming, soothing, giving her permission to enjoy the day without giving too much weight to what would happen next.

Buoyed by that thought, she went to finish getting ready, excitement tingling over her skin.

David glanced over at Nychelle as he steered the car into the river cruise parking structure. She looked relaxed, and that made his trepidation wane.

Bearing in mind their encounter in her office, he hadn't known what to expect, and when Martin had explained the situation his first impulse had been to suggest they postpone their outing until the whole family could go. But Martin had insisted Nychelle was expecting him, and David hadn't wanted to sound churlish, or make a big deal out of it when she obviously didn't care.

There had been a hint of tension in the air, but after a slightly stiff greeting at her door it had mostly dissipated.

"The riverfront area is nice to walk through. Good restaurants and shopping, if you're into that kind of thing."

She'd been acting like a tour guide, pointing out various places of interest, like the Broward Center for the Performing Arts and the Museum of Discovery and Science, along with a Jamaican restaurant she said was amazing.

While he parked in an empty space she continued, "I prefer to go there when it's a little cooler. Somehow the heat isn't as bad when you're on the water."

She didn't wait for him to open her door, but got out immediately and, closing the door with a firm snap, gestured toward the exit.

"Let's go find us a water taxi."

When he rounded the back of the car she'd started walking, but then suddenly she stopped and turned to face him.

"Listen," she said. "I know we should talk about what happened between us. It's the adult thing to do. But can we shelve it for now and just enjoy the day?" Her hands fluttered between them. "I just need some more time to get things straight in my head, okay?"

He should be thankful—and a part of him was. Rubbing the back of his neck, he once more contemplated just how confused and contradictory his feelings were when it came to her. Even though he'd repeatedly told himself the best thing they could do was pretend none of it had happened and maintain the status quo, the urge to push, to find out exactly what she was thinking, was strong.

Yet this was an opportunity to simply be with her, without worrying about what his emotions meant or what to do about them. So, accepting her request to put it all aside for the day, he nodded. "Okay. So where do we go from here?"

Nychelle looked around, choosing to ignore the less literal interpretation of his words.

"This way," she said, pointing down a pathway.

"Do we need to buy tickets?" David asked as they approached the riverside restaurant where apparently they'd board the taxi.

"No, Martin got them online and I printed the vouchers. I thought about booking one of the guided tours," she told him, leading him into the restaurant. "But this way we can get off and on the taxis whenever we want, without being tied down to a specific route."

"Wow, this place is…colorful." David looked at the ceiling, where all manner of nautical gear and beach-themed tchotchkes hung.

A large wooden mermaid caught his attention. When he raised his eyebrows at her suggestive pose, Nychelle giggled.

"It's a true tourist spot," she told him, petting a plastic parrot with an eye patch and still chuckling. "But although some these things are just kitsch, many things are real equipment used on boats in the past."

David smiled at that, his mood lightening even more with her laughter. "You don't have to tell me." Pointing at his chest, he went on, "South Carolinian, remember? I recognize the glass fishing globes and old-school breathing apparatus."

"Darn it." She added a pout to her disgruntled tone. "You're spoiling my tour guide spiel!"

"Okay, I won't say another word."

David mimed zipping and locking his lips, then throwing away the key. It was silly, and not something he'd usually do unless he was around his family, who knew and understood his lighter side, but it felt natural to show this aspect of himself to Nychelle.

"You nut."

Nychelle swatted him on the arm, and he hoped their easy camaraderie would last for the whole day. It felt so right.

"Do you want a drink before the taxi comes?" she asked.

"Mmph-mmm-hmm-mmm." Keeping his lips pressed

together was hard, with a grin trying its best to break through, and when Nychelle swatted him again David couldn't hold back his laughter. "Hey, I promised not to say another word."

"Oh, you…*you*…"

"Careful, Nurse Cory." He gave her a stern look, knowing his twitching lips gave away his amusement. "Let's not sully that sweet, professional disposition everyone talks about."

"Ha!" Turning up her nose, she replied, "At least no one at work calls me names like *Dr. Heat.*"

"Argh!" He was still smiling, but embarrassment made warmth spread across his face. "One of the other doctors told me about that and I thought he was kidding."

"Nope." She was giggling so hard she could barely get the word out, and she took a couple of hitched breaths before she continued. "In the nurses' lounge it's all, 'Dr. Heat said this…' and 'Dr. Heat is so dreamy…' It's a wonder your ears don't burn all day long."

"Now you're just being a brat." He lifted her hand and nipped the knuckle of her index finger. "Stop that."

"Ow." She pouted again, and tried to pull away. "Just because you don't appreciate being sexualized it doesn't mean you can be nasty when it's pointed out."

"'Sexualized?'" He groaned dramatically. "That's what I get for going out with a psychiatrist's daughter? Big words and overanalyzing?"

She opened her mouth, as though to make a scathing rebuttal, but instead broke out in giggles again.

David couldn't maintain his air of indignation either, and soon cracked under the strain of their combined silliness—so much so that when the water taxi drew up to the dock they practically reeled toward it, rather than walked.

The crew member who checked their vouchers grinned at them. "You folks look like you're already enjoying the day."

"It's a gorgeous one," Nychelle replied, and David nodded his agreement.

Watching her face, her brilliant smile, had him thinking the perfect, cloudless day was nowhere near as beautiful as she was.

They made their way to one of the seats in the shade, near the bow, and he settled onto the padded bench beside her, appreciating the breeze coming off the water. Around them the boat filled up, a cacophony of diverse languages filling the air as different groups came aboard.

"Do many locals use the river taxis?" he asked.

"Not really," Nychelle replied. "It's more of a tourist thing—although bar-hopping along the waterfront using the taxis as transportation can be fun. It's easier than trying to find parking if you want to go to the beach too." She chuckled and shook her head. "But most people are so used to driving they don't remember it's available."

David tipped his head back to catch more of the breeze. "The tourists have it right. I'd rather do this than drive in circles looking for a parking space."

"Me too." Nychelle was still smiling. "There's always a little wind to stir the air when you're on the water, so it really is a nice way to travel. Far nicer than being in an air-conditioned car."

"Ha!" He snorted. "Don't knock the air-conditioning. I've really come to love Florida, but the heat and humidity takes some getting used to."

"I'm sure it does," she replied. "Especially after being in Chicago."

As they chatted about the hazards of winter, and how different it was in the south, the boat pulled away from the dock and the captain set a leisurely course down the New River.

"Have you convinced your parents to come visit yet?" Nychelle turned sideways on the seat, so she was facing him to ask the question.

"Not yet." He gazed toward the north shore, his amusement waning. "I've got my sister working on them too." Thinking about his no-nonsense little sister made him smile again. "Of course, Mary-Liz says if they won't come she and the kids would be happy to take their place."

"Of course!" Nychelle chuckled, shifting to put her arm up on the bench cushion behind her. "Why don't your parents want to come?"

Again, not something he'd usually discuss, but talking to her was so easy. "They haven't traveled much, and just thinking about navigating through airports makes my mom break out in hives." She nodded, and he liked it that she showed no amusement about their fears. He continued, "Dad would never admit that's the case with him too, but he doesn't have to. I know the truth."

Glancing down at the hand lying casually in her lap, he wished he had the right to take it and hold it. Instead he looked out over the water again.

"He has heart problems, and I'm a little worried the strain may bring on an angina attack, so I'm not pushing too hard."

As though reading his mind, Nychelle gave his hand a quick squeeze. When she let go, he immediately missed the contact.

"Have you thought about going up and then having them fly back with you? Or, if they really don't want to fly, driving them down? It's about nine hours from Atlanta to here. How long a drive would it be from where they live?"

Emotion rushed warm and sweet through his chest and he couldn't help staring at her as he replied, "About the same."

Nychelle lifted a hand to smooth her hair, the gesture uncertain. "Why are you looking at me that way?"

"Why didn't *I* think of that?" He shook his head. Then, throwing caution to the wind, he reached out to thread his fingers through hers, and was ridiculously happy when she didn't tug her hand away. "You're incredible."

"Don't be silly." She dipped her head, as though shy, and the warmth in his chest spread out into his belly. "You would have thought of it sooner or later."

"Probably not," he replied, tightening his grip on her hand when she gently tried to pull it free. She stilled. "It's the kind of solution only someone with a completely empathetic soul would come up with straight off the bat."

She looked at him and said quickly, "By the way, keep an eye out for manatees. They're the reason the boat has to go so slowly, and every now and then you'll see a tail pop up out of the water."

"Okay," he replied, but his gaze never left her face and he felt no inclination to look away.

CHAPTER THIRTEEN

DAVID KEPT STARING, and Nychelle was the one who looked away first. It felt as though something important had just happened, yet she didn't know what. Rushing to speak, she tried for a much less intimate subject, hoping to curtail the tension flowing between them.

"By the way, while I remember, our patient Carmen Fitzpatrick released a statement to the media about having sickle cell disease."

"Really?" There was genuine surprise in his voice, and when she looked at him his eyebrows were raised. "I thought she was fanatical about her privacy?"

"She always has been, but maybe she decided it was better to do it when she wanted to, rather than have someone dig it up and blindside her—like you and her manager said might happen."

"Hmm." Leaning back, still staring intently at her, he asked, "How did you find out?"

"Martin's daughter, Leighann, told me. Once the news broke she looked up the disease and had questions." Nychelle shook her head. "Her parents are both doctors but she called me for information and to discuss it. Go figure."

"She probably knows you'll give it to her straight. Besides, you're both fans, so it makes sense to talk to you about it rather than her parents."

"I guess..."

She feigned interest in the passing scenery and pushed her sunglasses farther up her nose, still a little shaken by the strangely intimate moment they'd just shared. This man could upset her equilibrium like no one ever had before. The way he watched her, whether smiling or, like just now, with that serious, searching expression, just made her shiver.

Lost in thought, she was a little surprised when he reverted to their previous conversation.

"So, how do you know how long it takes to drive to Atlanta? Do you go there often?"

"A few times a year, usually, since my cousin Aliya—Martin's little sister—moved there four years ago. I don't always drive, but sometimes I just like the idea of a road trip."

"You're close?"

"Best friends practically since we were born." She smiled at the thought of Aliya and her craziness, and her excitement at the thought of being an honorary auntie. "We spent all our time at each other's houses...went to school together. Our families even migrated at the same time, so it was only when we went to college that we were first really apart."

"Don't tell me—she's a doctor too?"

Nychelle nodded. "Uh-huh. An hematologist-oncologist, specializing in research into childhood hematological cancers and the effect of known cancer treatments on kids."

David's lips quirked. "You really *do* come from a family of overachievers, don't you?"

Nychelle gave him a grin. "You know it."

The boat had already stopped a couple of times to pick up passengers and was now once more edging toward shore.

"Ooh," she said, pointing, hoping to distract him. "That's the Stranahan House Museum. It's reputed to be haunted and they sometimes have ghost tours, including a nighttime boat ride."

David seemed less interested in the historic house than he was in her life, though.

"Why was it that you decided not to become a doctor too? It seems as though it's a family tradition."

She hesitated, torn between complete honesty and a slightly less revealing version of the truth. Today wasn't the day to get too deep, she reminded herself.

Just keep it light.

"Overachieving requires a singularity of focus I've never truly been interested in. I wanted to have a life outside of work. Have room for days like today, when there's nothing more pressing than drifting down a river, having a laugh or two."

He leaned back against the cushions and even with his dark glasses in place she knew he was subjecting her to another of his intent stares. It caused little prickles of awareness to tiptoe along her spine.

"But I'm a doctor, and I'm here drifting down the river too."

"Sure." She nodded. "But how old were you when you finished your residency?"

"Thirty," he replied.

"There you go." She waved a hand for emphasis. "I'm not quite thirty yet, and I've been out of school and living my life for a while—whereas I'm sure you've had to put off a lot of stuff, make a lot of sacrifices, to get to where you are now. I've been able to do some traveling, save up for a house and advance my career, all within the frame of time it took you to graduate. That's what I wanted, rather than MD after my name. Aliya is brilliant—she graduated far earlier than her peers and has already made a name for herself—but she admits she wishes she'd had more of a life when she was in college."

There was much more to it, but she hoped he wouldn't dig any deeper.

Trying to steer him off that track, she continued, "And you yourself said my job is just as important as yours. Did you mean it, or were you just trying to annoy my father?"

"Not at all." David paused as the boat bumped the dock near Stranahan House, putting one large, warm hand on her arm as if to steady her. "I *do* believe it." He grinned. "Besides, if I really wanted to aggravate your dad I'd have said your job was more important than mine—and his."

She laughed at the thought of her father's face if David had said that to him, and turned to watch as more passengers boarded the boat. There was a family of seven: parents, another couple who looked to be grandparents, and three children—the oldest no more than eight or so, the youngest just a baby in the mother's arms. They all looked happy except for the baby, who appeared to be sleeping, and a pang of longing so strong it made her breath catch swept through Nychelle.

That was what she wanted. *That* was why she'd forgone the rigors of medical school for what her parents had called "a wasted opportunity." Of course they would never understand. The concept of not wanting to be called *Doctor*, of believing there was more to life than work, was alien to them both.

The water taxi rocked as more people climbed on, and as though reacting to the motion the baby awoke, squirming, her face scrunched up in objection. Nychelle couldn't help smiling, thinking about the life growing in her belly, and longing for the day she would be holding her own baby.

* * *

Nychelle was so focused on whatever it was she was looking at that David's gaze followed hers to where a young woman sat, holding a squirming baby. In deference to the heat the baby was uncovered except for a pink and yellow onesie and a pair of rather snazzy striped socks. Her face was red with temper, her hair plastered down on one side and wildly curly on the other.

David instinctively looked away, as he always did when seeing a baby outside of a work setting. Yet, he found his gaze drawn back.

It was only then he realized that the hard pang of grief he used to feel whenever he saw a baby was absent.

When had that happened?

Now he waited for guilt to take its place—was shocked when there was no hint of that emotion either. Was he the same man who, on the anniversary of Natalie's birth, suffered all the agony of losing a child as if it had just happened?

But that wasn't quite right, either. He remembered what it had been like when it had happened. The agonizing, almost paralyzing sense of loss. The inability to think about anything other than Natalie. The urgent need to somehow turn back the clock and save her, even though logically he knew it was impossible.

He'd mourned on her last birthday, and still thought of her often, but not to the exclusion of all else. Not in the way he had at first, and for a long time after, when it had been a Herculean effort to see past the pain so as to go on with his life. A little at a time he'd learned to live with the knowledge that she was gone and was never coming back.

"Look, Mom. *Look!*"

A child's excited shriek gave him a good reason to look away from the baby, to pretend interest in where the little girl was pointing, out into the river. Still lost in his ruminations, David hardly saw the ripples in the water, barely registered the flip of a large, dark tail and the lively chatter the brief appearance of the manatee had caused.

"Did you see it?"

"I did." He nodded, wondering if she meant the manatee or the baby, since she'd been as intent on the latter as he.

"The first one you've seen since you came here?"

"Yes, although I still don't think I've seen one properly," he replied, aware of a dual meaning to his words that she wouldn't understand, and gaining a chuckle from her.

"True. A tail does not a manatee make, right?" When he laughingly agreed, she said, "I've always wanted to go to the Three Sisters Springs, on the west coast, and see them where they winter. Apparently you can get a really good look at them there."

"Why haven't you?"

She lifted a hand to push her sunglasses firmly up on her nose. "My ex-fiancé didn't like the outdoors much—preferred to holiday at casinos and resorts. Although it's been a while since we broke up, I just haven't made the trip."

The news that she'd been engaged gave him a jolt, and it struck him then how little they really knew about each other. Their friendship had grown in fits and starts, without any of the revelations that would naturally have emerged had they been dating. He'd told her very little about himself too, so it wasn't one-sided.

They'd agreed to keep things light between them today, but he didn't think that meant they were barred from talking about themselves.

"You should go," he said, leaning back and putting his arm along the cushion behind her, so the end of her ponytail brushed his hand. "When my marriage broke up I went white-water rafting. My ex refused to even consider it when we were together, and it was something I'd dreamt of doing since I was a child."

"I thought I'd heard you'd been married but I didn't want to bring it up, in case it was too painful."

She was in profile to him, and he saw her eyes flick toward him behind her dark glasses. The sideways glance was accompanied by that habitual rubbing of her wrist, and it made him want to stroke her nape with a calming finger.

"It was a while ago, so not painful anymore."

The divorce had stopped hurting, although some of what Kitty had said still lingered painfully, but talking about it would lead to deep waters.

The boat moved on and, looking back toward the shore, he said, "Tell me more about Stranahan House. What makes it so special anyway?"

"The man who built it is credited with being the founding father of Fort Lauderdale." She visibly relaxed, turning to face him, her hands falling to rest on her lap. "It was built in the early nineteen-hundreds…"

As she gave him a mini-history lesson David took it all in—although it was less the story and more the sound of her voice and her expressive face that held his attention. When she'd finished the story, he said, "You know a lot about the history of the city."

"I like history," she replied. "If I hadn't gone into nursing I'd probably have become a teacher."

He could see her doing that—interacting with the kids, enjoying watching their young minds soaking up knowledge and growing.

"Why didn't you go into pediatrics? You obviously love kids."

"Aw, hell no." Even though she chuckled, she didn't sound amused. "My heart couldn't stand it. Give me an adult in pain and I'm fine, but if it's a child or, worse, a baby… I turn into a mess. My peds rotation was the hardest on me emotionally." She shook her head slowly, her face taking on a faraway expression. "I almost quit nursing."

"I'm glad you didn't." Talking about it seemed to be taking her to a dark place—one he wondered at. "It was that bad, huh?"

"Yes, it was."

She was still facing him, but David wondered if she was even seeing him.

"There were a couple of days that left me wondering what it was all about—if there was any reason to try to help. If it wasn't for Aliya, I'd probably have snapped."

He knew what she was talking about. He'd experienced some of those same emotions during his residency—times when he'd seen the worst human beings could do, and his faith and optimism had been stretched to breaking point.

Not wanting her to relive those hard times, he instinctively stroked her hand and said, "This must have been a fun place to grow up."

She shrugged, leaving her hand where it was, beneath his. "I know it was for some people. I didn't have the chance to enjoy it until I was older."

Another sore subject. He could tell by the way her fingers clenched into a fist. But this one he didn't want to skirt. "Why wasn't it for you?"

She glanced toward shore and he heard the sound of the boat's engines change. She'd said their stop was next, so hopefully she'd answer before they had to disembark.

Instead of answering, she asked, "You grew up poor, right?"

That was an understatement, but he simply said, "Yes."

"So what did you do during the summer?" Nychelle raised her eyebrows. "Probably worked, right?"

"Yes." He nodded slowly, wondering what she was getting at. "I helped my dad in his shop, and picked up whatever other jobs I could."

"What else? Did your family spend some time together? Were there times when you got to do other stuff?"

"Sure." Wasn't that what childhood was all about? She seemed to be waiting for him to elaborate, so he continued, "When we were little Mary-Liz, Donny, our cousins, and I spent as much time as we could outdoors. Every now and then, when our parents could afford it, we'd spend a day at the beach or go camping. When I was a little older I'd save up my money to go to science camp."

His parents had let him, instead of insisting he use the money to buy school supplies, although he'd done that too. Talking about it with Nychelle, he suddenly realized it had been a childhood of joy and wonder, despite the poverty.

"Sounds like hard work, but with fun to balance it out." She tipped her chin up in an almost combative gesture. "For us—Olivia and me—everything was geared toward our futures in medicine, being prepared to get into the best colleges and *'getting a leg up on the competition.'*"

The way she enunciated the last words told him it was something she'd heard often.

"There wasn't much room for good times under those circumstances." She gently pulled her hand out from under his and reached for her bag. "We get off here."

As they waited for the boat to dock he contemplated what she'd said. It wasn't hard to believe. Having met her parents, he could imagine the pressure they'd put on their children. He'd gone to school with some people he suspected had been raised in a similar way. If they hadn't got one hundred percent on a test, or aced a subject during a semester, they'd freaked, worried about what their parents would say. He'd even seen some of them crack under the strain, and knowing that made him admire Nychelle all the more. It must have taken immense strength of character to stand up to her parents and go her own way.

He'd had to work like a fiend to get to medical school—but not because his parents had been pushing him. For him it had been work to secure scholarships, to have enough money to get where he wanted to go. It was ironic to feel bad for Nychelle, knowing she'd come from such a wealthy family, and yet she had missed out on the joys of childhood because her parents were so single-minded.

"Well," he said finally, as they stood on the dock waiting for the other water taxi to come so they could continue their adventure, "why don't we make up for some of that lost time?"

Brow wrinkled, she asked, "What?"

"The fun times you missed as a kid." He grinned. "Let's make up for them."

The beginnings of a smile tugged at her lips. "How do you suggest we do that?"

"Personally, all *my* childish fantasies involved ice cream and clothes that were bought specifically for me. What did you wish you could do in summers back then?"

Even behind the dark lenses of her glasses he could see her eyes widen.

"I don't know," she replied quickly, but then she shook her head. "I do know. I wanted to go to the beach and build sandcastles, or go to a water park." She gave a little chuckle. "I was even jealous of my friends who complained they had to spend their vacations with their grandparents."

David took her hand. "Well, if you give me ice cream I'll build sandcastles with you. I'm pretty good at it, if I might say so myself. And if you don't believe me we can call my niece and nephew to have them verify that fact."

There was a moment of stillness between them, but

David could feel Nychelle's gaze almost drilling into him, as though she didn't know how to react to his nonsense. And then she laughed: a full-bodied, throaty sound, echoing with what sounded like pure joy.

"You're on," she said, giving his fingers a squeeze. "And your skills had better not disappoint."

"Oh, they won't." He gave her a jaunty grin for good measure, feeling lighter, happier than the simple moment really called for. "I promise."

CHAPTER FOURTEEN

How had she ever questioned David's character? He was one of the nicest people she'd ever known.

Leaning back on her towel, Nychelle watched as he added another tower to the sandcastle, expertly shaping it into a cylinder before starting to embellish it with crenellations.

"The trick is the amount of water you put in," he said, then glanced over at her and held up one sandy hand. "Aren't you going to help at all?"

Nychelle just chuckled and got up to shift the umbrella so it covered him better. "There. I helped stop you getting sunburned."

"Ha-ha." David shook his head and went back to decorating the castle with arrow slits inscribed into the sand with the end of his straw. "I thought this was something *you* wanted to do."

He tried to sound disgruntled, but couldn't stop the sides of his lips quirking, which spoiled the effect completely.

"I'm finding watching you even more fun than I'd have actually doing it. Besides, you're so much better at it than I could ever be."

His laughter brought a smile to her lips as she resumed her seat beneath the other umbrella and tucked her legs up under her. It was, she decided, the best day she could ever have hoped for. Simple pleasures, enjoyed together.

They'd floated along the Intracoastal, looking at the fabulous houses, critiquing the architecture and marveling at the luxuriousness of the surroundings and the boats berthed outside many of the residences. Initially Nychelle had planned for them to have lunch at one of her favorite waterside restaurants, but the smell of the seafood had made her feel queasy as soon as they'd walked in. David hadn't commented or complained when she'd changed her mind, and they'd strolled along for a couple of blocks more, until they'd found an up-scale burger joint.

Although their conversation had been light enough, she'd discovered a few things she hadn't known before. He'd talked a bit more about his marriage and, in true David fashion, had spoken of his ex with respect and regret, rather than acrimony.

Thinking the woman a fool for letting him go, Nychelle had wanted to ask for more details. But when he'd moved on to talk about something else she hadn't pressed the subject. After all, it had been her idea not to go too deep today.

After lunch they'd wandered along South Fort Lauderdale Beach Boulevard, browsing shop windows and craft stalls. He'd threatened to buy her an alligator foot keychain or a gator tooth necklace, both of which she'd politely refused through her laughter. But she'd stopped on her way back from the ladies' room and bought him a tropical print shirt in colors so wild she was sure he'd never wear it.

He had immediately put it on.

"Good grief!" she'd said, breathless from giggling. "I don't know if I want to be seen with you in that."

"Too bad," he'd replied, with a grin that just turned her insides to mush. "You should have thought of that before you bought it."

Then, true to their agreement, she'd bought him an ice cream cone, which had prompted him to suggest they cross over to the beach and build their sandcastle. With one more stop to get another round of cold drinks, they'd done just that.

It was surprising to realize the sun was sinking toward the horizon already, although it wouldn't get dark until after six.

"The day has flown by." She suppressed a sigh, wishing their time together could last longer. "We should think about heading back soon."

He looked up and gave a one-shouldered shrug. "If I wasn't so covered in sand I'd suggest making an evening of it, but I'm not fit to go anywhere like this."

Nychelle nodded in agreement. While it hadn't been very windy, the sea breeze had left her feeling salty and sticky. "You can explore the night-life another time."

Slanting her a quick glance, he replied, "Yes, we can."

Busying herself by pulling out her phone, Nychelle ignored his comment. "I need to take a picture of the sandcastle. It's amazing."

"One second." Using his straw, David wrote around the inside of the moat in neat script: *Queen Nychelle's Palace.*

"You're a disgrace to the medical profession, having handwriting that neat," Nychelle teased as she snapped several pictures, including a couple that featured him rather than the sandcastle.

"I don't believe in conforming to other people's expectations." He stood up and brushed at his sand-covered legs, with little effect.

"True," she said as she gathered up her bag. "Not doing so really does make life interesting."

She knew that for sure, having spent years doing what she felt was right for her rather than what others wanted.

She just wished she knew whether spending all this time with David was a good thing or not.

It had been an easy, uncomplicated day on the surface, but every time he'd smiled, or reached out to hold her hand, Nychelle had been aware of the undercurrents. As swift and strong as a riptide, they were rife with attraction, both physical and emotional—at least for her. Wishing she knew how he felt about it was futile. She wouldn't ask. Not only because she was leery of actually knowing, but because she didn't want to risk spoiling the day.

It had been wonderful.

Yet as they walked toward the shower at the exit near the road Nychelle looked back at the sandcastle and felt a sharp pang of sadness, knowing that it, like the day, would soon be gone.

Maybe it was the sun, or perhaps the amount of laughing he'd done during their day out, but as they wound their way back toward the water taxi stop David felt mellow. Happily tired. Nychelle looked pensive, though, and he could only hope it was because, like him, she was regretting the end of their time together.

As they hurried across the busy street toward the Intracoastal, where they'd catch the water taxi, he took her hand again. She gave his fingers a squeeze, then slanted him a glance.

"Why did you decide on general practice instead of a specialty?"

The question took him aback, and his first impulse was to avoid it. "Why did you? I would have thought with your family connections you would have gone in a different direction."

"Oh, no, you don't." She gave his hand a shake in emphasis. "Didn't anyone tell you answering a question with a question is an obvious sign of deflection? Why would you be defensive about something so simple?"

He groaned. "Analyzing me again?"

"Asking another question?" she shot back.

"Okay…okay."

He changed his grip on her hand, lacing his fingers with hers. It wasn't that he didn't want to tell her, just that he was sure she'd think he was nuts.

"I've always thought that eventually I'd want to move back to South Carolina and set up a practice near where my parents are. There aren't enough doctors in the area, and the hospital is a ways away—especially for some of the more rural communities."

He struggled to find the appropriate words.

"The people support each other every way they can, and my family benefited from that way of thinking. It's what neighbors do there, even when they have little themselves, so I've always wanted to give back."

He didn't tell her about the charity he'd been saving toward setting up since he'd first started making decent money, or that he had been talking to Dr. Hamatty about how he arranged his free clinics, hoping to do something similar one day. Yet even without that the look she gave him, so full of admiration and joy, made him feel as though he were suddenly ten feet tall.

"How lovely. I think that's wonderful!"

She beamed, as if he'd given her a gift, and his heart ached, feeling suddenly too big for its place in his chest.

There was nothing he could say; his throat was tight with emotion. During the day he'd opened up to her more than he had to anyone else for a long time, speaking about his parents and siblings, and the home he'd run from and yet often longed for. Even about Kitty, although he hadn't been able to bring himself to say why the marriage had failed. That was a conversation he thought might happen soon, but he'd prefer to have it somewhere other than in public.

He wasn't sure he wouldn't break down telling her about Natalie. Even though time had made the pain more bearable, there was something about Nychelle that brought all his emotions close to the surface. As though she were some kind of magnet, which drew from him all he sought to hide or hide from.

They were near the dock when Nychelle said, “Whoops!” Tightening her grip on his hand, she continued, “Look. The next taxi is coming. Let's go.”

She broke into a run and he fell in with her, the sound of her laughter, the gleam of her smile, making that sweet ache in his chest expand, filling him with contentment.

Breathless, they threw themselves onto a bench at the prow of the boat, exchanging smiles.

“Just a moment! Please—just a moment!”

At the shout from the dock David looked up and saw the same family they'd shared the trip with that morning running toward the boat, the two older members bringing up the rear. The taxi waited, and one after the other they clambered onto the boat, the adults red-faced with exertion.

This wasn't the calm, happy group of the morning, David thought. The older children were obviously exhausted and, as often happened with siblings, were squabbling and baiting one another. The father was now holding the baby, who squealed in outrage, while the mother and grandparents corralled all the various bits and pieces the family had needed for their excursion.

After watching them get settled—which involved the stowing of equipment, the swapping of the baby from hand to hand, and a few sharp words to the older kids from Dad—David turned to Nychelle with a wry grin.

"I always tip my hat to parents. Just watching the chaos sometimes makes me tired."

His own words took him by surprise. Normally he avoided any reference to children, and any jokes about what parents went through, since they brought with them regrets for what he was missing.

"It's wonderful chaos," she retorted, and there was an edge to her voice. "There's nothing I love more than taking care of Leighann and MJ. It's crazy, but rewarding."

"No doubt it is." Her vehemence was startling, pulling him out of his own contemplation. "I didn't mean it as a—"

"I look forward to experiencing it."

Her interruption was fierce. Although she still spoke softly, all pretense of indifference was washed from her tone, and the hand she held up was defensive, as if she expected him to object or argue.

"I don't understand why children are suddenly seen as a burden—something to be put off and a cause of problems in peoples' lives. No matter how chaotic, I think people should be *thankful* for their kids."

"They should be." That he knew for a fact. He took her hand, squeezed gently, wanting to calm her.

"Some aren't, though."

Now she just sounded sad, rather than angry, and an ache formed in David's chest.

"It's sad when so many people are longing for kids and can't have them. I can't wait to be a mother."

As she pushed her sunglasses firmly up on her nose and turned to look out over the water David was left wondering. Was that a general observation about infertility, or was she thinking of someone specific? Perhaps herself?

Before he could decide how to best broach the subject Nychelle rolled her shoulders, as though sloughing off the conversation. She drew in a deep breath and turned to him, smiling a somewhat wobbly smile.

"So, what do you think of Fort Lauderdale now you've seen a bit more of it? How does it compare to Chicago?"

He had no choice but to follow her lead, and yet her remark about longing for children of her own had cast a shadow over the day. Over his heart. She had no idea how that drive to be a parent, the longing to bring another life into the world, could cause an agony beyond anything she'd ever experienced.

The ache in his chest intensified, and even as he answered her question he felt the peace he'd only just experienced evaporate in the glare of the setting sun.

Nychelle's need to be a mother put paid to any hopes of him being anything more to her than just a friend. And that hurt more than he wanted to admit even to himself.

CHAPTER FIFTEEN

NYCHELLE'S HEART WAS POUNDING, and a sour taste settled at the back of her throat as David talked about the comparative merits of the two most recent cities he'd lived in. She nodded at what seemed to be the appropriate times, although she was only minimally following what he was saying.

What on earth had come over her to go on a rant like that?

But she knew what had caused her to lose her cool. David was, in her opinion, perfect father material. He was kind, calm, beautiful of spirit. The knowledge that he didn't want kids rankled. And when he'd seemed to be denigrating parenthood altogether…

She was overreacting. Also, *she* was the one who had imposed the rule about not discussing anything intimate, and she had broken it.

There was no way she could continue on the way they were. Too much simmered between them. Over the last few weeks she'd grown more and more intrigued by him, had felt attraction smoldering beneath her skin. Today had fanned it into a wildfire. He was all she'd ever wanted in a man. Yet once he knew she was pregnant there would be nothing left between them—maybe not even friendship—

so she wanted to get it over with. Deal with it now rather than later, as Aliya had so wisely counseled.

It was hard to find the words, though, hard to trust him with her news, even though in her heart she knew it was the right thing, and they switched over to the New River line in silence.

The loss of camaraderie was no doubt her fault, and she withdrew into herself, trying to come up with the right words to make her decisions make sense to him the way they had to her.

Finally she turned to David, still unsure, but determined to do the right thing. "Listen," she said, having to stop and clear her tight throat before she could continue. "I feel as though I owe you an explanation."

He raised his hand, but she didn't let him interrupt. If he said it was okay, she'd probably wimp out.

"From when I was a little girl I loved babies and other children. The ladies who looked after Olivia and I used to call me *Little Momma*."

She pronounced it *Lilli Mumma*, the Jamaican way, out of habit, and saw him smile.

"I would get up before school and go to check on Olivia before I got dressed or had my breakfast. It just came naturally to me. I wanted to make sure she was okay, and felt as though it was my job to ensure she was. I was even like that with Aliya—which annoyed the heck out of her, since she's actually a couple months older than me."

David leaned back, his intense focus on her causing distracting shivers to run across her shoulders and down her arms, as happened every time she had his full concentration.

"So you've wanted to be a mother from when you were a little girl?"

"Yes." She nodded, facing him head-on rather than

looking away, the way she really wanted to. Their stop was coming up. People were rising, preparing to get off the boat. There might not be enough time to tell him everything she wanted to.

"But there's more to it than that. You see, when I was thirteen I developed dysfunctional uterine bleeding. Eventually, because medication wasn't working, I ended up having a D&C and there was some scarring. The doctors warned I may never get pregnant."

The boat bumped the dock and people crowded around, getting closer to the exit point. Suddenly self-conscious about airing her personal business in public, she stopped talking. David was still staring at her, and she wished she could understand his expression, but he was keeping it carefully neutral; it was his professional face, as if she were a patient.

Tension making her feel almost nauseated, she got up. "Can we finish this conversation later?"

"Sure," he replied.

But his gaze lingered on her face, making heat climb up her neck and into her cheeks.

The family group, which had changed over to the second water taxi with them, were getting ready to disembark too, and she turned to watch them. The father had taken hold of the older kids, helping the eldest put on his knapsack and carrying the other one. Mom juggled the now squirming baby and the ubiquitous diaper bag until the older lady said, "Let me take the nappy bag," and relieved her of it.

As the younger woman said, "Thanks, Deana," the older gentleman reached for the stroller, which had been folded up and stowed beneath the bench.

"I've got the buggy," he said.

Nychelle was about to comment to David on the older

folks' English accents when the older man straightened, stroller in hand, took a staggering step back and then collapsed.

For a moment everything seemed to slow as the elderly man fell backward, and then she heard the *crack* of his head hitting the bench on the other side of the water taxi.

"George!"

The older woman was a step ahead of Nychelle, and fell to her knees beside the man's crumpled body. She grabbed his shoulders, but Nychelle held on to her hands, stopping her from shaking the unconscious man.

"Wait—"

"I'm a doctor." David was there, bending down, already reaching for the patient's wrist. "Let me take a look."

"Give us some room," Nychelle said to the woman, hoping she'd back away. When she only continued crying out her husband's name, and wouldn't release her grip on his shoulders, Nychelle turned to the rest of the family, who were standing as if turned to stone. "Someone help this lady up. And call 911 immediately."

There was a flurry of activity: the younger man rushed forward to pull the distraught woman away, one of the deckhands shouted to the captain to tell him what had happened. As soon as the other woman was out of her way Nychelle concentrated on the patient. He was partially seated, slouched against the base of the bench, held up by a jut in the gunwale.

"Pulse is elevated, but strong. Respiration within normal range. Pupils responsive." David straightened from his examination. "Stabilize his head. Let's get him flat on the deck."

Nychelle did as she was told, holding the gentleman's head and neck while David supported his upper torso, so as to shift him away from the bench without risking any additional injury to his spine.

"Gently. Gently…" he said. "And down we go."

As soon as they had the gentleman flat, Nychelle said, "Scalp laceration," although she was sure David would have noticed the blood on the bench, and the spreading pool on the deck where the man's head now lay.

David reached around to palpate the wound. "No obvious sign of fracture." He straightened. "Apply pressure."

None of the towels in her bag was clean, so Nychelle looked over her shoulder at the baby's parents. "Give me a clean diaper. Hurry."

The mother moved first, bending to scrabble in the bag for one, handing it over with a shaking hand.

Folding it inside out to create a pad, Nychelle pressed it to the wound, glad they didn't need to lift the man's head for her to do so.

David leaned closer to the gentleman. "George? George? Can you hear me?"

When there was no response, he flicked his finger on the patient's cheek and called to him again. It was only on the third try that George's eyelids fluttered and he moaned.

When his eyes opened a crack, David said, "Hey, there. You're all right, but stay still for me."

"Wh-what happened?"

Despite David's injunction for him to stay still George made a move to sit up, and David stopped him with a hand on his chest.

"Where am I?"

"You fell and hit your head. The ambulance is on its way, but I need you to stay still." David's calm voice had the patient relaxing, although his face was lined with pain. "Can you answer a few questions for me?"

"Y-yes." George scrunched his eyes closed for a moment, but then opened them slightly again.

"How old are you?"

"Eighty-three," he replied, with only a fractional hesitation before the words.

"Do you have a heart condition?"

"No. High blood pressure, though. Take pills for that."

"Any other medications?"

"No." He squeezed his eyes closed again, and a little groan followed his reply.

"Where does it hurt, George?"

"Have a cracking headache. And someone's using a damned blowtorch on my leg."

"Left or right?"

"Left."

Nychelle was glad to hear the distant sound of approaching sirens. There was only so much they could do for this gentleman. David had asked George to move his leg, and although he could a bit, it obviously caused him a lot of pain. Nychelle suspected a broken hip and, while most people might assume the fall had caused the break, she knew that more often than not the break actually happened first, causing the fall. Many older people weren't aware of the dangers of bone loss caused by aging and other chronic, sometimes undiagnosed, conditions until a situation like this one arose.

Having finished his exam, David offered no opinion other than to say, "The ambulance should be here any minute. Would you like your wife to keep you company until the paramedics get here? She's been very worried about you."

"Yes." George's English accent was even more pronounced than before. "Let her see I'm not done for yet."

David looked over to where the rest of family were all

huddled together on the dock. Everyone but a deckhand had disembarked in preparation for the EMTs' arrival. "What's her name?"

"Deana."

Nychelle knew that with each question and reply David was testing the injured man's mental abilities.

"Pretty name," David said, eliciting a small smile from the patient.

When David called and gestured to Deana, the deckhand helped her back on board and she hurried over. Kneeling beside her husband, she grabbed his nearest hand.

"It's all right, darling." George tried to be reassuring, although his voice was weak. "Just a little fall."

"What happened to him?" Deana asked David, her voice quavering. "Was it a heart attack?"

"The ambulance is on its way. They'll be able to better tell you what happened when he gets to the hospital."

"Why won't *you* tell me?" Her voice rose beseechingly. "You said you were a doctor. You should know what's happened. I need to know what's happened to my husband—"

"Stop it, Dee." George's voice was firm, and he gave his wife's hand a little shake. "Enough. The poor doc was just having a nice day out with his lady. I doubt he has a stethoscope or any other equipment hidden in his shorts, do you?"

His voice was a little breathy, and Nychelle was relieved that the wail of the ambulance had stopped. The EMTs should be there soon. The diaper was already heavy with blood, and Nychelle could see the first signs of incipient shock; George had paled, his respirations were quickening, and a touch of his face revealed he was clammy.

"It's okay, George." David was as calm as ever. "Deana, here come the paramedics. They're going to need you to go back onto the dock so they can do their job."

Instead of moving Deana added her other hand to the clasp she had on her husband. "No. I—"

It wasn't unusual to have family members be more difficult than the patients, so Nychelle tamped down her frustration. Looking Deana in the eyes, she said, "If you truly want to know what's happened to George, let the EMTs get him to the hospital as quickly as possible."

Perhaps it was her tone, or the seriousness of her expression. But something got through to the woman, who bent quickly to kiss her husband on the lips and then moved back toward the dock, just as the rattle of equipment heralded the paramedics' arrival.

"Forgive her," George muttered. "She's a firecracker. Always has been."

"It's fine," Nychelle replied in a reassuring tone. He'd grown even paler, and was beginning to shake. "Don't worry about it. It's not a big deal at all."

But she was still a bit steamed. She was used to having patients doubt her abilities—sometimes even rudely. It was part of the job, and it didn't bother her anymore. But somehow hearing someone seeming to question David's competence had just set her teeth on edge.

David rose, getting out of the way so the lead paramedic could take his place. As the EMT gave him a questioning look David introduced himself, then said, "Patient staggered and fell backward, striking his head. He was unconscious for approximately two minutes. Pulse and respiration are within normal range, although rapid. He sustained a scalp laceration and I suspect he also has a broken hip. With the way he fell, I'd check for neck fractures and TBI."

The second paramedic approached with a neck brace and backboard, and Nychelle scooted away, giving her room. The first paramedic was asking David more questions as the two EMTs worked in a coordinated rhythm to prepare George for his trip to the hospital.

There was nothing left for her to do, so Nychelle got up, gingerly picking up her bag as she did so, hoping not to get too much blood on it. Standing to one side, her attention wasn't on the paramedics or their patient. It was all on David: on his expression as he watched the EMTs fit George with the neck brace and backboard, on the timbre of his voice as he answered their questions. She was fascinated by the way his long fingers flexed, as though his capable, beautiful hands wanted to get back to helping the patient, and then by how quickly he moved to assist the paramedics lifting George onto the stretcher.

He was a man made for his profession; his desire to diagnose, to heal, was ingrained into his soul. Yet it was just one part of him—an important facet, but just one of many that added up to the most amazingly perfect man she'd ever met.

Suddenly, just as the stretcher was being moved toward the dock, he looked up and caught her staring. In that moment, as their gazes met, the chaos seemed to subside and a sense of almost surreal calm enfolded her. The spark that zinged between them couldn't be denied even if she wanted to. It wasn't the aftermath of the incident making her knees weak and her heart leap. It was him. *All* him.

The stretcher rattled past her and Nychelle blindly turned to follow its path. She vaguely registered the family milling about and hurrying off after the paramedics.

Then David was beside her.

"Let's get out of here."

All thoughts of their prior conversation fled. She didn't ask where they were going—didn't ask any questions at all. She just nodded, knowing she'd go wherever he wanted.

CHAPTER SIXTEEN

SOMETHING HAD CHANGED between them. It had sparked in her eyes when she'd looked at him on the dock. It had shimmered like heat off asphalt between them during the walk back to his car, and it still hung in the air, strong enough to have the hair rising on his arms while he settled into the driver's seat.

"Come home with me," he said, breaking the silence, trying to gauge her reaction to his words from her clear-cut beautiful profile.

He had it in mind to add his apartment was closer than her house, and that although they'd paused at the restaurant to wash their hands, it would offer her the chance to clean up properly.

But as he was about to say all that Nychelle turned toward him. "Yes."

For a moment it was as though time itself held its breath. Then David's gaze dropped from Nychelle's eyes to her mouth, snagged there, entranced. She wasn't smiling. Instead the curve of her lips was a little shy, but also knowing. It was like a siren's call…irresistible. Yet he didn't move, exerted a superhuman effort not to lean forward and kiss her the way he so desperately wanted to. If he did, he wouldn't be able to stop.

Instead he pressed the start button on the car and turned

his thoughts, as best he could, to backing out of the parking space. Neither of them spoke as he turned out of the parking structure and drove east toward his condominium, which was ten minutes away.

The radio played softly. The song was one David had in the past thought illustrated an unrealistic ideal—one in which a man loved all the different facets of his woman, even the imperfections. Now he heard it with different ears, tuned to a new frequency that understood what the crooning singer meant.

There was nothing about Nychelle he disliked, and so much that he admired. The tenacity and courage she'd displayed in following her own path in life, not the one everyone had seemed to expect of her. The reticence she hid behind her warm, engaging smile, which was unusual in these days when people overshared their every thought and feeling. He liked it. Being forced to dig beneath the surface to understand her and get to know what she thought important in life was exhilarating. Over and over he'd found new things to respect about her, including her grace in the face of her parents' disapproval and the calm, friendly way she interacted with patients and colleagues.

He'd fought so hard to resist the attraction between them, but now, with the knowledge that she was unlikely to be able to conceive, that resistance was melting away.

It was so selfish of him to feel her infertility was a sign, but he did. He hurt for her, knowing how much she wanted to be a mother. And if he were honest he wanted children too, but couldn't seem to get past his fear that somehow Natalie not making it to term had been his fault. Kitty had remarried, and now had two children with her new husband, all born without problems. Intellectually he knew it probably wasn't the case, but he wasn't willing to take the risk.

He was beginning to feel as though eventually he might be able to handle being a father through adoption, if it meant having Nychelle. Because having Nychelle in his life permanently would be heaven.

It took no effort to imagine her at his side, in his bed. He wanted to take her to South Carolina to meet his family, who he was sure would adore her as much as he did. Wanted to have her early-morning smiles, or her grumpiness if it turned out she wasn't a morning person, and her goodnight kisses. Wanted to see her face as she lost herself in ecstasy and know he was the one who'd given her pleasure.

The longing that last image conjured was a physical ache in his belly. And lower.

Was this love? He was sure it was. The song he'd previously dismissed as sentimental now made perfect sense. No doubt Nychelle had her faults—although if someone asked right now he wouldn't be able to name one—but no matter what they were, he couldn't see them making a difference to how he felt. He'd never been more certain about anything in his life. To him Nychelle was perfect—and perfect for him.

Pulling into the apartment complex, he drove around to the entrance to the underground parking lot and pushed the button to open the gate. Nychelle still hadn't spoken, but a quick peep at her showed nothing but serenity in the lines of her face. As he drove down the ramp he thought it seemed as though she'd come to a decision and was at peace with it. If only he knew what that decision was…

Trying not to wonder about that propelled him into speech. "The apartment isn't much. I rented it furnished and haven't made many changes. But it does have a really nice view from the balcony. I thought we could order in some food and just relax after that excitement with George."

Pulling into his space, he put the car in Park and turned to look at Nychelle, just as she slanted him a glance from the corner of her eye.

"Mmm-hmm," she replied, with a little quirk of her lips. "That sounds good."

He took her hand on their way to the elevator, and when he heard her indrawn breath he knew he wasn't the only one who felt the electric charge generated by the connection of his skin with hers. He tightened his fingers around hers, swept his thumb across the back of her hand, reveling in the softness of her, longing to feel her touch on his skin again.

They rode up to his floor in silence, and he resented having to release her hand to unlock his door. Need built beneath his skin, tightening his muscles, making it difficult for him to breathe normally. As they stepped inside he knew he should wait, but couldn't.

As soon as the door closed behind them he drew her into his arms. Reaching up, he took off her sunglasses and set them, along with his own, on the hall table.

"David…" It was a sigh: arousal, surrender and fear all intermingled. She looked vulnerable, and his heart twisted. "We shouldn't…"

Cupping her face, he said, "Maybe not." A light, lingering kiss sealed whatever she was planning to say next behind her lips, and as she melted against him, trembling, he lifted his mouth just far enough away to say, "But unless you tell me you don't want me I don't want to stop—consequences be damned."

"I…"

Her attempt at a reply ended on a muffled sound, rife

with desire, as he trailed his lips to her ear and nipped the lobe.

"Tell me you don't want me, Nychelle."

He whispered it in her ear, felt a shiver race through her body. Her nipples pressed, tightly furled, against his chest, demanding attention.

"Tell me to stop and I will."

Nychelle tried with all her might to say they shouldn't go any further, but couldn't get the words out. Knowing she needed to tell him the rest of her story battled with the desire making her head swim and her body tingle and thrum with desire.

"Tell me you don't want me," he said again, and she knew she couldn't. To do so would be to lie.

"I can't. You know I can't. But..."

He didn't wait to hear the rest, just took her mouth in a kiss that made what she'd planned to say fly right out of her brain.

Desire flared, hotter than the Florida sun, and Nychelle surrendered to it, unable and unwilling to risk missing this chance to know David intimately, even if it were just this once. Was it right? Wrong? She couldn't decide—didn't want to try to.

There were so many more things she should explain to him, but she knew she wouldn't. Telling him about the baby when she knew he didn't want a family would destroy whatever it was growing between them. It was craven, perhaps even despicable not to be honest with him, and she hated herself for being underhand, but her mind, heart and body were at war, and she'd already accepted which would win.

She'd deal with the fallout, whatever it might be, tomorrow. Today—this evening—she was going to have what she wanted, live the way she wanted. Enjoy David for this one time. There would only be regrets if she didn't.

His lips were still on hers, demanding, delicious. She'd relived the kisses they'd shared over and over in her mind, but now she realized memory was only a faded facsimile of reality. The touch and taste and scent of him encompassed her, overtaking her system on every level. Her desperate hands found their way beneath his shirt, and his groan of pleasure was as heartfelt as her joy at the first sensation of his bare skin beneath her palms.

His hands, in turn, explored her yearning flesh, stroking her face, then her neck. When they brushed along her shoulders, easing the straps of her sundress away, Nychelle arched against him. With a tug, he lowered her bodice and the bandeau-style bathing suit beneath it to her waist, and she rubbed her nipples against his chest, spurring him on, want turning to aching need within her.

Perhaps he felt the same way, for suddenly it was as though they had both lost all restraint. Arms tight around each other, their bodies moved in concert, their fiercely demanding kisses whipping the flames of arousal to an inferno.

Naked. She wanted him naked.

She set about achieving her goal, tugging at his shirt until they were forced to part so as to get it off over his head. Once it was out of the way David's lips came back to hers, and she breathed in the scent of him, the essence of it rising to her head, making her love-drunk. Already she had the knot of his board shorts untied, but she paused to cup the hard length of his erection through the fabric, a shiver racing along her spine, eagerness firing in its wake.

He made a sound in the back of his throat—something feral, predatory—and her legs almost gave way, trembling with anticipation. He lifted her, carried her easily into the bedroom, where he set her down on the bed. With swift, capable movements he stripped off her clothes, leaving her exposed. When his intent blue gaze stroked from her toes up to her head she felt it like a touch, and her body tightened even further, trembling with arousal.

Burning. She was burning from the inside out. She cried out as he fanned the flames of her excitement with his lips and hands, the slide of his body against hers. His mouth branded her breasts, her belly. His tongue slid and flicked over what felt like every inch of her torso, teasing and arousing, until she shook and writhed and yearned, caught on the edge of orgasm, slipping toward the chasm with every intent-filled touch he placed upon her body.

"You are so beautiful, Nychelle."

His torso was wedged between her thighs. His breath rushed over her belly, leaving a little trail of goose bumps. When he kissed her navel, swirling his tongue around the edge, her hips lifted and a pleading gasp left her throat. He smiled slightly, that beloved tilt of his lips, and although his lids were slumberous his eyes were dark, gleaming, and she felt his need vibrating through his body into hers.

"David," she pleaded. "Please. I want—"

He didn't let her finish—had already slid down as she spoke. And at the first touch of his lips on her most intimate flesh, the first swipe of his tongue through her folds, she shattered, crying out his name. Not a plea now, but a capitulation. A wild giving of herself—completely, utterly—even as she took the ecstasy he so freely gave and demanded…

"More…"

CHAPTER SEVENTEEN

DAVID FLOATED UP from a deep sleep and had one of those moments when, because of the quality of the light, he wasn't sure whether it was morning or evening. Then he took a deep breath, intending to yawn, but stopped as Nychelle's scent flooded his head.

'More...'

He heard her voice again in his head and, rolling onto his stomach, pulled her pillow over to bury his face in it. There had been more—and more. Lovemaking so intense, so utterly beautiful, a sensation of repletion filled him at the memory.

If he were a rooster, he'd crow as he remembered watching her straddle his body, taking him deep, her face tight with need. He'd cupped her breasts and she'd covered his hands with her own as she rocked above him, the connection between them so sublime it had thrown him into an altered state. One where all that mattered was Nychelle, the love swelling inside him, and her pleasure.

She'd cried out his name as her body had clutched his, her ripples of ecstasy catapulting him into an orgasm that had left him weak with pleasure. Just as the next one and the next one had, each pulling him further into love with her, making the bond between them grow stronger.

Thinking about it made him want to make love with

her all over again, although his stamina, as evidenced by his renewed erection, frankly astonished him. It was all her. Looking at her was aphrodisiac enough, but when he touched her, felt her touch in return, he reached a whole different level of arousal.

Where *was* she?

The bathroom door was open, but the door leading to the living room was almost completely closed. Sitting up, he reached for a pair of shorts and hoped she was out there ordering dinner. He was ravenous. Plus, he needed more energy for when he pulled her back into bed.

Stepping into the living room, he found her standing by the sliding door to the balcony, gazing out over the city lights. She'd found his bathrobe, which had been hanging on the back of his bedroom door, and he was glad she hadn't got dressed.

It would only mean undressing her all over again.

About to cross the room and embrace her from behind, he hesitated, something about her posture stopping him in his tracks. She turned, and her bleak expression made his heart stumble.

"Nychelle? What is it?"

"I have something to tell you. Something I should have told you before I… I slept with you."

"Okay…" But his throat felt tight, the word coming out rough and low.

Even from across the room he could see her inhale, and he already knew, from the habitual rubbing of her wrist, that whatever she had to say probably wouldn't be good.

"I had IUI a few weeks ago. I'm pregnant."

The words hung in the air and he was unable to make sense of them immediately. Reaching behind him, he found the arm of the couch with one hand and sat down before his trembling legs gave out.

That couldn't be right, could it?

"But you said..."

What had she said? His brain scrambled to remember.

"I developed dysfunctional uterine bleeding. The doctors warned I may never get pregnant."

She hadn't said she couldn't, just that she might never.

Everything inside him froze, ice filling his chest and spreading into his veins. Desperate, not wanting her to see what she was doing to him, he donned a stoic, neutral mask.

Her lips trembled slightly, and her eyes grew liquid with tears. "I'm sorry. I should have told you. I just—"

"It was none of my business." The distance in his tone made the words hollow. The breath caught in his throat, painful and raw, and had to be forcefully expelled before he could say, "I understand."

"Do you?"

It was, to him, a moot point. One he didn't want to discuss.

He would have told her so, but she said, "I don't think you do, and I'd like to explain."

He lifted his hand, gesturing for her to go on, humoring her, and for an instant he saw a hint of what might be anger in her eyes. Then it faded, and she sighed. Moving to the dining table, she pulled out a chair and sank into it. All this he watched as if from a distance, detached, refusing to allow himself to get pulled in. To feel.

"Two years ago I discovered that my fiancé, Nick, was cheating on me. He'd told me that while he eventually wanted kids he wasn't ready yet, and I'd agreed to wait. Then I found out the woman he'd been cheating with was pregnant. He tried to say it was a mistake, get me to take him back, but I think that was because he was worried my father would be angry."

She shrugged and shook her head, ruefulness evident in the gesture.

"Daddy didn't care, of course, and I won't bore you with the rest of the fallout, but needless to say I was reluctant to get involved with anyone else after that."

David forced himself to nod—a sharp, get-on-with-it motion—and Nychelle closed her eyes for a second. He swallowed, feeling bad for her but also hating how the woman he'd just made love with now seemed a perfect stranger.

Hating her for ruining the happiness he'd only just found.

"I didn't want to wait—take the chance of leaving the attempt to have a child until it was too late. With my problems there would always be risks, but the longer I waited, the longer the odds of my even conceiving would become. I didn't know..."

He winced, her words piercing the ice around his heart. What hadn't she known? That they'd meet? Fall...?

No. He couldn't think that way. Refused to. Wouldn't allow her to follow that train of thought in case she completely destroyed him. Instead, he asked the first question that came to mind. "What do your parents think about this?"

"They don't know. I didn't tell anyone except Aliya."

The sound that broke from her was bitter, but he didn't let it weaken the barriers he'd already thrown up around his battered heart.

"When the doctor told me, at thirteen, about the problems I'd have carrying a child I started crying. And my mother..." She paused, her hands clenching into fists. "Do you know what she said to me?"

"What?"

"She said I shouldn't cry. That it was a chance for me

to concentrate on my career without having to conform to what society deemed was my duty to procreate."

She looked away, but he saw the way she blinked, trying to hold back her tears.

"I remember wondering if she regretted having us, saw us as burdens she was forced to bear. It explained why she was hardly around—why she left our care to others and was only interested in how we were doing academically. Was so cold and uncaring."

"Maybe she was just trying to spare you the pain of trying and not being able to conceive." The instinctive words broke from him, tearing at his throat as they passed. "Or the pain of carrying a baby only to lose it later."

She stared at him, eyes wide, and he saw the tracks left by her tears. "You don't know..."

"But I *do* know." Trying to push back the pain, keep his expression stoic, took everything he had inside. "And that's the advice I'd have given you...as a parent who's lost a child."

The shock of his words left Nychelle frozen except for her hand, which crept to cover her still-flat belly. David's eyes flicked as he followed the movement, and then rose to her face again.

"What?" she whispered, a horrible, aching sensation filling her chest. "Oh, David."

"Yes." His lips twisted. "My daughter was born at twenty weeks."

The way he said it wasn't lost on her, and tears filled her eyes again. He didn't see it as his wife having had a miscarriage, but as his daughter being born too early to survive.

"It's soul-destroying, Nychelle. Something you never get over. I wouldn't wish it on someone I hate, much less on someone I care about."

The air she'd just inhaled stuck in her lungs. All she could do was shake her head and blink to clear the tears from her eyes as the enormity of what she'd done crashed over her.

David had gone through hell, and she was bringing it all back to him. It was there in his pain-filled eyes, and in the way his fingers gripped the arm of the couch until they turned white.

"So maybe your mother was trying to shield you the only way she knew how." A muscle jumped in his jaw. "She knew the difficulty you faced, the potential heartbreak, and she tried to stop you from doing something you might regret even more than you'd regret not having a child."

"Don't say that!" The storm building in her was a maelstrom of pain and anger, and they were both there in the ferocity of her cry. "I'll never regret trying."

"Really?" David got to his feet so quickly Nychelle gasped at the rapid motion. "Even if—God forbid—something happens to your child?" He turned away, his shoulders rigid, his fists clenched. "Believe me, at that point you'll feel nothing more than regret and heartbreak."

She saw it so clearly then: David's desire never to be a father again was really his need never to take a chance on losing another child. And she knew now there was no hope for them.

None.

Blissful numbness overcame her and she welcomed it, knowing she couldn't bear to fall apart in front of him. Feeling distantly amazed that her legs held her, she stood and walked toward the bedroom, unsurprised when David said nothing; didn't even turn to watch her go. Collecting her clothes from beside the bed, averting her eyes from the place where she'd experienced the greatest pleasure of her life, she went into the bathroom, quietly closing the door behind her.

Only then did her hands start to shake, and it took her longer than usual to get her swimsuit on, and her sundress, and to undo her ponytail, finger-comb her snarled hair and secure it again.

By the time she got back to the living room David was in the kitchen, as though it was important to put the width of the island between them. Her bag was on the table by the door, instead of on the floor where she'd dropped it earlier, and she figured he'd put it there so she wouldn't waste time searching for it.

So she'd get going quicker.

"I'll drop you home."

There was that distant tone again, and it struck her straight in the heart, threatening the calm encasing her. "No. I'll call a cab." She held up her hand when he looked as though he might argue. "Really. It's okay."

There were so many things she wanted to say, but couldn't. So many questions, too, that she would keep to herself. She'd destroyed whatever they might have had—even friendship. She didn't have the right to ask anything more of him.

But as she put her hand on the door handle there was one thing she had to ask. It was, to her, too important to ignore.

"What is her name?"

His expression didn't change, as though he hadn't heard her, but then his eyebrows went up in query.

"Your daughter," she clarified. "What's her name?"

The silence that fell was so profound Nychelle's ears hummed with it, and it felt as though she'd sucked the air from the room with her question. David's expression cycled through pain to surprise, and then to an almost beatific calm.

"Natalie," he said, so softly she almost couldn't hear. Then his voice got stronger. "Her name is Natalie."

"Beautiful." Her voice hitched, and she knew her control was slipping.

Without another word she opened the door to step through. When it closed behind her the click of the lock snapping into place sounded suspiciously like the crack of her heart breaking.

CHAPTER EIGHTEEN

ALL NYCHELLE WANTED to do was pull the afghan up under her chin and go back to sleep, but the insistent ringing of the doorbell wouldn't let her. Rolling to sit up, she groaned, wanting to disappear for a little while and let the world go by without her.

She'd made it as far as her couch the evening before. Haunted by the conversation she'd had with David, she'd replayed it over and over in her mind. The numbness which had allowed her to leave his place without breaking down completely had lifted, and she'd cried long into the evening. The pain she'd felt as she'd recalled David talking about his daughter had been visceral, and she'd wept as though Natalie were her own—as though David's agony were her own.

Finally she'd forced herself to eat some yoghurt and fruit, although her stomach had threatened rebellion the entire time, and then had fallen asleep in the living room, her dreams bedeviled by images of David.

"What time is it anyway?" she groused as she blinked to try to clear the sleep from her eyes.

A glance at the kitchen clock made her wince. Nine o'clock was far later than she usually slept, but who on earth was at her house at that time on a Sunday morning without letting her know they were coming?

David.

Her heart hammered at the thought, but looking through the peephole in the door brought a mixture of shock and disappointment.

Quickly unlocking the door, she opened it.

"Aliya? What are you doing here?"

Her cousin stepped in, letting go of her bag as she did so, and grabbed Nychelle in a hard, sweet hug. Tears immediately threatened and had Nychelle wiggling out of the embrace. Aliya held on to her shoulders, kicking the door shut behind her.

"I was worried about you, so I grabbed the first available flight out of Hartsfield." Her dark eyes flashed and her usually smiling mouth was grim. "I'm glad I did. You've been crying."

"But why were you worried?" Nychelle forced a smile. "We spoke a couple days ago. You knew I was fine."

Turning Nychelle toward the living room, Aliya gave her a little shove. "Yeah, well, when I get a call from your Dr. Warmington, saying he knows you're upset and is worried about you, and your phone goes straight to voice mail all evening, of course I'm going to drop everything and come see what's going on."

Shock made Nychelle stumble, and she grabbed the back of the nearest chair for balance. "David called you? When?"

Aliya moved the blanket out of the way, then plopped down on the couch. She patted the seat beside her in invitation, but Nychelle ignored her, still too surprised to move.

Aliya sighed. "Yesterday—in the evening. I tried calling you afterward—"

"I'd turned off my phone." Nychelle waved her hand. That wasn't the important part. "What did he say?"

"Just that you'd had a really upsetting day and he was worried about you." When Nychelle made a rolling *go on* gesture with her hand, Aliya shrugged. "Seriously, that was it."

Forcing her trembling legs to move, and still holding on to the chair for support, Nychelle stepped around to sink down into the seat. "How did he get your number?"

"Does it matter?" Aliya raised one eyebrow.

"You flew all this way just because—"

Her cousin's raised hand and fierce expression were enough to have Nychelle snap her mouth shut.

"Listen, you need me—here I am."

Her face softened, and Nychelle turned away from the love shining in her eyes.

"You know if the situation were reversed you'd be at my side in a flash. Besides, that stiff upper lip nonsense comes from your father's side of the family. This side is all about making noise and garnering sympathy. That's what I'd be doing, so I figured I'd give you the chance to have at it—even though apparently there's nothing really wrong with you. What I want to know is, what happened to make him feel he needed to call me?"

It all came flooding back, overwhelming her, and Nychelle covered her face to hide her tears.

"Tell me," Aliya said softly.

The words poured out of Nychelle then: how wonderful the day had been, how she'd started telling him about her medical issues and had been interrupted by George's accident. Even how, as she'd watched David minister to the other man, she'd realized just how she felt about him.

"You're in love with him."

It wasn't a question, but Nychelle didn't want to go there with her cousin, so instead she blurted, "I slept with him."

"Oh."

Aliya's shocked expression would normally have made Nychelle laugh, but she couldn't summon any amusement.

"Before I told him about the baby."

"Oh…"

"And then he told me he'd lost a daughter when she was born at twenty weeks."

She couldn't bring herself to say his wife had miscarried—not when David so obviously saw it as a premature birth.

"My situation brought it all back to him. I saw it on his face, in his eyes—the fear and the agony. The regret. And I knew, no matter what had happened between us, it was over. He'd never take the chance of going through that again."

"Oh, honey." Aliya got up and came over to perch on the arm of the chair, pulled Nychelle into a hug. "You can't know that for certain. It was a shock, and once he's thought about it…"

"You didn't see him. He was gutted." Nychelle buried her head in her cousin's lap, tears flowing to dampen Aliya's dress. "He'll never forgive me. And I'll never forgive myself for hurting him that way."

Aliya sighed and stroked Nychelle's hair, seemingly unable to come up with a reply. After a while, she sighed again, then said, "Listen, you're upset, and probably overtired. Did you sleep much last night?" When Nychelle shook her head, Aliya coaxed her out of the chair and over to the couch. "Lie down for a while. I'm going to cook some soup."

"I'm not sick," Nychelle pointed out as she allowed her cousin to tuck the afghan over her legs. "I don't need soup."

"Maybe not, but cooking clears my head and I need to

think about everything you've told me. And you need to eat. My goddaughter or godson needs nourishment, and Auntie Aliya is going to provide it."

Nychelle felt herself relax as the sound of her cousin bustling about in the kitchen filled the house. No matter how David had gotten Aliya's number, she was grateful he'd cared enough to make sure she wasn't alone. At the same time it was just more evidence of the kind of man he was, and the relationship she'd missed out on.

Shifting around so she was sitting up against the cushions, Nychelle said, toward the kitchen, "You can say it, you know."

Aliya glanced over her shoulder to ask, "Say what?"

"That you were right to tell me to wait."

Aliya put chicken in the pot. "I'll say *I told you so* if you want, but what good will that do?"

"I don't know. Maybe justify how horrible I feel about all of this?"

Aliya didn't answer immediately, and when she did her tone was musing. "If you had waited, and gotten involved with David, because of how he feels chances are you wouldn't even have tried to get pregnant. Is that what you would have wanted?"

"No!" Pushing herself farther up on the cushions, Nychelle glared at her cousin's back. "Of course not. I won't ever regret doing what I did."

"So, then, you're going to have to accept the situation as it is." Aliya's rueful and kindly tone softened the prosaic response. "It isn't like it's a binary situation, where you can only regret either trying for a baby *or* not being with David. You're going to have to deal with loving both the baby and David—even though it seems as if you can only have one but not the other."

Suddenly exhausted, ineffably sad, Nychelle slid back down on the couch and pulled the afghan up so only the top of her head was exposed.

"I kind of hate him right now," she mumbled, more to herself than to Aliya. "For being the perfect man and coming into my life at the worst possible time."

"No, you don't. It's yourself you're hating, and you need to stop. Poor David's probably as messed up about all this as you are."

It made sense. Too much sense. "I hate it when you're right." Sitting up, she grabbed a tissue and blew her nose in an effort to be able to breathe, but her next thought just made her tear up again. "I doubt he cares about me now."

"I don't know, honey, and neither do you. And you won't know until you talk to him. At least then you'll know for sure where you stand. You want to know that, don't you?"

It was on the tip of her tongue to deny even caring about where she stood with David Warmington, but they'd both know it was a lie. "Yes…"

Aliya chuckled at the grudging admission, then said, "Think about it. Talk to him when you're ready." When she continued, her voice was soft, yet serious. "I know you're in love with him, Nych, even if you won't come out and say it. You wouldn't have slept with him if you weren't. Maybe it's time to take stock, figure it all out, before you try to move on. He's all wrapped up with this period of your life, and sometimes you have to deal with everything that's happening rather than just bits and pieces."

"Okay, that's enough." Through her tears and stuffiness Nychelle found some laughter, let it roll over her. "You sound like a TV psychologist. Or your mom."

"Ha!" Aliya sounded suitably outraged. "Could be worse. I could sound like *your* mom."

Full-on giggles caused Nychelle almost to suffocate, since she still couldn't breathe through her nose. "That is too darn true."

He'd been unable to sleep, to eat, since Nychelle had left the night before, and finally David took his tortured mind and tired body down to the beach for a run. It made no sense for him to sit at home waiting for text updates from Nychelle's cousin. They obviously weren't coming. She'd been kind enough to let him know she was in Fort Lauderdale and on her way to Nychelle's house. He really couldn't expect more than that. After all, she didn't even know him.

But it didn't stop him from checking his phone every couple of minutes, anxiety like a tangle of barbed wire in his gut.

Pounding along the sand, he let the events of the last couple of days play over and over in his mind. It was surreal—life swinging from ecstatic to familiar nightmare in just a few hours.

Nychelle was pregnant. Not just pregnant but at high risk for miscarriage too.

Just the thought made him shiver, his skin pebbling with goose bumps despite the heat.

Hearing that had filled him with a fear so strong he'd felt nauseated. Memories of Natalie and the aftermath of her too-early birth had flooded his head; Kitty's screamed recriminations, coming at a time when he'd hardly been able to handle the loss of their baby. The slamming of the door when she'd left to go back to South Carolina, which had seemed to echo like a gunshot in his soul. The agonizing pain and guilt.

He'd lost everything when Natalie died, and now he was facing the same heartbreak all over again.

The fact that it wasn't his child didn't make a difference. It was Nychelle's child, and that made him or her special. Important.

He couldn't love a woman and not love her child.

And he loved Nychelle.

But he couldn't be with her, even if she wanted him to be. The terror pushing at him wouldn't allow it. The devastation he'd endured couldn't be repeated.

It would break him completely to go through it all again.

He'd felt the cracks opening in the armor keeping him safe as he'd listened to her. Her words had rendered him too broken to react—he'd barely been able to breathe. After she'd left the room he'd realized his hands were shaking, as though with ague. She'd been so upset by what he'd said, had looked so fragile as she'd walked into the bedroom, and his stomach twisted with anxiety as he thought of her being alone after she left.

He knew her independent streak, knew she wouldn't tell any of her family what had happened, and that spurred him to move.

Nychelle's handbag was on the floor, where it had fallen earlier, and he fished her phone out, glad to find she didn't have a lock code on it. He looked up her cousin's number, transferred it to his own phone, planning to call her once Nychelle had left. It was doubtful Nychelle would thank him for interfering, but there was no way he could watch her leave without knowing someone else would be checking on her.

He couldn't do it himself without falling apart.

When Aliya had said she would call Nychelle, and then, unable to contact her, that she'd be catching the first flight out of Atlanta, David had closed his eyes, fighting tears of thankfulness. Nychelle deserved to be taken care of right now, and he knew her parents wouldn't do it. They'd probably lecture her instead of nurturing her, and that was the last thing she needed.

Although he'd wanted to lecture her too—ask her why, with her medical problems, she'd taken a chance on getting pregnant. Didn't she know the heartbreak she was courting? Realize how devastating the loss of her child would be?

No. No. *No*.

He wouldn't think that—even as he feared it might happen. The baby would be fine. It had to be. She couldn't—wouldn't—go through the agony he'd experienced.

Gritting his teeth, he quickened his pace, even though his legs and lungs burned. Even as he prayed everything would work out for her, his anxiety built, growing to fill every nook and cranny of his soul.

"Stop it," he panted aloud. "Stop it!"

She would be all right. She had to be. The bright, beautiful light that shone in her eyes shouldn't be dimmed by that kind of pain. He couldn't bear to see that happen. Needed to force himself to believe everything would work out.

It was too hot to be running for this long. He knew he should turn back toward his car but he pressed on, the pain of overexertion a physical manifestation of his inner agony, tears mixing with the sweat running down his cheeks.

And when finally he collapsed on the sand, dragging air into his tortured lungs, there was only one thought left in his mind.

Despite everything, he wished he'd told her he loved her.

CHAPTER NINETEEN

NYCHELLE CHECKED THE blood pressure apparatus and, after jotting down the levels, smiled at her patient. "Everything looks good. You're really doing well, Mr. Comstock."

"Please—how many times do I have to ask you to call me Doug?" But he was smiling even as he groused.

"Doug," she amended, returning his smile. "You've lost eighteen pounds in two months, which is amazing—but most important, your blood pressure is down."

"Even better is the way I feel." He was grinning now, obviously pleased with himself. "I've been sleeping like a baby, and I'm determined to drop the rest of the weight as soon as possible. I've been exercising like a fiend."

"Just make sure you stick with the plan we worked out, okay? You want to make sure your nutritional needs are being met, and you don't want to risk an injury, which could set you back." Nychelle checked his chart again. "I see you have a follow-up appointment in a few weeks with Dr. Napoli, and that she diagnosed a herniated disc but deferred any treatment other than mild painkillers. Are you still having the leg pain?"

"It's nowhere as bad." Doug stretched out his legs and flexed his feet. "Dr. Warmington called that one, though, didn't he? Both the diagnosis and Dr. Napoli not being willing to do much until I got my weight under control. Hey, where *is* the doc anyway?"

At the mention of David, Nychelle busied herself adding another note to the chart. "Usually I handle the follow-up appointments, but Dr. Warmington will be happy to see you if you particularly want his input."

"No, no—that's okay. I don't necessarily need to see him. I was just wondering if he was around."

Both disappointment and relief washed through her, and she kept her eyes on the tablet a moment longer than necessary, hoping Doug wouldn't see any of what she was feeling in her expression.

"Well, let's get going on these blood tests, so we can keep track of how your body is responding to the new regime."

Steering him away from talking about David worked for a while, but after they were finished, and Doug was getting ready to leave, he said, "I honestly think you and Dr. Warmington saved my life." He fussed with his collar, making it lie flat, while he spoke. "The two of you make a great team. If this place ever closes you should set up your own clinic somewhere. Believe me—just as I've been telling everyone I know in this neck of the woods to come to Lauderlakes, I'd be sending patients your way if you did."

"That's very kind of you," she said, and resolutely held her smile in place until she'd left him in the reception area to head back to her office. Then her happy expression fell away.

Doug had been her first patient of the day, and she was already wanting to go home. It had been a long couple of months, and just hearing David's name had the power to send a jolt of emotion through her. It was exhausting—especially considering how many times each week she either heard people talking about him or actually saw him.

Hearing Doug praise the way they worked together made her remember David's hope to go back to South Carolina and open a practice. She'd actually imagined going with him, being an integral part of making his plan a reality.

That was her own pipe dream.

As she lowered herself into the chair behind her desk she sighed, wishing she'd had the courage to do what Aliya had suggested: talk to David about what had happened.

She'd meant to—she really had—but the first time she'd seen him at work after that fateful Saturday he'd given her a cool nod, his expression closed, unreadable. Frozen by that icy stare, she had felt her resolve shrivel up and die.

There was no way she could have braved a conversation with him under those conditions. And, although his attitude toward her didn't seem quite as bad anymore, there was still no evidence that beneath his distantly professional demeanor the David she'd fallen for still existed. Not even a hint that her behavior hadn't destroyed everything between them.

It still hurt terribly and, despite telling herself she needed to get over him, Nychelle's heart wasn't ready to listen to her head. Probably because her head wasn't actually fully on board with that concept yet either. Knowing she needed to move on wasn't the same as accepting it was time to do it.

Yet she'd promised herself she'd do the very best she could for her baby, no matter how she was feeling. Give him or her the very best chance. She needed to maintain a healthy emotional as well as physical balance, and doing so meant dealing with the reality of losing David.

It wasn't enough to cut back on her activities, like excusing herself from the free clinic planning committee. Although that, of course, had had the added benefit of eliminating one place where she'd see David while also allowing her the extra rest her body was demanding.

Who knew falling asleep could be so easy? It was as if when the baby decided it needed a nap, it involved Nychelle going to sleep too. Not an easy thing to deal with during her busy work days. Not to mention that many of her dreams, which were particularly vivid and included David, caused her to wake up either crying or sexually frustrated. Sometimes both. And her emotional mood swings were draining. Elation over the baby morphed seamlessly into desolation over David, leaving her almost shell-shocked at times.

Leaning back in her chair, she yawned as another wave of exhaustion washed through her. Rubbing her eyes, she thought maybe it was time to take another piece of Aliya's advice.

"You need some time off. Breathing room to get everything into perspective," Aliya had said. She'd insisted on video calling, since she wanted to see for herself how Nychelle was, and had always had the ability just to look at her cousin and know. "I'm sure you have some vacation time left."

She did. And now, as she reluctantly got up to go and greet her next patient, she made the decision to take a few days, maybe even a long weekend, to rest and get her head straight.

Clearing it with Human Resources wasn't as easy as she'd hoped, but she was able to take the following Friday as a personal day, plus the next Monday and Tuesday as vacation.

When she left the office on Thursday she was feeling lighter than she had in ages, determined to use her days off to concentrate on the baby. Nothing else. She already had plans on how she wanted to rearrange the house. It was time to put them into effect.

By the Monday afternoon of her vacation she was feeling both rested and accomplished. The hall cupboard, which was to become a small library, was cleaned out and ready for the organizer she'd ordered to be installed. Now she turned her attention to culling her books, which took up almost a full wall in the smallest of her three bedrooms—the room now used as an office, but soon to be the nursery. She assembled packing boxes for the books she planned to donate, and got down to it.

She'd just taped the last box closed when the doorbell rang.

"About time," she muttered, getting up off the floor. As the chimes pealed again, she called, "I'm coming." Adding, under her breath, "Impatient, much?"

She opened the door, expecting the shelving delivery man. Instead her heart leaped as she gazed up at the man standing outside.

"David."

His name was torn from a throat already closing in shock, coming out high and surprised. He didn't reply, or greet her, just stood there, his lips tight, his posture ramrod-straight. He looked leaner than usual, his face almost hawkish in its severity, and his hair was disheveled, as though he'd been running his fingers through it. When his gaze raked her from head to feet and back up again Nychelle's skin heated, tingled with awareness, and her heart seemed set to leap clear out of her chest, it was thumping so hard.

"Are you all right?"

It wasn't so much a question as a demand, shot at her like a bullet, making her jump.

"What? Yes." The words stuttered and stumbled from her lips.

"And the..." His gaze dipped again, only as far as her belly this time, and his jaw clenched an instant before he continued, "And the baby?"

"Fine," she replied softly, her heart aching. "We're both fine."

David exhaled, the breath leaving him in a *whoosh*, and he visibly sagged, reaching out to hold on to the doorjamb as though in need of its support.

"Thank God," he muttered, rubbing the back of his neck. *"Thank God."*

Stepping back, she asked, "Do you want to come in?"

He came through into the foyer, and instead of going into the living room stepped close and pulled her tight to his chest. As he buried his face in her hair Nychelle realized he was trembling, and instinctively wrapped her arms around his waist. Melting against him, inhaling his beloved scent, she allowed herself this moment, even though she didn't think the joy coursing through her veins would last.

"I was so worried about you."

It was a whisper against her temple. "Why?" she asked, just as softly.

"You weren't at work on Friday, and then again today. I thought..."

His voice faded and for an instant more she savored the sensation of being held so tenderly. Then she gently disengaged herself from his arms and stepped back.

David didn't try to stop her, just leaned against the wall and watched as she backed up far enough to perch on the arm of a chair. The door had swung shut, and in the quiet of the house they faced each other. She took a deep breath, trying to steady her heart, to be realistic, before she spoke.

"You thought I'd lost the baby?"

He nodded—just a single, staccato dip of his head, and she sighed.

"I just took a few days off. There was no need for you to worry. Besides, you could have just called or texted me before you got so upset."

The sound he made was indecipherable: a snort of what might have been interpreted as laughter, except there was no sign of amusement on his face. "You make it sound so simple."

"It *is* simple," she said, sad to think of having once more brought pain into his life.

Her heart ached to think of him suffering a moment more, even when she knew alleviating that hurt definitely meant them going their separate ways.

Lifting her chin, she looked straight into his eyes. "You need to stop torturing yourself because of my situation. You've dealt with enough without worrying about me. Just know that no matter what happens I'll be fine."

"And you're so rational," he said, as though she hadn't spoken, or as if he was offering commentary on a conversation that he wasn't really a part of. "Unfortunately there's no rationality left in me when it comes to you."

"David—"

Whatever she was planning to say was forestalled by his upheld hand.

"I need to explain."

He gave her a smile so sweet her heart melted.

"When I lost Natalie and my marriage fell apart, it made me question everything. What kind of doctor was I that I couldn't tell something was wrong? What kind of husband that my wife blamed me for her unhappiness both before and after we lost our baby? Had it been my fault Natalie was born too soon? It changed me in a fundamental way—made me fearful. Just the thought of going through something like that again made me lose all hope of having a family, of loving anyone again. Then I met you."

Nychelle could only stare at him, wondering if this were some kind of dream. David pushed away from the wall and paced closer, stopping about an arm's length away.

"I didn't want to get involved with you—fought it every step of the way. But you got under my skin and into my heart. It frightened me, made me want to run. And then..."

He faltered, and she saw him swallow before he went on.

"I hope you won't hate me for this, but when you told me about your medical problem I was elated. I saw it as a sign that we were meant to be together. We would grow our family through adoption, and I wouldn't have to worry about losing another child prematurely. Wouldn't have to risk my heart that way again. When you told me about the IUI I didn't know how to handle it. It didn't matter that it wasn't my child. It was yours, and I knew I would love your baby as if he or she were my own. I froze—was terrified."

Even as he said the words she could see his fear reflected in his eyes, in the tightness of his face, and her heart ached anew.

"It's okay," she whispered, wanting to put her arms around him again, comfort him, but knowing she shouldn't. If she did, she wouldn't want to let go. "I understand. I never meant to hurt you. I would have never done it on purpose."

The look he gave her was one of tenderness, and the softening of his face was so dramatic her heart leaped.

"Don't you think I know that?" He took another step closer, reached out to sweep a finger over her cheek. "You're the kindest, most amazing woman I've ever met. I know the last thing you'd want to do is hurt anyone. It's one of the things I love most about you."

He *loves* me?

He'd intimated it, but hearing it said so bluntly made her tremble, had tears welling in her eyes. Yet the barrier of his past still loomed between them, and although she'd love to ignore it, and pretend happily-ever-after was assured if they loved each other, she had to find the courage to face it head-on.

"David, you know there are no guarantees with this pregnancy." She searched his gaze, trying to gauge his reaction to her statement. "Look at how upset you were, thinking I might have lost the baby. And I still have such a long way to go. You don't need that kind of stress in your life and, believe me, I'll understand if you don't want to sign up for it."

Without breaking eye contact, David cupped her face, tilting it up toward his. She found her lips softening, longing blooming and spreading through her body. When his fingers settled, warm and strong on her skin, a little groan of need rose in her throat.

"I won't say it doesn't frighten me, but we'll get through it together." He caressed her lower lip with a sweep of one thumb. "I've allowed fear to rule my life too long. When we were apart I was consumed with wanting you, seeing you smile, hearing your voice, just being with you, and it was tearing me to pieces. I guess you could say my love for you is far stronger than my fears, and I'd rather be with you, no matter what, than try to exist without you."

"Suppose you change your mind?" she whispered, hope warring with her own fear to bring on a wave of insecurity. "What happens then?"

His smile was beautiful, open and happy. "You don't get it, do you? I'm yours—heart, body, mind and soul. Driving over here, half crazy with worry, I had to accept that I'll never be free from loving you. I thought if I just stayed away my feelings would fade, but now I know that will never happen."

His hands slipped from her face to her shoulders, urging her to stand. When she did, he wrapped his arms around her waist, but kept just enough space between them so they were face to face.

"I want to be the one who makes sure you're fine, no matter what. I want to be there for you every day, to hold your hand, or rub your feet, or tell you off when I think you're overdoing things. Say you love me again. Tell me you'll have me for the rest of our lives."

The love they shared washed over her, chasing away her trepidation and filling her with joy. "Yes. Oh, David, I love you so much."

And then, enfolded in his arms, she lost herself in his kisses, completely secure for the first time in her life and exactly where she was supposed to be. All doubts cast aside.

EPILOGUE

"I WAS THINKING," David said, in a casual voice that Nychelle knew meant he was feeling anything but relaxed. "You should stop working soon."

This wasn't really a promising start to what she'd hoped would be a busy and productive Saturday. So many changes were coming, and coming so quickly her head sometimes felt as though it were spinning.

In less than eight weeks they'd welcome their baby, and as if that weren't enough they also had to sign the papers to purchase a practice close to David's home town. While he wouldn't take over from the retiring doctor there for another six months after that, Nychelle was determined to have as much dealt with on the home front as she could before the birth.

She had a to-do list as long as her arm, but David didn't seem inclined to go anywhere or do anything other than lie here. Or rather, he was probably inclined to have *her* lie there all day.

Lying across the bed, his head resting on her thigh, he rubbed her distended stomach, pausing every now and then to feel the baby turn or kick against his palm.

"Sweetheart, I'm just at thirty-two weeks," she replied. "And in good health. I don't want to stop working yet."

She'd been waiting for this to happen ever since she'd

had a scare at twenty-two weeks and her doctor had diagnosed placenta praevia. Dr. Miller was monitoring it carefully, and had scheduled Nychelle to have a Caesarian section five days before her due date, but David's stress levels had been climbing ever since. However, even though she wanted to alleviate his fears, knowing that she wouldn't be returning to Lauderlakes after the baby came made her want to maximize her earnings before she left. It was a *Catch 22.*

"I know," he answered, keeping his focus on her belly, his hand sliding around and around. "But it's something to think about."

Nychelle sighed, but made sure he didn't hear it. He'd been so good through her pregnancy up to this point—not hovering too much or allowing his doctoring instincts to take over; being concerned and engaged but not smothering.

Of course she knew he watched her when he thought she wasn't looking, and was sure he sometimes stayed awake at night to keep an eye on her when she wasn't feeling well. No matter what the doctor said, or how often she told David she was feeling wonderful, she knew he wouldn't really be okay until the baby was safely delivered.

She'd planned to work right up until the week before her C-section, but it looked like it was time for a compromise, and Nychelle carefully considered her words before saying them. "Well, why don't we—"

"Hang on," he said, his head coming up off her thigh. "Hold that thought."

He rolled to stand with a motion so fluid all she could feel was envy. The very last vestiges of grace had deserted her at least a month ago, and it often felt as though she needed a block and tackle to do the simplest things.

Like get up out of a chair or push herself up to sit higher on her pillows.

Moments later he was back, carrying Jacqueline, who'd just woken up. Like her mother, it took the toddler a while to face the day and become fully human again, and David was patting her back and joggling her gently, the way he knew she liked.

"Here we are," he said, placing a kiss on the top of Jackie's head. "Here's our beautiful girl, ready to rise and shine."

Nychelle chuckled when she caught sight of Jackie's expression. "Rise and shine" indeed. If the pout on their daughter's face was anything to go by, she had no intention of doing any such thing anytime soon.

"Mama," the little girl mumbled, reaching out with one arm while still keeping a tight grip on David's neck with the other.

Lowering himself and Jackie onto the bed with practiced ease, David lay down so the little body was snuggled between them.

"Good morning, my sweet girl," Nychelle said.

She was just reaching down to kiss Jackie's sleep-warmed cheek when the toddler abruptly sat up.

"Good morning, little bruvver," she said, in her scratchy, first-thing-in-the-morning voice, before leaning close to kiss Nychelle's tummy.

As Jackie flopped back down and rolled over, pulling at David's hand so he embraced them both, Nychelle knew a fullness of heart that never failed to make her eyes misty.

Looking across Jackie into her husband's beautiful blue eyes, she saw reflected there all she was feeling and more. And she smiled, knowing she was the luckiest woman alive.

"One more month," she said, moving her hand to cover

his, which was back to circling her stomach. "Then I'll stay home."

"Two weeks," he said, as she'd expected.

"Three," she countered, her smile turning into a grin when he reluctantly nodded.

"Why do I feel as though that was what you'd decided from the outset?" he grumbled, turning his hand to link his fingers with hers. "To you and Jackie I'm just a pushover, aren't I?"

She giggled, wrinkling her nose at him. "At least at the clinic you're still Dr. Heat, the man who has the nurses falling over themselves to do his bidding."

"Stop it," he growled, even as he swooped in to kiss the laughter from her lips. "Why can't I be Dr. Heat to *you* instead? I'd like that better."

"Oh, you are," she murmured against his mouth, surrounded in happiness, basking in the warmth of his love. "And you always will be."

* * * * *

MILLS & BOON

Coming next month

REUNITED WITH HER BROODING SURGEON

Emily Forbes

The gorgeous man with amazing bone structure stepped forwards and Grace's heart skipped a beat and her mouth dropped open.

Marcus Washington.

She could not believe it.

It had to be him. Even though he no longer resembled the twelve-year-old boy she once knew, it *had* to be him. There couldn't be two of him.

She hadn't thought about him for years but if she had she never would have imagined he would become a doctor. She knew that sounded harsh and judgemental but what she remembered of Marcus did not fit with her image of someone who had clearly ended up in a position of responsibility and service to others.

But what did she really know of him? She had only been seven years old. What had she known of anything?

Her father was a doctor and, at the age of seven, everything she knew or thought was influenced by what and who she saw around her. Particularly by her own family. And Marcus's family had been about as different from hers as a seven-year-old could have imagined. But she knew enough now to understand that it wasn't about where you came from or what opportunities you were handed in life, but about what you did with those opportunities, those chances. It was about the choices you made. The drive and the desire to be the best that you could be.

She would never have pictured Marcus as a doctor but now, here he was, standing in front of her looking polished, professional and perfect. It had to be him.

She knew a lot could change in twenty years and by the look of him, a lot had.

She was still staring at him, trying to make sense of what was happening when he looked in her direction and caught her eye. Grace blushed and, cursing her fair skin, the bane of a redhead, she looked away as his gaze continued on over her. She finally remembered to close her mouth.

Had he recognised her?

It didn't appear so, but then, why would he? She was nothing like the seven-year-old he had last seen.

Continue reading
REUNITED WITH
HER BROODING SURGEON
Emily Forbes

Available next month
www.millsandboon.co.uk